Also b

MEAGAN BRANDY

Bloom books

Published by Bloom Books, an imprint of Sourcebooks
P.O. Box 4410, Naperville, Illinois 60567–4410
(630) 961-3900
sourcebooks.com

Cataloging-in-Publication data is on file with the Library of Congress.

Printed and bound in the United States of America.
PAH 10 9 8 7 6 5 4 3 2 1

For those whose choices remain their own secret. Never let the world push your off course. Your patience will pay off in time.

CHAPTER 1
CAMERON

"You've either got bigger balls than the ones I saw or you're looking to get your ass kicked." I cross my arms over my chest, not giving two shits that the door he needs is the one behind me. In fact, I'm purposely blocking this entrance to keep my friends inside and this fucker out here on the lawn. If he gets by me or follows my ass inside, the boys will pounce, and it won't be pretty. From what I've heard, they're already giving him shit on the practice field, and the season hasn't even officially started yet.

Wait, why am I protecting him from that?

I sidestep, leaning against the doorframe, and decide that, if he wants to go in, I won't hate what happens after. We both know he deserves to get reamed.

Alister's shoulders fall, and he shuffles closer. "You haven't returned any of my calls and I didn't see you all summer."

"And somehow you convinced yourself that meant I wanted to see you face-to-face rather than understanding it for what it is: a big, fat sign telling you to back off."

His green eyes are crestfallen, and he nods, a sad tip to his lips. "I tried, Cam. I left you alone after you told me to fuck off on Christmas."

"You called and texted me all summer long, Alister."

"I said I tried, right?" He gives a pitiful smile, and I hate that he looks cute when he does it. "I gave you space after everything that went down and didn't bother you all spring semester. That was hard enough when you never even let me apologize, so when June rolled around and I realized you went home for the summer, I couldn't help myself. It's been almost eight months, Cam, and look at me." He lifts his hands, tilting his head slightly as his eyes hold mine. "Still over here missing you and wishing I didn't fuck things up."

I regard him for a long moment, despising the vulnerability the sight of him stirs and hating how I'm standing here wondering if what he's saying is true.

Does he really wish he didn't fuck things up?

Does he miss me?

Or is he just doubling down on the pretending, this time to get his teammates off his ass?

My bet is on the latter, even if the thought bothers me a little more than I'd like, so of course I remind him of how we got here in the first place—me hiding out from him and him doing his best to track me down on the daily.

"You lied to me, used me to get insider information about my family."

"Mason isn't your family," Alister snaps instantly, and by the way he scrunches his face, I'd say he regrets it just as fast.

A humorless laugh leaves me, and I shake my head. "Yeah. This conversation is over."

"Cameron, wait!" He reaches out, latching on to my wrist. "I'm sorry, okay?"

I yank myself free, quickly spinning to face him with a glare. "Clearly, you're still sour over the *lie* that your ex-girlfriend told you, but honestly, Alister, get over it! You spent your first season as a college football player hating your team captain instead of leaning into him as a mentor like you should have. You made enemies you didn't have to make all because a shitty girl—who clearly never cared about you by the way—was too much of a pussy to tell you she fucked some random guy she met at a bar and ended up pregnant. So I'll say it again: get over it! Mason isn't the enemy here."

2

"You don't think I've tried?!" He throws his hand out, a strain pulling at his brows. "I have, Cam."

"You've said that word twice already: *tried*. Well, you know what? Try harder." I narrow my eyes, moving farther into the house. "Because Mason isn't just my best friend's twin brother. I've known him all my life. He *is* my family. They all are." I point to the stairway behind me, knowing he's smart enough to realize it's not only Mason up there waiting for me but also the rest of our core friend group. "If you can't even handle my saying the words, then you're wasting your time talking to me."

Why did I agree to step outside to talk to him?

Oh yeah, 'cause he said he would just knock on Mason's door if I didn't, and yeah, that wouldn't end well.

Alister's shoulders fall. "Nothing about you is wasted, Cameron."

"Yeah, well, the two months I spent with you sure as hell were."

I turn away, trying to hide the way my hands are shaking by tucking my hair behind my ears, and stomp up the stairs that lead to the captain's quarters of the football house, hoping Alister gives up, if only for the moment.

But the gorgeous dickhead of a man waits until I've gotten one foot over the threshold of Mason's room, every eye in the place now pointed my way, and shouts, "I'm going to change your mind, Cameron Cox, and I won't give up on us until you do!"

I tense, my attention shooting to the couch, where Mason and the other boys I've known all my life are eating pizza from the box. Sure enough, all three of their glares swing toward the open door.

Of course, it's not at all surprising when the one who flies to his feet first is the big, burly protector of our group.

His heavy feet pound against the floor, and I throw my arms out, palms pressing to either side of the frame, blocking his path.

Yes, I talked a big game about letting my boys eat Alister for lunch, but at the end of the day, he's not worth the trouble they'd get into with their coach.

He reaches me in three Goliath-sized steps, so I raise a blond brow, and he raises one right back, his massive hands closing over my ribs in the same second. He lifts me with zero effort, shifting and preparing to deposit me to the side, but I'm not going to make it that easy.

I curl my limbs around him until I'm a full-on frontal backpack.

He tenses for a split second, then his chuckle fills my ear. "If you think that's gonna stop me from getting down those stairs, you're wrong."

"He's probably already tucked his tail and ran off."

"Staring right at him."

My head yanks around, and sure enough, Alister is standing right there at the bottom of the stairs, looking right at me. Or more at me latched and locked on the tree of a man that is Brady Lancaster.

My lips purse and I bug my eyes as if to say *what the hell are you doing?*

Alister smirks, crosses his arms, and just…stands there.

A low rumble vibrates against my chest, and I curl my arms tighter. "Brady—"

"Nope." He cuts me off, his hands moving to the underside of my thighs to support me as he starts taking the stairs down two at a time. "Warned his ass."

"Well, I think it's established he's not the brightest."

"I take offense at that," Alister drawls.

"You were meant to," I snap. "Why are you still there?!"

"Waiting for him to put you down."

Brady grips me tighter. "I'm gonna drop-kick his ass," he mumbles for only me to hear, and I know we must be but two steps away now. He may very well do as he wishes.

I wrap my arms tighter, shimmying to get my mouth to his ear. "If you turn around, I'll do your laundry for a week."

4

"Nope."

"I'll cook you breakfast."

"You don't wake up till noon. I'm up by five."

Not true.

Well, not *entirely true.*

"Ugh! Fine, I'll give you a massage after the game."

Brady jerks to a stop midstep, tugging back to meet my eye. His narrow. "Not the next morning. On game night."

"Yep."

"I'm talkin' right after."

"I'll come to the locker room if they let me."

"Locker room?" Alister asks, stepping closer.

"No." Brady scowls, his voice low. "Your dorm. I want quiet and that smell-good shit."

"Wait, her dorm for *what*?"

I smile at Brady, pretending Alister doesn't exist. "Lavender and chamomile."

"What the hell are you two talking—"

Brady tears me from him, winding me to his back like nothing, and I latch on, my head snapping forward just as Brady places himself on level footing with Alister, cutting the asshole off.

He doesn't say a word, just stares down at Alister a moment before chuckling and spinning on his heels. Brady leaps up the stairs with me on his back, and when we reach the room once more, my bestie Ari and the boys are waiting for us.

As we step inside, he spins, both of us now staring down the narrow stairwell at the blond...who is still standing where we left him.

Brady pats my thighs, now woven around him from behind, so I lower them to the floor, but before I can step away, he twists his torso and reaches back until he can wrap his arm around my waist. He hauls me against his side, speaking to Alister. "Cameron will call you if she wants to talk, but I wouldn't bet on it. If you haven't figured it out yet, she's a stubborn one."

"I'm well aware," Alister bites back.

"Then you're aware she's not in the business of second chances."

Alister crosses his arms. "Which will make it all the sweeter when she awards me one."

"Don't hold your breath."

"Don't fall for my girl."

My brows snap together, but Brady only laughs, shaking his head at the guy who can't take a hint—or refuses to. But it's not the words that Alister spoke that linger long after Ari and I head back to our dorm.

It's the look of sheer determination that was etched across his attractive face as his eyes met mine.

He's not going to walk away from the idea of us so easily.

The question is, What the hell am I going to do about it?

CHAPTER 2
CAMERON

"Remind me why I agreed to this again?" I whine the second I drag my feet out of my dorm and spot Brady right where he said he'd be waiting. "It's like the witching hour."

Brady grins, pushing off his shoulder and walking closer with his arms behind his back. "It's eight in the morning, baby girl."

"Like I said: the witching hour." My lips poke out in a pout, shoulders drooped and all. "The sun isn't even fully in the sky yet."

"If you took those giant saucers you call sunglasses off, you'd see the sun is nice and high, but either way, you know I got you." He brings his hands forward, revealing what he was hiding.

I freeze on the spot, eyes glued to the familiar to-go cup. "Is that an iced Caramel Cookie Crumble with extra cookie and extra crumble?"

"You mean is this a whole-ass sugar bomb for the sugar queen? Yes. Yes, it is."

I squeal, erasing the distance between us, and take the large drink into my hands, inhaling the addictive scent of toasted chocolate chip. My eyes close, and I go in for a decent-sized suck through the straw, so I won't get brain freeze. "I fucking love you, Brady Lancaster." He merely laughs and I can't be bothered to open my eyes, just sigh, leaning forward and letting my forearms rest against Brady's chest with a smile. "Such a good boy, you are. Let's make Ari jealous." I pull my phone out, putting my straw to my lips, and Brady lifts his drink into the frame too, pressing his chin to my cheek with a smirk.

I snap the photo and send it to my best friend.

Me: Proof. He loves me more.

"Wait!" Brady tries to snag the phone, but I dodge his grabby hands and spin around, straw stuck between my lips.

"Girl." He points a finger at me. "If you just cost me that plate of spicy spaghetti she promised to bring me tomorrow night, you're getting an ass whoopin'."

"You mean the way I'm about to whoop your ass in Communications."

"Oh no. I'm talking a full-on, over-the-knee ass whoopin', Cammie Baby." He steps in close. "No one messes with my food."

I hum, cocking my head to the side, straw stuck between my teeth. "Is that what you tell the girls at night, Big Daddy?"

"Wouldn't tell you if it was, Little Mama."

"Original," I tease.

"I was trying to be matchy-matchy."

A laugh spurts from me, and Brady's chuckle follows.

He shuffles back only to lock his arm around my neck so he can tug me along at his pace. "Come on. I think the sugar is kicking in, so we should hustle our asses to the library before the good spot is gone."

"Good spot," I deadpan. "At the library? Aren't all the tables in the same area?"

"You'd know if you ever spent any time in there."

"Hey, number ninety-eight," a group of girls calls out, giggling and waving at Brady.

"Ladies," he damn near croons, glancing back at me with a laugh he swallows for their benefit.

I, unfortunately, accidently let mine slip but continue with our conversation. "Why would I do a thing like that when I have a perfectly good dorm room?"

"Uh-huh, and how much studying did you get done last night?"

"None. I watched a whole season of *The Last Kingdom*."

Brady throws his head back with a laugh and mine follows. "Thanks for making my point, even if I have no idea what that is."

"Vikings. Big ones. *Hot* ones." I side-eye him, peeking up at his dirty-blond hair. "Actually, you would make a good Viking."

"That right?" His lips quirk, and he nods at someone who walks by, guiding me along the walking path.

"Oh yeah, I can see it now. You would be right at home— eat meat with your hands, never have to wear a shirt, and fuck whoever you wanted."

Brady's head snaps my way, and he gives me a teasing glare. "First of all, I don't eat meat with my hands."

I raise a brow. "Three weeks ago. Santa Monica Pier."

"It was a food truck festival, and they had turkey legs!"

"That you..." I lead.

He grins, tickling my side, and I duck out of his hold, pointing my drink at him.

"See? Right at home." I laugh.

"You're a brat, Cameron Cox."

"And you still love me."

He scoffs, but it's playful, and this time when he hooks his arm over my shoulders, he curls it, using his other to make a mess out of my hair.

"Shithead!" I shove, but his big-ass body goes nowhere and then we're both laughing, but as I face forward, I instantly pout, realizing we reached the steps of the dreaded library. "Curse you for dragging me here...but bless you for feeding me sugar first."

"You didn't really think I'd expect you to make it through the walk here, let alone the rest of the morning, without a pick-me-up did you?"

"I would very much like you to pick me up right now, thank you."

Brady shakes his head and starts up the steps. "Come on, girl." He chuckles.

I follow like a sad puppy and blindly drop into the chair that Brady pulls out for me, glancing around as he lowers into the seat at my side.

I frown at the space, looking over my shoulder at the mostly empty tables—because only crazy people come to the library to study *before* morning classes. Well, at least not this early in the semester anyway.

Honestly, what do I know?

"I thought you said you wanted the best table. We're literally at the front where everyone and their mom has to walk right by us to even get in here."

"Everyone and their mom and…" He trails off, stretching his head to the right, and I follow his line of sight but see nothing. When I look back to him, his smile slowly stretches, so I glance over again just in time to watch as a short, cutesy redhead comes out of the aisle, pushing a cart of books.

I follow her progress, my lips pressing together to fight a smile as she parks her cart at the podium-style desk *right* across from us.

The moment she hops up into the barstool-style chair, I glance over at Brady, who is focused on her.

"Good spot, huh?" I deadpan.

"Best one in the house." He grins, breaking his gaze away from the little librarian and meeting mine. "She wants me."

"Does she even know you?"

"Not yet."

We both start laughing.

And then we get to work.

A little over an hour later, Chase slides up to the table, scoffing when he sees where we're sitting, his attention moving to the redhead a moment before coming back.

"I see he's still hoping to catch the quiet one's attention," Chase jokes.

"More like demanding her attention."

"Hey. Don't forget, we're here for you." Brady looks my way as he pushes to his feet with a tip to his lips and shoves his shit in his backpack. "I'm a God at Communications, and you know what they say about killing two birds with one stone."

"That only future serial killers throw rocks at innocent animals?"

Chase chuckles and Brady tosses a crumpled paper at my head. "That's it, brat. You're Chase's problem now. I'm out of here."

He hustles away, and I leave my bag, trusting Chase to snag it as I speed after Brady, jumping up on his back.

Brady catches me around the thighs instantly, used to my habit of making myself his backpack. "You're getting scary good at that."

"It helps that my landing spot is built like Bane—the Tom Hardy version, of course."

"Not sure if that's a compliment or not, Cammie Baby."

"At least she didn't compare you to Chad Michael Murray," Chase says as he catches up.

Brady and I start laughing, glancing over at Chase, and just as I figured, my bag is hanging from his left hand.

"To be fair"—I grin—"I was *trying* to be an asshole. You needed a haircut and were acting like a douche."

"Hey." He raises his free hand in surrender. "I'm not saying it wasn't deserved, just a low blow."

"What's a low blow?"

A frown instantly forms along Chase's brow, and we all face forward just as Paige walks up, her flowy, pastel-pink dress meeting her knees, paired with cute flats a sparking pearl-like color.

I smile at the little fairyesque girl we met our first year here at Avix. She's a good friend of Ari's boyfriend, Noah, and he introduced us to her not long after he and Ari started hanging out. After my best friend's near-death accident at the end of our freshman year, we got to know her better, and she's been a part of our ever-growing group ever since.

"Telling everyone about Chase's secret man crush on Chad Michael Murray," I joke.

Chase groans and Paige tucks her hair behind her ear with a laugh.

"I'm going to call my mom back real fast," Chase mumbles, moving ahead of us, and I notice the way Brady turns his head to follow his friend's path.

Paige looks from Chase's departing form to us, a small, possibly forced, smile on her lips, and we fall in step beside her, walking slower as we wait for the rest of the gang to come around the corner as planned.

"So did you figure out if you can come with us to the game on Saturday?" I ask Paige, resting my cheek on the back of Brady's head.

Paige's shoulders fall and she shakes her head. "I don't think I'm going to make it."

"The womb donor's parental still asking to see you?"

She gives an uneasy smile. "More like demanding. Why a man I've never met thinks he has a right to tell me what to do is beyond me."

I don't know all that much about Paige's life before Avix, just that she was raised by a single dad, her mom having overdosed just after she was born. But I do know she likes to please people.

So I'm not surprised when she says, "I'm just going to meet him for dinner, let him say whatever it is he wants to say, and hope he leaves me alone after that."

"Is your mom's side a bunch of assholes?" Brady asks.

"I have no idea." She looks off, seemingly lost in thought. "My dad told me my mom had no family. He either had a good reason to lie to me or he didn't know."

Neither Brady nor I comment. Like the twins and Chase, the

two of us also came from full, loving homes with more support than we could ask for.

I don't think Paige lacked love from her dad. If I remember right, Noah said they were really close, and it couldn't have been easy to only have one person in your life you could depend on. It had to be even harder to then lose that person. But her mom, I know, was a different story, so it must be hard to learn she had family out there she never even knew about.

"Anyway, I might make the party after the game, but I won't know for sure until the time comes."

Mason and Ari walk up, and Chase rejoins us, his frown still present.

"All right, let's go eat before all the good shit is gone." I reach back, smacking Brady on the butt. "Giddy up, horsey."

Brady looks to the boys. "Last one to the steps has to save the table and gets their food last?"

Mason smirks and bends at the knees, and Ari instinctively hops up on her brother's back. "You're on, Lancaster."

We all look to Chase.

His gaze snaps between his friends, settling last on Paige, who chews her lip and looks the other direction. His eyes narrow on the tiny blond. "She's wearing a dress."

"So cup her ass. Nothing will show." Brady laughs and I smack him on the arm.

Chase stares at Paige, and finally, she gives a little shrug.

He drops our bags onto the grass and pulls a hoodie out of his, gingerly wrapping it around her waist.

"I could do it," she says softly.

Chase ignores her and ties it low across her belly. He turns, silently lowering to one knee.

Paige climbs on and he pushes to his feet as if she weighs less than a butterfly.

Brady grabs my bag and Chase takes his once more. "On three?"

13

"One."

"Two."

All three guys cheat, breaking out in a full sprint before the count is finished, and we can only laugh.

This.

This happy-family feeling is the one I want to hold on to.

But there's a pattern that seems to be following me here at Avix U.

Everything I try to hold on to...I have to let go.

Let's hope this year it's not something I can't live without.

CHAPTER 3
CAMERON

"Yes, Mason, I made sure to swap out the scratchy blanket he fell asleep with to the soft one from his bag." I prop my phone between my shoulder and ear, shoving my textbooks in my bag and setting it on the counter. "You act like this is my first rodeo. Little D and me are like best buddies at this point."

"I know, but—"

"But for some reason, he likes the scratchy one and fights his sleep without it. Again. We're best buddies. I know all the things." I laugh, waving at Junie, my boss—or, I guess, professor—at the child development center on campus. "He's good. I'm God given, and you and Payton are so lucky to have me here with him for two hours a day. I know. You don't have to say it."

He chuckles and my smile blooms wide. "All right, all right. I'll leave you alone."

"Until Monday, you mean," I tease. My phone beeps and I reach up to pull it back and check the screen. I sigh, fighting a grin. "Well, gotta let you go, whipped boy. The one who holds your leash is calling now."

"Don't tell her I called again—"

I hang up on him and answer his girlfriend's call. "Well, hello, Payton. Your son is sleeping like an angel and had a fantastic day, and I just reported to Daddy Mase."

Hauling my backpack onto my back, I snag my watered-down iced coffee and head out the door.

"Have I mentioned how amazing you are lately?" she sighs.

"Literally every day, but as I told you guys a thousand times, it's no big deal. I have a million hours to put in for here, and doing a little each day is so much more manageable than two or three full shifts. Honestly, it's the best change I could have made to my schedule. I ended last year with double the hours I had my first year."

"Thanks, Cam. I don't know if I could have committed to moving here full-time without someone I trust being there with him."

"Uh, yes, you would have. And the reason is a six-foot-ish, dark-haired quarterback who would have probably talked his mom into moving here to be your sitter just so he could have you and little man with him."

"Yeah." She lets out a second happy sigh. "That sounds about right."

Laughing, I head for my girl, who's waiting for me outside the lecture hall building. "K. Gotta go. There's a super-stimulating lecture about the effects of backward thinking waiting for me."

"That sounds…"

"Like a shit way to end the day?"

Payton chuckles. "I'll talk to you later. I still have to help break down the set before I can pick up Deaton."

"Love you, bye." I hang up, jogging over to Ari and bowing when she holds out a fresh iced coffee. "Thank you, bestie."

She takes the old one from my hand, tossing it in the trash before tugging the door open. "How was baby Deaton today?"

"Cute as ever. I can't believe he'll be two soon."

That familiar wave of longing weaves through me, but I force it away.

You aren't ready to worry about what the future might not bring yet anyway, Cam.

"Stop trying to speed up time." Ari nudges me. "It's only August."

16

"And November before we know it. You know how football season is. Our lives are a rat race for the next few months, even more so now that we're not only trying to make all the boys' games here at Avix but as many of your superfamous *fiancé's* NFL games!"

"Cam," she hisses, head whipping around.

"What?" I grin, glancing her way. "Afraid the world will find out what literally *everyone* is waiting for?"

"We're not engaged."

I cock my head, blinking hard at her, and her cheeks pinken.

She looks away, whispering as we enter the giant room. "We're not engaged as far as the rest of the world knows. You know *The Avix Inquirer* is on a crazy kick right now. It's gone from a fun school page to a damn gossip column. All we need is for them to start spreading rumors."

"Not a rumor if it's true."

She snaps her mouth shut, fighting a grin as she shakes her head. "You're annoying, and if we were engaged, we sure as hell wouldn't want our friends to read about it on social media."

"So tell us."

"Oh my god," she laughs, letting me go and moving ahead of me.

Smirking, I follow behind her, dropping into the seat on her right.

"Like I've told you a hundred times." She leans in close so only I can hear. "We want to keep it to ourselves until I graduate and can be with him full-time."

"That way, the pro huntresses don't go hard on him?"

"Pro huntresses?"

I shrug a shoulder. "Better than football groupies or cleat chasers, don't you think?"

She scoffs, grinning as she opens her book bag.

We pull out our materials, and I scroll on my phone as we wait for class to begin.

17

A few minutes pass when she nudges my elbow, and I follow her gaze.

My eyes land on a blond head at the front of the room, a white slip of paper in his hand.

"Coincidence?" I whisper.

In my peripheral, Ari shakes her head. "I'm going to go with no."

Alister stands at the front of the class, chatting with the professor.

A class I've already attended twice, seeing as it's the second week in the fall semester, so I know for a fact he's most definitely not in this class—at least not at this specific hour. I try to remember if I saw his name in the queue on the online hybrid portion, but I don't think I would have forgotten if I had.

Alister shakes the professor's hand and turns to walk away, but before his feet move a single step, his eyes lift, instantly locking on mine.

I give him a blank expression, and he smirks in response, winking my way before exiting. "Jackass," I mutter.

Ari chuckles beside me, and we all face forward when the professor speaks.

"Just a reminder, everyone. Two missed classes across the first three weeks and missed log-ins to our online blackboard, and you will be dropped from this course. If you're on the wait list, you should not be seated in the class. We're a full bunch this semester, so only those registered are permitted."

"He's trying to get into this class," I whisper.

"Seems like it."

"Why would a business major want to be in Instructional Design class?"

"I'm going to ignore that because there is no way you're actually asking that question."

I glare at my best friend, who hides her smile by sucking on her straw.

18

The professor starts his lecture, and I do my best not to die of boredom.

It's easier said than done.

Just like ignoring the existence of Alister freaking Howl.

Why is he being so…I don't even know what to call it.

I mean, the guy pretended to be into me, followed me around like a little lover boy for weeks. I laughed him off at first, assuming him to be like Brady—a massive flirt by nature—but then, I don't know. At some point and without my own knowledge, I realized I looked forward to those random pop-ups across campus. It wasn't long after that we started hanging out. Hanging out led to hooking up, and hooking up led to a boatload of self-pity.

Considering my obsession with *Dateline,* I should have caught on sooner. I mean what are the chances the superhot football player just so happened to be in the quad, café, and gym at the same time as me nearly every day?

I squish my lips to the side.

Okay, well, it's not exactly uncommon. I see a lot of the same people every day because anyone who has classes related to mine is on a relatively similar schedule. But still.

He was outside the damn child development building when I was headed in and near whatever building I was headed to on my way out, but now that I think about it, it was only when I was alone.

Never in front of my friends.

Because he was using you.

I sigh, propping my chin on my palm.

Like I said, I should have known, but at the end of the day, I enjoyed his attention. I needed it, having been in a funk since the first guy who made me feel more than attraction left me for something bigger, as he should have.

My heart aches a little at the thought of the boy—no, the *man* I met the summer before my first year of college. Little did I know he'd be in the same school come that fall. Had I known,

I probably wouldn't have gone full summer fling with him but rather taken things slow out of fear of what might happen once we had to see each other around campus. A small smile graces my lips as I think of Trey Donovan.

Maybe one day I'll find my way down south, catch one of his prime-time games. Last I heard, he was already breaking records as a rookie in the NFL.

I couldn't be prouder of him. He had a dream, and he made it come true.

He's exactly where he's supposed to be.

We can't all live the Hallmark movie plot. Sometimes people really do have to go their own ways in the end.

This time, I hold back the sigh desperate to escape.

I'm over this pity-party shit and ready to move back into boss-babe mode.

Which is why the second class ends and we're clear of the building, I spin and walk backward in front of my bestie, my hips rolling from side to side in my best attempt to be Shakira.

"Uh-oh." Ari teases with a small smile.

"Uh-oh is right."

The words register just before heavy arms come around my shoulders, and I reach up, locking my hands on Brady's forearms. Tipping my head to the side, I look up at him.

I'm not short, standing a whole-ass heel higher than Ari at an easy five ten, but Brady is beastly, so I still have to lift my chin a bit to meet his eye fully.

"I take it we're going out tonight?" He lifts a brow.

"Aw, cute. You think you're invited."

"Aw, cute." I face forward as Mason steps up, Chase at his side. "You think you girls are allowed to go anywhere without one of us."

"Us?" I scoff playfully. "Please. Like you won't be knee-deep in baby shit by seven. You wouldn't know if we did or didn't go out."

Mason grins. "Why do you think I said one of us?"

Ari laughs, and when she looks my way, it's written across her pretty, little face.

My shoulders fall. "You have a date with a hot jock, don't you?"

She squinches her nose, guilty. "FaceTime at six thirty."

I perk up a little. "Does that mean I get something good to eat tonight?"

She smiles. "We're making something called beef bourguignon." Pulling her phone free, she winces. "Actually, I need to head back to the dorm. He said the ingredients are being delivered around three."

"Fine. I'll allow you to ditch me so long as you keep feeding me."

"I'll go." Brady releases me with a shrug. "Can't get fucked up 'cause we got practice in the morning, but I can play bodyguard and dance partner."

"Tempting." I nod slowly. "But I think I'll see if Paige is back yet."

"Back from where?" Chase asks.

Glancing his way, I open my mouth to answer when I spot an interesting little scowl pulling at his forehead. "Why do you want to know?" I draw attention to his question, enjoying the way he straightens when all eyes move his way.

"Yeah, why you wanna know?" Brady doubles down with a chuckle.

"I don't," Chase answers swiftly. "She mentioned it, so I figured I'd ask."

I cock my head, and he scoffs.

He waves us off. "I've got a meeting with Coach. I'll see you girls tomorrow."

"Later," the boys call out while we wave, and I turn back to the others.

"Payton wrapped up her shoot with the new squad today,

so I'm taking her and little man somewhere tomorrow, get off campus for a bit," Mason says.

"No invite?" His sister pouts.

"Love you, but no." He chuckles. "I'd like to actually get to play with my son, and if you're there, I have to compete for his attention."

The way he says *my son* so fluidly and thoughtlessly is…I don't even know. What a man he is and at just twenty years old. He loves that little boy like his own, and he has maybe even since before he was born.

"This one's just for the three of us," he continues. "But we'll both be at the party after the game tomorrow."

"Mom and Dad decided to stay the night?" Ari asks.

"Any excuse to get to hang with Deaton." Mason smirks. "They're coming to the game and taking him back to their Airbnb from there. It'll be the first night Payton has spent without him—if she makes it all night."

Ari scoffs. "Please, it will likely be you who calls Mom and wants to pick him up in the middle of the night."

Brady smiles. "I'd bet on that. My boy hasn't spent a single night in his room since we got back to campus."

Mason only grins, his eyes sliding to the side. "Don't look now, but there's a Lancaster fan club coming."

We all turn to look, and the girls smile, not caring they were caught looking at football's finest.

Mason chuckles. "See you guys Saturday."

We nod, and Brady pins me with a hard look.

"If you go out tonight, I better get a call and *not* only after you're buzzin' and need a ride home."

"Whatever you say, Big Guy."

"I mean it." He frowns.

"I know."

That frown deepens. "Why do I feel like I'm being played right now?"

The twins laugh and my own follows. I take my fave twin and loop my arm through hers.

"Later, boys!" I shout when we're a few feet away.

"Swear to god, Cammie Baby, if you don't let me know you're going out!"

"What's he gonna do, spank me?" I say to Ari, and the two of us laugh.

We might be out of earshot, but he hears our laughter and shouts again.

"I didn't mean you can't call if you get buzzed! Swear, girl, your ass better if you drink somewhere! Do not walk home alone!"

Shaking our heads, we make the five-minute walk to our dorm building.

My mood is uplifted, and I decide a night in with some chocolate pudding, Scooby-Doo! grahams, and last week's episode of *Dateline* sounds like a nice way to end my school week.

I'm so glad I didn't sign up for hours at the child development center on Fridays. I'm living for these three-day weekends.

Perky and ready for a good face mask and junk food, I add a little skip to my step, and Ari chuckles, following along.

And then we walk around the corner, coming face-to-face with Alister freaking Howl.

He grins and I growl.

Of course, that only makes him grin wider.

But why does it have to be such a good grin? All curved and cool and gorgeous and shit.

"Hey, beautiful. Ari."

Ari gives a tight-lipped smile before glancing my way and motioning with her head to let me know she's going to go inside.

He watches her a moment, making this even more awkward, then looks back to me.

"How was class?" he asks, stuffing his hands in his pockets.

"Peachy. How's Allana?"

He winces, nodding as he glances away. "I deserve that."

Not exactly an answer that clears up if he's still playing the scorned, stalking lover.

Did he love her?

Better yet, does he love her?

Girl, stop.

You don't care.

I cross my arms. "Why are you waiting outside my dorm, Alister?"

"This is our thing, isn't it?" He gives a sad smile. "I follow you around until you pay attention to me."

A hint of warmth slips over me, yet it's swiftly followed by that bitter burn of betrayal, freezing out everything else.

Alister sees it, knows that his words backfired, and takes a step toward me. "Cam…"

He reaches for me, but I evade his touch, spinning and putting myself behind him, forcing him to turn too in order to keep me in his sights. A dejected sigh leaves him. "Can we please just talk for a bit?"

"No, Alister, we can't." I keep walking backward toward my dorm building entrance and he stays planted where he stands. "I told you before to just let it go. We were hooking up and now we're not. We're done. No hard feelings."

His eyes narrow at that. "I don't want to be done, and yes hard feelings. Cameron, I hurt you, and I'm sorry."

I jerk to a stop, my emotions bubbling up inside me and making it hard to tell which is stronger: the feeling of being the pathetic, oblivious girl or the pissed-off, burn-the-world-down one. "I said I was over it. I'm good, so just…go back to whatever it is you did before playing my shadow became your favorite pastime."

He watches me closely, his green gaze unsettling and making my palms start to sweat. When he finally does talk, it's not what I want to hear.

"I can't do that, Cam."

"And why is that?"

He gives a woeful smile. "Because I realized something in the last several months."

"That you're a royal dickhead?"

"That I'm pretty sure I'm falling in love with you."

My face falls.

My lungs shrivel.

My knees fucking shake.

"Fuck you, Alister." I hurry toward the dorms.

I don't look back when he calls my name and I don't wait around for the elevator, instead running up several flights of stairs until I reach my and Ari's floor. Shoving the door open, I rush inside, tugging at my long, blond hair as I search for my best friend.

She pops up off her bed the second she sees me coming, her arms open and waiting.

I fall into them, and together we sink onto the mattress.

She doesn't ask questions, and I don't offer answers. Words aren't necessary for us.

She just lets me pout and hugs me while I do it.

I feel the threat of tears burning my eyes, but I won't let them fall.

I'm not lovesick and broken by what Alister did to me.

Was I hurt and confused and angry when I found out I was a pawn in his little game of revenge seeking? No shit I was. Maybe, more than likely, still am, but mostly that's only when I think about it. It's not this dark cloud following me around like a thunderstorm of misery.

The fact of the matter is I was starting to really like the guy, but I wasn't in love with him by any means. I mean, shit, we were still sort of undercover when everyone found out I was but a fool who fucked a fool.

Yeah, that sounds bad. I mean, it's college. We all have sex we regret at some point.

Right?

How dare he say he's falling in love with me.

No, that he's "pretty sure" he's falling in love with me. Like, boy, fuck off, 'cause guess what? I'm "pretty sure" I hate you.

I groan, covering my face with my hands.

Pretty sure that's a lie.

CHAPTER 4
ALISTER

Game days in the locker room are an experience like no other, especially when it's a home game. It's that first part of the day you look forward to.

There's the juice of waking up knowing you get to take to the field for real that day, ready for all the hard work at practice to pay off. Then there's the drive or walk to the stadium, where you rock out to your favorite hype music, feeling those nerves starting to bubble up. Reaching the parking lot is when the excitement starts to kick in.

Coach gives a single time to arrive, so most everyone is piling into the parking lot within minutes of each other. That's when the earbuds are ripped out and the shouting and shit begin, amping up to the next level of anticipation. But that's nothing compared to when it comes time to suit up.

The locker room is pure chaos. It's loud and overstimulating and carries a sort of magic. There's anxiety and anticipation and every other emotion in existence.

Your buddies are screaming and shouting across the space, calling you out for a fuckup last week with a grin or jacking you up more by asking for a repeat of some sick-ass play you pulled off the week before. There's dancing and singing and videos being made for social media. There's bickering and shoving and full-on fights sometimes, but when Coach comes around that corner, it's forgotten. Done.

You don't snitch and you don't bitch.

You turn to your boys and get back to the good shit, running down all the ways you're going to attack or defend against the jerseys you're facing on the field.

I've always looked forward to the pregame locker-room nonsense.

Which is what has me clenching my jaw as I enter on my own, groups of players at my front, a few not far behind, and as I round the final corner leading to where my locker sits, another good dozen—not a single one acknowledges my presence, looking through me as if I'm a goddamn ghost.

The shitty part is I deserve it. Everyone knows you don't throw punches at your starting quarterback without consequences. Hell, hit him by accident on the field and you get the cheap shot you had coming.

Coming at him off the field at the football house no less?

Yeah, I'm officially iced out like a kicker on a crucial play, only worse.

My own damn team is against me.

Not that it's *my team*.

I could have had my own team. I had a starting quarterback position of my own, and I turned it down to come play second-string here at Avix U.

Why?

Why else do men do stupid, poorly-thought-out shit?

For the love of a girl.

My high school sweetheart, who graduated a year ahead of me. We made all these plans about what our future would look like, and when she went off to college, it was okay. I played my heart out on that high school football field and it paid off.

My offers had offers.

I knew coming to Avix meant I'd have to, one, battle it out for the starting position and hope I earned it or, two, prepare to play a few downs a season until it was my time. I didn't care. I just wanted to be with my girl.

Imagine my surprise when *my* girl was clearly pregnant and I hadn't touched her in a lot longer than what would have made that possible.

Grinding my teeth, I unzip my bag, shoving my phone inside, but I don't take out my earbuds just yet.

She could have thrown out any random person—Joe Blow at the corner store would have been better than the route she took—but instead, she told me the quarterback who I'd have to go up against for playing time was the man she was having a baby with.

Mason Fucking Johnson.

Cameron's best friend's twin brother.

It was all downhill from there.

Sighing, I shake my head.

I can't fucking *believe* Allana lied the way she did, but I had no reason to question her. After all, she was already pregnant with someone else's kid when I thought she was over here missing me like I was missing her. She cried throughout the entire conversation, told me he didn't know and would likely want nothing to do with her. And stupid fucking me, I became upset on her behalf.

I was pissed at her and him and my-damn-self.

I'd like to blame her for ruining what should have been one of the most exciting times of my life, but the truth is it's my own fault.

I should have just walked away, gave her what she deserved—absolutely nothing.

I didn't, and then I met a girl who was more than I knew was out there.

Soft and kind yet full of fire and sass, and she gave it all away freely.

I'd had to earn everything I had in my life, Allana included.

Cameron is different.

It's too bad I realized this after the fact.

I don't know why I didn't just let Allana go when I started to feel something real for Cameron, but I didn't. I guess four years of firsts and loyalty to someone messes with your head more than you expect.

It's a poor excuse, but it's all I've got.

I want to prove to Cameron that I—

My train of thought dies when I'm jolted from behind, and I whip around, a frown instantly in place as I tear my earbuds out, the rowdiness of the room making my ears ring for a split second. "What the fuck, man? You mind?"

Brady Lancaster, the O-lineman turned defensive end, cuts me a glance over his massive shoulder for nothing more than a lazy blink before facing forward and yanking his shirt over his head.

Because of course Mason's and his two best friends' lockers are directly opposite mine.

Shaking my head, I go back to getting dressed—and being ignored as conversation after conversation happens all around me.

God, I sound like a whiner.

It's not that I don't have guys I talk to on the team. They're just few and far between…and happen to be on the opposite side of the locker room.

I'm almost fully laced up and preparing to shoot to my feet and hit the field early for some stretches—anything to get me out of here—when I pick up on the conversation behind me.

"Girls are already here. Payton wanted to bring little man to meet the mascot and walk him around for a bit, hopin' he'll nod off during the game." Mason tells his friends, "Kind of want him to stay awake and watch."

"Dude, he's what, almost two? He'll watch for all of five seconds, and he ain't gonna have any idea which one of us you are once the helmets are on anyway. He's more likely to get excited by the frozen lemonade guy." Brady chuckles. "Let her wear the kid out the way you're gonna wear his mama out tonight."

"I don't know if that's fucked up or not," Chase adds. "So your parents are taking the baby. You walking over with me and the others or hanging back and waiting for Cam and this guy?"

Mason asks exactly what I'm wondering: "Why are you and Cam coming late anyway?"

"Gotta get her ass back to the dorm. She has a debt to pay, and I can't wait to cash in." Brady chuckles, and the others join in.

I frown at my locker, blindly picking up my bag and setting it inside.

What's that supposed to mean?

"She waiting for you after the game or what?" Chase asks.

"Nah. She's going back with the buddy-walk crew so she can get shit ready for me. She doesn't want to stick around here longer than she has to."

I wince at that, knowing those words are for me and not missing how they all go silent the moment I stand.

I should walk away. I know that.

The last thing I need is to stir up more shit with three starters and my team captain. I've already been hit by two of these guys. I'm not looking to add a third.

For some reason I spin, plastering on a careless, asshole-like grin as if I'm completely unbothered, and I'm met with three hard stares.

I quirk my lips up higher. "So no need for me to show up early tonight, huh?"

Brady shoots to his feet, but Chase catches him around the collar and Brady clenches his fist, allowing his buddy to tug him back down.

I don't want to hear what might be said after that. I hustle out of the room, stepping into the tunnel that will lead me to the field.

I can't think about this shit right now. There's a game to play soon, and I need to focus just in case I'm called off the sidelines.

Right now, I'm going to worry about the plays on the field, and tonight, I'll decide which ones to use off it.

Win the game, then win the girl.

That's the plan.

We won't talk about how every plan I've ever made for my life has failed miserably.

Damn it.

CHAPTER 5
CAMERON

I shuffle back, smoothing out the final edge of the towels, and stand. Staring at my arrangement, I purse my lips, wondering if I should have set us up on the floor. In the end, I shrug and move into the kitchen. "He'll just have to put his arms at his sides if they hang over the edge."

Opening the fridge, I peer around the drinks in search of some of Ari's leftovers from yesterday, but there's no luck. All that's staring back at me is several bottles of chocolate Ensure shakes and fresh ingredients I want nothing to do with. One of the best parts about being away at college? My parents aren't hovering over my shoulder every couple hours, asking what I've eaten so far today. It's sweet and I'm blessed with a family who cares, but sometimes I just want to pretend it doesn't matter if I'm having too much fun to remember to eat.

I was thirteen and still hadn't hit puberty when my parents and I realized something might be wrong with me. I wasn't overly active like the boys, so we knew that wasn't the cause of the "late blooming" as Mom called it, and then there's the fact that I was, and still am, an eater—I eat all the time and I'm almost never full. Well, at least not for long.

I was hungry after breakfast but before lunch and then raiding the fridge before dinner just to do it again before bed—sometimes twice. Not just snacks either but actual food, though I have always been a bit of a snacking queen, too. There is never not some sort of munchies in my purse or backpack, and it's always been that way.

All that food down the hatch, and I was stick skinny, sometimes sickly so. My clothes had to be sewn or pinned if I wanted to wear what others my age were wearing. If not that, then I was stuck in leggings meant for a seven-year-old and what looked like oversized T-shirts, but that was before it was an actual trend to do so.

Kids were assholes until Brady and Mason chased them around the playground, and my teachers thought I was neglected or underfed. It didn't help that I was taller than all the girls in my class at that age.

Turned out I have an overactive thyroid. They say I'm "one of the lucky ones" because I can manage my disease with meds, and I didn't learn about the other challenges the disease would leave me with until I was a little older. *But we don't think about that part, Cameron.*

I don't remember to take the pills every day, but I remember enough that I don't have hardcore issues, and I'm no longer worried about blowing away with the wind. It helps now that I've forced myself not to hate weight training and have built muscle over the bones to help me look fit rather than frail, but it takes a good amount of carbs to manage. I still have to down some less-than-desirable shakes a few times a week and eat some nasty greens here and there, though.

Yeah, I am not feeling either of those options at the moment.

I sigh, staring longingly at the empty shelf meant for leftovers in the fridge.

Ugh! Does the dream couple have to be all into health shit right now? What a girl wouldn't give for him to start teaching Ari how to bake. Maybe then I wouldn't have to drink shitty shakes at all.

There's a hard rap on the door, and I frown, moving to look

out the peephole. My eyes flick to the ceiling, and I tug the damn thing open, blinking at the guy on the other side.

"You look…" Alister grins, eyes traveling over my game-day outfit. "Damn."

Today I'm wearing the white AU T-shirt that I turned into a fun, fringy thing. I cut the bottom nearly up to my bra line, the pieces even with each other and about a half an inch wide. The AU is outlined and bedazzled with little diamonds, also in the matching colors of the lettering.

To go with the cowgirlesque style I created, I'm wearing my cutoff jean shorts, some dark blue fishnets underneath, and short cowgirl boots. My hair is up in a high pony with glitter helping to slick it back, and my lips are so pink they'd make Barbie jealous.

Too bad none of it was for him.

I just like to dress for every occasion.

"What are you doing here, Alister?"

"I heard you were headed home right after the game…" He trails off, a strange look in his eye, as if he wants to ask me something but isn't sure he should.

I'm gonna call that progress.

"Well." I lift my arm, motioning to my living room. "Looks like you heard right."

His lips form a tight line, and he just continues to stare.

I raise my brows. "Okay, well, I wish I could say thanks for stopping by, but considering I asked you to back off a bit and you're here, I—"

"A bit?"

Confusion bubbles within me. "What?"

Alister steps forward, and I hold my breath. "You said you want me to back off *a bit*."

"Um…" Did I say that? "I didn't mean that…like—" I cut myself off, flustered, and my cheeks start to pinken when Alister's grin slowly grows, showing off his perfect, pretty-boy teeth. It's like he had braces twice or something. And monthly whitening appointments.

And a lifetime membership to the gym…

Alister chuckles, coming so close I don't notice his hand lift until his palm is closing over my hip.

I curl my toes in my boots, hating how familiar his touch is and the reminder of the last time his hands were on me.

It just so happens the last time we had sex was also the same day I learned he pretended to like me to try and get dirt on his competition.

My face must show where my mind has gone, as Alister's grin begins to fall.

His free hand comes up then, attempting to cup my cheek, but I turn away at the last moment.

"Please," he whispers, and to my disgust, I feel the heat of tears building.

And to my absolute horror, the most protective man in our entire crew appears.

Even with my head turned away, my eyes find mossy brown ones over Alister's shoulder.

I'm not sure what he sees, but my fun, flirty guy turns red and then his fist is locking around the back of Alister's neck.

Alister tenses as he releases me and tries to yank free, but Brady's hand is wider than the guy's neck, his fingers curling around so far, they press against his throat.

Brady jerks him backward, and his eyes meet mine, silently asking me what I want him to do.

Alister is bitching, but I don't hear anything he's saying.

I give Brady a subtle shake of my head and step to the side, opening the door up more. That's all the answer he needs, tossing Alister into the hall like he's nothing but a rag doll and not a five-eleven football player.

He gives Alister not another moment's attention but slips inside and eases the door closed behind him.

With the soft click of the lock, he completely transforms, his giant smile and glittering gaze now staring down at me. "You look like Ken's wet dream."

A laugh flies from me and Brady's smile widens. He kisses my temple and shuffles by, dropping onto the carpet, his back hitting the ground with a loud thump.

That's when I actually get a look at him, realizing he's still got eye black smeared all over his face and turf tape up to his elbow.

I look to the clock above the TV and back. "Rush out tonight or what? You told me you'd be here closer to nine thirty–ish."

"That was before fuckface booked it from the locker room before I could even get my damn pads off."

"Ah," I chuckle. "Yeah, I figured he must have overheard something."

"Yeah, and then I got stuck on my way out and it took me even longer."

"Let me guess, Lancaster Ladies in waiting?"

"That's good. You should lead the fan club, suggest an official name. Maybe suggest they take a couple days off a week."

I scoff a laugh, but it's light.

Brady's smile slowly falls as he looks at me with a gentler expression. "You good, Cammie Baby?"

I manage a half grin, grabbing his shoulder and giving him a little squeeze. "I'm good, mountain man. Go shower and I'll order us something to eat."

He shakes his head as he kicks his shoes off and digs into his bag for a fresh outfit. "Delivery drivers won't be able to get through the shit show of traffic for another hour. If we wanna eat, we'll have to scrape something together here or walk somewhere before the party."

"Ugh, fine, fine. Hustle your ass."

"Yes, ma'am," he chuckles, disappearing into the bathroom and closing the door behind him.

Back in my room, I light the candles and jump up on my bed,

spraying the misting spray I decided was free—seeing as it was on the counter of the hotel we stayed at in Denver when we went to Noah's preseason game the week before school started—up into the low spinning fan.

It gets in my mouth and I cough, hopping back down and fixing the towels on my mattress again.

Less than five minutes pass and Brady slides in, in a pair of boxers, flopping right onto my makeshift massage table. "Ready, Glinda the Good Witch. Work your magic on me."

I toss my phone onto the pillow and climb over him, sitting down on his thighs because I'm too lazy to stand.

I get straight to work, pouring some warm oil along his spine and slowly working it into his muscles. He's tense, likely sore from playing a kick-ass game tonight, so I take it easy to start but press into him a little firmer as I go on.

I'm almost positive he's fallen asleep after about ten minutes of nothing but his deep, even breaths, but then he lets out a satisfied moan.

"You should be paid for this," he mumbles, his face half pressed into the towel beneath him. "I mean, not from me but…"

I chuckle and press the tips of my fingers along his spine, working up and down. "In another life, I would totally open a day spa."

"Why not in this life?"

I shrug, trying not to think about what it could mean for me if I didn't choose a career that allowed me time with little ones, and press my palms into the space below his shoulders, kneading out the knot there.

Brady groans long and loud, and I smile to myself. "You're too sweet to be so mean with your hands twenty-four seven, aren't you?"

"Ha!" I mock and Brady laughs, but it's quickly cut off when I dig my knuckles along the tension line in his shoulder blade, his sharp hiss following. Biting back a laugh, I bend down, whispering in his ear. "You were saying?"

"I take it back. You're not Glinda. You're Maleficent. Evil, evil woman."

I do laugh now, easing my touch and gliding my hands down, collecting a little more of the oil and sliding back up until my fingers are curling around the front of his shoulders. I skate them out and down his biceps, then back again.

"Jesus. No I take it *all back.* You're not allowed to be a massage lady. Stick to the hot kindergarten-teacher thing. None of you girls are ever doing this professionally. This shit is bonerfide."

"Bona what?"

"Boner. Fide. As in boner inducing. As in dudes will be getting hard anytime you—"

"I think I get it." I smile, shaking my head. "Honestly, I only took that class this summer because I was bored. Ari stayed with Noah most of the time, and you guys were doing all your offseason training shit, so when Paige told me about the little studio near hers offering it right there in Oceanside, I figured why not. We signed up that same day."

"So what you're telling me is I should tell Chase that Paige has magic hands too?"

My mouth gapes and I slap him, sliding off his ass so I'm beside him and can meet his eye, a laugh bubbling up my throat. "Oh my. Shit, I fucking knew it! He wants to bone her down, doesn't he?"

Brady's whole body shakes with his chuckle, and he shifts, lifting an arm and tugging me up higher so we're face-to-face. "I mean that's the vibe I get, and I can usually tell when someone's fuck meter is full, but I mean, if I asked him, he'd probably say he more wants to strangle her than straddle her."

"And because you're a fantastic fucking friend, you would then remind him that that very frame of mind will lead to the best of sex." I smile wide.

Brady coughs and releases me, pushing up and swinging his legs off the bed. "What are friends for, right?"

Why does that sound so evasive?

I push up into a sitting position, meeting his eyes when he glances at me over his shoulder.

"Come on, girl. Let's get some food and get to the party before all the good beer is gone."

I roll my eyes but do as he says. "We're in college, Brady. There is no such thing as good beer."

I slide my boots back on, checking myself quickly in the long mirror as Brady pulls on some pants and tugs a T-shirt over his head. He runs his fingers through his golden-boy, dirty-blond hair and gives his head a little shake.

"Do you even have to try and get laid, or do girls just fall from the sky and land on your dick?"

"What the fuck?" Brady laughs, looking up at me as he drops down to put on his shoes.

"You're like hot jock mixed with the naughty pool boy. Like Scott Eastwood, the *Suicide Squad* and *The Longest Ride* versions mashed together. But somehow even hotter."

"Somehow, huh?" He climbs to his feet, making a show of running his hands down his torso and doing a little stripper hip roll.

"Okay, Magic Mike. Save it for the dance floor." I head for the door, and Brady reaches past me, tugging it open.

Once outside, I let out a little yawn and Brady laughs, wrapping his arm around my shoulders. "Food first?"

"Food first."

The two of us head over to the small pizza place across the road, and just as we're walking through the doors, the others call, saying they're starving too.

Forty-five minutes later, we're sitting on the patio of the place with our best friends, a couple pitchers of beer being passed between us and three empty pizza trays.

We never make it to the party.

And I forget to remember that this time last year, I was like Ari and Payton and had a man I considered my own.

I'm oh for two at college.

Here's to hoping junior year won't make it three.

CHAPTER 6
BRADY

The treadmill slows as I switch it into cool down mode, and I tug my earbuds from my ears, letting the wires hang from the lip of my hoodie. The gym was pretty empty the first forty or so minutes I was here, but people started shuffling in about twenty minutes ago, and in another twenty, there will be so many that some will be waiting around for certain machines. Yet another reason I like to be the first through the doors each morning.

That and I don't sleep all that much. When I was younger, my mom would have to give me melatonin to get me to pass out, and even then, it still took me a few hours of staring at the dark ceiling and counting the number of times the fan went around before I'd pass out. It didn't matter how early I woke that day or how much I ran around and let out energy, my brain just never could quite shut itself off.

Now that I'm older, it's not so much that it's hard to fall asleep but hard to stay asleep. Hence the four a.m. mental wake-up call.

I'm at the gym before five every day and gone before most even know I was here. It's funny, even Coach questioned me a couple months into my first season here freshman year, asked if I was skipping out on the weight room and my mandated workout plan because when they were asked, none of the other coaches could remember spotting me more than a handful of times.

I happily started snapping them inappropriate pictures of me slick with sweat at five thirty in the morning, and after a good reaming on the field, they quit asking.

I laugh thinking about it, deciding I should get up to that shit again and wondering who would appreciate a sweaty, sexy motherfucker like me being the first person they laid eyes on in the morning.

For some reason, Cameron comes to mind first. Probably 'cause she's good for my ego, not that I have a problem with that. I know what I am and what I'm not. And I'm not ugly or out of shape or hard on the eyes.

It's with that thought that I tug my shirt over my head and drape it over the back of my neck, my dad's first set of dog tags ever given to him hanging between my pecs. I lift the camera screen up and turn slightly, so no other bodies are in the pic, and flex, my muscles so slick with sweat, it looks like my back did after the massage—slicked up and ready for a ride. I stick my tags between my teeth, running one hand through my hair, and take the photo.

A couple guys laugh from the left and I only smile at my screen.

It's the perfect thirst trap if I've ever seen one. Grinning, I fire it off to Cameron without a single word before stuffing it back in my pocket.

It's true what she said the other night.

Girls do tend to fall, sometimes quite literally, right on my dick. I can't tell you how many college girls decide my lap is free for the taking and straddle me right then and there in the middle of a party. I don't hate it, but they're coming around a little more aggressively now after that damn post on the *Avix Inquirer*'s social media page. It was a photo Payton took of me on the sidelines after a game, sweaty and grinning like a fool after a win. It said something about landing Lancaster and referenced Noah— basically a sneaky way of using Ari and Noah's relationship and teasing who would be the girl I took with me all the way to the top, assuming I go pro.

Again, I don't hate the attention.

I'm a flirt by nature, and I like being a part of the reason others have a good time. Most call me the party boy, the good time guy, and let's be real, I'm both those things. From what I hear, my roster is longer than Casanova's.

If they only fucking knew.

I smirk, nodding at my boy Xavier when he walks by, and head into the locker room. I'm tearing my bag off the shelf when fuckhead across from me shuffles in, his face paler than his usual pasty-ass self.

"What's up, man," he mumbles, pulling shoes from his bag.

"You're blood alcohol level by the looks of it." I glance his way as I tug my bag over my shoulder, deciding I'll shower back at the dorm since I don't have class until eight. "Looks like you could use a few hours in the sauna." I go to walk past him but pause to meet his eye. "Not that that will do you any good. Karma never gets it wrong."

Alister glares and I bump his shoulder as I walk past, frowning at the door ahead.

I hate being an ass to my teammates—it fucks with the team dynamics—but I can't find it in me to be nice to the guy. Not now.

He fucked with my friends, and in my book, that means he fucked with me.

If his ex-girlfriend carried her lie any further, it might have messed things up between Mason and Payton, and that would have broken my best friend. His girl and the family he's created with her and her son—no, their son—are his entire world now, and Alister threatened that by acting like a child about everything instead of coming at him like a man should. You just don't fuck around when there's a child involved. To top off the asshole sundae, he went and used our kindhearted Cameron to try and get to him.

I know the girl is fierce. Hell, she's a handful of a woman

on her off days, forever keeping us boys on our toes, but she's dreamed of opening a day care or running a kindergarten program for years, and while she hasn't said what it was—at least not in front of us guys—something happened our senior year of high school that pushed her determination to reach her goals even further. And *he* threatened that by messing with her head and altering her focus. She nearly failed her finals that semester.

The girl might be hell on wheels, but at the same time, she's soft as the sunset. Shit, she cries at those car commercials during the Super Bowl.

That dickhead made her cry—even if she didn't allow us to see it, I know it's true. I told that fucker to stay away from her, and as far as I've heard, he's finally getting the hint. Thank fuck for that, 'cause as much as I'd enjoy doing it, I'd hate to have to kick his ass.

A scoff leaves me, and I smile as I push out the double doors, stepping out into the early morning sun.

That's a fucking lie if I ever told one.

I'd thoroughly enjoy getting to kick Alister Howl's ass.

And we're not going to think about why the thought alone brings me satisfaction.

What is it they say, ignorance is bliss? I'm sure it is up until the day you're blindsided by the truth you never saw coming, because once you know the truth, there's no turning back.

No forgetting or letting go.

After that it's just the truth…and the lies you're forced to tell yourself.

CHAPTER 7
CAMERON

"If it isn't the ultimate boy toy."

Brady spins around, his grin wide and devilish. "I take it you got my picture this morning, Sleeping Beauty?"

"I like to think I'm more of Merida, little wild, little out there, hates to do what she's told. And what were you trying to do, give a girl a quivery clit first thing in the morning?"

Someone fights a laugh, and I lean to the side just as Brady moves one foot to the right, revealing another guy from the team, Fernando, I think his name is, standing there.

I feel my face start to flame and purse my lips. "Well…okay, so this is your fault." I glare at Brady.

His smirk grows and he puts a hand over his heart. "My fault? Pray tell, princess."

"You can't just…stand there and hide people behind your big-ass shield of a body. If I can't see him, then I don't know when to censor and keep my jokes to myself."

"I vote never." The guy raises his hand, and I scowl at him.

"Aw, come on," Brady teases. "It's not my fault I'm so…thick and long." He fights a laugh.

His friend *fails* to do the same.

I narrow my eyes at him. "You know what? All right. Keep throwing those words out there, and I'm going to feel the need to call your bluff. Better think twice next time you wear drawstring bottoms to class, Brady Lancaster. You never know when you're gonna find your pants around your ankles."

His grin is a full-on smile now. "Hey, just make sure there's a lot of people around when you go in for the kill, okay? Street cred and all."

I hum, raising a brow. "I'll make sure it's cold out."

His mouth drops open in horror, and I laugh, bumping my shoulder into his arm for the sake of doing it, and head into the coffee shop without him.

He can order his own damn protein muffin.

I've been in line for about five minutes when my name is called out by the barista, and I look over to see who shares a name with me, only to find Brady smiling my way as he walks by. He picks up a drink that looks suspiciously like my order with one hand, and he brings a giant chocolate muffin to his mouth with his other.

Eyes on mine, he bites into it obnoxiously, and I scoff, tearing out of the line and snatching my drink from his grasp. He laughs around his mouthful, kissing my temple and making me cringe when warm chocolate is left behind.

"You little shithead!" I laugh, pushing him away. "And you could have told me you ordered for me already...before I came in and waited in line for no reason."

"Meh, that takes the fun out of it."

"Well, you're forgiven, and thank you. I'll Apple Pay the money over later."

"I'll just send it right back."

True.

I'll make sure to tie us up next time there's a chance.

"Ready for the first quiz today?" he asks.

"Ready as I can be." I nod, smiling over at him. "Thanks again for studying with me last week."

"Always. Now come on. We've got A's to earn."

"I like asses to kick better."

Brady chuckles and into the building we go, ready to make the first quiz of the year our bitch.

47

"God, that woman is such a bitch." I shove the door open, stomping out into the sun and tipping my head back. Maybe I suddenly turned into a vampire, and it will turn me to ash so I never have to go back into that damn class again.

My brow furrows.

My luck, I'll become a vampire and fucking glitter in the sun.

Brady chuckles, and when I hear him move past me, I open my eyes and fall in step beside him. "Your phone went off during the quiz," he says.

"It happens." I shrug.

"Three times."

"Not my fault. I didn't text myself."

He glances my way, brow raised. "After you told her you turned it off."

I growl, crossing my arms. "Whose side are you even on?"

He only laughs harder, checking the time on his screen. "Come on, I'll walk you to the child development center on my way out."

"I can't believe you're already done with classes for the day."

"That's what happens when you can function like a real human and take early classes."

"Sounds like a drag."

He shakes his head, lips tipped up. "So who was texting you anyway?"

My eyes snap his way, and I pinch my mouth to the side, facing forward once more. I walk several feet before I realize he stopped, and I'm too chicken to turn all the way around, so I peek over my shoulder instead.

"Cameron," he drawls.

I smile, wide and fake. The man can't stand lies, even tiny ones that don't affect him, and I don't know what it is, but there's something about him that refuses to allow me to even try.

48

It's how the boys always knew what party to burst into when we were growing up—neither me nor Ari could lie to the man. And well, even if we tried, he'd see right through us midattempt, and we'd fold like origami.

"Is that asshole seriously still bothering you?" He starts walking again and I loop my arm in his, dragging him along the path.

"It's fine."

"It's not fine. You told him to leave you alone. We fucking told him to leave you alone when he decided not to do what you asked." Brady shakes his head, glaring at nothing ahead.

"Brady." I give him a little jiggle. "Stop thinking of ways you're going to deal with this."

He grins. "But there're just so many good ones to choose from."

I laugh at that but pull him to a stop a few feet from the student entrance. "For reals. Freshman season, things were fucked with the Chase drama. Sophomore season, Mason was a walking zombie when Payton wasn't around. It's our junior year, your third season on the university football field. I don't want you guys to have any bullshit to stress over where I'm concerned."

"Baby girl, don't make me tackle you right here." He glares.

I chuckle. "All I'm saying is you don't have to go all alpha for me. None of you boys do. I can handle a groveling flirt with my eyes closed."

Brady cocks his head, eyes narrowing in that gauging way of his, and I realize what I said. "Wait. Are you… Do you like that he's still trying?"

I bite into my lip and look away, pulling in a deep breath. "Um…" *Do I?*

"Yo!" is shouted, and we both look left to find a few guys from the team waiting at the edge of the building with their bags hung over their shoulders.

"Fuck. I forgot I told some of the guys I'd step in to spot for the afternoon session."

"If you keep adding a random third workout to your day, you're going to reach Hulk status."

He makes a show of flexing his muscles, moving from one pose to the next.

"Yeah, yeah." I roll my eyes with a grin. "You're enormous. Perfect. Zero percent body fat."

Brady sticks his tongue between his teeth and winks, jogging off with a laugh when I shove at his shoulder.

I head inside through the employee and student entrance, smiling at Granny Grace behind the counter.

"Morning." I move toward the lockers in the left corner.

Granny Grace shakes her head with a grin. "Honey, it's eleven thirty."

"And I'd likely still be in bed if it were up to me." I grin, swiftly putting my things away and tying up my hair as I walk around the back counter. "How many we got this morning?"

"Afternoon, and twelve right now, but we have three pickups in the next hour and five drop-offs a bit after that."

I sigh happily, washing my hands and nudging the swinging door with my butt. "Well, I better get in there. See you in three hours!"

Granny Grace waves without looking my way, and I smile as I move into the main care room. I hope I'm still smiles and kind eyes fifty years from now.

"Hey, Junie!" I call when I spot her.

"Hello, trouble."

"Trouble? Me?" I tease, spotting my favorite little guy—not that I can say that out loud, not that it's a secret. I swoop Deaton up before he has a chance to turn around, giving him a little wiggle. "Never, huh, Little D?" I kiss his chubby cheeks, turning him in my arms, and he wraps his hands around my neck, squeezing.

"Calmy!" he squeals in his little baby voice, his attempt at saying Cammie the cutest thing ever. The nickname is adorable, and the others have started to use it more and more because of it.

"I've ball!" He lifts the little football in his hands, patting it softly against my chest.

"Yeah, you do!" I beam, kissing his cheeks one more time before setting him back down where he was standing. I look up at Junie as she comes over, making crazy baby faces at little Bella, the new one-year-old who joined us this semester.

"Look who is here early."

I wiggle my fingers, and Bella reaches out, leaning into my hands. I take her from Junie, bouncing her softly as I sing my words for my boss slash professor, "Anything specific you need from me to start?"

"If you want to take over here, help them wash their hands, I'll get the lunch table ready. Ashley and Melanie are with the infants, so it's just me and you with these five until the others come in. By the way, we've got some new girls starting here pretty soon. Just waiting on their papers to be signed and sent over from the director's office. You and Ash are my only third-years, so they'll take turns shadowing you."

"Sounds good. Just let me know if I need to change any times or anything."

"Yep." She waves me off, and I move over to the little washing station and toss a towel down, lowering onto my knees and setting Bella on my lap.

"It's time to wash the baby, wash, wash the baby…" I start to sing as I turn on the warm water, and of course, Deaton is the first to run over, his two little buddies right on his heels.

Playing with all the little ones make the hours go by in a flash. Before I know it, Payton is here for pickup, letting me know I went a little over my three-hour mark.

She beams at me as I step into the pickup area, Deaton's hand in mine. She bends, her camera bag weighing her down further, and opens her arm for her baby boy, who doesn't hesitate to throw himself into her chest. She laughs lightly, burying her face in his neck.

51

"Time for home?" He pats her cheeks.

"Yeah, time for home." She kisses his cheek, looking back to me. "You coming?"

"Go ahead. I still need to sign out and grab my things."

"K. Mason is picking him up the next couple days, but I'm sure I'll talk to you in between."

"Sounds good." I wave at Deaton, but he's already dragging his mama out the door.

Smiling, I make quick work of saying bye to everyone and grabbing my things, skipping out the back door again as I leave.

I pull my phone from my bag, texting Ari, but before I can hit Send, I slam into a wall with an oomph. Sturdy hands close around my biceps, and I look up into a pair of green eyes. "Alister."

"Hi, Cam."

For a moment, I just stare at him, my attention falling to his mouth when it forms an annoyingly gorgeous grin. I've kissed that mouth more times than I'd care to admit. I know exactly how full and soft those lips are. How skilled.

How they feel against my skin—

Fuck, shit. No.

No!

I pull away, blinking to clear whatever the hell expression took over my face to make him smile like a spider who's already caught me in his web.

"I hate spiders."

"What?" He grins.

I blink again, clearing my throat. "What?"

Alister chuckles, and when I start walking, he falls in step beside me.

"You know, stalking is a criminal offense."

"What's criminal is going to bed without talking to you first."

Do not flutter, oh weak and needy heart of mine.

"Yes, well. We could talk all day and all night." I pause, glancing his way in time to watch his smile spread and not looking away so I get to witness as it falls. "You know, if you weren't playing the role of Brian O'Conner, making me Mia Toretto in this scenario. You know, the guy with the hidden agenda, fucking the girl who was none the wiser."

And there that smile goes, a sharp pinch of his lips taking its place.

Alister reaches out, gently taking my hand and tugging me to a halt. "Cammie," he whispers, a low, tragic sound.

Treacherous tears sting my eyes, and I gingerly tug myself free. "You don't get to call me that. That nickname is reserved for friends only, and we're not friends."

"I don't want to be friends, Cameron. I want to be more."

"Did you learn nothing last year?" I grip my backpack straps before he can try and reach out for me again and take a few backward shuffles away. "We don't always get what we want." Alister stares at me, and because it's clear his determination hasn't dissipated in the slightest, I add, "If we did, you wouldn't be standing here. You'd be skipping across campus, holding hands with the girl you *came here to be with* in the first place."

He opens his mouth and closes it before he finally says, "Not fair, baby."

"I'm not your baby."

"I want you to be."

"Jesus!" I shake my head, my cheeks getting warm for some reason. "Are you even listening to me?!"

Alister smiles, and I want to slap it off his face. "I am, but I don't like what you're saying, so I'm choosing to ignore it."

"You're... Ugh!" I growl, spinning and stalking away. "Stay away from me, Alister!"

"That's going to be tough for me, Cameron!"

"Life's tough. Get a helmet!" I shout back, whirling to glare at him once more. "Oh wait, you have one...not that you'll be getting any use out of it!"

I wince at my own words, this time walking away so fast, one might call it running.

Damn it, that was a low blow, but I mean, so was fucking a girl he just pretended to like to get close to someone else. Several times, I might add. And well.

Fuck. No. Stop it!

It doesn't matter if he supposedly caught feelings along the way, making his own plan fall in on himself. It means nothing that he's sorry now. Even shitty people feel remorse every now and again, and I refuse to be the dumb girl who gives a man a pass only to get hit in the heart even harder the next time.

I won't forgive him.

I can't forgive him.

I drag my hands down my face with a groan.

Jesus fuck, why do I sort of kind of want to forgive him?

CHAPTER 8
CAMERON

With a squeal, I toss the Ziploc full of plastic forks back in the bag and dash across the quad the moment my parents come into view.

My dad smiles wide, his arms already outstretched, and I jump, letting him catch me and twirl me around the way he always does.

He chuckles, lowering me back to my feet, and I tear away instantly, wrapping my arms around my mom's neck, hugging the life out of her before moving back to my dad.

He smiles, his whiskers scratchy against my face. "And here I thought you didn't need me and your mama anymore."

"Pshh. Yeah right." I tug back, smiling at the two of them. "Who else is going to pay my tuition?"

My dad laughs loudly, slinging his arm around my mom and tugging her closer as I start to lead them toward the quad.

I wrap my arm through my dad's free one, smiling down at the two of them. "How's Zeus?"

"He's getting grayer around the whiskers but still bringing your mama mice as gifts when she's trying to relax on the back deck." My dad grins when my mom makes a face.

"Don't make that face, Mother dear. You're going to cry like a baby when I take him after I graduate."

I don't realize what I said until both my parents' feet falter, and they turn to look at me fully. Shit.

My mom's features soften, and she reaches out to take

my hand. "So you've decided? You're moving out right after graduation?"

"I mean…" I look for an out. Moving out wasn't *exactly* what I was thinking, but I don't want to get into that yet. "Look, it's not like it's happening tomorrow. It's only September, and I've still got another year after this and—"

"Pumpkin, it's all right." My dad tries to smile reassuringly, but it just looks a little sad. "We've known since you were two feet tall that the pigs and chickens wouldn't be enough for a girl with a heart the size of a blue whale."

My scowl is instant. "I love the farm."

"I know, but we moved to the house in town for a reason. You're a people person, Cameron, and we've known that for a long time." He pauses, looking over at my mom. "Actually, your mama and I have been talking about selling the house, moving back to the one on the property."

My face falls, my eyes instantly finding my best friends across the yard. "You're selling the house?" They're moving onto the farm property?

"Don't look so sad. We both know if you're not coming home, Ari isn't coming home. Hell, I'd be surprised if any of you do since you're all sharing the beach house in Oceanside."

Sadness fills me at the thought of not going back to my child-hood home, my best friend's place just a skip away, but I get it and it makes sense. I look back to my mom and dad. "You know"—I cock my head—"I should have seen this coming."

My dad smiles, wrapping his arm around me and steering us over to where Ari has finished unpacking the bag we brought of paper products, spreading them out along the picnic tables piled with items others contributed.

"Hi, guys!" Ari beams, hugging my parents and pointing them in the direction of where hers are already settled alongside Brady's, Deaton the center of attention as he runs between them, forcing them all to take chip after chip that he offers.

"Man, to be a baby who can make anyone do anything that they want." I sigh dramatically and Ari chuckles, hip checking me. "You bummed your boo thang isn't here?"

Her smile grows a little sad, and she looks out across the quad, gaze settling on her brother manning one of the many grills, as per usual, Payton at his side. "Last year was tough, but with everything going on with Mason, me, and Payton, I had a distraction. This year though..." She pinches her lips to one side. "I mean we're only a few weeks into the semester now and I just feel like I'm—"

"Swear to god, if you say missing half your soul or something else super Hallmark like that, I might actually vomit, and the wedges I'm wearing are way too cute for that."

The longing melts off Ari's expression and she grins, both of us smiling softly, no words needing to be said. She knows I know what she means, even if I can't possibly understand how it must feel to be apart from someone you'd literally cut your heart out for and hand it to them if the situation demanded it.

She sighs, but it's not a gloomy sound, and wraps her arms around me. "Thanks, Cam."

"Welcome, sister. What am I good for if not the art of distraction? Now let's go rescue the 'rents before Deaton fills them up on Funyuns."

She laughs, and we make our way over, dropping down into the grass between our parent's chairs, and chat about school, their work, and every other random topic that comes up.

About half an hour later, Chase returns from picking up his parents at the airport.

"Chase, honey, it's so good to see you!" Ari's mom jumps up, always the first to take her "second children," as she calls us all, into her arms. She holds on to him a moment longer than she did us, and I know it's because she senses he needs it.

We like to joke Brady is more like her than his own mom, what with his perceptive-ass self.

I sneak a peek at Ari, and she meets my gaze, her shrug only noticeably to me.

I wonder if it's because she still feels for Chase after everything that went down between him, Ari, and Noah our freshman year.

Ari's mom whispers something, and he nods, pulling back with a soft smile.

Chase makes his rounds, saying hello to everyone else.

I glance around for his parents, but it's Brady who hops up from his spot on the grass opposite me. "You lose your parents from the parking lot to here?" He lifts baby Deaton and puts him on his massive shoulders.

Chase's chuckle is tense, and he nods toward the buildings. "Nah, they paused at the restrooms. They'll be over here in a minute. I'm going to see if Mase is ready for a break."

"We'll come too," Brady offers, and his dad pushes to his feet so their standing side by side.

The difference between them is stark and always makes me smile.

While Brady is built like a heavy-weight champion, wide and broad along the shoulders, tapering down into a thick, strong waist, his dad stands about five inches shorter than him, his build more that of a runner. He's lean, and while he is very fit for his age, he looks skinny in his shirt and jeans when side by side with his son. He's a military man with impeccable posture and his son basically has a master's in that hot, lazy-man slouch. I have never seen Ben slouch.

Like me, Brady got his hair and eye color from his mother, though I'm tall like my dad. Genetics are fascinating, and the thought has my eyes lifting to the dark-haired baby boy on Brady's shoulders.

He has the eyes of his mama, but his hair is the shade of his biological dad.

What if I never get the chance to see what my child would look like?

"Brady Lancaster," Ari's mom shouts, pulling me from my thoughts. "You be careful with my grandson up there like that."

"Yeah, Jack the Giant, careful." I grin. "His little legs can hardly curl around those massive delts."

"I'll show you giant!" he shouts back.

"Brady!" all the moms scold at once, making the rest of us laugh.

His mother sighs, shaking her head, but there's a smile on her lips. When her attention moves back this way, her eyes pop over my shoulder. Two seconds later, she's elbowing my mom the way I do Ari.

Both of them look to me, my mother's sly smile making me anxious.

"What?"

She lifts a shoulder, sitting back in her chair.

"Mom!"

"You'll have to look if you want to know, but I will say, that dessert table is looking mighty…appetizing."

Now I glare at the pair, and they laugh harder, lifting their drinks to their lips.

Ari looks between us three, trying to put it together, when she too spots something over my shoulder. She sighs and I tense at the sound.

"It's him, isn't it?" I mumble, but our mothers have the ears of bats, and they lean in.

"Him?"

"Him who?"

"Are you seeing someone?"

All our nosy-ass moms fire off questions at once, eyes glittering.

But I only wait for my friend to confirm my assumption, which comes as a low, "Yep."

Vivian squints. "He looks familiar."

"He looks divine," my mom mutters.

59

My mouth drops open with a laugh. "Mom! OMG, you guys, stop staring."

"Why? He hasn't."

"Look how bold he is." Brady's mom smirks. "Ben was like that. Drilled me with his eyes before he drilled me with his…well."

Everyone laughs, one even sputtering from me before I can stop it.

"You horny old bags." I squirt them all with Deaton's abandoned water gun, and they squeal, jumping up and moving back, gaining the attention of the others.

I smile at them and then the men in our lives, their laughter a comforting sound.

Mason calls out that the chicken is done, so we move over to grab some plates.

This is the third annual cookout the football team has hosted that we've been a part of, something we were told the team has been doing for decades now. It's when the team comes together with open invites for friends and family, and we all hang out, making or bringing our fave dishes to share, potluck style.

An hour or so passes when my mom catches my eye, a gleam in hers. "Cammie, honey, let's go get some of that homemade ice cream I see over at the dessert table."

My eyes narrow on her and my dad chuckles, patting my head. "Help your mama get some ice cream, pumpkin."

"And by that you mean don't forget to bring you some back?"

My dad grins. "Perks of having a child. I no longer have to get my own shit, and I haven't had a chance to reap the benefits of all those years of hard work in a while."

Mason's dad fights a laugh and my dad's eyes crinkle in amusement at his own comment, his words finally clear in my own damn mind.

"Ugh! Dad!" I cover my ears. "Do you want me to bleach my ears?"

Payton smiles, looking between us in question, and Ari takes pity on her.

"It took them, like, five years to get pregnant, so when he says hard work..." Ari trails off, and the two of them laugh.

I fly to my feet, yanking my mother from her chair, and not only to avoid hearing about my parents' sex life but the reminder of how hard it was for my parents to have a child when my mother is the picture of health. "Ice cream. Let's go."

"Oh, I'm not missing this!" Vivian jumps up, rushing to my side with a huge smile.

"Don't forget the sprinkles!" my dad shouts.

The women laugh, linking their arms in mine and steering me. We get in line behind two Avix U football players, waiting for our turn to make a sundae, when my mom squeezes me suddenly.

I look down at her, a small frown building, when she waggles her brows. And then a throat clears from behind and ruins all the fucking fun.

The traitorous women who most definitely did *not* want ice cream giggle and gawk, eyes bouncing from me to the person I refuse to acknowledge who, shocker, was sitting on the bench right next to the ice cream table.

"Cameron!" my mom mutters through her teeth, a big fat smile on her face. It's a reminder not to be rude. Too bad she doesn't know he deserves it. Unlike Vivian, she's not the most perceptive person in the world, but to be fair I don't think Vivian has picked up on it yet either, and I haven't given them any sort of interaction to study.

They will most definitely analyze the shit out of this now.

Lips pinched in a tight line, I spin around, not expecting him to be so close. I stumble slightly, and his hands shoot out to catch me, latching on to my waist.

Our eyes lock and he smiles. For a moment, I forget to be angry, the chill of his hands on the sliver of exposed skin just below the hem of my shirt short-circuiting my brain.

61

"Wait, I know you!" Vivian approaches, and I can hear her smile. "You're a quarterback as well, right?"

"Yes, ma'am."

Both moms seem to melt, and I flick my eyes to the sky.

"You play well. Quick on your feet," Vivian says, complimenting him.

"Thank you." His eyes fall to mine, and I glare at him, my back to my family. "I didn't mean to interrupt—"

"So why did you?"

He pushes a little closer, and I hold my breath as his arm moves around me, only to lift once more and reveal he's picked his phone up from the tabletop. He gives it a little shake before stuffing it in his pocket. "I was sitting here."

Yeah, no shit.

My mom fights a laugh, and I whip around to find her hand on her mouth, though she quickly spins, facing *literally nothing* behind her.

"Are we even getting ice cream?" I ask.

Vivian nods. "Mm-hmm." She moves forward, scooping some into a bowl at a snail's pace. "So what's your name again, young man?"

"I'm—"

"Alister, this is Mason's loving and devoted Martha Stewart of a mother, Vivian," I say, jumping in.

Alister's face falls and he lowers his gaze, having enough sense to look slightly guilty.

"And I guess I'm chopped liver, also known as Clair, Cameron's mom." My mother's voice is teasing, and she sticks a hand out to shake his. "It's lovely to meet you, Alister."

"You too, ma'am."

I step aside, so I'm not sandwiched between the two and have enough space to turn if needed—or drag one of them away should it come to that.

"So why have you been staring at my daughter all afternoon?"

Dear god. I sigh, pinning her with a look.

"She's impossible to look away from," Alister says, and my head whips right back around.

I glare at him, and he fucking winks.

Winks!

I swear, if my mother still had her uterus, it would be fluttering. Country women, man. They love a good wink.

I'd like to tear his eyelashes off one by one.

"So how do you two know each other?" Vivian asks, making a second, smaller ice cream bowl that can only be for baby Deaton, what with the Froot Loops she adds to the top.

"We were fuck buddies all last year, and he wants to be again," I deadpan.

Alister's eyes shoot wide in horror, and after a single second, my family responds exactly how I anticipated.

They laugh loudly, shaking their heads, completely undeterred and used to my shit. I am my father's daughter after all. If only they knew I wasn't teasing.

It takes a moment, but Alister relaxes—though only a little; his laughter is stiff and fake.

I scoot forward, slapping two giant scoops of vanilla into a bowl and dumping a mountain of sprinkles on top.

There's a shuffle behind me, and I don't have to look to know he moved closer. Then his lips find my ear.

"Don't forget the chocolate syrup," he rasps.

The memory sends heat through me, and I don't mean to look to the side, but our gazes catch regardless.

His eyes soften, regret and longing so easily seen that I become instantly aware of the audience we have.

Vivian and my mother have gone quiet, but I see them out of the corner of my eye. There will be no missing *that*.

"Cam," he whispers, stepping in more.

"Don't."

"Baby, please," he murmurs, reaching for me.

My eyes start to close, the anticipation of his touch making me warm and fluttery, but then a sound somewhere to the side snaps me out of my momentary lapse in sanity.

I tear back, jerk away from the table, walk around my mom and Vivian, and speed back toward our group. Of course, that would be too easy, and this man clearly intends to make himself hard to forget.

"Wait." Alister's heavy footsteps follow. "Cameron, wait. Please just—"

I spin around, slapping the ice cream into his neck, smearing it down his chest.

His hands go up, shocked at the cold or the act—maybe both, I don't know—but I only blink at the man.

"Is Allana a fan of sprinkles? Maybe she can lick it off you later," I whisper, saying without saying *fuck him and his memory of warm chocolate combined with the softness of his lips.*

When I rejoin the group, my dad notices my empty hands and Brady notices my mood. I avoid my dad's gaze in favor of Brady's. He goes to launch himself up, but before he can, I shove his shoulder, dropping onto his lap.

His lips find my ears instantly and I know he spotted Alister. "Get up. Now."

"No," I mutter.

"Cameron."

"Brady."

"Get. *Up.*"

I shift, meeting his eyes, and whisper, "If I get up, you're going to make a scene...in front of our entire family, his family, everyone on your team's families. Just leave it."

"Tell me what he did."

I sigh. "He...made me miss him." I scoff, closing my eyes at how dumb it sounds, and when I reopen them, Brady is staring down at me.

His mouth presses in a firm line, tiny worry lines forming

64

along his forehead, but he settles back, no longer trying to escape me.

"Okay, I'll leave him be today," he concedes in a whisper. "But tell me I can lay him on his ass at least once next practice."

I huff and face forward, leaning into his warm chest. "Ask me tomorrow."

Brady chuckles, though it's rough, and gives my sides a quick squeeze. As he goes back to his conversation with his dad, his lips slide across my temple in support. I drop my head onto his shoulder, staring up at the clear blue sky, trying to make sense of my thoughts.

When I turn to the side a few minutes later, catching my dad's eye, he cocks his head, studying me closely, so I give him the most reassuring smile I can muster.

His frown is instant, but then he shifts his gaze to the man behind me, and when he finally does look away, it's with a secretive smile on his lips.

Sighing, I close my eyes, my current reality becoming clear: I still have feelings for Alister Howl.

What's worse, no matter how much I wish they would, I'm not sure there's anything that will make them go away...

Is there?

CHAPTER 9
ALISTER

I shouldn't be smiling.

I should not be smiling as I hide behind the old brick building, sticky, melted, and now slightly dried ice cream all over my damn clothes, but I can't help it.

Cameron Cox, the girl I never saw coming, still cares.

She doesn't want to, that much is clear, but she does. I saw it in her eyes when I touched her, the chemistry we've had since the day we met—the desire not only for more but for a clean slate. She wishes I didn't fuck up and create this rift between us, but the reality neither of us can escape is that I did.

I made her feel dirty, used. I made her feel like a worthless toy.

She has every right to hate me—but I'm damn glad she doesn't. My chance with her might be slim, my time to convince her I want her for real narrowing thinner and thinner with each passing day...but it's not gone yet.

The opportunity is still there, and as much as it might piss her off along the way, I'm going to take it. I'll not waste a single moment, the risk of what could happen if I do is far too dangerous. I'm already at a disadvantage, as her entire friend group—*family* as she calls them—is here and far more dedicated to the girl than I'd like.

They hover, demand, and "rescue" her at every turn. It's frustrating, but she seems to appreciate their meddling. Moreover, she seems to think it's normal.

Then again, maybe it is.

I sure as hell wouldn't know, but what I *do* know is that Cameron Cox is more than worth the time it will take to prove how much I want her, and it has nothing to do with sex. I want the girl with the bright smile and sharp comments, with the flirty mind and flirtier demeanor.

I want her, and I'm going to get her.

I move around the building, my eyes instantly finding her bright blond ponytail.

She's laughing now, throwing her head back, and she hops to her feet, taking her best friend with her. They sing something I can't quite hear, heads moving back and forth as they give their group a little show.

She bends then, lifting the little boy in her arms and spinning him around, an infectious sense of happiness on her face.

I can't help but chuckle at the sight.

"So." A voice snaps me out of it, and I spin around, finding a dark-haired man with a tight-lipped smile and assessing eyes. "That's what happened to my ice cream."

Well, shit.

CHAPTER 10
CAMERON

"Tell her to be nice to me, Noah, or I'm going to put a cup to my ear the next time you give her a little late-night call and—"

"Cameron!" Ari cuts me off, shoving me away and swiftly moving in the opposite direction of class to finish her FaceTime call.

Laughing, I yank the door open and head down the hall, taking the steps two at a time until I reach our regular seats. Best part about college, there's none of that assigned-seat, awkward get-to-know-your-desk-partner shit.

Okay, not *best* but a def plus.

I lift my legs, crossing my ankles so my shins are against the desk, and pull out my phone to scroll until class starts.

Biting on my straw, I take small sips of my soda, determined to finish it before it starts to get watered down. I've been getting headaches more often lately, and I'm convinced it's my lack of caffeine, not because my thyroid hates me, so I'm doubling down like a proper college student.

Pausing on a video where a college baseball team breaks out in a full dance on the field right before the pitcher throws a nasty curveball, I laugh out loud, quickly hitting the Share button and sending it to the group text thread. The boys won't see it until later—all three are currently stuck in a shitty math class together— and Ari likely won't give up the fifteen seconds it would take from her call with Noah, so she won't see it until after class either, but oh well. I send a second message to go with it.

Me: Whose ass do we have to kiss to make this happen at
     our games?

"I saw that one."

I tense, hide my screen against my chest, and drop my head back so I'm looking up at Alister from upside down, seeing as he's standing behind my chair. I frown, and he smiles, holding out a candy bar.

I face forward, dropping my feet to the floor, and stare straight ahead.

"Oh, come on. You know you want it. Don't allow the fact that I'm the one who brought it to you stop you from enjoying a sweet snack," he says, laying it on thick.

And it's working.

It's a free candy bar, and I'm fresh out of sour gummy bears in my backpack.

I look away, and he chuckles, setting it down on my desk, and I fight a small smile, then freeze.

Ugh, how does he know what I want him to do?

Facing forward again, I look down and fake a gasp. "Wow, would you look at that? Someone left a perfectly good chocolate bar right here."

I rip it open, tearing off a piece and popping it into my mouth.

"It must be your lucky day." He smiles, lowering into the seat beside me.

Ari's seat.

I turn toward the door, watching as the professor slips in, a little brown satchel bag hanging over his shoulder.

Where is Ari?

The professor looks up then, scans the room, and pauses once he's staring in this direction.

He lifts a hand, motioning with his fingers.

I freeze, looking to my candy and half-empty soda.

Wait, is this the class I'm not supposed to eat in? I start to stand, but then notice that Alister is taking the stairs down two at a time and the professor is no longer looking this way.

Alister pulls a paper from his pocket and the professor grabs a pen, scribbling something on it before dismissing him.

With a huge smile on his face, Alister heads back this way, the class having filled up around me.

He drops into the seat beside me again just as I spot a familiar head of brown hair pop into the class.

Ari starts this way but freezes, her eyes growing wide when she realizes Alister is in her seat.

I spin my glare on him. "That's Ari's desk."

He raises a brow. "They're assigned?"

"Yes."

A laugh leaves him, and he shakes his head, slouching back in that same lazy, hot-boy way Brady does. "Nice try, beautiful."

"Don't call me that."

"Shh, class is starting."

"You're not *in* this class."

He holds up the paper the professor signed, the class access code scribbled across it. He smirks, his gaze traveling across my face. "Am now. Someone dropped, and what do you know? I was next on the add list. I just have to make up a couple assignments, and I'm good."

I put my straw between my lips and slurp obnoxiously, but the man only laughs harder.

Professor Gilroy flicks on the monitor then, and I tear my gaze from the man beside me, spotting Ari a few rows lower.

She shrugs, and I cross my arms in a pout.

"All right, everyone. As you can see on the class syllabus, we've finished the review and basic introduction, and we're moving right along. This is when things will start to get tough. Take a few minutes, even number chairs turn to the left, odd to the right."

Wait. No, no...

"Take your phones or a notepad out, swap numbers."

I sit forward in my seat, literal sweat building in places I'd rather not mention as I—the person in the even-numbered chair—look left, right into Alister's waiting eyes.

"This person is your new best friend. Your lifeline. Introduce yourself and get familiar."

Alister sticks his hand out, and I glare at the offending appendage, looking back up at him just as the professor blows up my Avoid Alister Plan when he says, "Say hello to your course partner for the remainder of the fall semester."

Alister smiles wide, and my head falls to the desk with a groan.

———

I keep speed-walking, chin lifted high into the fucking sky and thoroughly ignoring my best friend's laughter as she does her best to keep up with me. Too bad for her, her legs are shorter.

"Cam, come on!" she chuckles.

"You and your man are officially on my shit list."

"Liar."

"Nope." I shake my head, hustling across the path and onto the large strip of grass. "This is all your fault."

"Is it, though?"

I cross my arms and spin, my fake-mad face breaking when she literally slams into me, bouncing back with a cackle.

I groan into the air, then take her arm and yank her with me, trying to get away from this area as fast as possible in case the ass himself decides to follow me across campus. "Why is this happening, Ari? He just…gets into class today and then bam, he's my partner? It's like he's the stallion and I'm the broodmare getting fucked."

She laughs, but when she looks over, her features mollify a bit, making me frown even harder. "Tell me the truth."

My lungs shrivel a bit as I wait for her question.

"Is it that you don't want to be near him because of what he did to you…or is it because when you are around him, you aren't sure you care what he did anymore?"

"Of course I care," I snap, tugging my arm from hers. "You know how fucked up all that had me." What's sad is it wasn't even really about the guy but the fact that I was so blind to what was happening. A hit to the pride, I guess you could say, and if anyone had asked before then, I wouldn't have assumed myself to be prideful. Guess I was wrong. I felt pathetic when I learned what I'd fallen for, and now when I look at Alister, sometimes that's all I see—a tragic me staring back.

So which part of what she's asked is the right answer?

Do I not want him near because of what he did…or because he sometimes makes me feel like I'm not mad at all?

Ari and I both stop, and my best friend tips her head, staring me down.

I glare at her, not wanting to answer, but she holds her ground and my eyes snap shut in confession, my palms lifting to press into my eye sockets. "Fuck me, Ari. Why am I like this?"

Her arm comes around my shoulders, and she steers me as she starts walking again. "No one is going to judge you if you decide you want to try again with him, you know."

"I'm going to judge me, Ari. I deserve better than a lying asshole who only approached me for personal gain."

"So he's not swaying you in the slightest with his little pop-ups and gestures?"

"I'm pissed off, not a robot. The guy's practically throwing me a touchdown every time he looks at me, and all I've got to do is take it to the end zone."

"And do you want to score?"

"I want to slap him and kiss him at the same time."

"Kinky."

I whip around, cheeks growing pink as Alister steps up. I open my mouth to yell at him, but he simply holds out a flower.

Hesitantly, I reach out and take the wilted, I don't even know what kind of flower, trying to plan exactly what I'm going to say after he lets it go, but I don't get that far.

I no sooner accept his little gift than he dashes past.

Ari and I both spin, watching as he jogs over to a small group of guys—baseball players, by the looks of it.

He doesn't look back once, but me?

I watch him until he's gone, and unfortunately for me...I think about him long after that.

CHAPTER 11
CAMERON

It's Saturday night, the boys just won 29–18, and while we haven't even made it out of the parking lot yet, I'm already on my second shot. It pays to have a rowdy group of boys who drive to the stadium rather than walking like most of us—we get to stash our stash beneath their seats.

Ari climbs up in the truck bed as I spin, squeezing my torso through the small back window, and turn up the radio. When I stand again, she's passing me a fresh lemon wedge, dancing her way to me as music blares through the custom speakers in Brady's Chevy.

The parking lot is bursting with energy, our entire row more or less a mirror of what we're doing: getting the party started early and celebrating what sportscasters predicted would be a loss.

Joke's on them. The Avix U Sharks are a force to be reckoned with, and this season is proving to be no different than the last.

I take a third—small—shot, biting down hard on the lemon before tossing it into the bag hanging off the mirror. Arms up, I sway my hips, spinning and enjoying the chilled night air.

It's been a fucking *week*—hell, it's been a month, and I'm so ready to just…let it all go tonight. I haven't been properly wasted since the week before the semester began, and that's a college crime if I ever heard of one.

I'll pay for it tomorrow, but right now all I can think is *worth it*.

My limbs are loose, and the only thing on my mind is the music blaring in my ears.

Payton is the first of our friends to make it out of the stadium about a half hour later, her camera bag slung over her shoulder.

She smiles as she approaches, drumming her hands on Brady's tailgate in excitement.

"So, Miss Media Queen, how does it feel to be officially on the field taking candids?"

"Unreal…and feverish!" she teases.

Ari and I both laugh, dropping down on the tailgate to sit as she stands behind the truck.

"I bet, shit. The testosterone alone must be lickable."

Payton grins, shaking her head, and looks to her watch. "I have to get going. I told Paige I'd be home before ten, and it's going to take me a good twenty minutes to get out of this parking lot."

"Which is precisely why we're having the party here!" I raise my empty shot glass necklace, and Ari spins, grabs the water bottle full of lemon vodka, and pours a half shot. "That and because we don't have to drive."

"Have fun, guys, and do your best to get Mason to stay and enjoy his win," Payton says.

I scoff, and Ari looks over and smiles, shifting to face me.

"Hey, Mase, Payton would like you to stay with us and party so you can enjoy your win."

I put a deep frown on my face, pursing my lips, and use my most Masonlike tone I can muster, "No."

Ari laughs, shaking her head. "No?" she mocks. "That was the best you could come up with? We're role-playing here."

"Sorry, little freak-a-leak. Some of us haven't gotten to the role-playing stage in life, *Miss I've been practicing the sexy sous chef and the lowly little dishwasher he falls madly in love with.*"

Ari's jaw drops open and then she shoves me off the tailgate, making Payton catch me as we all laugh.

I simply spin and start dancing again, pointing up at my best friend with a teasing grin. "Anyway, that's essentially what Mason would say, right? With a few other words like *it means nothing without her* and *she's who I want to celebrate with* and *I don't care that my son is asleep. I want to watch him breathe because apparently that's a thing parents like doing.*"

I can't even keep a straight face, but the others are laughing with me.

"Technically, that all sounds about right, if worded a bit oddly," Payton jokes, nudging me in the arm and waving at Ari. "Okay, I'll see you guys at Sunday dinner tomorrow."

We wave our goodbyes, and when a guy from the truck beside us drunk dances his way over with a grin, flapping a giant AU foam finger in the air, I take the bait and indulge him until the end of the song.

Ari hops back up, swinging around the tailgate and tugging a few of the girls from our dorm up with her, and before the next song can start, there's a good ten of us girls singing loudly to some Carrie Underwood.

We're living our best damn lives right now, and it's everything.

Not sure how much time goes by, but when the students around all start to whistle and yell, we know who's stepped out and spin to cheer along with the others as we watch the team file through the crowd, the top trio headed right toward us.

People clap Mason on the back, reaching out for high fives and bro daps of all kinds, and Ari grabs my arm in excitement, her eyes misty as she stares at her twin brother.

He deserves all that star praise he's getting, and it's such a cool-ass thing to witness.

People chant Brady's name too, others screaming out about Chase's touchdown with three seconds on the clock.

I let out a whoop and spin back around, taking Ari with me, getting lost in the group of girls once again. A few minutes pass, and then the truck bed dips, making us stumble a bit and then big-ass arms are around me, lifting me in the air with a laugh.

"Tell me you got me" is whisper-yelled into my ear as my feet hit the bed again.

I chuckle, sneaking an arm through the little back window and lifting a soda bottle full of honey-flavored Jack Daniel's from the seat, twisting to hand it to Brady.

"Always." I smirk.

"My girl." He beams. "Careful with the clear stuff. If you start to feel overheated, tell me. I'll get you some water and we can swap to beer, yeah?"

I don't bother to point out I could get my own water, and he wouldn't have to swap to anything just because my skin rebels against clear liquor sometimes. He'll just give me that sharp stare of his, and I'll crumble like a cookie anyway.

"You got it, Big Guy."

Satisfied, he kisses my cheek and shuffles away, jumping over the side of the bed instead of weaving his way back through the gang of girls piled in it. He turns back when someone calls his name and grins up at a brunette wearing an AU tank top. He opens his arms in invitation, and she jumps into them, letting him carry her to the truck to our left.

I catch Mason's eye, and he waves, making me shake my head with a knowing grin. Payton is so cute, thinking there was any chance he'd stay.

A few minutes pass and most of the girls clear the back of the truck bed, heading off to join whoever it was they were waiting for, so we drop down too.

Slowly but surely, everyone piles into their vehicles. Chase, our DD, drives us back to the football house for the after-party.

When we get there, the music is already reaching the curb, and inside, we find the keg stands are in full effect.

We pause just inside the entry, and I smile at the chaos. "Bros. Bros everywhere."

Ari laughs, and we look up at Brady when he and Chase shift to stand before us.

"You girls know the rules," Brady begins. "No—"

"Taking drinks from anyone but you," both Ari and I say at the same time, and I lift the plastic bottle of liquor we brought for ourselves.

Chase raises a brow. "And no bathroom breaks alone."

"And no leaving with anyone without talking to us first," Brady adds, and they all look to me.

"Hey!" I defend, but Ari's giggle has my head whipping her way.

"Well, I'm *not* going to go home with anyone, and Paige isn't here tonight. That only leaves you."

"Love Noah, not a fan of being the only single female in the gang. Paige needs to get her shit together and act like the twenty-one-year-old she is, not a forty-year-old divorcée."

"I like a good MILF." Brady grins.

"We know, Big Guy." I pet his shoulder. "We know."

Ari grins, wraps her arm around my shoulder, and drags us away from the guys.

"Okay," she shouts. "What's the plan? People watch in the corner, sit by the firepit out back until our buzz becomes something more, or hit the dance floor and figure the rest out later?"

"Option three, baby!"

She smiles, dragging me into the dead center of the makeshift dance floor. We dance to several songs, jumping up and down when "Shots" by LMFAO plays, getting lost within the people around us, swapping from partner to partner and utterly enjoying ourselves.

We pause, take another mini shot, offering some to a couple girls who shuffle in close at the sight of the bottle.

We cheer and get back to it.

Ari grips my arm, and I look up to see her lift her phone in the air, Noah's face on the screen.

"Hey, best friend's boyfriend!" I shout, blowing a kiss, and Noah smiles, waving back, a few guys who must be teammates crowding closer to see what all the noise is, I'm sure.

"I'm going to go out back and talk for a minute!" she shouts. "You coming?"

"Nope. I'll be right here."

She nods and walks off, and I watch as she makes her way toward the patio door, flagging Brady down on her way. He extracts himself from the girl who was using him as a barstool, smiling as he follows Ari out back.

I grin, forgoing the little shot glass around my neck and finishing off the last little bit in the water bottle before smashing it, dropping it, and kicking it off to the side. It's fine—I usually come in the mornings to help with clean up anyway.

I close my eyes, moving to the beat as I gather my hair and tie it up in a high pony. Before my arms have even begun to lower, a pair of warm hands find my hips.

The guy doesn't get all up in my space, so I allow it, swaying a little more intentionally, my knees bent slightly as I get more into the movements.

The lights cut out then, and several strobe lights kick on, making everyone shout in excitement. It's not dark by any means—there's still plenty of light coming from the other rooms around—but it's a vibe.

The liquor starts to kick in, inhibitions out the window, and I press closer to my dance partner. Hands come around my front, closing around me and pressing to my ribs in a way that I'm not too drunk to recognize as intimate.

Still sexy but in a familiar, deeper way.

I peek behind me, meeting a pair of green eyes.

"Hey, beautiful." Alister smiles assuredly, but I can feel the unease in his hold on me. His fingers twitch the slightest bit, unsure that this is okay.

I'm not sure it is either, yet I keep dancing, my eyes apparently glued to his over my shoulder.

Little by little, his grip tightens, and when I don't protest, he tugs me into him until there's no space between us.

His hand comes up, fingers running along my jaw, and my lips part.

The moment he loosens his hold, I spin, our chests now pressed together, as if we both not only knew exactly what to do but when to do it, our bodies in tune with each other's in a way only lovers—*past lovers!* my hindbrain shouts—are.

We keep dancing, my leg between his and his between mine, and with every dip of our hips, I grind against him; he grinds against me.

I'm sweaty and probably drunk and most definitely turned on.

I haven't had sex since the afternoon I left his bed nearly two semesters ago, and my body is remembering the way he treated it.

Very, *very* fucking well.

Alister's eyes flare, his tongue slipping out to wet his lips, and I can't take it.

Ripping myself away, I tear down the hallway, clenching my eyes closed.

Stupid girl, what are you doing?

"Cameron!" he shouts, his calls never growing more distant because, like I knew he would, he follows.

You're an idiot, you're an idiot, you're an idiot.

People are scattered all around, but I ignore them, quickening my pace.

I get to the end of the hall, then take the stairs two at a time, rushing up and around the mini library.

Just as I pass it, my wrist is caught, and I'm yanked around, Alister having been hot on my heels.

"Please don't run—"

I shove him against the wall, silencing him when I crash my lips to his.

He freezes, but only for a split second, and then he's on me.

Gripping and squeezing, smashing me to him, his tongue pressing into my mouth and tangling with mine.

My skin prickles with need, my body burning with it.

I tear away, and he stares at me with pink smeared across his mouth, eyes dark, pupils dilated.

He frowns slightly, but then he hears the soft click of the knob, and his head snaps over his shoulder, realizing where we are. Where I led him.

To the very place I left him—his bedroom.

His eyes slice to mine again, but I don't give him time to speak. I shove him into his room and kick the door closed behind me.

I knew he'd follow me, just like I knew where I was going.

Smart? Probably not, but the decision was made, and I'm good with it.

I tear at his clothes, and he helps me peel his shirt from over his head. I push him to the mattress, throw my own top somewhere to the side, and we scoot back until I can straddle him near the headboard.

My hands dive into his hair, and I kiss him hard, drowning in his familiar taste. I moan into his mouth, and he pulls free, dipping down to kiss my neck. He sucks lightly, his hands coming up to cup me over my bra, and I roll my hips into him, chasing the heat.

"Damn, baby," he groans, pressing his erection up against me. "God, I've missed this."

"Stop talking."

"Yes, ma'am." His hands tug at my bra, freeing my left breast, and he takes me in his mouth.

I shake against him, pulling on his hair but pressing him farther into my chest. My head falls back, and I reach behind myself, fingers going to the clasp of my bra as his undo his belt.

It's a tantalizing sound, and my toes curl into the comforter beneath me.

I sit up slightly, and he drags his jeans down. I barely allow him to get them past his hips before I'm lowering again, bra sliding off and tangling around my wrists.

He chuckles, helping it off before pushing my skirt up over my ass and moving my boy shorts aside, lining himself up at my entrance.

Closing my eyes, I sink down onto his hard shaft, heat zinging up my spine at the stretch. "Yes," I moan to myself, hips pressing down and rocking slowly.

This is what I needed.

"You feel so good," he groans, seeking out my lips, but I bite into his and tear away, my eyes focusing on his dick.

I watch as it slides out just a couple inches, then press back down, moaning when my clit meets his pelvis and then do it again.

"Shit," he hisses, fingertips pressing into my thighs and urging me to move faster, but I don't.

I keep the slow, torturous roll. His hips buck up into me and he moans, muscles bunching beneath me.

My limbs start to shake, my orgasm building slowly, painfully.

I clench in anticipation. *Yes.*

Please. I need—

A loud bang shakes the door, and we both freeze, Alister's hands instantly going to my hips.

"The door isn't locked," he whispers raggedly.

We wait a second to see if they'll go away, but then it pounds twice as hard.

This time, the person doesn't wait more than a moment for a response. The door is thrown open, an angry Chase on the other side.

"What the fuck, Harper?!" Alister lifts me off him, his dick sliding out and leaving a mess all over my thighs. He tugs his bottoms up as he pushes to his feet, the clink of his belt like a deafening church bell in this small, silent space.

He shifts, attempting to hide me behind him, but my skirt has fallen back into place, and I've already got my breasts smashed in my hands.

Chase ignores him, walking my way as he reaches over his head, peeling the shirt from his back with one swift pull. He gently tugs it over mine next, then takes my hand, softly yanking until I'm forced to stand, and leads me to the farthest corner of the room.

My cheeks burn in embarrassment, my breath ragged. "I'm fine," I rasp.

"Are you drunk?" he asks with a firm tenderness that's void of judgment.

"I would never—" Alister booms.

"Fuck off, Howl. I'm not talking to you!" Chase shouts back, not taking his eyes off me. "Cam?"

I swallow, looking away from him. "I'm sober enough to know what I'm doing."

Jesus, Cameron, you're embarrassed to admit as much. Does that not tell you something?

He stares at me for several unnerving moments, and I don't look away, letting him see the truth in my eyes.

"Okay," Chase finally whispers. "In that case, am I walking you out of here, or am I leaving you?"

My throat starts to feel tight, and I can see Alister crossing the room in my peripheral, so before he can get to me, I meet his stare, speaking to Chase. "Walk me out."

Alister's shoulders fall, and he shakes his head. "Cameron, don't go."

I offer a tight smile. "See you in class."

I move ahead of Chase.

"Cameron."

We both ignore him, stepping out into the hall. This time, he doesn't follow.

Chase tethers his hand with mine, and I let him steer me to

the front corner of the house, knowing where we're going before we get there.

He takes the keys from his pocket and opens the door leading to Mason's studio suite, our safe spot here now that Mason mostly spends nights with Payton and the baby—not that it wasn't our safe spot the last few years, even when the room belonged to Noah. It just happens to be empty more often than before. I drag my ass up the narrow stairwell and push myself against the wall when I reach the final door. Chase steps up, pushes it open, and freezes. But before he can tug it closed once more, I press on the frame, and it whips open with a bit of a crash, and I realize why he was going for a stealthy backpedal when I'm met with Brady's naked back.

Oops.

He whips around and only when his torso twists do we spot the girl sitting on the counter in front of him. He scowls at first, then looks down at my shirt, Chase's lack thereof, and steps back. He deposits the girl on her feet and smiles down at her. "Rain check?"

The giggly girl nods, unoffended, and lets out a little yelp when he swats at her booty.

As she passes us, she gives Chase a seductive grin and winks at me. "Nice catch."

"Thanks," I say, laughing lightly when Chase does as well.

I shrug, and we push inside.

Chase moves into the mini-hallway, and I drop down on the foldout couch that's still made into a bed from movie night the other night and close my eyes.

When I open them, Brady is standing there with a bottle of water and Chase is pulling a fresh shirt over his head.

"I'll come back up and check on you when things die down downstairs," he says.

Brady kicks his shoes off, undoing his jeans and chucking them to the side. "Don't worry about it. I'm cooked. I'll stay."

I raise a brow at the beast. "You were five seconds from getting yours. You sure you don't want to go find that before she finds someone else?"

Brady smirks. "I did my duty. She's prepped and primed. Someone will have a great time, and they'll owe me one."

I scoff, tugging the blankets up over myself until I'm tucked in to my neck.

"Speaking of getting some…" He raises a brow.

I look to Chase, but he shakes his head, unwilling to tell my dirt for me.

"I'll see you guys later."

He starts to take off, and I panic, flying up out of bed. "Oh my god, Ari!"

"Paige picked her up, and they went to get something to eat. She's taking her back to the dorm and making sure she gets inside safely before taking off."

I settle instantly. Of course they made sure she was good. That's what we do.

Clearly.

Brady climbs into the bed, his body nearly too big to fit, so he's forced to sit up. He hauls me closer so I'm half lying on him, half beside him, and starts scrolling through Netflix.

"So…" he leads once the door closes behind Chase.

"Yeah," I confirm. Saying his name isn't needed.

"Not sure if this means I should want to kick his ass even more or find a way to let it go and be his friend."

"Nah, don't be his friend."

Brady chuckles, tugging my hair from the messed-up, just-got-fucked pony and brushing his fingers through it until it's strewn out behind me. "Sounds good to me."

I smile even though he can't see me, replaying the evening in my head and wondering if I'm supposed to regret any of it when I find that I don't. "You know what the worst part is, Big Guy?"

"What's that, Cammie Cam?"

I press on his chest, looking up at him in misery. "I didn't even get to come before Chase burst in."

Brady freezes, then explodes in laughter, and I can't help but join in.

"You and me both, Cammie Baby. You and me both."

CHAPTER 12
CAMERON

"You are getting pretty good at this cooking stuff." I stare at my girl from the other side of the kitchen bar, fork pointed at her.

Ari smiles down at her bowl of only slightly sticky risotto.

"Seriously, these weeknight FaceTime cooking sessions you guys keep doing are paying off big-time. I've actually managed to keep some weight on this semester."

"I did notice the Ensures haven't been disappearing from the fridge as often as normal." She looks up at me. "How are you feeling?"

"Good. Fine. Meds are down the hatch most days, and I didn't turn the shade of a lobster when we had vodka after the game, so that was nice. Just keep feeding me all this starchy shit, and we'll be good." I don't mention I haven't had a period in four months or that my headaches are back. There's nothing to be done about either, and both are nonconcerns that come and go. Just part of life at this point. I change the subject back to her. "You're literally on your way to becoming the ultimate wife."

"I'll never be the cook of the family, but it will be nice to feed him something other than pizza and sandwiches when we do finally get to live together."

I stare at my friend. "Ari, you know you can live with him now, right? You're an adult. He's a fucking NFL player, not the guy stuck living in the football house anymore."

She sighs. "I know, but I made a commitment to you guys."

Her eyes meet mine. "Me, my brother, you, Chase, and Brady made this plan years ago, and we actually achieved it. We got into the same school, and they chose this one because I was able to get in when they could have gone somewhere with an even better team than the one they've helped build here. I'm not going to leave now. We've got less than two years. I see him a few times a month and more than that in his offseason and literally every day on-screen. We've talked about all this, Cam, and he gets it. Honestly, he's happy I'm not alone in a big house somewhere while he's on the road for 'work.'" She makes air quotes with a smile.

My own forms, and I give her hand a little squeeze as I get up to rinse my bowl out.

Ari's phone buzzes, and she looks down at it, chuckling as she follows me from the kitchen into the small living room.

"Do I even want to know?"

"Maybe. Maybe not."

I scowl, snapping my head her way. She answered that way on purpose, so I turn her wrist toward me, looking at the screen. It's a message in our group thread from Mason, a picture attached of Alister with his earbuds in, wiping his eye. Clearly, they just took it at the right time, but the caption makes me snort.

Mase: I take it she's still ignoring him?

I groan, dropping down on the sofa. "Why couldn't I have just gone out onto the back patio with you when Noah called?"

"Because you were determined." Ari plops down on the cushion beside me, smiling over at baby Deaton, asleep on the pile of blankets on the floor.

I wait for her to look back this way before responding, that way my frown isn't wasted. "And by that you mean?" I narrow my eyes.

"I could have told you exactly where you were going to end up that night if you'd asked."

I gape at my best friend, and she beams brighter, squealing when I hit her with a pillow.

"Stop." She tries to rein in her laughter. "You'll wake him, and he only just fell asleep."

"Yes, well, if you had told me I was on a self-destructive warpath Saturday, I wouldn't have skipped my round at the child development center just in case Alister was waiting outside it as he's been known to do, and Deaton would be napping on his little cot over there and not here."

"One, I like him here better because I don't get to see him when you're both there, and two, it was not self-destructive, so don't be dramatic."

"I had sex with the guy I'm trying to hate."

"Is it still considered sex if you don't make it to the grand finale?"

"Can you not even say the word *come*?" I snap back.

Ari chuckles, pressing her shoulder into mine. "Okay fine, but it still counts."

I scoff, shifting on the couch and putting my head on the pillow pressed to her side.

Ari looks down at me, lips pinched, and I scowl up at her.

"What?"

"You said *trying* to hate."

Huffing, I face the TV, watching without listening. "I don't hate the man. I...dammit, I like him."

"But?"

"But I'm not so sure I want to."

"Because of what he did?"

"It's more than the scheming," I admit. "Obviously he fucked up, but it wasn't just some little white lie. He was intentional in finding my soft spot. Kissed me the first time to get closer, not because he wanted to." I pause, remembering the day we met last year and hating the bitter notes that roll across my tongue. "Our whole...nonrelationship relationship was built on fake interest. It's tainted and I don't know if, one, I can let that go and, two, if I even want to try."

Ari is quiet for a moment, considering my words before asking, "Do you think he's a bad person?" Her tone is one of genuine curiosity.

I sigh, closing my eyes. "Nope, and that right there just makes it all worse. I mean, we all do stupid shit when we're hurt, right?"

"Not all of us," she says, and I look up at her. "Not you."

"Please." I sigh. "I'm not a saint."

"No, but you don't hurt people when you're hurt. You don't act out. You accept it and you move on."

I groan, kicking the blankets from my legs. "Then why the hell can't I move on this time? I did just fine when Trey left for bigger and better things."

Ari fights a smile, and I fly up, settling on my knees beside her.

"Knock it off. I did and you know it."

"Okay, fine, you did, but maybe that's because Trey left town and Alister is still here fighting for you."

"It sounds like you think I should forgive him."

"No, it sounds like you are waiting for someone else to tell you that you can, but you must already know that, Cam. If you want to forgive him, none of us are going to judge you."

"Brady literally wanted to know if he should start befriending him."

She smiles. "See?"

I stare at my friend a moment, then throw my hands up and move toward the kitchen. "In case you were wondering, this isn't helping."

"So what are you going to do, hide out here forever?"

"Seems like a solid plan."

"Until Thursday arrives, and you have to be his partner in class."

My face falls and the traitor laughs.

"Forgot about that, did you?" She smirks. "At least it's a hybrid class so you don't have to see him in person twice a week unless you have project work to do."

I pout some more. "I just want to pretend he doesn't exist for a few months and see if I care at the end of it."

"Uh-huh, and did you decide this before or after Saturday?"

"Fuck off," I mumble, ignoring her amusement and heading to my room.

Plopping down on my bed, I stare up at my ceiling, wondering what to do from here.

It's not that I regret being the aggressor and taking a ride on Alister's disco stick, as Lady Gaga so expertly put it. I don't. I wanted what he had to offer in that moment, so I went for it, and he obliged.

Does that complicate things even more now? Probably, but it doesn't change anything. I'm still fucked in the head, and he's still an ass for making me feel that way. To be fair, I'm an ass for taking things to the end zone at the party, but if I know Alister the way I think I do, he's not upset with me over it, and therein lies the problem.

I guarantee I didn't deter him by running out and ignoring him after.

No, if his string of unanswered calls and messages tells me anything, it's quite the opposite, which only makes shit harder.

I wanted time, and then I erased it at the first feel of his erection. Now I have to start over in order to figure out what the fuck it is I'm after here.

I pick up my phone for the first time today and open my and Alister's message thread, but I don't read over them. I back out and, with one long inhale, swipe my finger to the left.

I delete the entire thing.

And then I ditch class on Thursday, fully aware that Friday morning, the entire Avix U football team will be loading up on a bus for an away game, and he'll be on it.

ALISTER

She's avoiding me. I've called her a dozen times, texted her twice as many, and the girl either turned off her read receipts or she isn't even opening my messages.

I don't blame her, but I think it's fair to want to have a conversation after Saturday night when she blew my damn mind.

Man, having her in my arms again felt right. For the first time in months, I was able to forget about all the other bullshit that is my life, and it had nothing to do with alcohol. That might be what settled her nerves when I first approached her on the dance floor, the same way it was what made me decide to go to her at the risk of getting smacked upside the head—if not by her-damn-self, then by her helicopter friends. Not saying it's bad to have a gang of people looking out for you, it's just not something I'm used to.

The door to her dorm building opens for the hundredth time this morning, and my lungs swell in anticipation, only to deflate when, yet again, the person who steps out isn't the right shade of blond.

I look down at my phone to check the time.

Shit. If I don't take off now, I'll be late to the bus, and if Coach has to delay our departure time because of me, that will be a whole different kind of a disaster.

Sighing, I shove to my feet, stuffing my phone in my pocket and hauling my overnight duffel off the grass. With one last glance up at the window that I know is hers, I head in the opposite direction.

The only thing that keeps me from turning back around and sweet-talking my way into the building is the fact that she can't hide from me forever. I've got her entire schedule memorized, know all her favorite places on campus, and I'm not afraid of a little coercion if it comes down to it.

One way or another, we're going to talk about what Saturday night means.

And I refuse to believe that the answer to that is a resounding *nothing*.

CHAPTER 13
CAMERON

It's been a good Monday, which is saying something considering I hate waking up to an alarm, hate having to get ready right when I wake up, and hate long lines at the coffee shop.

Today was great, though. I woke up before my alarm—something that *never* happens but is attributed to my lazy ass not getting off the couch all day yesterday and falling asleep "for the night" around four in the afternoon.

I was showered before Ari, so I didn't have to bang on the door to tell her to hurry the hell up *and* the café's mobile order is thankfully still on, so I slid past the line, feeling like that meme where the hyenas snarl at the little lioness as she sashays by with a smile.

My professor canceled my first class, so I went to the childcare center early, and all the little ones were in the happiest of moods today. So yeah, it's been a nearly epic Monday as far as Mondays go.

That should have been my sign the world was not in order and I needed to brace for what the moon had coming.

I hear him before I see him and clench my eyes closed.

"Have you seen Cameron?" he asks, getting right to the point.

Damn it. The way I don't want to deal with him right now.

Leaning over the pretty pink sink in the Sigma sorority kitchen, I peek out the small window facing the front yard, and sure enough, there he is in all his glory, Ari and Paige standing before him.

I grin when my girls cross their arms, Ari looking away, ignoring him completely, while Paige is too damn poised to be so direct about it. But she does bring a smile to my face when she hits his ass with the best glare she can muster. Honestly? "Needs work, girl," I muse, hopping up a bit to put a knee on the countertop so I can damn near press my ear to the glass to eavesdrop.

"I haven't." Paige smiles then; it's too wide and purposeful, so she flutters her lashes his way, going the only route she knows how when it comes to confrontation—sweet as fucking pie. "But if I do, I'll let her know you're looking for her."

Yeah, she will.

She will so I can hide from his ass some more. Cameron and controversy? We don't mix. We pivot.

"Give it a rest already, Alister the Asshole," I mutter, not quite feeling the power behind the words this time, especially as I accidently take him in from head to toe and a pout draws to my lips. "But why do you have to be so hot?"

"I was born that way."

I squeal, lose balance, and fall right into the sink, ass cheek stabbed by the stem of a spatula and sending me jumping forward.

Brady catches me on the edge, his head falling back with laughter, and when he faces forward again, his glossy eyes meet mine. "Cammie Baby," he purrs, mischief gleaming in his gaze.

"Big guy." I raise a brow, looking behind him at the barrage of babes waiting to regain his attention. "Having fun?"

"Am now."

I scoff, then remember what I was doing and swiftly spin my torso, only to find the driveway now empty. I press my lips together, unsure if I'm happy or annoyed.

"Let me guess." He cuts a quick glance to the window where I have the blinds sneakily open and back. "That little fucker showed up uninvited again?"

"I mean, he is on the football team, and this is technically a party for the football players but yes. Yes, he did." I sigh, letting my body fall against his big-ass one, and stick my lip out. "I can't shake him, Brady. I've tried and he just...won't let me."

Brady's eyes search mine, a question I can't read written in his own, though I'm not sure it's the one he asks. "Do you really want him to? Let you shake him, I mean."

"Yes." My answer is fast—maybe too fast—and when that brow of his raises, I groan, covering my face and burying it in his chest. "No. I mean I don't know," I mumble against him.

God, I sound pathetic.

Opening my eyes, I meet Brady's. "Am I having one of those dumb-girl moments?"

"No. He's just a dipshit." Brady's attention snaps over my head, his eyes narrowing and his lips flattening. "But you need to decide what you want to do, 'cause he's about to walk through the door in five, four, what do you want?"

Panic curls in my belly and I tense up. "I don't know."

Brady's eyes slice to the right, and I hear the front door opening before they then cut back to mine. "Okay, then what do you need?"

"Time." I swallow.

"Time?" He sets his can down on the counter, standing to his full, massive height.

"Time to figure it all out, I guess."

Brady nods, slow and several times, his eyes never leaving mine. "I can help you out with that."

The door closes, and in my peripheral, I see a streak of blond headed right this way. "How?" I rush, my heart rate spiking.

Brady pushes closer, not that there was much more room to go. I'm literally sitting on the edge of the counter, his body still positioned between my legs from when he caught me. Still, he manages to get even closer, and when his knuckle presses against my throat, dragging up until he's hooked me by the chin, my head falls, my long hair tickling my lower back.

Suddenly his eyes fall, and if I didn't know any better, I'd say they landed on my mouth.

"Brady?" We're running out of time.

He swallows, and a small frown builds across my brow. "Trust me?" he whispers.

"Always."

I get no warning. No explanation. No period to process.

The unthinkable, the utterly unexpected happens, and it happens fast.

Heavy, demanding lips drop to mine, and they waste not a second, coaxing them open with a swift flick of the tongue.

And what a hussy my mouth is, opening wide without a word of protest. Suddenly, my hands are around a thick, strong neck, and hands so massive they reach from belt to bra lock around me.

Our tongues tangle, my fingers jealous of the action and seeking the tips of his hair to do the same thing, but I never make it past the nape.

He's shoved from the side, but he's massive and pure muscle. He doesn't budge an inch—he simply lifts his head, and my eyes are locked on his face, shock setting in at the sight of his swollen lips when he says, "Do you mind?"

Oh my god, those are Brady's lips. Those are Brady's lips because this is Brady before me, and they're swollen from my kiss.

Our kiss.

"What the hell is going on?" This comes from Alister, and the question might be for me, but I've got no words. Only thoughts.

Holy shit being the loudest one.

"What's going on is you interrupted us." Brady glares, his hands still sealed on my sides. "Now if you don't mind"—*good God almighty, I kissed Brady Lancaster*—"I'd like to get back to kissing my girlfriend."

I can't believe that just—

Wait.

What?

BRADY

Wait.

What?

What did I just say?

I look down at Cameron, whose cheeks are flushed and whose gaze is jumping from my lips to my eyes, not a single word coming out of that little mouth of hers.

I've rendered the little hellcat speechless, and I kind of want to tease her about it.

"Cameron!"

That snaps me out of it, and I let her go, moving to shield her from his view. "Watch yourself, pretty boy. That tone isn't gonna fly with me."

"Oh, fuck you. What the hell is this?" Alister throws his arms out, bending to try to look past me, but I move with him, stepping close.

"Did I not tell you?" I pause. "I just got here, my girl is here, and you're interrupting our night."

He glares, standing taller. "She's not yours."

"Kind of feels like she is."

Alister's fists ball, and he looks toward the living room, no doubt our little exchange having gained some attention. Suddenly, a mocking laugh leaves him. "Right. Okay. Your girl, along with every other girl in here, right?" To prove his point, he looks left again.

My eyes decide to follow, and I fight the frown threatening to take over when my gaze lands on the Sigma sorority girls, each wearing a plain white shirt with a single letter on it.

I saw the post online today. Like always, the game was being broadcast on a large projector in the quad. After the win, the Secret Shark, the person who runs the AU Instagram page, took a shot of the girls all dolled up and in a line, my last name spelled out across their chests.

"You've probably slept your way through half of them already, so why don't you drop the bullshit and move aside? Maybe see if you can knock a couple more off your list tonight."

Little prick has no idea what he's talking about, and normally I don't give a shit what people say—clearly, considering what everyone thinks of me when it comes to women.

So why is a strange heat burning the nape of my neck, and why do my eyes cut to the side, sneaking a look at Cameron to catch her expression?

I don't fucking know, but the ball of tension that I didn't realize had formed in my gut untethers at the sight of her wicked glare narrowed in on Alister. Instantly, I relax.

"Nah." I lift a shoulder, sliding back until my hip is between Cameron's thighs, and drag her to the counter's edge. "I'm good. But if you don't want to see what happens next, I suggest you move along."

Alister scoffs, eyes narrowed and angry, but then he looks back to Cameron.

Slowly, surely, a smirk slides across his lips. "Yeah, okay." He chuckles, and I hate the sound.

Annoyance pricks at my skin as I stare at Boy Wonder, wondering what he sees to make him look so…confident.

By the time I look her way, she's facing the opposite direction, her grip on my forearm growing tighter by the second.

Fuck this guy. He's making her hide—that's bullshit.

I hoist her up, and wide blue eyes meet mine before they settle, her legs coming around me.

"Let's get you out of here," I whisper for only her to hear, pulling back to make sure that's what she wants.

Her small smile says it all, and she buries her face in my neck.

Without a second thought or a single look back, I carry her from the house and straight to the bed of my truck. Before her ass meets the cold steel, she starts laughing, and I can't help but join in.

"Well, that was one way to go about it." She smiles, pulling her legs up and crossing them beneath her. "But I do feel a little bad."

"Don't." I shrug. "It wasn't a *complete* hardship to kiss you, only a small one."

She smacks me before I'm even done talking and I chuckle, hopping up beside her and tugging my hoodie off, tossing it at her.

Cameron pulls it on, the sleeves dwarfing her hands as she plays with them. "I had sex with him nine days ago, and I've ignored him ever since…yet I only feel *a little bad* for messing with him just now."

A sharp sting of…something hits my chest, and I face forward to hide the frown it draws.

"He deserves to stress a bit," I tell her. "You're a lot to lose, baby girl. He needs to feel that, and chasing after you all this time ain't the same. He needs the threat of another to really feel it, you know." That's how it goes, right? We want what we can't have?

Her smile is gentle. "So you're saying it's a necessary torture?"

"Only if you want it to be." I hold her gaze, a strange bitterness coating my tongue as I force my next words to leave my mouth. "You can go find him right now and tell him we were fucking with his head the way he did yours, or you can let him sit on it for a night and tell him tomorrow."

"Why do you sound like you think something's going to happen tomorrow?"

My grin is slow, and there's a weight behind it I can't explain. "Why are you pretending like it's not? The dude is coming for you. And now he's going to come harder than before."

Her eyes narrow, but it's playful. "I can't tell if you're intentionally being dirty or if it's a natural part of who you are."

"Silly girl." I hop down and tug her to her feet. Taking her right hand in mine, I grip her waist with my other hand like some old-school waltz or some shit, swaying her a little. "You know damn well it's in my DNA. Now hush it and let me dance with my thirty-minute girlfriend a little."

She laughs, dropping her head back with a grin, and then she lets me twirl her around the grass a bit.

"Hey, Brady," she whispers, her head falling to my chest when the song ends.

"Yeah?"

"Thanks for rescuing me again tonight."

"Always, Cammie Baby. Always."

CHAPTER 14
CAMERON

I spot Alister the moment he walks in the door, blond hair shining like a damn Pantene commercial. Of course he chooses that moment to run his fingers through it, eyes snapping up and skimming the aisles before he even makes it to the first step.

He finds me almost instantly, and a slow smile pulls at his lips. With each tiny tip higher, my heart pounds a little harder in my chest.

Okay, so he's not mad. That's a good sign, but I'm not sure I like this particular sparkle in his damn eye.

My phone vibrates in my hand, and I look down to see a message from Ari, who's stuck in that random row closer to the door beside her new partner, thanks to Alister and his little game of musical chairs.

Bestie: Someone looks a little cocky.

Me: Little and COCK-y don't belong in the same sentence where he's concerned.

I look up, smiling at the back of Ari's head when she hides her laugh behind her hand.

Bestie: Is that why we took a little secret trip downtown this weekend for your revenge jewelry?

Me: Not revenge jewelry. Ravaging jewelry in case the next is
   working with a worm and not a snake.

This time, I hear her laughter and set my phone down with a smirk.

A second later, Alister's voice warms my ear. "Hi, beautiful. You look stunning, as always."

I tip my head to the side, meeting his gaze, mine narrowed. "Thank you, Alister. Can you sit down now?"

"Why, is having me this close making you nervous?" he teases, bending so we're eye level. "Or maybe it's because your 'boyfriend' won't like it?" His tone is mocking, amusement written across every inch of him as he calls me out on the lie without calling me out.

God, Brady was right—we only encouraged him more.

I run my tongue along my teeth, trying to find something else to focus on other than the heat of his nearness, and finally, the professor walks in. Alister straightens and takes his seat just as our professor begins going over the focus for the remainder of the semester, and a little buzz of excitement zings through me. I sit up straighter in my chair, Alister's presence forgotten as I lock on to every word Professor Gilroy has to say.

Finally, I'm getting to the good stuff.

My first two years here, I focused on the basics: math, English, history, and all the other standard prerequisites only. Meaning I saved all the good stuff for my last two years.

This is the class I had been most looking forward to, and it's exactly what I was hoping it would be: I get to build my very first lesson plan and not just any old lesson plan but one that is engaging and meets the needs of diverse learners.

I've known since I was young that I wanted to work with kids in some capacity, and the plan only grew more concrete as I got older and learned more about myself, but listening to Professor Gilroy speak, I can't stop smiling. This is the first time I've felt like my dreams are within reach. My best friend glances over her shoulder then, a softness in her eyes and a smile on her face as she looks at me because she knew this is what I was waiting for—a way for me to learn how to truly connect with kids when I may or may not have any of my own.

This course is good for her too. Before Noah, Ari always secretly hoped she could one day be just like her own mother—blessed with the opportunity to stay at home with her kids and raise a family. Thankfully, that is the exact life Noah can give her down the line. All the random classes she's taking with me will help her with that, seeing as she hopes to be able to teach them to read and write before they go off to school. And like her mom did us, be their study partners the years that follow.

Even if I was to become a mother one day despite the challenges in my way, I don't think I'd be cut out to be a stay-at-home parent. It takes a very special kind of person to dedicate your life in that way, and I'm just not sure I'd be up for the job. Maybe that's part of the reason why I want to run some sort of facility, to know that there is one more safe place for kids who do have working parents to go and still feel the warmth a home should bring.

"Go ahead and break off with your partner for the rest of class," Professor Gilroy says, pulling me from my thoughts. "I'll be making the rounds, so if a question comes up, flag me down and ask. Confusion will not be an excuse for late work."

My smile falters, and I look to Alister, only to find he's already staring at me and who's to say for how long.

"This class is important to you." Not a question.

I can't help but scoff as I shift my legs in the chair so they're angled toward him and flip my notebook open. "Reality reminder, Alister? I'm not an athlete waiting around for something bigger than what college has to offer. All my classes are important to me."

"Cameron, I didn't mean—"

"I know," I sigh. "Let's just not talk about our future dreams and aspirations, all right? I was supposed to be doing this with my best friend."

"And now you're stuck with me." He's not being an ass about it. In fact, he looks a tad remorseful, his next words confirming as much. "If it means anything, I feel a little bad right now."

My smile is sad. "You seem to do things you regret quite often."

Shame falls over him. "More than I'd like to admit, Cam, but I am sorry I took away your fun for this class."

"But not sorry enough to offer to swap," I guess.

His grin is a bit sheepish and a low chuckle escapes.

"And now I'm stuck doing it with a guy I'm not sure I can trust with my grade."

He leans forward then, all hints of remorse wiped from his face, something wicked washing over him. When he speaks, his tone is low and raspy and only loud enough for me to hear. "Can't trust me with your grade, but you can trust me with your body?"

I match his movement, meeting him halfway until we're way too close to be considered appropriate for class. "Trust is not a word I would use for you. Do I know I can give you my body? Yes. Any other part of me?" I lift my brows, shaking my head.

"Giving me your body. That's trust, is it not?"

"No. It's not. It's a bad decision I knowingly and willingly made."

"I'll take you anyway I can get you, you know." He stares into my eyes. "If that means you only come to me when you need someone you can give your body to, then so be it."

"Nothing has changed, Alister." I sit back, cursing myself. "God, none of that was fair to you. I was being selfish, and I'm really sorry about that."

"I'm not."

I frown at him. "You should be. Clearly, I gave you hope where I'm not sure there is any. I shouldn't have led you on like that."

"We had sex." He grins. "That's like the opposite of leading me on."

A low laugh leaves me, and I look away a moment, slowly facing him once more. "I'm just trying to apologize for any confusion that night might have caused."

"There's no confusion, only clarity."

My brows snap together. "See?" I whisper. "You think it means something."

"At the very least, it means you still want me."

I chew the inside of my lip, considering something. "How honest do you want me to be with you?"

He has the common sense to tense at the question, taking a few moments to consider what it is exactly that I'm saying. He looks around, and I wish the professor would come over and interrupt us already. Tension tugs at his eyes, but he nods. "Tell me."

Nerves tangle in my stomach, a towing sensation I try to push away but can't quite manage to. I don't want to be vulnerable with this man, not after everything, but maybe I need to be. Maybe he needs to hear it.

"I like you, Alister. I really, really do. You're smart, talented, dedicated. You're hardworking and funny. Being with you felt like having something special all my own, and that's not something I'd ever had before. My family and friends, we're all so intertwined that most of our lives are shared with the next person, but with you..." I lift a single shoulder. "I had my own little world, and when I was in it, nothing on the outside mattered. I didn't need to label what we were. I was happy just quietly hanging out and hooking up, and toward the end, I realized I wouldn't mind there being more to it." I pause. "And then it all blew up in my face and you became the one thing I regret most about college so far."

His expression was on a downward spiral the more I continued to speak, but it falls fully as I say that last line.

Harsh? Maybe, depending on who you ask, but it's real, and he asked for honesty.

Alister stares at me in silence for several moments, and then he moves his focus to the empty page of his notebook, zoning out on it for several more. When he does finally look up again, the despondent expression is washed away, and while it seems a little forced, he smiles. "You still like me."

A surprised scoff leaves me and I shake my head.

"You still like me, and I'm going to win back your trust by becoming your friend."

"What makes you think I want to be your friend?"

"Well, we've got to start somewhere. Friends seems fair."

"It's not. You're basically the enemy right now."

"I don't believe you."

I glare. "I don't care. We are partners in this class, and outside of it, we are nothing."

"Why? Afraid to be alone with me again? Or wait, I wonder"—he smirks, the mischievous glint behind it making my muscles tense for what might follow—"are you worried your 'boyfriend' will get jealous?"

Boyfriend?

Oh yeah. Boyfriend.

I actually laugh, and he smirks like the Cheshire Cat. "Please. Brady?" I can't help but laugh again. "That man wouldn't even be jealous of Adonis if he stood beside him."

That smirk of his falls away instantly, and he leans forward again, his reaction catching me slightly off guard. "Are you really going to sit here and pretend the two of you are seeing each other?"

Wait, what? I didn't do that.

Did I?

I replay the last sixty seconds, and well, shit. I guess my response should have been more along the lines of "I don't have a boyfriend," but I seem to have messed that part up, haven't I?

"Cameron," he snaps.

"What?" I snap back.

"You're not dating Brady."

I purse my lips, glaring due to the nerve of this guy. Obviously, it's not a command, more him stating what he thinks is a fact. Technically, it is one, but he doesn't know that. Well, not for certain anyway. "Who I do or don't date is none of your business."

"Bullshit. I want you, and I'm not giving up on the idea of you being by my side when all this is over."

"By the time what is over?"

"I don't know, this class, this year. I don't really have a timeline here." He grins.

"I'm asking you for space to figure out what I want."

"Space will push me further away. I can't give you that."

"You will respect my choices, Alister."

"You just said you like me!"

"I like you but I don't trust you!"

"Let me prove to you that you can."

"Stop."

"Please, Cameron."

"I said, stop," I hiss, noticing a few eyes pretending not to look this way now.

"Just tell me you'll give me a chance. Go on a date with me. A real date and I'll show you—"

"I swear to god."

"—that I'm not that guy. I can be what you need—"

"I have what I need!" I shout as I shoot to my feet.

And then I freeze.

"Is there a problem back there?" Professor Gilroy calls out, standing from where he's helping another pair.

My face is turning red, from anger and embarrassment and straight-up frustration. I swiftly shove my shit in my bag and take off down the steps, vaguely aware of Alister telling the teacher everything is fine as I push out the double doors and into the hall.

I run to the end, barging out into the afternoon sun, and then tip my head back with a growl.

My god, why is he so damn...I don't even know!

I groan again, gripping the straps of my bag, and hustle toward the café. I need some caffeine. And sugar. Maybe some carbs.

Yes. Coffee and a cookie and then to the cafeteria I go. I'm aware I could get coffee there, but I'd rather not have the stuff that tastes like my dad made it at five in the morning and reheated it five hours later.

I don't bother preordering my drink, since I left class with about ten minutes to spare, and as soon as I have my goods in hand, I stomp on over to the dining hall. It doesn't open for dinner for another two hours, but hopefully there's still some items on the grab-and-go wall.

"Cameron!"

My head whips around, and I glare, quickening my steps toward the building. I'm so close I can taste the processed cheese from here.

"Cameron, wait, damn it!" Alister yells, yet again gaining the attention of those around us.

I can tell he's jogging by the sound of his voice and use my long-ass legs to my advantage, speed-walking like a motherfucker.

"I'm going to catch you! No reason to avoid me."

People snicker, and I feel my face heat.

I'm almost there, my hand shooting out to grip the railing and use it like a catapult, but just as my palm closes around the painted metal, I catch something out of the corner of my eye to my left.

There's no time to think it through, no time to second-guess.

I cut to the right, and I'm only about four feet from them when they notice me.

Mason smiles, but I'm pretty sure a frown begins to form just as fast. I can't say for sure though because I'm already launching myself at his best friend, one of my best friends, and the man doesn't let me down—not that I thought for a moment he would.

109

Not that I had a second to think this through much at all if we're being real.

Instantly and without hesitation, Brady catches me under my thighs. My legs lace around him like I'm a spider monkey, and his chin lifts just a bit, so he can meet my eyes, a hint of worry working its way into his own.

"Sorry," I manage to mumble as my hands weave their way around his neck, and then I crush my lips to his. I kiss him, and I don't stop, putting on a good and believable show. And Brady doesn't disappoint, simply trusting me in the moment and following my lead.

Only when a few people shout out catcalls do I pull back.

Brady licks the seam of his lips, brow lifting as he stares at me.

"Am I gonna fuck up your bed game if I ask to stretch out your fake boyfriend idea for a while?" I whisper.

Brady shakes his head, a question in his eyes, but then I'm yanked from his arms with a yelp.

Brady drops his shit, shoving Alister so hard, he falls on his ass, but Alister gets back up, and before I can move, Chase's arms lock around me, holding me still.

"Quit with this shit already!" Alister seethes, not cowering from the man who has a good sixty pounds on him, not to mention being nearly a head taller. "I get it. Leave her alone. Wait for her to come to me. Just...stop fucking kissing her."

"I'll kiss her anytime I want...any*where* I want, if you feel me." Brady smirks.

"See?" Alister shouts. "And you're supposed to be her friend! Everyone knows you're nothing but a player. You screw anything that walks and then you do the walking. There is no way she would actually *date* you."

Chase's hand clamps over my mouth before I even get a chance to attempt to speak.

I look to Brady, hating Alister's words on his behalf, but settle a little when I find his smirk is still in place.

"You done, bitter baby?" Brady cocks his head mockingly.

Alister turns my way, his eyes seeming to dive deep down and search for the truth of what's really happening here. He must not find the answer because little creases form along his forehead.

I wait for him to snap at me, to call out more lies in front of all the people watching, and there are *a lot* of people watching, but he doesn't do that.

He clears his throat and offers a small smile. "I'll make sure my part is done for the project. I'll see you Thursday, okay?"

I try not to frown as I nod in response.

Alister nods back, grabs his backpack, and walks away.

It's not until he's far, far away—Ari having made her way to us and the rest of the onlookers going back to whatever the hell they were doing before we became a sideshow—that the boys look between Brady and me with wide, *what the fuck* eyes.

"Right." I clear my throat, wiping the lipstick that must be all over my mouth if the sight of Brady's tells me anything—really need to switch to the long-wear shit. "So...I guess Brady is my boyfriend now."

I've never wanted to have a camera at the ready more than I do in this moment.

Their expressions are priceless.

Brady tells them what happened at the party the other day, and they start to laugh. They don't ask questions, don't offer opinions, but simply wrap their arms around me and Ari and lead us toward the cafeteria.

Guess the boys need a sandwich too.

After we all find food to grab, we make our way over to a long table and set it out in the middle to share.

Everyone starts to sit, but I pause, facing Brady.

"What's the matter?" He reads the concern in my expression with ease.

"I'm sorry he said all that about you."

Understanding dawns and he shakes his head. "Don't stress on

111

my behalf. People can say whatever they want about me. It doesn't change anything."

"How are you not bothered? I'm pissed."

Brady smiles, tugging my hair gently. "Because it's a bunch of bullshit, Cammie Baby. That's how."

I frown and he grins wider, motioning for me to sit, so I join the others on the picnic-style table.

Brady sits with one leg on either side of the bench seat, tucking me back into his chest, and whispers in my ear, "I'm gonna be so good at this fake-boyfriend stuff."

I laugh as I settle into him, and I can't help but look around the room with a smile.

This, right here, this is what we talked about for years.

It's a random Thursday, we're in a cafeteria sharing pound cake slices and nearly soggy sandwiches, but it's exactly what we were looking forward to all our teenage years. I think it's safe to say that junior year here at Avix University is guaranteed to be an interesting one.

The question I want the answer to the most, though?

How the hell is it going to end?

CHAPTER 15
ALISTER

It's hilarious. Comical, really.

She could have chosen any other guy, and I might have believed her, but dating Brady Lancaster?

Yeah fucking right.

The man has his own harem, and Cameron isn't the cleat-chaser type. There is no way she would be okay with being one of many. And there are *many*. I may not know him on a personal level, but I'm his teammate, and I have eyes.

On the flip side, I'm well aware of how close they are. They've been friends since they were in grade school, maybe longer. I'd have said Brady was like a brother or cousin to her if anyone asked why my girl was always hanging around another guy, but he sure as shit didn't kiss her like he would agree.

I wonder if they've hooked up before.

I scoff to myself, shaking my head.

No. They're just messing around, trying to discourage me by putting on a show.

It's not going to work. I know it's fake.

Cameron, while in tune with her sexuality and unashamed of it, doesn't bounce around. The fact that she and I just recently hooked up tells me all I need to know.

This thing between them isn't real.

All I have to do is wait it out, and if my assumptions are correct, I won't be waiting long.

The guy has always had a girl chasing after him, he's just charismatic like that, but this season it's doubled with the help of the Secret Shark. They come to him in flocks, his name and number painted all over their bodies, and I mean *all over*.

I've never been to a single party, at the football house or otherwise, where he's been in attendance when he didn't take the offer of at least one of them.

I'm not saying he's a womanizer, but he is definitely a women lover.

So while he tries to figure out what it even means to be someone's boyfriend, pretend or not, I'm going to be Cameron's friend. I'm going to use this time to take a step back and really get to know the girl the way I wish I would have in the beginning.

We pretty much jumped right into things. We flirted and danced around each other for a few weeks, and yes, a lot of that was because, at the time, I had no intention of finding out any single thing about her. It's true, she was a means to an end, but that didn't last long.

Our chemistry was instant. We fell into bed first, and the rest came after—or it was beginning to anyway.

My stomach turns, regret burning up my insides like acid, but it's all good—or it will be because there is no way Brady is going to be able to stick to their little plan for long. He'll find someone new he can't say no to, and that will be that.

I bet he doesn't make it through the week.

I step into the locker room, and three pairs of eyes snap my way, drawing a sigh from my lips.

Practice is going to be even more interesting now, that's for damn sure.

BRADY

The snap is made, and I throw my weight around, twisting my torso and tossing Kroger to the turf, hands shooting up and smacking the ball straight out of pretty boy's hold, my shoulder pads knocking into his and sending him stumbling back.

Coach blows the whistle, and Alister spits out his mouthpiece opening his lips to pop off, but Chase shoulder-checks him as he gets back into position to run the play—or attempt to—for the third time.

The punk clenches his jaw, glaring at me, and I wink under my helmet, shimmying my way backward until I'm in position once more.

"Same play!" Coach Rogan shouts. "Alister, fire the fucking ball off!"

Not on my watch.

I smirk around the hunk of plastic in my mouth, chuckling when Alister shoves his mouthpiece back in with angry, jerky movements.

My eyes do a swift scan of the field, watching as Chase and our other receiver swap places, spreading out until they're on opposite sides of the field.

Alister's knee is bouncing slightly, a tell of his I learned last year. He's letting his anger get the best of him, and it's affecting his play.

He'll never be able to lead a team at this level if he can't find a way around that, and he'll never even get the chance to lead this one after Mason's time is up if he doesn't find a way to gain the respect of his teammates. Where he stands currently, he doesn't have it, and it's got nothing to do with his annoyance at me or the shit he stirred with Mason last year.

Nah, it's all him and his inability to trust those around him. He's a quarterback who wants to run more than throw, and that makes no fucking sense, especially not with Coach Davies, who runs the offense here. He's all about the passing game, and Alister doesn't trust his receivers enough to make the catch, let alone trust his line to block well enough to allow him time to read the field.

Now *that* I will take all the credit for.

I'm in the backfield more often than not, and practice is no different. When Coach first asked me to make the transition from offense to D-end, I wasn't so sure. It's always been me and my boys on the field together: Chase as the receiver, Mason the one throwing him the ball, and me, the guy who makes sure they can't fucking touch him. But man, that very first week practicing at the new position, something just clicked.

This is where I was meant to be.

I got three sacks in the very first game this season. My first fucking game at a position I'd only been practicing at for *weeks* rather than the twelve years I'd spent on the other side of the ball. That is just wild. Some people go full seasons without a sack, and I managed three in one game.

We're six games in, and I'm already at seven sacks, tied for the division's leading spot.

I'm 'bout to make it eight, not that this will count toward my real stats.

Coach blows the whistle, and Alister steps up, casting a look across the line. He lifts his foot once, twice. The ball is snapped, the line holds strong, but I shove my way through just as Alister steps back.

He's in full windup, but before the ball leaves his fingers, I wrap his ass up, taking him to the turf with a satisfying thump.

The ball rolls out of his hands, and I snatch it up, jogging toward the end zone for what would be a defensive touchdown, but just like I figured—hence the jogging—Coach is already blowing the whistle, and I fight a laugh when he starts to chew me out.

"Goddamn it, Lancaster, what the hell are you doin'?" He stomps out on the field, clipboard held out and pointed in the air. "You don't take the fucking quarterback down!"

"Sorry, Coach!" I shout, shrugging like an innocent school-boy, and bite back my retort that Alister isn't our real quarterback. "Couldn't stop my momentum."

He scoffs loudly, slapping his leg with the thin plywood. "Take a lap, asshole."

"Yes, Coach." I grin, jogging back over to where Alister has pulled himself off the ground, turf stains on his ass. I toss him the ball, and he bats it away, his glare following me as I take off for my lap. I'd bet money he knows exactly where I'm headed.

I go wide on the field, running along the edge without getting my cleats on the track, and when I reach the benches on the opposite side, I cut a quick look back. Good, Coach ain't watching...but guess who is.

I smirk, tear my helmet off, and run over the small walking path, jumping up until I'm half hanging over the ledge to the bleacher.

The girls laugh, textbooks and notebooks in their laps, having come out to study while we practice, something they've been doing since high school.

"Ari, Paige." I smile at them, then turn to Cameron. "Hi, Fake Girlfriend."

Cameron crosses her arms with a playful narrowing of her eyes. "Hi, Fake Boyfriend. I take it laying him on his ass wasn't satisfying enough?"

"Not nearly. Wanna make out, celebrate our eight-day anniversary?"

She laughs, but I'm already jumping down, having only been teasing.

"Gotta go. Don't let my hot body distract you from studying too much, okay?"

"Oh, however will I manage that," she teases, still looking at me as I turn around and finish my lap.

We run a few more plays, Mason back out on the field this time before practice is called.

I drop onto the bench, tearing my helmet off, and take several long pulls from the water hose. I sit back, swiping a towel across my face and neck, my chest heaving from exertion.

I fucking love this feeling, the hard work, the grind, day in and day out.

A ball hits me in the chest, and my head snaps forward to find Alister stalking over.

A grin splits my lips. "Uh-oh, pretty boy's pissed."

"Fuck you." He frowns. "You're the one acting like a dick because you're pretending to date my fucking—"

I'm on my feet in a second flat, bent at the knee to make us eye level. "You're…what, huh?"

He seethes, lip curling, but says nothing.

"Your biggest regret? Your biggest fucking loss?" I press my forehead hard into is, driving him backward. "'Cause we both know that's all she'll ever be to you now."

He pulls back and swings, clipping me across the jaw.

My teammates rush in, pulling us apart, and I let them, keeping my eyes locked on his with each foot of distance put between us.

I shake the guys off, glaring at the asshole who made my Cammie Girl cry. I knew I'd hit a nerve with that one, but at least I know for sure now Cameron is right: he's decent enough to feel bad about what he did.

"That was your one free shot, Howl," I warn with a grin. "You won't get another."

He opens his mouth, but Coach appears, and he clamps his mouth closed like a good boy. Coach looks between us, eyes narrowed, but when no one says a word, only going back to cleaning shit up, he doesn't ask.

"Harper!" Coach calls out instead.

I look over just as Chase lifts his head.

"Coach?" his brows pull.

"My office after you're all done out here."

Chase meets my gaze with a slight frown, his chin jerking in a nod as he looks back at the man. "Yes, Coach."

With that, he walks away, and we hurry through our tasks,

cleats crunching against the concrete as we head back into the locker room.

It's not until I get back to my locker, Alister's shit still hanging in his, that I realize he didn't come in when we did.

No. He stayed out on the field, and I only need one guess as to why.

Determined little dickhead.

CHAPTER 16
CAMERON

"What's the matter, baby boy?" I ask Deaton, slowly lowering onto the couch beside him, little Abby in my arms.

He rubs his eyes, tears smearing across his cheeks as his lip starts to wobble.

"Aw, Big Guy." I reach for him with one hand, and instantly, Abby starts wailing again. "Shit. I mean crap." I shift her, picking up Deaton in my left arm, and stand, trying to bounce them both. "Baby boy, what happened? You okay?"

He buries his face in my chest, and Abby lifts her head, pushing at his shoulder to try and get me all to herself.

"Abby, honey, be nice to Deaton. He's your friend."

She starts kicking, her cries getting louder.

Thankfully, Junie walks in two seconds later. When her eyes meet mine, wide and begging for help, she chuckles and walks over.

"Is that my friend Abigail I see?" Junie softens her tone, and slowly, Abby looks over at her. Junie smiles, putting her hands on her hips. "It is you! I'm so happy you came back to play today."

Abby's cries start to soften, though now she's hiccupping from crying so long. Poor baby nearly breaks down every time her daddy drops her off for day care, which seems to happen more than her mama dropping her off lately. She's been here for twenty minutes, and this is the first deep breath she's taken.

Junie comes up with her arms outstretched, and after only a

moment's hesitation, Abby leans over into her arms. "And now what happened to this little man, huh?" She rubs her hand along Deaton's back, and I hoist him higher, kissing his temple.

I freeze, rubbing my cheek along his forehead before quickly pulling back and pressing the back of my hand to his face. "Junie… please tell me he doesn't have a fever."

"Okay, don't panic on me, Cameron. Babies do get sick, often this time each year and when they're in day care."

"But he's never been sick before."

"I'm sure he has. Like I said, children get sick." Junie looks him over and hums. "His cheeks are a bit flushed. I'll get the thermometer, poor guy."

Deaton tucks his arms in, hiding his face in my chest, and I lower into the rocking chair with him, patting his back. "It's okay, D. Marley, honey, no throwing toys," I call out.

Junie is back as fast as she disappeared, and Abby finally lets her put her down, all tears forgotten as she runs over to play with the plastic kitchen set.

"Okay, let's see." Junie presses the button, rolling the little ball across Deaton's forehead. The machine beeps, and she frowns at it. "Definitely a fever. I'll grab him a Popsicle and we'll need to call his parents. Unfortunately, he does have to go home."

I nod. "And he can't come back until he's fever free for twenty-four hours, right?"

"Good job. Now should I call, or do you want to?"

I scoff. "I don't want to. Payton is in the middle of a shoot with the cross-country team, which means she's tagged Mason in while she has to have her phone off." An idea sparks. "Oh! I'll just call—"

"You are not calling Arianna, Cameron." She frowns. "Parents. Always parents, your family or not."

She starts to walk off to get that Popsicle, so I shout, "Hey, remember you said that when he shows up with an ambulance!"

Now she scoffs, disappearing through the door.

I bite the bullet, dial Mason, and prepare my most peppy voice possible.

"What's wrong?" he answers on the first ring.

"He's fine—"

"Cameron."

"Okay, he has a little fever so—"

"I'm on my way." I hear some shuffling, then the sound of a door opening and closing. "Can I talk to him?"

Junie comes back in then, and I look up at her, unsure what the protocol is on this but wanting to let him anyway. Thankfully, Junie nods, peeling open the Popsicle and handing it over to Deaton.

"Sanks, Jujie."

We both chuckle at his pronunciation, and I think I hear Mason's exhale at the sound of his son's voice.

"It's on speaker," I tell him.

"Hey, little man," he breathes, and Deaton's eyes light up as he puts his free hand over mine on the phone.

"Daddy?"

"Yeah, buddy. Cammie said you're not feeling good. What's the matter?"

He licks his Popsicle, tucking back into my chest, and shrugs his shoulder, not fully understanding Mason can't see him.

"He's enjoying his Popsicle." I let him know so he doesn't panic.

"Can you, I mean are you allowed to just hold him until I get there?"

I smile. "Of course, Mase. I won't let him go."

"I'm leaving the library right now," he tells me.

"You gonna get in trouble for ditching study hall?"

"Nah, Coach just watched me get up and go. I'll put in more time next week or something. I'll be there in five."

We hang up and, Deaton pops his head up. "Daddy coming, Calmy?"

"Yeah, baby. Your daddy's coming."

I rock him a little, and then I sneak him another Popsicle.

As promised, Mason is signing Deaton out not six minutes later, and I should be shocked when my best friend walks in right behind him—I'm not—her cheeks heaving like she ran here—she probably did.

"Aw," she coos, sticking her lip out. She walks over, holding her hands out. "Come to Auntie Ari."

Deaton holds on to Mason's neck, the Popsicle rubbing sticky shit all over the back of his skin, but Mason doesn't even flinch.

He smirks at his sister. "Nice try."

Ari shrugs, then grabs the diaper bag and looks my way. "Okay, Mom gave me a list of stuff to ask."

She rattles off her questions, and I answer, letting her know when we noticed, how he was acting, what kind of thermometer we used, and what it read.

The twins walk out, and I sink against the counter, exhaustion setting in even though I still have two hours left.

Granny Grace chuckles, shaking her head as she slides the artwork from last week into the pickup cubbies. "Busy day back there, hmm?"

"You have no idea." I fold my arms, lowering my head to settle on them. "I need a nap."

"Honey, I've been here since before you were born. I think I have a bit of an idea what a rough day feels like by now. And you know it's only gonna get worse. The weather's changing, which means snotty noses and no patio playtime."

"I love kids, but so glad I get to go home without one at the end of the night."

"I bet you are, what with the hubba-hubba hunk of man meat you take back to your bed with you."

My head snaps up with a frown, and she swats at me, spinning to the cubbies on the opposite side. "Don't give me that look. I saw you and your…friend, though you two don't look strictly friendly anymore."

I try to remember if they have met, but I'm almost positive they haven't, at least not officially, face-to-face. She's likely just seen us all around campus or them waiting outside a time or ten.

"He's a…big boy, ain't he?" She waggles her eyes.

My mouth drops open and a laugh follows. "You dirty bird."

"Well, is he?" she presses.

I push off the counter, smiling at her. "I'm not telling." Because I don't know.

Well, I mean I do. I've seen him in his boxers a good hundred times, not to mention he's not one of those guys who wears underwear under swim trunks.

The chilly ocean water never played as the witch, casting any disappearing spells. No, his wand was forever present, not that I would sit and stare, but girls notice these things. But I haven't actually seen the size of the stalk—only the outline of the bean before it's watered.

"Look at you, picturing his pecker while standing in a child care center. You should be ashamed."

I gape, and Granny Grace smiles. "Now shoo. Junie is all alone back there. No more of this *needing a nap* nonsense. You've got two hours left, girl. Suck it up."

"Yes, ma'am." I smile, pushing through the double doors again and stepping through to the other side.

Thankfully the next couple hours go by quickly, and I'm out the door.

I check in on Deaton on the way home, Ari telling me she's still with them and Payton's home now too. Apparently, they're all going to have dinner and stare at him for a while.

Back in my dorm room, I'm only just plopping onto my ass, Cup Noodles in one hand, remote in the other, when my phone dings on the coffee table.

Brady's name is on the screen. I open the message.

Brady: help.

I scoff, typing away.

Me: I'm gonna need a little more context, my dude.

Brady: Mean. Thought you'd do anything for me?

Me: I have uneaten food in my hand.

Brady: Shit. Okay, but what if I promise to buy you real food cause we both know you're eatin something from the microwave.

Brady: Don't make me mention it is, in fact, your girlfriend duty to be there when I need you.

I smile, shaking my head.

Me: You had me at real food. What's up?

The three dots pop up, and I wait for his next message, but his location comes through instead.

I frown. "What the hell do you need help with at 7-Eleven?" I look at the time. It's only four.

Me: Do you need a gas can or something? Cause I have to tell you, my no car having ass is fresh out.

I wait a minute, but he doesn't respond, so I stare longingly at my spicy shrimp noodles and then groan. "Okay, fine!"

I look at myself in the mirror and cock my head. I've already changed from my jeans and the top I was wearing, now in a sports bra and an oversized T-shirt so big you can't even see the spandex shorts I have on underneath. I'm wearing thick, scrunchy Avix U socks up to my damn knees and a pair of Minnie Mouse Crocs Payton brought back for me from Disneyland last year.

"Ah, fuck it." I throw on some sunglasses and walk out the door. "Call me Rescue Ranger."

BRADY

Sweet mother of baby Jesus, what in the actual all hell did I get myself into?

I swiftly flick the lock on the bathroom door, dropping my head against it.

I called her ten minutes ago, and her dorm is the closest to the main road. She should have been here by now.

I can only hide out in the damn bathroom for so long, and this isn't my first trip in here. It's my third. Ari claims that I have a baby bladder, and I do, in fact, have to take a piss again, though that's not why I'm in here.

Damn, *do* I have a baby bladder? Maybe I should have that checked out.

"Oh, Brady." A voice so sickly sweet I'll have to go to the dentist after today calls out to me, clearly not concerned with offering me any privacy as one should when the other person is inside the damn restroom.

"Is this the line?" I hear someone else ask from outside the door and a curse leaves me.

Damn single-bathroom businesses, man.

With a deep breath, I wet my hands and grab a paper towel, force a smile on my face, and step out, drying my hands for show.

I grin at the elderly woman waiting for a turn. "It's all yours, ma'am."

She looks at me, her lips pursing, and steps a little farther to the side than necessary to allow me to pass.

Well, okay, then.

Must be because I'm shirtless and oiled up like a prized trophy.

Sarah, or maybe it's Sasha, slides up right then, looping her hand through my arm—because women seem to think they can touch me whenever they want. She smiles up at me, slurping through her straw a little aggressively.

"Need my help again?"

She nods, and I push open the front door, pulling myself free so she can step out first.

"Aw, you're such a gentleman. And yes, we do. Three more people pulled up, and two are big, tall trucks."

My eyes go over the parking lot, and sure enough, there are two pickups sitting there, a little Nissan wedged between them.

The moment I'm off the steps of the convenience store, several girls turn toward me, some rushing over, the others just calling out and throwing up their hands.

"Brady!" The one with the bright-yellow tank top that's tied just below her bra line beams, jogging over with what feels like very intentional movements, being she's only about ten feet from me. "Help me with the big red one?" She sticks her lip out in a pout, and I wonder if I'd find that sexy if it were a Friday night.

A loud, familiar laugh reaches my ears, and I whip around, seeking the source.

"Oh, thank fuck," I mutter, slipping away from the girls around me and meeting Cameron where she stands a few feet away.

She looks me over, her smile growing, so I give her a little show.

Doing my best stripper hip roll, I make the straw skirt around my waist crunch and move, and run my palms down my ribs in tune with the girly music blasting across the parking lot.

Cameron laughs harder and I join in, lifting her off the ground and spinning her before lowering her back to her feet.

Her eyes trail over the parking lot before landing back on mine. "So sorority car wash, huh?"

"Yep."

She nods, smirking a bit. "So, like, am I playing the jealous-girlfriend role? Do I make a scene and get mad that you're here with all these girls and I had no idea, stomp off, and force you to chase after me?"

My brows crash together, horror stricken. "You crazy? Some of these girls have had to hear the rumor that I'm someone's boyfriend now. Do that and they'll take it as us splitting up, and it will be worse. No, no. I need a partner in crime here, Cammie."

She chuckles, nodding her head. "All right, so what do you want me to do? And why aren't they in bathing suits if they're having a car wash? Every girl knows jean shorts get baggy once they're wet."

I shrug. "Something about not wanting half-naked women out here to scare off store customers. Not sure they've realized all the girls have their shirts up to their bellies yet."

"So how is it you're allowed to be out here shirtless?"

"'Cause I'm Brady Lancaster, Cammie Baby," I tease, and when she only lifts a brow, a laugh leaves me. "The owner has season tickets to our games. He saw me here and asked for an autograph for his kid."

She shakes her head with a grin. "Of course he did."

"Brady, come back!"

"Yeah, Brady, help me with the hood?"

"Wait, I asked for his help first!"

When we both glance that way, Yellow Top asks, "You'll lift me on your shoulders, right? I have really flexible legs."

Cameron coughs to hide a laugh and I look back at her with pleading, puppy-dog eyes.

She stares a moment, trying to figure her plan out, and I wait, praying it's a good one.

I take her hand and tug her in closer. "So what's the move, fake girlfriend?"

128

Cameron winks, then steps back, tearing her shirt over her head, revealing a skintight, light pink sports bra with a little zipper in the middle that's halfway down, and teeny tiny...

Hold up.

"Yo." I crowd her, take her shirt, and wrap it around her back, hiding her booty from view. "Are those underwear?!"

"No," she chuckles, gently shoving at my chest.

But my feet are planted firmly, and I don't budge, cocking my head and stretching my neck to get a better look. "You sure?" I stare at the spot they stretch around her toned thighs, literally *right* at the edge of her booty.

And girl's got a booty. Ever since she and Ari did that Booty Bootcamp thing, whatever the fuck that is, it's been poppin'. She's most definitely kept up the routine. It's high and round, and I've got the sudden urge to give it a little tap. Maybe a squeeze or two, you know, just to see how soft it is.

I glare harder at the offending underwear. "Pretty sure when your leg stretches to take a step, them things are gonna slide up and out will plop a cheek."

Her laugh is loud, and she gives me a saucy grin.

My brow raises and she pushes up on her toes, tongue flicking across my lips, and there's a little twitch in my toes.

A frown threatens to form, but then a shadow falls over us, and we both look left.

The girl flicks her eyes at Cameron, then turns them back to me, batting her long lashes. "Come on, number ninety-eight," the brunette singsongs. "We need our big, strong mountain man's help."

Cameron's hands, still on my chest from attempting to push me back, span out, and she runs them slowly and steadily down my abs, making my muscles twitch at the feeling. She looks to me, but her words are for the interrupter. "He's not *your* anything." She holds my gaze steady. "He's mine."

My feet shuffle closer on their own, but she's already pulling back, smiling wide at the sorority girl.

I think Cameron's going to say something, maybe introduce herself, but she doesn't. She simply walks past, tugging her hair from the messy bun it was clipped up in.

I watch as it falls in long, tousled waves, the tips nearly touching the swell of her perfect, peachy ass, and I've got the sudden urge to tug on it.

To wrap it around my fist and pull just enough to—

My muscles lock, my frown instant.

No.

No, no.

I don't want to do that to Cammie Girl.

I don't.

Cameron walks past the group of girls staring at her, not all out of maliciousness, some seemingly just curious, and takes two buckets full of soapy water, tossing a sponge inside one. We all watch as she sets it on the open tailgate and hops right up. Taking the other bucket, she dumps it over the roof of the truck, flips it upside down, and climbs on top.

Then she leans all the way over in those goddamn underwear—fight me, that's what they are—and starts scrubbing, hips swaying to the music that I'm suddenly tempted to turn off.

The girls are frozen for a moment, some looking over their own jean shorts and tops, and then they laugh, tearing their own clothes off and revealing bikinis hidden underneath.

"Yeah, ladies," a few guys shout, clearly other AU students, and I decide they are the owners of the trucks. "Wash it real nice."

Not a single one turns back to me, and a smile spreads across my lips.

I move over to the truck Cameron's washing and hop up, sponge in hand, then crowd her from behind. "You're, like, freakishly good at handling women."

She smiles over her shoulder at me, big blue eyes bright. "Sometimes we just need a little inspiration. Now, you just gonna stand there, or you gonna help me wash this ugly-ass truck?"

I raise a brow and make a show of dipping my sponge in the water, and she smiles, spinning back around and getting to work. I take the sponge and, instead of scrubbing the window with it, swipe the soapy water across her sides.

She gasps at the cold, jumping down with a squeal, her wide eyes meeting mine. They narrow quickly, and then she's on me, rubbing the sponge across my neck and chest.

I juke left, spinning until I'm behind her, and pick up the whole-ass bucket.

Her mouth drops open. "Don't you *dare!*" she shouts, but there's no venom behind her words.

I bite my lip, smiling, and lift the bucket up high.

She yelps, taking a chance and rushing forward, bending and slipping under the bucket until she's pressed to my body, arms wrapped tightly around me, head tucked in, plastering herself to me.

"You really think that's gonna save you?" I tease.

"No, but at least this way——"

I pour it over both our heads, and she shouts, trying to break free, but I tossed the bucket the second it was empty, and now I'm holding her to me.

She laughs, her body shivering a bit before she looks up.

Her hair is soaked, hiding one of her eyes completely, and the other is only just poking through.

Grinning, I push it out of the way, and she shakes her head with a low laugh.

"You're an ass."

"Oh, but, baby, I'm your ass," I coo.

She slaps me on the arm, and I let her go, shaking my hair out as she finger-combs her own before making quick work of a braid.

"Careful, or I might make a scene and break up with you right here."

"You wouldn't dare."

Her hands fall to her hips, and she raises an eyebrow.

My eyes accidently fall to her light pink sports bra and narrow to slits, but she spins before she notices.

Cameron turns once again, hopping down with our now empty bucket, but before she can reach the hose, I'm there, gripping her shoulders from behind.

"Cameron Hope Cox," I drawl in a low, scolding tone with a hint of playfulness woven in. "What in the fresh *hell* did I just see?"

I can sense her confusion, and it takes her a moment, but she looks down to where the material of her top has softened a bit, revealing a dirty little secret behind it.

A dirty little secret that should not make me curious, yet here I am, wondering what exactly I'd find beneath the soft pink fabric because, I swear to God, it looks like two tiny toys right where her nipples would be.

She spins there, her eyes meeting mine, a small blush creeping up her neck, even if she does smile in response.

"Cameron."

"Brady."

"Tell me."

She cocks her head. "And why would I do that?"

"'Cause what kind of boyfriend doesn't know what's under his girlfriend's shirt?"

She leans in close, whispering teasingly, "A fake one."

I frown and she laughs, giving up on filling her empty bucket and instead grabbing a new one.

She spins, and my eyes fall to her chest. "Come on, Boyfriend," she calls out loud. "Let's wash the *headlights next.*"

I glare, and she beams brighter, spinning and adding a little extra sway to her hips.

"Swing those hips this way, honey," one of the guys hollers.

My head snaps toward the group gathered by the picnic tables, a warning on the tip of my tongue, but I don't have to let it out.

No, Cameron does it for me.

"Sorry, boys," she teases, meeting my gaze over her shoulder with a grin. "But I belong to someone else."

I smirk from her to them. "She belongs to me."

CHAPTER 17
BRADY

"Come on."

"No."

"You can't just leave me in suspense!"

Cameron laughs, pushing through the doors before I can hold them open, and I follow her ass toward the tables.

"Look, just tell me I'm right."

She gives me a blank stare, and my grin grows.

"That means I am."

She scoffs. "Like there was any room for doubt."

"There most definitely was not."

She faces forward as the blush starts up her neck and picks the table closest to the back, folding her legs beneath her the moment she lowers into the seat.

I drop in the one across from her, watching as she tosses her book onto the table between us, my eyes locked on the swell of her breasts in her purple top. There are pierced nipples under that shirt. On Cameron's body.

I can't believe she has her nipples pierced.

"What do we—Brady!"

My attention snaps up, and she crosses her arms, cocking her head at me.

"Really?" she deadpans.

My hands lift into the air in the universal sign for *I didn't do it* when I oh so clearly did, and she groans and laughs at the same time.

"Can we get down to business please?" She fights a smile. "I only have an hour."

"Yeah, yeah." I take my own things out, and we start on our assignment, breaking the questions in half and swapping answers.

It only takes thirty minutes to get through it, so we move to the section review, only pausing when she starts to grunt and grumble.

"I hate this class." She sighs, finishing off her bottle of water and taking mine.

"I hate most of my classes, but we still gotta pass them."

"You mean, *I* have to pass them. You'll be drafted at the end of the year, along with Mason and Chase, and leave us girls here like peasants, all alone while you go play for some big, bad pro team." She smiles then. "OMG, you'll be the second boyfriend I've had to leave me to become a pro athlete." She laughs good-naturedly, but there's a little something in her voice she can't hide—a small edge of sorrow maybe.

It's not for me, of course, but the real boyfriend she had freshman year. Now that I think about it, I'm not so sure I realized he was her boyfriend. Guess I figured they were just seeing each other a bit. I wonder how serious they were.

I'm about to ask when she beats me to speak.

"Unless I dump you before you can dump me," she jokes, stretching those long legs out until her heels are balancing on my knees. "That way, I don't look like the girl who was left behind when you climb that ladder."

"I, um…" I clear my throat, scratching the back of my neck. "Yeah, I don't…I mean I'm not…" I just stop talking, not wanting to get into that.

Cameron eyes me closely, pausing a moment, and I wonder if she's going to call me out, make me say what I didn't mean to start saying in the first place, but instead, a small smile covers her lips, and she looks to her phone with a sigh.

"I have to go. Are you hanging here a bit or want to walk out with me?"

"Nah, I'm going to go check on Chase. Coach asked to see him after practice again last week, but he still hasn't told us what it was about. Any ideas of a bet I can make him to force him to talk?"

"One that I would give up to you and not save for my own future benefit?" She smirks. "Negative."

"Brat."

"You love me."

"Uh-huh." I glance at my phone, pulling up a text from Mason and firing one off real fast before turning my attention back to Cameron. "Make sure you spend some time going over those sections this weekend. I have a group project for my finance class on Sunday that's going to kill, so I might be brain fried after that."

"Wait." She frowns. "The test is next Monday?"

"Girl, do you pay attention to that poor woman at all?"

"I try really, really hard not to."

I laugh at that, gaining a few glares from around the room.

"She's so annoying," Cameron whines. "How do I know what to memorize if she doesn't give us the questions?"

"You're not supposed to be memorizing. You're supposed to be learning."

"And you're supposed to be helping me study so I can pass this class, but so far I've had to do all the readings my damn self."

"What?" I gape. "Girl, I have worked over every section with you since week one. What do you want me to do, read it to you?"

She gasps, smiling as her brows jump.

"For real?" I grin. "You want me to read it to you?"

"Imagine, I can lie back, rest my eyes, and just listen." I see the moment she decides this is the best idea ever, her eyes lighting up at the thought alone, and oddly enough, a sliver of eagerness races down my own spine. "Okay, yes. Let's do that. Fuck this library. It's distracting anyway. Ari is in class during this time, so my dorm is perfect."

"Your ass will fall asleep," I tease. "There's a reason I made you come out of your dorm to study in the first place."

"Pleeease," she begs, pouty lip and all.

I want to lean forward and bite at it...but that would be weird, so instead I flick her pretty mouth, my own twitching. "All right." I nod, and she starts to get excited, but then she sees it, the mischief in my gaze.

Her eyes narrow just as I say, "On one condition."

———

CAMERON

"Cammie," he singsongs, his long strides easily keeping up with my own.

I don't get so much as a single pace ahead of him. No, the man stays on me the whole-ass time, and he doesn't give up.

"We already established you're a closet freak," he says, laughing and dodging my hand when I reach out to smack him. "And while I'm shocked by this latest development, I'm not surprised."

"No?" I raise a brow.

"Nah." He grins, and it's the infamous Brady Lancaster grin. Intentionally slow, hooked high on one side, showing just a hint of white teeth and maybe making the dimple on his left cheek pop. It's full-on playboy, screaming *baby, come get me.*

I glare, and he chuckles tauntingly.

"Fine! Just tell me when you got 'em done, and I'll leave you alone," he suggests.

"Liar."

"Okay, I'll leave you alone...for today."

I almost snort, spinning in my sandals and giving him my back. "Bye, Brady!"

"See you later, Favorite Girlfriend!"

I can't help but laugh, tucking my hands into my hoodie as I make my way to my Free Art class, my first ever elective.

When I first registered for the semester, I assumed this class would be my easiest. Unfortunately for me, it's quite the opposite. It's hard as shit, and apparently, I suck at all things art.

So far, we've only played around with several different types of artistic expression, searching for our "niche," as Professor Lorraine called it.

I officially suck at drawing, photography, digital design, *and* painting. To be fair, we did swap to something new each class, so it's not like there was time to learn a whole lot, but I guess that's the point. Dabble in them all and find that sweet spot.

I may very well fail this class if I can't find something I'm half-decent at, but by the looks of it, it's going to be a close call. I'm sitting at a solid D at the moment, having been unable to complete a single assignment from start to finish. But hey, at least I've got the 10 percent of my grade coming from attendance and participation points going for me.

Ugh.

Slipping into class, I smile at my station partner, slowly making my way over.

"Hey." Lilly beams, her pink hair in two adorable, spiky pigtails.

"Hey." I stuff my bag in the cubby drawers under our station and tie my apron over myself before looking over the supplies stacked on the table.

There's some weird gray powder, a little plastic tray, and some makeup-brush-looking things with sharply cut points.

"What are we doing, making dust angels or something?"

She laughs. "My guess is sculpting." She pokes the gray, dusty-looking stuff. "This looks like the making for some sort of clay."

Sure enough, when the professor closes the door, officially locking anyone who isn't yet in their seats out for the day, she confirms Lilly's guess.

I huff, grumbling internally.

Yay, another thing for me to suck at.

I get to work, adding all the components together until a thick, slightly sticky clay is formed. It grows denser and denser with each roll of my hands through it, and then I glare down at the mess, wondering what the hell I should try to create.

I look to Lilly, who seems to be making an actual lily, the lines of the flower already forming and obvious. Another girl has a basic heart with an arrow through, while the guy beside her puts us all to shame with his cat-making skills. To my right, the guy whose name I can't remember but who told me at the start of the semester he joined this class on a whim, same as I did, is making a simple football, but the texture he's adding to it looks legit.

I smile as an idea sparks. I think it over for a moment, take a deep breath, and laugh to myself.

"Here goes nothing," I mutter and get to work.

Starting slowly, I create a lower base using my pointer fingers, pressing the clay in a deep curve on each side, rounding it out toward the top. As soon as that's done, I smile because I know this is actually going to work.

For the first time, class comes to a close too fast, and I nearly pout, but I take an extra minute or two to put my final touches on.

Stepping back, I beam at my work, looking over at my professor as she comes up.

"Is that…" She looks to me.

I laugh. "Yep."

"Nice work, Cox. I think you might have found your element. Get it in the kiln and get your station cleared."

"Yes, ma'am."

I do as I'm told, thinking maybe this class won't be so bad after all.

With a little extra pep in my step, I head out and over to the cafeteria for some lunch.

Burrito bowl with extra guac in hand, I take a seat. I no sooner take my first bite than a pair of thick thighs appears across the table.

I look up, following the tight stretch of a deep green T-shirt, molded perfectly to a firm chest, and into a pair of green eyes that still spark something inside me, making me swallow my tongue. He knows it too, his lips twitching at whatever he sees staring back at me.

"Hi, Cameron," Alister all but purrs. "Think your *boyfriend* would mind if I joined you?"

CHAPTER 18
ALISTER

Her face is so expressive. That was one of the first things I learned about her.

She can't hide how she feels, but more than that, I don't think she tries to. She doesn't shy away from her likes and dislikes, her desires, and the look in her eye tells me she feels a little of all three of those things for me.

The dislike sucks, but it's outweighed by the others. I can work with that.

"So will he?"

Cameron blinks up at me, going the silent route as she takes a big bite of her food, her teeth scraping her fork to drive the point home—I'm on her nerves already. But that's fine. At least she's no longer telling me to fuck off.

I take a seat across from her, and she folds her feet beneath her, sitting up a little higher.

"Glad to know he's not threatened by me," I tease.

"Please." She stabs her chicken, lifting her fork as she smirks at me. "He's threatened by no one."

"Because you're so in love?" I joke. "Or because he wouldn't know how to take a relationship serious enough to know he should be threatened?"

"You know nothing about him," she snaps.

A small frown builds, her quickness to defend him rubbing me the wrong way, but I have to remind myself that they're like family. Of course she'll stand up for him, probably until she's blue in the face. It doesn't necessarily mean anything.

I lift my hands in surrender. "All right, my bad. I guess I assumed having played on the team with him for a season and a half, I might have some idea—"

"What exactly are you getting at, Alister?" She pops the top of her soda, taking a small sip.

"Oh, nothing, I was just going to offer to keep an eye on him for you at next week's game."

"Why not this week, oh savior of mine?" She flutters her lashes mockingly.

"Well, this week, we're playing at home again. Next week, we're on the road. No one to report back to you if *your man* decides to go back to his player ways and shacks up with someone."

"He won't."

I cock my head. "You sure?"

Cameron licks her lips. "You know, if this is your idea of being friendly, you suck at it."

I laugh, unwrapping my roast beef sandwich, and take a couple bites.

We eat in silence for a few minutes, and it's nice. I miss just being near her.

Cameron finishes too soon and starts to stand, but I swiftly reach out, gripping her wrist before she can, and her blue eyes pop up to mine.

"Come on, Cam. Hang out with me for a few minutes."

"I should really—"

"Just until I finish eating," I interrupt. "Please."

She stares at me a moment before a fake sigh leaves her, and she lowers back onto the seat. "Fine. I still have a brownie to eat, I guess."

I let her go, grinning widely, and she hides hers by looking down at her tray.

"So what classes did you have today?" I ask.

"You mean your initial stalking skills from the first few weeks didn't tell you all my secrets?"

"Only where to find you, but I did refrain from approaching all your professors."

"Oh, yeah, so only the one in the class I was most looking forward to then, huh?"

"Hey, Thursday afternoon was my only free spot, and it's hard to find a class that's only in person once a week. You should feel flattered I want to spend what could be my afternoon off with you instead."

She laughs, tearing off a corner of her brownie and tossing it in her mouth.

"You eat like a bird."

Her smile brightens. "That's what Brady says."

My brows twitch, but I force my lips to stay tipped up. "Well, I guess we have more than just one thing in common."

"Football?"

"Wanting to be your boyfriend."

Her eyes snap up, narrowing. "Alister."

"Sorry," I chuckle, finishing off my sandwich and opening my fruit bowl. "You know you could just admit you're not really dating, and I wouldn't have to lay it on so thick."

"It would have to be true for me to admit such a thing, which it isn't."

"And do you plan to still be dating him at the end of the month?"

"Even if I wasn't, I already told you: I don't want this." She waves her fingers from herself to me. "I can't trust you, and if I can't trust you, I can't be with you."

I drop my gaze to the watermelon piece I spear with my fork, hearing what she's not saying.

If I hadn't fucked things up, then she would not be pretending to date some other guy just to keep me at arm's length. Because that's what she's doing.

Not that she's admitted it, but it's like I said.

Brady will hook up with someone else at some point, forgetting or maybe too excited about the prospect to worry about a fake relationship, and then she won't be able to hide the truth anymore.

I look up, meeting her eyes and hating the hint of sorrow that I'm responsible for that clouds those baby blues. "I know I've said it already, Cameron, but I truly am sorry for what I did to you. I hate myself for hurting you. If I could go back…"

Cameron stares at me a long moment. Hesitantly, she reaches across the table, and I take the offer, locking my hands with hers. She squeezes slightly, a small, sad smile on her lips.

"We can't go back, Alister."

I nod, my throat growing thick as I ask, "But do you think we can ever go forward?"

She opens her mouth, so for the sake of this conversation, I add, "I mean if you weren't dating Brady anymore." *Fake dating.*

She swallows, eyes dropping to the spot where my thumb is running along her wrist.

"I'm not sure," she admits quietly.

She may as well have screamed the words into my ear because there wasn't a no in there. That's a maybe, and maybe will always make trying worth it.

We're not done.

I just have to convince her of as much, and I think I have an idea of where to start. I shift closer, holding on a little tighter. "Hey, so—"

A large figure wraps around her from behind, and I look up to find Brady.

She tears her hand free, quickly dropping it to her lap as her cheeks flame, but he's already got his face buried in her hair, and if the silent shake of her shoulders a moment later means anything, he's whispered something to her.

She tips her head back, smiling up at him, and I note the way

144

it reaches even beyond her eyes. There's a tenderness there I never noticed before, and it has my stomach turning.

They're just friends, I remind myself, slowly starting to feel like the outsider here when that's my girl he's holding on to.

Was your girl.

Damn it.

I clear my throat—loudly—and her head snaps this way as if she forgot I was here.

The tint coloring her cheeks makes me wonder if she did.

"Alister," Brady drawls, his arms moving from where they are folded around her shoulders to her waist. "Mind if I borrow her?"

"If she were really your girlfriend, you wouldn't have to ask."

Brady chuckles, and he hauls her up with one swoop. "I got your bag, Cammie Baby. Ari and Paige are waiting outside."

Cameron nods, looking back at me with a tiny smile and a wave before heading toward the door.

Brady watches her go, same as I do, and only when she's out the door do we face one another. He bends down, placing his left fist knuckle down on the tabletop. "That little *if she were your girlfriend* line hurt your case, not the other way around."

When I frown, he scoffs and stretches to his full height.

"If you knew her like you think you do, like *I do*, you'd know that was a really fuckin' stupid thing to say." He starts to leave, but something has him pausing and his shoulders seem to fall as he looks back toward me. He opens his mouth but closes it a moment later.

Brady shakes his head and walks out, shoving the door a little harder than necessary. And because I'm a masochist, I rise, moving over to the window to watch his next move, to see if he keeps up this boyfriend act when he doesn't know I'm watching.

To my surprise, he doesn't rush her and wrap her up.

It's she who steps up and takes his hand, her other moving animatedly in front of her face as she tells him something that has him grinning her way.

My eyes slide to Cameron's friends, searching for any hint of scrutiny or, I don't know, something that tells me this is new or not the norm, but both are smiling and laughing alongside their best friend as if it is.

As if her holding hands with the campus playboy is normal.

As if this little farce is real when it's not.

She's just playing a role.

Cameron is not *dating* Brady Lancaster.

She throws her head back and laughs, and he smiles down at her, wrapping his arm around her shoulders to tug her closer.

Is she?

CHAPTER 19
CAMERON

"Honestly, Payton going back to the beach house with Deaton this weekend worked out."

I skip down the cement stadium steps, bypassing our seats and moving all the way to the first row, something you can only manage to do when you show up the second the gates open, or the staff will play hard-ass and not let you pass. I'm aware they're only doing their jobs, but it still sucks when your friends are the ones on the field. Though I guess hundreds could likely claim the same, seeing as this is college and all.

I spin around, smirking at Ari. "Do you feel like a traitor wearing someone else's number?"

"My twin's number?" She raises a brow. "No."

I raise one right back and she chuckles.

"Okay, somehow it does feel a little strange," she admits. "I haven't worn anyone's number but Noah's for a year now." Ari looks beside her, only to frown and turn completely. "Why are you hiding behind me?"

Paige shrugs, smashing her lips to the side.

I reach out and tug her down the last stair to stand beside us. "Stop stressing," I tell her.

"I don't know." She glances down anxiously. "This just feels... He's going to be mad."

"Doubtful."

"We're not... I'm not like that with him. We don't even talk."

"You and the dozens of other fans that will be here today."

She scowls, and it's such an innocent look on her, I can't help but give the girl a giddy hug.

We watch as the final prep is done across the field, the guys likely having already been out here today for the first round of warm-ups. We pretend the seats in the first row are ours, not moving as others start to file in around us.

Across the stadium, red and gold start to fill in the space, and I peek behind me to make sure our side is coloring up just as fast.

As always, it's raining blue and yellow, as it should.

Some people shout from the upper deck, and I face the field just in time to watch the team jog out. We hop to our feet, shouting and clapping as they all fall into formation at the forty. As in sync as always, they form parallel lines, moving right into stretches before breaking up into groups for pregame drills.

A quick glance at my phone a bit later tells me it's twenty minutes to kickoff, and right on time, the boys file to the sidelines, ditching their helmets to fuel up on water and electrolytes.

It's Mason who spots us first, his grin spreading as he jogs over.

"How the hell did you score these seats?" He scopes the area.

"Shhh," I scold, and he laughs, looking back and catching Brady's attention.

Brady frowns at him, but then his eyes move left.

He spots Ari first, then Paige, and finally, his eyes land on me.

His cup freezes halfway to his lips, his smile slow. Then he's tossing the paper product, water flying all over as he lets out a loud whoop that gains us the attention of everyone around.

I beam brightly, putting my hands on my hips, and give several poses.

"And here comes the boyfriend," Mason teases, throwing me a smile.

Brady doesn't simply lean against the edge. No, he hops up, kicks one leg over, and sits his ass there. His eyes move from my top to my cheek and back. He opens his mouth, but I spin, doing a little shimmy, and then before I know what he's doing, he's yanking me over the edge.

I yelp, legs flying in the air as I feel like I'm about to fall backward for a split second before my boots hit the ground.

"Brady, what the hell!" I laugh, but then I'm in his arms again, this time bridal style, which is kind of awkward with his already-massive body and the pads bulking his shoulders out even more. "You're going to get me in trouble!"

"Nah. Coach loves me. Besides, this is too good. My name is on your ass, Cam. This has to be documented."

I raise a brow. "Documented?"

"Oh yeah." He starts jogging down the sideline, and I grip him harder, my ponytail flying around and whipping me in the face when he spins suddenly and takes off the other way, flying past his team, who yell and root him on. "You ready for this, Cammie Girl?"

"Ready for what exactly?"

He stops and sets me on my feet, twirling me around and then yanking me to his chest. He grins wildly. "For this."

And then he kisses me, hard and greedy and not at *all* PG, his tongue sweeping in instantly, teasing and tasting mine one second, then he's yanking back in the next. He's full-on cheesing now, his laughter mixing with my own.

"Did you mess up my face paint? 'Cause I'll have you know writing backward in the mirror is not easy."

He leans away, gaze traveling the shape of his number on my cheek, then the little shark on the other side. "Nope. Still perfect. Shirt too." He smiles down at my outfit. "So. If I weren't wearing these pads right now, would I feel a little metal poking through?"

I laugh, teasing, "Brady Lancaster, are you asking if you made my nipples hard?"

"What? No! I meant... Wait." He grins slowly. "Did I?"

I chuckle, shaking my head, and answer the question he was

really asking. "It's called a padded bra. A must when you have what I do hiding underneath."

"And how long exactly have you had to wear said padded bra?"

"Nice try, Big Guy."

"Worth a shot. Imma get it out of you, you know," Brady swears, his attention shifting over my head. "Here we go, girl."

Before I can ask what that means, his name is shouted gleefully from my left, and I turn to look that way.

"Brady! Can you give us a minute? Tell us who the lucky lady is!" A microphone is shoved between us as a gorgeous, dark-haired woman steps up. "And she's wearing your number!"

"My number, my name." He throws me a quick wink. "My heart on her sleeve."

I fight a laugh, and he squeezes my side, his lips pinched tight to hold in his own.

"I know we've all heard the rumors there was a love story kicking off, but can we take this as a sign that our favorite party guy has settled down?"

Brady smirks, takes my hand, and looks into the camera rather than at the reporter. "Wish I could say sorry, ladies, but I'm not."

Before the woman can say anything else, he's tearing down the field again, my hand locked tight in his own and forcing me to jog with him.

We're both laughing as we get back to the others, and Mason bends down, offering me his knee. I climb up, and Brady pushes my ass until I can officially leap over.

Chase jogs up behind them, clapping Brady on the shoulder with a grin. "That was smooth, man. Hopefully they got the message and no one tries to pay off the staff to get a copy of the key to your room like at our last away game."

"No!" I gape. "They do that?"

Brady scoffs. "You have no idea."

"Bitches."

"Jealous?" he teases, and I give him a hard eye roll.

Chase grins, glancing over the group, and I see the moment he notices my little Paige's surprise. His eyes snap back to the other blond, holding for several solid seconds. His lips twitch slightly, and I give myself a mental high five, but then he quickly turns away, so we never get to see it fully take shape.

I share a look with Brady, and he wiggles his brows knowingly.

"Come on. Coach is about to flip out if we don't get settled." Mason tugs Brady away by the sleeve, and I look back to Paige, Chase's number printed across her T-shirt.

Her cheeks are pink, and she suddenly starts messing with her shoelaces, but there's a small smile on her lips. Ari and I face the field, clapping and cheering as everyone gets ready for kickoff, but just before the team takes the field, the players shift around, and I see him.

Standing there in the middle, holding on to the collar of his pads as he stares right at me, an expression I can't quite read blanketing his face, is Alister.

I offer a smile and a wave, but his eyes fall to the turf, and then he turns around.

My smile falls instantly.

His dismissal shouldn't sting. I have no right to feel hurt after all that I'm doing to try and let him go, especially after the little show Brady and I just put on. Though to be fair, I didn't even think about Alister being here to witness it as it was happening.

So why is there a little ache in the center of my chest?

I'm the one who asked for this.

I wanted to let him go and asked for Brady's help to make it happen. Well, after he successfully sparked the idea, but still. I'm the reason we're doing this fake-dating thing. By the looks of it, it's working.

Alister is starting to believe our time has passed.

That thought shouldn't send unease skittering through my veins.

So why does it?

Chase and Hector, another AU football player, are getting down on some video game. Ari and Paige both sit in the recliner on the other side of the room, searching the internet for costume ideas for the Halloween party coming up. Mason and Brady are in the little kitchen area with a few of their other friends, laughing and talking about tonight's game while finishing off the last of the frozen pizzas we made about two hours ago.

Thankfully, the team took the after-party down the block to one of the fraternity houses. It worked out since we were already planning for a quieter night in. The boys all have to fit in a study group tomorrow because their schedules will be different next week due to an away game. It's not an overnighter, but they won't get in until around three in the morning.

I don't realize I've zoned out until Brady drops beside me on the carpet, spinning a football around in his hands.

We look at each other, and he tips his head slightly. "You okay?"

I nod, and Brady frowns instantly.

"Cam. Don't lie to me." He tucks the ball under an arm. "Was tonight too much?"

"You mean was your helping me sell the story of us the way I asked you to too much?"

His response is instant: "Yes."

I shake my head but leave it resting against the wall, a small tip to my lips. "You didn't do anything wrong, Brady."

"You say that, but something's wrong, and I know this sad face you've been wearing the last few hours isn't 'cause we had no pineapple for those cardboard-tasting pizzas."

A small laugh manages to escape, and he grins, though it doesn't meet his eyes.

"Cammie Baby, I'm sorry. The girls, or fans"—he rolls his eyes—"or whatever you want to call them, have been hounding my ass a lot more this year. It's kind of a lot to deal with," he mutters, almost as if there's a little more to it than what he's saying. "When I spotted you all decked out in my name tonight, it seemed like the perfect opportunity to try to tame the packs, since we were already putting on a show on campus. I had a good time, and you were smiling, and shit, I don't know. I'm sorry," he says again.

"There's nothing for you to be sorry for. We were having fun, and you have as much right to use this arrangement to your benefit as I do. I want you to."

He scowls, shaking his head. "Not at the expense of hurting you."

I drop my eyes, sliding my fingers over the smudges on the screen of my phone before looking back to him with a shamed smile. "You didn't hurt me, Brady."

He stares, gauging me a long moment. As I knew he would, my perceptive friend figures out what I couldn't bring myself to say. He nods his understanding, his voice a little lower than normal when he says, "He didn't mean to hurt you either."

Embarrassment warms my cheek. "I know," I concede. "At least not in this instance, right?"

"Maybe not in either," Brady adds, almost hesitantly. "Not that that takes away from the fact that he did."

"Yeah. I think maybe you're right, but..." I break off with a sigh, propping my head on the wall once more.

He takes my hand, drawing it up to kiss my knuckles, and my eyes shift his way, my lips tipping up slightly.

"Should we call this off?" he mumbles. "You can slap me and call me names for everyone to see. I kinda always wanted to see how one of those public breakups felt anyway. The chick flicks you guys used to make us watch always made them seem so interesting."

A laugh bubbles out of me, and he grins, but it falls pretty quickly.

"For real, Cameron. Do we need to end this? I don't want to hurt anyone. Especially you."

Warmth washes over me, but it's not enough to thaw the tension my muscles have held since Alister gave me his back at the game.

God, I'm so messed up. I hate that you can't just turn off feelings. Life would be so much easier if you could.

"I don't want to hurt him either," I tell him. "That's not why I wanted us to pretend." Slowly, I meet his gaze and decide to be honest. "I don't think I can let go of what he did to even be able to *try* to be with him, Brady. I've attempted it. I've found myself enjoying his attention here and there since, but then suddenly it all comes back, and I can't get away from him fast enough. Like in the back of my mind, I know we can't get over the past, but then shit like this happens, and suddenly I'm confused again. It's like a part of me isn't convinced I don't want him, and I'm not sure how I feel about that. I was hoping he would accept this for what it was and distance himself, but he did the opposite."

"Until tonight."

"Until tonight," I parrot with a sigh, feeling dumb for being all torn up about this. "This is what I wanted, but I guess I didn't anticipate the feelings that would come with it all, you know?"

"Yeah," Brady whispers. "I know."

When I look over at him, I find he's staring at his lap. After a moment, he looks up, a ghost of a smile on his lips.

"So we're still doing this or…" He trails off.

I take his hand once more, entwining our fingers. "I'm all yours."

He scoffs lightly, nodding his head. "From now on, I'll let you lead this whole relationship thing."

"Nah."

"No?" He raises a brow, pinning me with a skeptical expression.

"I mean"—I shrug a shoulder, a true grin beginning to form—"where's the fun in that?"

Brady chuckles, bumping his shoulder into mine. "Where indeed?"

CHAPTER 20
CAMERON

The week flies by in a wave of uneventful boringness. Since Mason is on lockdown to prepare for midterms, Payton used her days off and left for the beach house with the baby to visit her brother and the others. Paige had an emergency at her dance studio back in Oceanside, so she ended up heading that way, too. Ari has been hit and miss with her own classes, so we mostly hang out at night before bed. And while Chase is in the same boat as Mason, Brady has gone full force into training.

I guess the team we're playing this weekend has one of the strongest lines, and he's determined to break his way through it to keep himself neck and neck with that guy from Brighton. The two have been trading each other for first each week in stats, but only one can take the record for the most sacks at the end of the season.

So yeah, my entire crew is busy, and basically, I need more friends.

I didn't even see Alister in class today. At first, I thought maybe he didn't show because of the whole *me and Brady kissing on the field* thing, but then I remembered the boys have an early away game on Saturday, so they'll be traveling tomorrow. Because of that, they get to take some midterms early. There were several players I know who were not in the classes I have with them all week.

I smile at the little figure in my palm as I make my way to the weight room. My professor let me stay a little later in art yesterday to finish my second clay project, since I didn't need my station to put the final details on it. So I missed my usual study session on the bleachers yesterday afternoon. In all fairness, I might not have gone anyway, since Ari was busy, but it's whatever. If I hurry, I can catch Brady just as he finishes up.

With a little more power behind my steps, I get there in no time, and as the gym comes into view, I slow my pace.

Brady is already outside, shirtless and sweaty, with a towel wrapped around his neck, hanging over his pecs—and hanging all over his arms are two volleyball players, if the kneepads they're wearing are anything to go by.

I mean, those pads could be pretty useful for extracurricular activities too…

When Brady laughs, I decide one of them told him exactly that, even if I have no idea what was actually said, because I seem to have stopped walking altogether, instead watching the three of them like a creeper from a distance.

Brady grins down at the blond one, so tiny her head hardly reaches his shoulder. If he tucked his arm around her, she'd fit under it like the perfect little puzzle piece: Goldilocks and the big, badass bear.

Man, I must seem like an ogre compared to her. Pretty sure my chin can rest on his collarbone. I bet she's so small, she couldn't even manage a proper sixty-nine position. I mean unless his dick is massive.

My eyes fall to his gym shorts, and I tip my head in thought.

They are pretty long, and now that I think about it, I've never seen him wear those short shorts some of the guys like to run or workout in. So yeah, there's really no telling what could be hiding under there.

Not that I'm wondering.

Okay, yeah, time to walk away, Cameron. What the hell?

I spin, yelping when I'm met with a hard chest.

Soft hands wrap around my biceps to steady me, and I meet Alister's gaze.

"Hi." He smiles.

I guess I didn't know I needed him to smile at me again, as the moment he does, my muscles ease.

I smile back. "Hey. Missed you in class."

His brows jump and I tense all over again.

"I mean," I rush out, "I didn't miss you. I just meant it—"

"It's all good." His expression is gentle. "I know what you meant, but I will admit that I wouldn't mind hearing you missed me if it were true."

I look away a moment. "You're not...mad at me, right?"

Maybe I shouldn't care if he is, but I can't help that I do, and to be frank, I would understand if he was.

The expression on his face seems to mirror my thoughts, as if he's not sure why I would care—though he's not upset that I do. The opposite, really.

His smile is forgiving. "I'm not mad, Cammie. A little sad for myself, but I can take it, and I'm well aware I made the bed I'm in."

"I don't want to intentionally hurt you, Alister. I'm just..." *Doing what I can to let you go? Using Brady to help me do that? Enjoying being with someone I can trust, even if it's not real?*

I don't know what I want to say here.

He reaches out, pushing my hair behind my ear, and my eyes close of their own accord. When I reopen them, he's gazing sweetly at me. "I know you don't. That's not who you are and that might be part of what's so hard about all this. You're good. Sweet. Spicy." He smirks a little, and a low chuckle escapes me, but a hint of sorrow falls over him in the next moment, though he tries to hide it. "What I mostly feel is regret."

I swallow. "Is it okay if I say same?"

"Yeah," he whispers. "It is. Is it okay if I say I'm a little worried about you?"

158

A small scowl builds. "Why?"

"Why did you stop where you did?"

I open my mouth but then close it.

I didn't stop for any reason. I was just…watching.

Alister holds my gaze a moment but then curses as he looks down at his phone. "I hate to run off, but if I don't go now, I'll be late for my session. I'll see you in class next week?"

I nod, watching him walk away.

I spin back around to find the girls are no longer standing there, and neither is Brady.

With a deep breath, I tuck my little trinket back in my bag, head to my dorm, and crawl into bed with the TV remote.

And that's where I stay all weekend.

BRADY

"What the hell do you mean, you're injured?" I jump up from the chair I only just planted my ass in, my frown snapping from Mason to Chase to Coach and back to the man in question. "How? You kicked ass out there. Walked off with your head high and got on a damn bus. How did you get injured in your fucking sleep, because I know for a fact all you did was go straight to Payton's and crashed when we got in last night?"

I'm sure they fucked first, but that has no bearing on this damn conversation, so I don't mention it.

Coach sighs, uncrossing and recrossing his legs where he's perched against the desk. "Sit down, Brady, and lower your damn voice."

My head snaps toward Chase, who stares at Mason with a scowl that matches my own.

"What happened?" he asks.

"Woke up about five this morning with a pounding headache

and started throwing up. Called Coach to give him a heads-up that I might not make it to practice tomorrow if I still felt like shit in the morning. He hung up on me and thirty minutes later sent me this clip." Mason turns the tablet in his lap around, and we both lock on to the screen.

Mason presses Play, and I watch as the Sabers' D-end breaks through our line, knowing what play it is before the clip finishes. Mason gets sacked, stays on the ground for a split second, his eyes closed, but hops up a heartbeat later.

My eyes move to Coach, then Chase, then back to the screen when Mason zooms in, replaying the last four seconds in slow motion.

We watch as Mason's head hits the turf before his body, bouncing once, twice, his neck crooked to the side slightly when it finally comes to rest against the grass.

"A concussion?" Chase says, and we both look to our best friend.

Mason nods. "None of us even realized how hard of a hit I took until Coach went to check the game film after I told him how I was feeling. Honestly, I should have put two and two together, but it didn't even cross my mind."

"Fuck." I rub my hands together. "Concussion protocol puts him out for two weeks," I say, stating the obvious.

Chase looks to Coach. "Why did you call us in here to tell us this?"

It's a fair question. Normally, these are private conversations we're none the wiser about, and unless a buddy of ours tells us beforehand, like Mason would have done, we find out who's on the IR list as a team at the start of Monday's practice.

Coach looks at us both, sighs, and kicks off the desk, moving behind it to drop into the seat. "Because the three of you are a unit, and that plays a huge factor in how the team has responded to Mason. With him out, that means—"

"Alister."

Coach nods, a glare quickly forming. "The kid is struggling with the camaraderie of things. That won't make leading this team these next two weeks any easier on him."

"What do you want us to do, kiss his ass? The guy is a dickhead half the time, Coach," Chase complains, crossing his arms.

Coach isn't aware of the beef we have, but it's obvious we have one. Shit, we wouldn't be in this office right now if it weren't.

"Not kiss his ass but listen when he speaks. Offer ideas. Show the team you're willing to follow him, and in turn, they'll follow you."

Chase looks to Mason, who nods. He lets out a sigh and turns to Coach. "Yeah, all right, whatever. This week should be an easy win even if we don't use pass game, but next week will be tough."

Coach agrees, pinning me with an expectant expression.

"What?" I shrug. "I'm on defense now. This has nothing to do with me. I don't have to hold his hand."

Coach scoffs, shaking his head. "Wrong, kid. I'm moving your training schedule to align with his."

"What?" I shoot forward in my seat. "Coach. No."

Mason laughs and I flip him off.

"Coach, you do know Brady's sleeping with Alister's ex, right?" Chase smirks.

Dipshit.

Coach groans, scrubbing his hands down his face. "Of fucking course you are, Lancaster."

This is one of those times I don't mind all the rumors.

"See?" I grin. "I'm more likely to let him get crushed by weights than help him any."

"You worked Mason through his program all last season and, from what you yourself told me, all offseason too." He raises a brow.

"I did. Been doing that since I was twelve. This is different."

"It's no different. The kid needs someone who will push him, and if it can't be Mason, it has to be you."

"Why not Chase? He knows the entire routine."

Chase throws his hands up as if to say *what the hell, man*, but I ignore him. If someone's getting thrown under this bus, I'd rather it be him.

Love him, but no.

"It's done and you won't argue." Coach has laid down the law, pulling out a folder and flipping it open. "I already checked in on your grades, and you're on top of shit, so I'm excusing you from all study hall sessions for the next two weeks. You'll spend that time working with Howl."

"Damn, Brady, how good are your grades to get a two-week pass?" Mason looks over. "I had to make up the hour I missed when Deaton got sick."

I shrug, but Coach is eager to share.

"Your boy here has a 4.0. Ended last semester with the same."

My friends' brows jump, but I just shrug again and change the subject. "When are you telling the punk?"

He glares at my word choice but looks at his watch. "He'll be walking in while you're walking out."

"You mean we don't get to see the look on his face when you tell him I'm his new backpack?"

"Out, assholes. Mason stays."

Together, we head out of the coach's office. As Coach predicted, we're exiting the main doors just as Alister is approaching.

He frowns in confusion but quickly wipes it away, nodding hello before slipping inside.

Chase and I stop a few feet from the entrance, both of our shoulders falling.

"Fuckin' great, man," he mumbles, running his hands through his hair. "I was supposed to get a good boost in my receiving yards next week against Brighton."

I shake my head, knowing that's not likely anymore. Fucking Alister won't pass half as much as Mason does.

"You gonna tell your girlfriend her ex-boyfriend is your new buddy?"

I shove Chase, and he chuckles.

We start heading back to the football house in silence, and I catch Chase staring at me from the corner of my eye a few times.

"What?"

He shrugs and looks away, but I scoff.

"Just spit it out, asshole."

"Just wondering how all that's going...you and Cam."

"It's all fun and games, man."

Chase points his grin forward, nodding lightly. "Okay."

"Okay." I nod back.

But I guess he's right—I should probably let her know I'm going to be working with Alister this week. Not that she'll care.

She's not worried about what he's got going on, so it's not like it will matter anyway. She won't suddenly want to wear his number or hang out with him again now that he's going to be the starting QB.

Not that I would mind if she did.

My lips pinch together, and I frown forward.

Nope, I wouldn't mind it one bit.

CHAPTER 21
BRADY

I mind. I fucking mind, and I don't know why.

I also don't know how to stop. It's dumb.

Really fucking dumb. And thinking about it is pissing me off even more.

The dickwad is over there, leaning over the ledge of the fucking bleachers, his arms folded, the skin of his arm touching her jean-clad thigh as she's sitting on the thick cement wall that separates the field from the stands.

He shakes his head, sending the water he poured over himself like some fucking model boy spraying out. I know that move. Hell, I probably invented it back in youth football days.

It works every time, and what do you know? Cameron squeals, throwing her hands up as her head falls back on a laugh. Even Ari and Paige are laughing.

Unoriginal prick.

Chase steps up, hands on his hips as he narrows his eyes in their direction. "Guess no one is mad at him anymore?"

"He won one fucking game—with our help, I might add."

"Not like we threw the ball for him, my man," Chase laughs.

"Shut up. You're just happy you got your yards after all, and that's only because I put their starting QB down in the first quarter, thank you very much."

Chase chuckles. "And you're just mad he's still after your *fake girl*."

I hate when they say *fake* like that. They should just stop saying it. I mean, you never know who might overhear, right?

My brows pull in a little more. "I just don't want her to fall for his shit and get hurt again. That's all."

"Maybe he won't hurt her…"

"Maybe he will."

"I think she's smart and won't let that happen."

Sometimes it's got nothing to do with that.

I shake it off, turning away and grabbing my gear off the sidelines.

"Maybe he's over it, admitted defeat to the bigger, better man," I joke, sneaking a side glance at Chase from the corner of my eye. "Could be over there testing the waters with an entirely different blond, if you know what I mean."

Chase's head yanks back toward the stands, and I swallow my laugh, leaving everyone out on the field. I decide to skip the shower last second and quickly tug on some sweats. I pack up my stuff and head out to my truck. Tossing my shit in the bed, I climb inside and get a good playlist going. Maybe I'll drive for a bit, clear my head, and go catch the end of the junior college's football practice ten miles up the road.

It's always good to stay in the know. Never know when some random transfer might pop up and fuck up the whole dynamic. I'm only as good as the next D-end to come through.

Before I can even put my truck in drive, my favorite blond steps in front of my hood, leaning her elbows on it with a smile.

I can't help but smile back, rolling my window down to yell at her. "Excuse me, miss. Imma need you to move. This is harassment."

She starts to climb up the bumper, and my eyes are glued to her as she crawls across the hood in playful movements. "Meh, I think you might like to be harassed by me."

I just might…

Wait, what?

I clear my throat. "Sorry to tell you, but my girlfriend is going to get mad if she sees you."

"Is she now?" she laughs, holding her balance on the hood as she folds herself over the driver side mirror so she's face-to-face with me rather than staring at me through the glass.

"Oh, yeah. Real possessive." I pause, hesitating, but decide fuck it. I spill a small secret. "So much so that she had two little magnets implanted on her body so she could stick to mine…"

Cameron frowns, my words running through her mind a time or two as she tries to connect the dots.

And then she gasps, grips my mirror, and pushes her torso up. "Your dick is pierced?!"

I bust up laughing, fold myself forward, and grip her under her arms.

She squeals, laughing as I maneuver her like a little toy until I can tug her straight through the window, dropping her across my lap, her calves and feet still hanging out of the truck.

She's cracking up so much, she loses her breath and just lets herself fall, her shoulders on the seat in the middle, ass on my lap. Her hair spreads out behind her, all over the thick leather of my seats.

It looks good like that. Enticing.

"That was fun." She grins, bending her legs and doing a full backward somersault until she's on her knees beside me. She crosses her arms and glares. "Brady Lancaster, you know about my nips, and you've been hiding a dick piercing?"

"Have I?" I tease, buckling my seat belt, and she does the same but stays in the middle.

"Yes, you have, but how have I not heard this? How are the girls not running around spreading this like the word of God to the other girls who want to climb on you? I am, like, mind blown."

I can't stop laughing, for more reasons than she knows, but I just let her go on.

"Okay, but like you, I'm not shocked. It makes total sense.

166

You're like a messiah. Or Buddha. A vag whisperer. *Of course* you have actual magical equipment on your wand." Her eyes gleam as she looks over at me, gaze dropping to my sweats. "What kind is it? Did it hurt? When did you get it?"

"Nope." I shake my head, pulling out of the parking lot. "Not telling you a word."

"Hmm."

I look over, and her gaze is still hooked on my lap. "Quit looking at my dick," I chuckle, shifting my leg in case a little something decides to grow with all the attention it's getting.

"Oh my god, I have something for you! This just reminded me."

"You trying to become the newest X-Man with X-ray vision reminded you that you have something for me?" I raise a brow, making a left and heading down the main road toward town.

"Yep. I made it last week in art."

"Wait, you *made me* something?"

"I did." She grins, tugging her phone out and typing something before tucking it away again. She looks up. "Wait, where are we going?"

"To catch the end of the JC practice, then maybe the food trucks for some grub?"

She nods and kicks off her shoes, reaching behind her to pull the little blanket tucked in the back over her legs.

I smile from her to the road. "By the way, you're buying."

Cameron laughs, and when she leans her head on my shoulder a moment later, I move as little as possible so she'll keep it there.

———

Cameron shivers, running inside the building with the blanket wrapped around her head. I hold the door open for the girls jogging up behind us, then step through, passing Cameron her soda when she holds her hand out.

"Let me take the food too." She reaches for the bag, but I turn my shoulders so she can't try and take it. "Brady, you've got your backpack, your gym bag, your drink, and the food. All I've got is one cup."

"And a blanket."

"That is hanging over my shoulders just fine. Let me help."

"Shush and push the button, or we'll just be hanging out in the hall all night."

"Oh shit," she chuckles, turning to the elevator. "It's getting cold fast."

"It is almost the end of October."

"I know, but last year I was Becky Lynch for Halloween, and I don't remember it being cold. This year's going to call for a freaking parka."

"Or maybe you just don't remember how cold it was cause you pregamed pretty hard."

"That…sounds legit." She chuckles, unlocking her door and stopping short, making me bump into her. She grins over her shoulder, holding her finger to her lips.

I slip in behind her, spotting Ari knocked out on the couch, her phone in her hand. I'm so glad their parents insisted they keep the flat-style dorm all four years, even though it comes with a higher price tag.

Quietly, we make our way back to Cameron's room. I set the food down on her little desk and drop my backpack to the foot of the bed.

"Wanna shower first?" she asks, tossing the blanket on the floor by the door.

"Yeah, I'll be fast, but eat. I don't want your food to get cold."

"Then be Speedy Gonzales, and it won't be."

"You don't have to wait."

"OMG, are you still here?" she jokes, tearing her closet doors open and digging around in the little dresser tucked in there.

I slip out and into the bathroom. I'm in and out in five

minutes or less, stepping back into her room as I scrub the towel across my head to get the excess water.

She's already changed into her pj's—a big shirt and shorts—and has arranged our food, having set us up on laptop pads with something playing quietly on the TV.

Her head pops up, gaze landing on my bare chest before lifting to meet my eyes. "Well, are you just gonna stand there and play the role of the Greek god statue or…?"

Smirking, I quietly close the door, hanging my towel on the little hook on the back of it. Picking up both of the laptop pads so our plates don't fall off when the mattress dips, I climb onto the bed beside her, setting our food back down.

Cam opens up her tri-tip sandwich and is digging in before I've even gotten the lid off my pulled-pork mac and cheese. We eat in silence for a few minutes and then she wipes her mouth, reaching over the side of the bed to grab her drink.

"So our little outing was super random." She shakes her cup a little and goes in for a sip.

"Well, you did crawl onto my hood uninvited."

Cameron grins, tossing a salt packet at me.

I swat it away and she raises a brow.

"Obviously, I wasn't referring to you and me, since we're at the food trucks at least once a week. I meant the practice."

I take another bite of my mac and cheese, and Cameron groans dramatically, picking up a piece of tri-tip that fell out of her roll.

A low chuckle leaves me, and I nod, swallowing my food before reaching over for my own drink. "I just wanted to see what was up. They start after us, so they're always practicing later."

Cam nods. "And you know this how?"

I shrug, stealing one of her Tater Tots and tossing it in my mouth. "I go and watch every now and then. Maybe once or twice a month."

"Really?" she asks curiously. "Why?"

I shrug, focusing on my food. "Just wanna stay aware, you

know? See what they've got on their roster, listen for any rumors I might pick up about transfers that might come in next year or whatever."

Cam studies me, pushing her tots my way as she settles back against the pile of pillows along her headboard. "Brady," she begins, a hint of hesitancy in her raspy tone. "We're juniors. You know what that means. You're going to be drafted come April. You won't be here next year, let alone next season."

"I...ugh—" I cut off, clearing my throat.

"What?" she asks softly, tucking her legs up so she's in a little ball.

"What if I told you I don't think I want to be drafted?"

Her eyes widen, and she sits forward, a little frown creasing along her forehead.

With a small smile, I reach over and wipe it away, my eyes falling to hers. "I kinda want to go home, Cammie Girl. Go back and work on the farm like in high school."

Surprise covers her features then. "With my dad?"

I shrug. "Or start my own, I don't know." I shrug again, busying myself by reaching over to grab the bag and throwing our garbage away. "It's just a thought. I mean, I don't really have a plan or anything."

"Brady." She waits until I look at her. "Are you afraid?"

A choked laugh leaves me, and I clear my throat, shifting on the bed so I'm facing her fully. I contemplate my words, but the longer I look into her big blue eyes, at the tender smile on her pretty lips, the more they untangle.

"If I get drafted, if I'm somehow that lucky and make it to the biggest stage the sport has to offer, it would be a literal dream come true. Hundreds of thousands of people have that same dream, but only handfuls get to live it. If I get drafted, I could get hurt in the first season, hell the first game or play, and just like that, everything could be gone. I don't want that for myself. I worked way too fucking hard, not only on the field but in the classroom. I won't cut out the first semester I'm eligible to enter the draft—not that there's anything wrong with that. There isn't, but for me and what I want in life?" I shake my head, my words stronger, more sure as I focus on Cameron. "I'm gonna graduate, Cammie Girl, with honors, and I'm going to have a degree under my belt. And if football comes after that, then I'm even more blessed."

Cameron stares at me, her eyes growing a little glossy. When she speaks, it's a one-word whisper. "Wow."

"Stop."

"No." She shakes her head, reaching out to take my hand. "This deserves a moment because honestly, Brady. Wow."

She tugs, and I shift, dropping back on the pile of pillows. Cameron settles against my chest, pulling the blanket up over us.

"I've never told anyone any of that," I admit after a moment.

Cameron shifts, looking up at me with a sweet smile. "Just so you know, luck would have nothing to do with it. Football will wait for you because you, Brady Lancaster, are that good. You'll have the jersey and the farm and anything else you could possibly want."

I run my fingers through her hair, looking down at her. "Think so?"

She smiles, burrowing her head in the crook of my shoulder, tugging the blanket up to her chin. "I know so. Now don't move. I'm way too comfortable, and I want to stay just like this."

"Oh yeah?"

"Yeah."

Would it be weird if I asked for how long?

CHAPTER 22
CAMERON

I kiss his cheek, his forehead, his cheek again, and then Mason is stealing him from my arms.

"Okay, I'm taking my son now." He chuckles, lifting little D and settling him on his shoulders.

"No fair. Today is the only day he was with me all week, and *you're* picking him up early."

"Because I took my midterms last week, so now I have the afternoon free until practice."

"Maybe I'll leave early too. I don't have class for another two hours." I smile suddenly. "Yes, I'll leave and come hang out with you guys." I can test out my lesson plan, see if I can keep baby D engaged, and—

"Sorry, Cammie Girl. This is a boys-only trip."

I whip around to find Brady sauntering in, his AU hoodie up, the drawstring hanging from the collar and tucked in his mouth. It shouldn't be hot, but it kind of is. Like backward-hat hot.

He grins when my eyes meet his earthy-brown ones, and I don't know why, but I just...stare, my head lifting little by little as he comes closer. A fly caught in his trap.

Granny Grace coughs, and I jerk my attention toward her, narrowing my eyes when she's simply smiling at the pile of papers in front of her.

Wait. I turn back to the boys, noting Chase has stepped in behind Brady. "Trip? What trip?"

"We're going to the Halloween store just outside town," Mason shares, glancing from Brady to me. "Paige made Deaton's last year, and she started on this year's, but I guess that flood from last week messed things up pretty bad at her studio, and Payton didn't want to add to the stress, so we're going to see what we can find."

"And why can't I go?" I cross my arms. "I need a costume too."

"Liar." Brady smirks, leaning back on the high desk. "Ari told me she ordered you guys something. Rude, by the way. Aren't we supposed to be, like, Barbie and Ken or something?"

"Sure, if you want to guarantee that someone else will be wearing the same outfit. You might as well go as Hugh Hefner and put a tail and bunny ears on me."

"I don't know, I think you'd look good hopping around with that booty out."

A scoff sounds, and we all look over to the source.

It takes Granny Grace a moment to realize and she glances up. "What?"

"Nothing," I chuckle, passing the diaper bag to Brady, who passes it to Chase, his grin pointed at Granny Grace.

"Oh, no." Brady spins, fully facing Granny Grace, and places his forearms on her desk, giving her his full attention. "I want to hear this." He gives her his best crooked grin.

She scoffs again but sets her pen down, pushing her glasses up on her head, and mimics his position from her side, leaning close the exact same way.

"Hello, Granny Grace," he drawls, peeking my way to confirm that she is, in fact, the person he is guessing she is based on our chats.

"Hello, Brady." She makes his whole-ass day by knowing his name, his growing smile the proof. "I'm going to go ahead and save you a whole lot of trouble. How does that sound?"

I bite back a smile, and Brady flicks his eyes to Chase in amusement before looking back to her.

"If that girl right there wore nothing but a leotard and a puffy little ball on her ass, with those curves and that gorgeous, golden hair of hers, the night would not go the way you wanted it to."

"Yeah?" He grins.

"Yeah. She'd be cold, and some poor fool would be knocked out cold."

Brady frowns for a split second before his head falls back on a laugh, the other boys joining in.

Granny Grace doesn't let him see her grin but buries it as she looks down at her papers again.

Brady steps over, taking Deaton from Mason's shoulders, and Mason unfolds the stroller.

Brady comes closer, turning so Deaton is in my reach. "Give Calmy hugs, little man."

Deaton leans over, and I squeeze his little body.

"Don't worry, Girlfriend." Brady smiles. "My costume of choice will not disappoint. I might even tell you what it is during our lunch date tomorrow."

"Do you already know what you're going to get?"

"Nope, but whatever I *do* pick out, it will be with you in mind."

I roll my eyes dramatically, taking his shoulders and spinning him around, pushing him toward the door. "Okay, jerk faces. Bye. Go have your man time."

The others wave their goodbyes, but Brady pauses by Granny Grace's desk once more, looking down at the photo of her and her late husband sitting on top.

"Nice picture, Granny Grace." He leans forward. "I drive a Chevy too."

Granny Grace looks up, small creases deepening her wrinkles at first, but then her soft smile falls on the frame. "He always said the smart ones do."

Brady places his hand over hers, and she glances up at him, but he's already walking out.

I watch his form as he walks through the door, a sense of warmth settling over me.

Just before the doors begin to close, I hear him ask, "Either of you know what the hell a leotard is?"

My lips tip up, and this time when I look over at my friend, because that's what she is, Granny Grace is looking at me.

"What?"

"That boy is gone on you."

I laugh, shaking my head. "Oh no, we're…" I pause, not wanting to say *fake dating* because that would be a whole-ass story to get into. "Just having fun."

"Oh, honey." She stands, taking her stack of papers with her as she rounds the desk, patting my shoulder on her way. "Bless your little heart."

———

"Okay, but don't we have to add in learning to read or write or something?" Alister stares down at the partial lesson plan I created without him last class.

"You can't make lemonade without the lemons."

He blinks at me and I laugh.

"Did you even read over the instructions?"

Alister smiles. "I just figured I'd let you lead."

I scoff. "You sound like Brady."

Alister stares into my eyes. "What can I say? The man clearly has good taste."

Not sure *taste* is the right word here, but this doesn't feel like the time for a vocabulary correction, so I pretend neither of us said a word. "So basically we are creating a yearlong lesson plan for preschool and transitional kindergarten. Last week's assignment was to complete the introductory phase."

"So going over the basics?" he guesses.

"Not really 'basics' because that can be subjective. Some kids will come into preschool with zero knowledge as far as academics go. They might not even recognize shapes fully yet or colors outside the primary ones. Tons of kids are still learning to speak confidently or at all at ages three and four. Our job is to create a lesson plan for all types of learners. It's like creating a foundation to build on."

"So kind of testing the waters, seeing where everyone is and what needs to be done to get them to the next phase?"

I nod with a smile. "Exactly. So you just have to go through that and add any ideas you might have, and this week we have to work on *explore and engage*. Which one do you want?"

Alister shrugs, a cute little crease forming along his brow as he reads over the instruction sheet. "Can we just do them together?"

My pen freezes over the diagram, and I look over at him, slowly rolling the pen between my fingers. "I don't think we'll get much of anything done today. There's only twenty minutes left."

Alister's eyes glitter as he watches me. "You afraid to see me outside class all of a sudden, Cox?"

I pin him with a playful glare. "You wish, Howl."

"I really, really do."

My mouth opens but nothing comes out, and then I'm chuckling. "Okay, fair. I fell right into that one."

Alister grins, taking his own pen in his hands, and starts making little notes in the column of the document. He's just finishing when class ends, and when I go to take the papers, he tugs them back. "Just send me the file, and I'll add this all in tonight after practice."

"No, it's fine. I can't really move on to the next part until I know this one is all tightened up anyway."

"But you're not going to work on the next one because we're going to do it together."

Right. Partners.

I squash my lips to the side. "Are you sure? I can have it done before you're even out of practice. I have nothing else today after this."

Alister considers my words, a mischievous grin growing. "How about this? You come and watch practice today. No studying. Just watch and I'll get this done *and* set us up for the next section." When I hesitate, he adds, "You can even just add me to the document instead of sending it to me. That way you can see in real time if I'm getting it all done, which I promise I will."

I chew on my lip. "If I come to practice and watch?"

"Yes." He smiles.

Ha. He has no idea he just got suckered because I was already planning to go to practice, and despite my studying in the bleachers, I always do a little watching.

Alister has been kind of hard not to watch this past week.

My best friend calls me out on this very fact not two hours later when we're sitting in our usual spots, blankets folded over our laps.

"I'm not staring at him," I defend. "I'm staring at the team."

"Right."

I frown at my friend, but Ari only laughs, a gentle expression on her face.

"You doing okay?" she wonders.

"I'm fine." I face the field again, my gaze trained on the quarterback.

"You know it's okay to be happy for him, right? It doesn't mean you're happy that Mason can't play."

"I know." My attention is trained forward. "It's just sad, you know. He gave up a starting position to follow his ex here, and the day he arrived, it all blew up in his face. Now he's stuck at second-string, and I mean, look at him, Ari. He's good. Really good. Sucks he…believed in love so much and Cupid just shit on him."

She huffs a laugh. "Yeah, that does suck but…everything happens for a reason, right? Me and Chase, Payton and Big Deaton."

177

My brows pinch as I try to make sense of her words, and when I can't, looking to her in confusion, her smile seems to soften even more.

"Has Mason talked to you about the draft?" I blurt out suddenly.

She frowns, studying me. "No. I assume he's all prepared. Why?"

"No reason." I face forward, yelping when suddenly Alister is there.

"Thought I said no studying?" he scolds teasingly, looking to my lap.

I show him the screen of my phone, nothing but a picture of Ari and me at Noah's game last year on the screen, and he nods approvingly.

"Good. Just double-checking."

"Looking good out there," Ari tells him.

He looks to her with wide eyes, making her smile in return.

"Hey, I can still compliment you on your game even though my brother is out."

"I appreciate that, thank you. It's...tough, not going to lie, but I think I'm doing even better than last week."

Ari nods. "I bet your family is happy for you."

Alister gives her a tight smile and looks to me. "I'll get all that done tonight. Promise."

I nod, watching as he runs off. He disappears into the tunnel, and I look at the rest of the group, but it looks like Brady is already gone.

"Okay, I need to head back. Paige is picking me up to take me to the airport in a half hour, and I want to change first."

The two of us get up, heading back to the dorm.

"You'll call me when you land?" I ask her, helping her toss her bag in the back of Paige's car.

"Of course." Ari hugs me. "Have fun at the party without me."

"Have fun at your party without me! I can't believe you're going to a freaking celebrity party. Who even are you?"

"You never know. The way things are looking, all three of us might be the next hit show." She lifts her arms, palms up, and pulls them outward slowly as if to reveal something. "I can see it now, Housewives of Oceanside."

I frown, meeting Paige's matching one, and look back toward my best friend. "I don't get it."

"Ditto!" Paige calls.

Ari only laughs. "'Kay, bye, love you!"

"Love you!" I close the door, and just as she pulls away, a familiar truck rolls into the parking space across from the curb, the window sliding down as I walk over to the driver's side.

Brady's brown eyes gleam. "Fancy seeing you here."

"Yeah, fancy seeing me outside my dorm building at the exact same time Ari has to leave."

"What are the chances?" He grins. "If I offer to buy dinner, will you share your bed with me again tonight?"

"What's wrong?" I tease, crossing my arms and leaning in a little closer, against the door. "Chase stop letting you sleep in his?"

"I like the feel of your body better."

I drop my eyes to the ground for some reason, then peek back up. "Do I get to pick what we eat?"

"Only if I get to pick the movie."

"Deal."

Brady turns the truck off, rolls up the window, and climbs out, stepping right up to me. "Lead the way, Hellcat."

I stare up at him, a strange...something swirling in my stomach.

Only when he raises a brow do I remember to move.

His chuckle heats my neck as I slip by, but the shiver that runs down my spine is because of the cold.

I mean...what else would it be?

CHAPTER 23
CAMERON

An alarm beeps softly, making my eyes peel open. The room is still dark, not a hint of light creeping through the sheer purple curtains hanging behind my bed. I blink my eyesight into focus, stretching slightly, and a small smile crosses my lips when I realize why I'm so warm.

Brady is my personal electric blanket.

I don't even remember falling asleep last night, but I know when I did, he was still in his sweatpants and hoodie. Now it's nothing but warm, soft skin pressed against my cheek, my entire body pressed to his side. My face is in the crook of his shoulder, my arms tucked in like a damn baby.

I press my forearms into his ribs, nudging him slightly.

His only response is to wrap his arm around me and haul me up higher until my head is on his chest. His lips brush across my forehead, and he holds me to him like his favorite pillow.

"Brady, your alarm." I try to push up, reaching over him to grab his phone from the bedside table. Just as my fingers brush the edge, he rolls us until he's hovering above me, his muscles somehow working already as he holds his weight over me.

Sleepy eyes the color of fall leaves fall on mine, a lazy smile on his lips. "Morning, Cammie baby."

I snuggle into his warmth but pout. "It is not morning. It is the ass crack of dawn, and if you don't turn that thing off, I'm going to reach down and show you how hard I can squeeze."

"Unfortunately, that sounds like fun, so Imma need you to come up with another threat."

I give him the best scowl I can manage while still half-dead, and my hand takes a little dive, ready to call him on his bluff.

His eyes hold mine, a playful spark dancing within them—a mischievous dare.

My knuckles brush his stomach and his muscles flex.

Before I can get any farther, his gaze still holding mine, he says, "There's a reason I'm holding myself up, Hellcat, and it's not for fear of squashing you."

It takes a second, but then his words sink in, and my hand freezes where it's at, falling to flatten on my stomach. But a split second later a thought hits, and I narrow my eyes.

"Okay, but are you holding yourself up because you think it's appropriate or to keep your secret about the kind of junk jewelry you've got going on?"

His laughter is thick with sleep, and he rolls off, finally turning off that god-awful tinkling sound of his alarm. He climbs from the bed, and I discreetly try to get a look at his boxers as he does, but he's already walking out of my room.

A moment later, I hear the shower turn on and let out a huff, yanking the covers over my head.

It is way too early for this shit.

I roll over, trying to get comfortable, but unfortunately for me, the bed isn't half as cozy as it was five minutes ago. I do my best to fall back asleep, pretending that I have when Brady quietly slips back in to get his things.

His lips ghost my temple on his exit and then the door closes with a soft click.

I don't fall back asleep after that.

———

"You look surprised." Alister grins, holding the door to the café open for me.

"I am. I thought for sure I'd have to kick your ass today."

"So you didn't follow along with me last night, watching my progress from your side of the screen?"

"Nah. I was knuckle-deep in fried garlic noodles watching *Galaxy Quest* for the hundredth time."

"Really?" Alister chuckles. "I never would have taken you for a sci-fi fan."

"It's Brady's favorite." I shrug, scanning the menu with rapt interest even though I always get the same thing. "Have you ever tried the Cookie Butter Latte?" I glance his way, frowning when I see he's staring at me with a crease between his eyes. "What, does it suck?"

Alister pulls in a full breath, a smile appearing a moment later, but it seems a little forced.

"Dang, that bad?"

A low chuckle leaves him, and he shakes his head, the upward tilt of his lips real this time. "I've never had it, but I'm not big on the stuff. I usually stick to the banana protein smoothies."

"Typical."

"Why, is that Brady's favorite too?"

My attention snaps his way, and he steps up to the counter and orders, giving me a sheepish glance as he looks to me to add my drink to his tab. I do but I don't let him pay, setting a five-dollar bill on the counter before moving toward the pickup side of the bar top.

Alister walks over, hands in his jeans pockets, eyes on mine, but he doesn't say anything until his name is called, and we're tucking into a diner-style booth in the back corner of the café. "I'm sorry."

"For what?"

"Being jealous of everything that has to do with you and Brady."

182

My muscles tense, and I should look away, but I can't. He just admitted that like nothing.

Maybe it shouldn't come as a surprise, seeing as he has said directly that he wants to be with me, but I guess I assumed that things had changed, that we weren't in the same place we were a few weeks ago.

He told me he had regrets. He said he understood where I was at.

I thought he was letting things go.

I mean he still could be. It's like I said, you can't just turn your feelings off, and jealousy is definitely a feeling.

But why does it have to be such an attractive one?

Jesus. Proof I'm a damn hot mess.

Aren't I supposed to hate jealousy? If I am, then something is broken in this little mind of mine 'cause…yep. Even after thinking it through, it's still hot.

Not that I want him to hurt or be angry or whatever way he processes that specific emotion. In reality, he has zero reason to be jealous, least of all of Brady. We're basically family, and our relationship is as fake as Professor Gilroy's hair color.

Brady's sneaky smile from this morning flashes in my mind.

Fake but fun.

Okay. Cameron. Focus.

I give Alister an apologetic smile. "No, I'm sorry. I didn't mean to throw Brady's name out earlier. I didn't even realize I'd mentioned him until you did, but I have to say, I feel like my sorry might not seem like it means much because I can promise you it's going to happen again. It's just second nature to talk about my friends when I think about them, and I don't want to have to try to censor myself around you. I want to be able to be your friend, Alister, but I think it's fair for us both to understand that that might come with some hiccups."

His eyes are pinned to mine, sharp and assessing, and I squirm a little.

"Like I said before, I have no interest in hurting you. I'm just doing what's best for me."

Alister just continues to stare.

"Let's just get our work done, okay?" I mumble, pulling my laptop and notebook from my backpack and pretending I'm not a little uneasy now.

Maybe I was wrong.

Maybe it's not so simple between us and we can't be friends—

The thought freezes in my mind, my eyes snapping up to his.

He sees the moment realization hits, that I finally figured out why he was so stuck after my little speech—my speech where I called Brady my *friend*.

I rub my lips together anxiously, and his green eyes fly to the movement, holding for several long seconds.

Goose bumps pebble along my arms, making me glad it's sweater weather these days. I don't need him calling me out at the sight of them. Besides, I have a boyfriend and that would look bad.

I tug the sleeves of my hoodie over my hands and flip open my laptop.

A million years later, he does the same, and we jump right into phase two of our project.

Surprisingly—to me—Alister has a lot of good concepts when it comes to physical activities for learning, having come to our session today with ideas in mind. It's obvious he's been paying attention, understanding the importance this class holds for me.

We've been at it for a few hours already when we pause for a break. I sip on my second coffee of the day, smiling as Alister heads back to our table from the café's front counter.

Alister sets down two toasted bagels and large ice waters, sliding in on my side of the booth this time. Without a word, he turns his laptop toward us and opens a new file, excited to show me what he's come up with.

"So after I went over what I missed last week, I went back and read the text again. If I'm honest, I wasn't really sure what it was trying to tell me, so I had to play around on Google a bit."

"Oh?" I fight a smile, not really sure where this is about to go.

"Yeah. And it's pretty interesting actually. I realized I'm the type of learner you're looking to cater to."

Attention officially caught, I shift in the booth, leaning my back against the wall so I can face him fully.

"Okay so, this is embarrassing, but I'm bad at school—as in I fail more than I pass, and it's mostly because I pretty much hate everything about learning."

A laugh leaves me, and Alister grins.

"I'm serious. The only reason I did any assignment in high school was to stay eligible. A 2.0, that's it. I had a waiver one year because I couldn't even manage to halfway pass."

"I don't love every class either, Alister, and I have to work pretty hard to get the grades I'm after."

"Exactly." He snaps his fingers, clicking on the document inside the folder he pulled up. "So what better way to *explore and engage*, as you called it—"

"Because that is what it's called," I laugh.

He grins. "Right, so what better way to explore and engage and test kids' ability to learn than finding their point of interest? Because I can tell you right now, if a teacher ever told me to take a hundred yards of open field and split it between two teams, then find a way to get one team to the hundred using x, y, z, whatever the hell, I would have known exactly what to do."

"Football brain."

"Since I was seven."

"Seven?" I take another sip of my drink. "That's even longer than my boys."

Alister smirks. "At least I'm beating someone somewhere."

I give him a blank blink, and he chuckles, nudging my knee lightly with his elbow.

"Anyway," he says, going back to the screen, "since we're

working on kindergartners and whatnot—I had to google what they learned too, by the way—I broke things down into colors, items, and places. Basically, the idea is it will give them an option of three to five colors, and they pick the one they are drawn to the most, then it moves to the next image based on the color they choose, and they pick from that and so on."

My fingers are dancing along my cup, my mind swimming with what he's saying. Alister's eyes are bright, gauging me and seemingly liking what he sees.

He scoots closer, and I move in too, fully intrigued with what he's about to show me.

"So check this out: obviously I don't have a program to make this work like I see it in my head, but for the sake of a good grade, I think this can do."

He pulls up the first set of images; four cubes, each a different color, are on the screen, and he even added little text blocks that spell out the color above the shape. It's smart, a way to help with potential letter recognition. I wonder if he even realizes this?

"Pick a color."

"Purple."

He pretends to click the purple before backing out and clicking the folder labeled *purple,* and another page pops up. Four more boxes are on this page, but this time they are items.

A doll with a purple bow, a basketball with purple swirls, a paintbrush with purple dripping from the tip, and a little book with a purple elephant on the cover—toys, sports, art, and reading.

I look at the four boxes again, which can be interpreted by a child as either an interest in the animal on the cover or the book and idea of reading or having a story read to them. It really covers all the basics in an extremely profound way.

I pretend to click this time, choosing the little book, curious as to where it will lead in this test of his.

Alister smiles, scrolling to the last page, but it's unfinished.

There's a diagram he's created, little color-coded text bubbles breaking down his thought process.

I nod, reading over his random thoughts, and it's pretty impressive. It's easy to see what he's trying to showcase.

"Alister, this is…" I look his way, not realizing how close we are until we're both facing each other.

"It's not the sharpest concept."

"It's perfect, simple in a complex way, and it makes sense. You're breaking things down intellectually and for a purpose, but at the level a child can process, having no idea it's essentially a test they're taking, even if it is just one that helps the teacher rather than the child. This is really, really good."

"Yeah?" Pride shines bright in his eyes, and I have the urge to reach out and touch him. To feel the smile lines along his temples and the hint of stubble on his jaw.

I hold my cup a little tighter. "How long did you stay up to work on this?"

He shrugs, glancing back at his computer, but I wait, and a few moments later, he faces me again. "I couldn't really sleep so…"

My smile is slow, and the giddiness he has been known to stir inside me does its thing. "You wanted to impress me today, so you stayed up half the night to work on this." It's not a question, and Alister doesn't answer because he sees it—what this means to me.

He can apologize until he's blue in the face, make promises only time can prove the truth of, and shower me in honesty, but to embrace something I'm passionate about when he's only just realized that I am?

It's more than words. More than physical action.

It's care in a rare sense.

He really is trying here, and his effort isn't going unnoticed.

Quite the opposite as I think, maybe for the first time, that I'm seeing a side of him he's never shared before.

There is no arrogance in his eyes, no cocky tilt to his lips. He's not all about the game, and this thing between us isn't a chase. I was already caught, after all, though the line broke before he could reel me in due to his own mistake.

No, this is a backward crawl, a pebbled path to friendship island. The only problem is we've already lost our shoes and the rocks on the way back are sharp.

Do I want to walk across them to meet him on the other side?

Alister offers a gentle smile, and I realize I'm staring right into his green eyes.

"Will you tell me what you're thinking?" he whispers.

I swallow. "I'm not so sure if I should."

Alister reaches out, pushing my hair from my face, his soft fingers gently grazing along my temples, tucking the loose, straight strands behind my ear.

His hand holds there a moment, and I find myself leaning into his touch, my eyes closing.

"I miss you, Cameron."

"I know," I breathe, forcing my eyes open, but when I do, it's not Alister my gaze locks on.

It's the brown-eyed man behind him.

CHAPTER 24
BRADY

She's with him.

She's with him and that should be perfectly fine.

It *should* be, so why exactly does it feel like I swallowed a balloon that's blowing up inside me, taking up all the room, until all the air from my lungs is forced out like a solid hit to the chest?

That's just fucking…weird.

I swallow, offering my best grin, and watch as Cameron's posture pulls in, her shoulders hunching a bit.

Feeling guilty, baby girl? Why would that be?

I slide into the booth across from them, and Alister's head snaps my way, only now realizing I've joined their little party. "Howl. Cammie Baby. What are we up to?"

I cringe on the inside, the notebooks right here, laptop open and blocking my fake girlfriend's body from my view.

Okay, I guess I'm just out here sounding like a jealous boyfriend.

Which I'm not.

My eyes fall to Cameron's phone, sitting right there on the table beside her. Not two inches away from her, face up and all.

She must see me looking, because pretty purple-colored fingernails tap the screen, and in my periphery, her head snaps up. "Holy shit, it's already one."

Yes. You forgot our lunch plans because you're busy with him.

I shrug, keeping my grin in place when really, I want to show teeth like an animal and piss on what's mine. I mean, for now, but mine nonetheless. I flick my hand toward the plates with nothing but a few crumbs on them. "It's all good. Just glad you had time to eat."

"Shit, Brady. I'm so sorry." She starts shoving her things in her backpack hastily, and slowly, very fucking slowly, Alister does the same.

"Don't be." I knock my knuckles on the table, looking over as my boy Xavier steps up to the counter to order, his bat bag on his back. "I'm with X. We're just coming to get a shake before we hit the cages over at FunWorks. I didn't even know you were in here. Happy accident." *Fucking cringe again, my man.*

I climb out of the booth, and her baby blue eyes follow me the whole way, narrowing slightly. "I'll call you when I get back, see where you're at," I decide to add, because I think that's what a real boyfriend would say—not that she seems too worried about pretending she has one at the moment.

"I'll come with you," she rushes to say, looking at Alister expectantly.

He stares, like the fucker forgot he has to move for her to be able to, having caged her in like a smart little prick.

"Nah, it's good. Stay. Looks like you guys were getting some good work in."

Why the fuck did you say that?

Cameron quickly drops her attention to her backpack, long, golden hair hiding her face as she moves a few things around to slide her laptop in with ease. "I am coming with you, Brady," she says, laying down the law. Straightening, she offers Alister a small smile. "You did more than your half. Let me finish the section and we'll start the next one together in class on Thursday."

I can't believe he joined her class as a late add. The dude is taking fifteen units now. That's rough with the already-crammed schedules football gives us.

He nods, gets out of the way so she can exit the booth, then goes back to packing his shit.

Cameron comes up, pushing into me, and I give her hip a little squeeze.

"Sorry," she mumbles quietly.

"For what?"

She gives me a little glare, so I give her hip another squeeze.

"You're all good. You don't have to leave just because I came over and showed my ass."

She huffs. "No, I'm glad you did. Come on." She grabs my hand and leads me toward the door, where Xavier is already waiting with our shakes.

"I'll see you later," Alister calls.

"Sure," Cameron says at the same moment as I call out, "Yep."

Both our heads yank toward each other, small frowns written across both our brows.

Xavier chuckles, pushing the door open, and we step out into the chilly October air.

"Why are you seeing him later?" she wonders.

"Why are you?" My delivery and grin are all teasing.

Huh. Would you look at that? All that tension my body was holding went away in the fresh air. Nothing to do with seeing them sitting there alone, looking at each other and touching and eating.

"I'm not." Cameron frowns. "I just said that to be nice."

"Maybe I did too."

"Oh, please. You're more likely to tell him to kiss your muscly ass."

"I knew you were looking this morning."

She shakes her head with a smile, and when her blue eyes meet mine, I realize I was waiting for one. Sort of like when you haven't had something for a while but you know it's coming soon, so you look forward to it. *Fucking strange.*

"You guys are cute. It's gross." Xavier winks at Cameron when she looks his way. "Wanna take my car since we have a third wheel?" he jokes.

"Nah, she can sit bitch." I glance her way. "You really don't have to come with us. I can drive around campus, drop you at your dorm. I think Paige is still at Payton's if you want to go hang with the girls and play with the baby?"

"Trying to get rid of me?"

I shake my head slowly, tugging her hand to get her to stop walking and wait for Xavier to get a little farther ahead. "Cameron." I hold her gaze. "Why did you leave just now? You do realize that wasn't necessary, right?"

"Yeah." She nods a little too hard. "But no, it's fine. We were only supposed to spend a couple hours working on our assignment. I completely lost track of time."

"You lost track of time because you were enjoying yourself."

She starts shaking her head. "It wasn't like that, Brady."

I study her, words I can't quite form working their way up my throat before knotting there, forcing me to swallow so I can speak them. "Tell me you know it's okay if it were."

A gentleness falls over her, and she steps into me, her warm palms moving to rest on my chest as she raises on her toes. She presses a kiss to my lips—a quick, barely there peck—with another smile to follow, and suddenly I really wish I hadn't said that at all.

"I know, Brady. Now come on. Let's go hit some balls."

A low chuckle leaves me, but for some reason, my feet feel a little heavy as I lead us toward my truck.

A few minutes down the road and we're climbing out at FunWorks.

Xavier runs in to add some money onto his players card, so I unpack his helmet and bat, setting it up against the fence of the fastball cage.

"Don't we have batting cages on campus the baseball team

can use?" Cameron asks, picking up the highlighter-green bat and inspecting it.

"Yeah, but there's something about the good old-fashioned cages at a place like this. Remember when me and Chase played baseball that one year? What was it, seventh grade?"

She smiles. "You literally tried to quit after the third game, but your dad wouldn't let you."

"No way he was going to let his son be a quitter." My words settle in my chest, a mix of pride, love, and sorrow creating a whirl of emotions within me. "He always said don't commit to something in life you're not one hundred percent sure about and can't give your all to."

The rest of his words run through my mind.

No one deserves half-assed, even if that's all they offer you. Be better. Do better. Be the reason someone else smiles, even if all you want to do is cry, and you can cry, Son. All good men do from time to time.

Cameron looks over her shoulder, a soft tip to her lips, somehow sensing I might need it.

Turns out, I did because the heaviness falls away, and I grab a pink helmet from the cubbies along the fence line, tugging it over her head.

She puts her hands on her hips as if to pose. "How does it look?"

"Perfect, Cammie Girl." I toy with the hair sticking out the bottom, my eyes meeting hers. "You look perfect."

And she does. Her eyes are bright, her cheeks a little pink from the chilled air, and that smile—all wide and true and pointed at me. I want to kiss her, pull her close, and be the reason for a whole different sort of flush to her skin. I want to thank her for choosing me, promise her things and deliver on them, because that's my job as her man.

'Cause, fuck me, I think that's what I am. Hers.

And she's mine.

If only for a little while…

CAMERON

"No, don't drop me off!" I slap at his arm quickly when he flicks on the blinker. "I don't want to go home alone."

"I've got a training session, but I can come over after if you want?" he offers, rolling into the middle lane, intent to ignore my request.

A scowl builds, and I unbuckle, scooting over into the seat Xavier just vacated.

Brady looks over, doing a double take. He frowns at first, then with a hesitancy I don't quite understand moves back into the regular lane and heads straight.

We follow the road down and around the block and turn into the parking lot of the training center. Not twenty seconds later, a second familiar vehicle pulls in two spaces away.

"Coach asked me to go through some routines with Alister a couple times a week. Since I work with Mason all the time, he figured I was the man for the job."

Brady's heavy exhale fills the cab, and I watch as Alister unfolds from the driver seat. "So that's what he meant when he said see you later. He was talking to you."

"Disappointed?"

"What?" My head yanks his way. "No."

Brady's smile is tight. "I'm only playing, but yeah, I've got to train with him for a little over an hour. You want to bring your bag in or anything? Work on some school shit?"

"I'm schooled out for the day. I'll just play on my phone or something."

Brady's brows drop low, but he nods, climbing out, and I follow.

We walk into the building, neon lights and a giant AU sharks logo greeting us. You can hear the clink of weights from here, and I look through the thick glass of the hall as we pass the different rooms, spotting several others in with trainers or teammates, working on various things.

Brady leads us all the way to the end, and we step into a wide-open space. There's a giant strip of blue turf lining the floor, markings like a standard football field made across it with a dusty yellow.

Alister is standing in the center, setting out some bright orange cones. He puts the last one down and looks up, eyes instantly snapping to mine. He smiles, and I can't help but smile back.

An echoed thud sounds, and I turn to see Brady crouching down to grab some things out of the bag he just tossed to the floor. I walk over, drop beside his bag, and lay my head back on it as he digs in the other side.

He raises a brow, and I grin up at him.

"Got a hoodie in there?"

"For you?" He digs around, tugging one out and tossing it at my face. "Always."

I sit up, pulling it over my head. It's so big, it's like one of those blanket robes. I tuck myself all up, inhaling his cologne and rubbing my cheeks with the thick cotton of the inside. "Oh, this is a new one."

"Coach just passed 'em out yesterday."

"Okay, so tell him you never got one, and let me keep this one."

Brady chuckles, stretching to his full height, and chucks his hoodie over his head, tossing it in my lap. He had no shirt on underneath, and in the next breath, he pushes his track pants down his legs until I'm staring up at him in nothing but a pair of briefs.

My eyes fall straight to his package, but he's already bending and tugging on a pair of athletic shorts.

Brady laughs and my eyes meet his. "Don't pout, Cammie Baby. You know this is all yours anytime you want it."

He's teasing—I mean, he has to be because he's Brady Lancaster, but my blood decides to heat at his words anyway.

I chew on my inner cheek, looking down at his massive legs. They're like tree trunks, thick and protruding, dusted with hair that's a few shades darker than the shade on his head. Curious, I look to his stomach.

I never noticed his happy trail before, at least I don't think I have, but he does have one, and it's not that sandy-blond color either. It's darker, which seems so fitting for the love machine that is my boyfriend.

I mean friend.

My eyes snap up to a pair of bold brown ones. "Your jewelry is black, isn't it?"

Brady throws his head back and laughs, his muscles bunching as he does, and now I'm looking at his abs. It's really not fair how cut and carved he is. They're so perfectly sculpted, they defy the laws of physics…or I bet they would if I understood the subject. They're sharp as granite, yet there's this smooth, velvet-like quality that's inviting all sorts of curious thoughts to my little, inappropriate mind. They're otherworldly. Godly. World champs.

I mean I'm not saying he's part superhero, but those abs could save the world, one glorious flex at a time.

Those masterpieces start to constrict even farther.

He's bending down again, and this time, his smirk is downright dirty. "Tell you what: I'll tell you what color mine is if you tell me what color yours are."

"Oh my god, your gift!"

His brows jump. "Gift… Wait. What's that got to do with body jewelry?" he asks.

I cross my arms, smirking up at him. "I'll tell you what it has to do with body jewelry if you tell me—"

He leans in so quick, I don't even see him coming, cutting me off with a quick press of his lips to mine, only he doesn't pull back—he keeps our mouths pressed together and whispers against mine, "Nice try, Hellcat."

Heat.

It slithers down my spine and back up, tingling the nape of my neck the way a blush might, but I'm not blushing.

There's absolutely zero reason why I would be.

CHAPTER 25
ALISTER

She's watching him, and the worst part is I'm not even sure she realizes it, but she is.

He runs through the cones, his footwork somehow graceful despite his massive frame. Just like with the ladder drills, he starts slow, showing me how to follow, what moves to make first, how the bend in my knee can determine my speed and overall delivery, things I've heard before, but watching someone his size do this? Coach clearly knew what he was doing when he tasked him with helping me, forcing me to take note of where I have to improve.

With each pass through, Brady speeds up, and not once does he trip over what must be a size-thirteen shoe.

This shit is effortless for him and I'm over here knocking over cones and messing up the setup. Again, I fuck up, this time sending the cone flying in the air on purpose. Of course, that gets her to look my way, and I try not to make it too obvious she's in my line of sight.

It's hard to do when his number is draped across her, and if she were to turn, I know I'd find his name on her back because I have the same sweatshirt stuffed in the bag to her right.

Allana used to wear my letterman's jacket all the time, and I wonder if Cameron understands what doing such a thing like wearing a name or number means to a man. She probably does, since she's been around football players most her life.

But she's never loved or been loved by one in that way, so maybe not.

Allana was always proud to show my name and number off, even though she was a year older than me. That first year she was here at Avix, my senior year of high school, she came back several times, mostly during holiday breaks, but she managed to make a few of my senior season games, and each time, she'd have my name or number written across her in some way. I'm not really sure when she started being unfaithful and stringing me along; all I know is, when I showed up on campus that first year, she was already cheating because she didn't come home that summer. *Summer school* she'd said.

I should have seen the signs.

I should have let her go instead of doing what I did and allowing my hurt to turn to anger, then taking it out on other people—on the girl I think could have loved me the way I know I could have loved her.

My eyes slide to Cameron, but guilt has me quickly looking away. That damn hoodie swallows her whole.

The worst part is there's no one to blame for that but myself. Too bad that fact doesn't make this any easier.

When I first saw her here, I was excited. That lasted all of ten minutes when we stopped jogging around the room as a warm-up and her eyes no longer warmed my skin but rather shifted over to him.

I can understand why. It's like I said—he's effortless in his movements, his body fluid for a man his size, and he is a *big* fucker.

I'm not small, and I put a lot more time in the gym than I'd like to admit, but next to him I feel like the Robin to his Batman.

"You've got it down, man. Stop stressing."

"I need to shave another second off my release. If I can't do that, I'm never going to get a chance to fire the ball down field against Brighton on Saturday."

"You'll be fine."

"Come on, Lancaster." I shake my head, running my hands through my sweaty hair before wiping my palms on my shorts.

I don't hold back my concerns. That will do us no good. "We both know we're not getting much for rushing yards against their defense. We're strong in receivers, but our running backs are lacking compared to theirs. We *have* to play a passing game to stand a chance at winning," I stress. "That means if I don't cut time off my own performance, the line will be broken through, and I'll be on my ass, upping that asshole Jetson's stats for every sack they make."

Brady grimaces, reality setting in. "Fuck."

I scoff. "Yeah. How'd you like to lose your lead in the division to that guy when he's playing your own damn team?"

He scratches his neck, his face tight in thought before his eyes meet mine. "I've got an idea, but you might have to back me up here."

"I'm all ears, man. I've hardly touched the field this season, and with Mason coming back next week, who knows when I'll get to play again after tomorrow? I need all the highlight reels I can get."

Brady looks off before bringing his gaze back to mine. "You're doing good, Alister. Don't let anyone tell you you're not," he forces out, but it's easy to see it's not because he is incapable of giving a compliment. No, it's another reason entirely—that and the man really doesn't want to like me on principle. "Just…keep your head up and all that." His features tighten again as he looks at me, but he sighs a moment later, his shoulders falling as he heads toward the girl I want to call mine.

I stand there, staring, as he grabs her hand and hauls her to her feet like she's nothing but a feather, her smile bright, hair now piled on her head.

She turns, bending to shove his things in his bag, helping him get ready to go without being asked, and when she stands again, he wraps his arms around her, his body cradling hers completely.

The laugh she lets out at whatever he tells her reaches my ears, and my chest tightens. It's sweet and easy, so different from how she laughs with me now. The laughs I earn from her these days are thick and hard-won.

I force myself to turn away from the pair, piling the cones one on top of another before moving to put them back on the racks. I stand there a minute, staring at nothing and waiting to hear the door close, letting me know they're gone, when my name is called.

I look over, and she's not in his arms anymore but standing beside him.

Ken and Barbie.

"You coming or what?" Brady shouts.

My brows snap together, and I want to ask where and what he means, but I don't. I just grab my shit and jog toward the new—hopefully fake—couple, letting Brady lead the damn way.

CAMERON

"No."

I wince at the sharp finality in the older man's tone.

"But, Coach," Brady tries again but stops when their coach raises his hands.

"You are not playing both ways, son. That's too risky, and I need you on the defensive side until the final second ticks. You get hurt, and they're going to get twice as many yards on us as predicted. I need you there to force the quick pass."

"I'll be good, Coach. I can do this," he tries to assure him.

"You'll burn out."

"I'm a fucking stallion. I've got stamina for days."

I choke on a laugh, and suddenly, several pairs of eyes land on me, even where I'm tucked away in the back corner. "Sorry," I mumble, lifting the collar of the hoodie so it covers my mouth.

The coach narrows his eyes at me, then looks to Alister, Brady, and back to me. He takes note of what hoodie I'm wearing next. "I take it this is the girl…"

"Yes, Coach." Brady looks my way, a gleam in his eyes that has mine narrowing. He winks and turns back. "Wanna ask her about my endurance?"

"Come on, man," Alister complains.

Brady only laughs, and their coach scoffs, rubbing his hand along the back of his silver hair. "Just think about it. Colorado's got a guy doing it, and it doesn't have to be every play. I just need in there to protect Howl when we're going deep and to give our receivers a chance to get down the field. They hit their routes right, which they will, Howl will get the ball in their hands. He can make the throw, probably with his eyes closed—he just needs that extra second. Put me on the line and I can give him that."

Their coach looks between the two men, a slow nod of his head following. He pins Alister with his gaze. "Two weeks together and you've managed to gain full confidence from a man whose best friend is our first-string quarterback."

Alister stands taller, and a small smile tugs at my lips.

"I hope that means something to you." Their coach gives Alister a stern, fatherly expression.

"Yes, Coach," Alister responds.

The man huffs, then waves his hand to dismiss them. "I'll talk with the rest of the staff, but no promises."

"Fuck yes." Brady gives a hard jerk of his head.

They both thank him, and I sneak out first when Brady holds the door open.

In the parking lot, Alister turns to us.

I can tell he's not sure what to say, his hands sliding in his pockets almost restlessly, and Brady, being the bighearted man he is, makes it a little easier on him.

"Watch game film tonight, man—ours and theirs. If they agree to this, and I think they will, they might have to call some unexpected plays. Make sure you're prepared for that. Learn who your threats are based on what they run."

Alister eats up his words, determined to learn the way he knows how.

He would have picked the basketball in his little test.

"I will," he swears.

Brady nods, glancing between Alister and me. He holds my gaze a second longer, and I see the beginnings of a small frown forming along his forehead just before he turns and walks away.

He's giving me a minute alone with Alister in case I need one.

The thing is, I don't think I do, so I just curve my lips up at Alister. "Good luck tomorrow, not that you'll need it," I offer, jogging to catch up with Brady.

He's tugging his door open as I reach him, his eyes widening when he realizes I'm right there, slipping under his arm and onto the seat.

He follows with a smile.

As we park in front of my dorm not five minutes later, I wait for him to meet my gaze. "Thank you."

"For what?"

"For being all the things I know you to be and more."

He reaches over, hauling me up until I'm sitting sideways on his lap. "Don't give me too much credit, all right? Coach pretty much forced me to work with him, and if I let him get his ass kicked tomorrow, it's only gonna hurt the team. I can't have that. Mason secured us a spot in the playoffs, and I'm not going to let anything mess that up."

"I know." I smile, twisting the strings of his hoodie around my finger. "Just like I know the kindness you're showing him has nothing to do with what you just said."

"Oh yeah?" he teases, tickling my sides lightly, making me squirm.

"Yeah." I settle against the steering wheel at my side. "It's a part of your nature and for *my* benefit. Layers upon layers, you have, Mr. Lancaster."

I've known this man since he wasn't one, since we were babies, then gangly little kids, both he and I taller than the others for a few of our younger years.

I was awkward and he was strong.

He's only stronger now—mentally, physically.

I wonder if there are still things I've yet to learn about him?

"What's with the frown, pretty girl?" he murmurs.

My eyes lift to his, and it's like there's a little magnetic pull that wasn't there a moment ago. It's trying to tug me in closer, to whisper something I can't hear, as if I'm a little too far away—only that makes no sense. I'm right here.

"Do you have secrets, Brady?" I ask suddenly.

Brady tenses beneath me, and it takes him a moment to respond.

"A couple," he rasps, brown eyes bolted to mine as he almost unwillingly admits, "maybe one more now than I had before..."

He says it so softly, I almost miss it. I'm about to ask him before what, but he doesn't give me the chance.

"Why do you ask?"

"Will you tell me one?"

I watch as an array of emotions wash over him—fear, uncertainty, anxiety, and the most confusing...guilt.

Suddenly, I don't just want to know why all those worries rose at my question.

I *need* to know. "Tell me."

"I'm not so sure I should."

"Do it anyway."

He inhales, long and deep, and I wonder if those gold flecks have always been in his eyes and I've just never noticed them before. "Not tonight." He pushes my hair from my face.

"Not tonight, but some other time?"

His lips tip up but only on one side. "Yeah, Cammie Baby. Some other time," he whispers.

And for the first time in my life, I'm not so sure I believe him.

CHAPTER 26
BRADY

Pouring water over my head, I give my hair a good shake, squirting more into my mouth and swishing it around before spitting on the turf.

Fernando comes up, so I pass him the bottle and wipe my face with the towel hanging from my waist.

We're in the third quarter, and Alister is getting hammered. My eyes fly to the clock, quickly focusing back on the field just as the ball is hiked. It's third down, Alister drops back, curls left, and prepares to fire the ball, but the line breaks, forcing him to scramble forward so as not to lose more yards. He manages to get back to the line of scrimmage before he's tackled, and the whistle is blown.

"Fuck, man," someone mumbles, and I frown, tracking Alister as he jogs off the field, the punting squad taking his place. Another fucking turnover.

Alister tears his helmet off, slamming it to the bench as he takes the tablet and pulls up the film.

He's shaking his head when I drop beside him. He doesn't look up, just glares hard at the screen, watching as the line splits and he's forced to make the call he did, abandoning the play and trying to get the few yards he nearly lost back.

"I fucking told you," he spits. "I'm not quick enough. I need more time on the field or I'm never going to get better."

I can't argue with that. It's the only way to level up from

a great high school player to a good college one. Alister hasn't gotten the opportunity he was hoping for, being second to Mason both last season and this one. Practice helps, but there's nothing like live game play when everyone is coming at you with 100 percent effort, not something your own teammates will give you when you're preparing for a game. We go hard but with the understanding that we don't want to injure our own guys.

Out here, everyone on the opposite side of the ball wants to take the others' heads off.

The punting team is coming off the field, and I have to jump up, shoving my own helmet on and buckling my chin strap. Alister looks up, watching me as I push through the team on the sideline and grip Coach's shoulder.

He looks up at me because, yeah, I'm taller than he is, a frown of frustration etched across his face.

"I'm not coming off the field when we turn the ball over." I run out, not letting him respond.

He knows we need to try something. We're down two touchdowns, our offense turning over the ball an embarrassing number of times the first half.

There's only four minutes left in the third quarter, and it's not looking any better.

I take the field with the rest of the defense, getting into position. I meet the eyes of some of our guys, nodding.

We've got to stop them to have a chance to win.

Shoving my mouthpiece in, I get ready, eyes snapping across the field, reading the play. The ball is hiked, swiftly passed off to their running back, who bulldozes his way through, getting wrapped up after a five-yard gain.

Fuck. "No more!" I shout, pointing at our defensive tackle.

He nods, and we get set. The quarterback kicks his foot back, the receivers fan out; the left has his body angled the slightest bit to the right, telling me where the ball is about to go—rookie mistake.

The ball is snapped, and I drive forward, juke a little to the left, then shoulder my way through.

Their quarterback already has his arm pulled back, foot stepping forward and prepared for the release. Going for a sack won't work, so I jump, arm stretched as high as it can go, fingers spread wide.

The ball tips my ring finger, toppling, and changes trajectory. From the corner of my eye, I see our safety, Thompson, fly up, the ball landing right in his fucking hands.

The crowd goes crazy, and we run down field, blocking, but he's shoved out of bounds at the thirty.

Still, the AU pride is going wild, the stomping in the stands echoing all around us.

The defense jogs off, but I stay right where I fucking am, meeting Coach's gaze on the sidelines.

He gives Alister the play, and Alister runs out, but I frown when I spot Chase and Hector still on the sidelines.

"What the hell?" I frown. "We have to pass."

Alister shakes his head. "He wants to push up the middle."

"It's first down and we're already losing time!"

"It's not my call."

Shaking my head, we get into formation.

Unlike Brighton, we only get a single yard, the line too fucking strong for our guys to break through. Second down, Coach calls the same thing, and now I'm getting pissed. The clock is still running.

I'm about to get in fucking trouble.

The ball is snapped, and I rush forward, grabbing the D-tackle, and I hold the fuck on.

The play ends with our guy getting tackled, and flags are thrown.

"Goddamn it, Lancaster!" Coach screams on the sideline, the white hat turning on his mic and making the penalty official.

"Holding, offense number ninety-eight. Ten-yard penalty, repeat third down."

Gotta pass now, don't you, Coach?

Coach points at me, aware of what I just did now that he's had a second. I'll get chewed out for purposely causing a penalty later, but oh fucking well. No more bullshit.

I look to Mason, dressed in his AU sweatsuit on the sidelines, a ball tucked under his arm, to see what his reaction is, and he gives me a nod.

I blow him a kiss in response, grinning around my mouthpiece.

The new play is called, and thank fuck our running backs jog out, exchanging places with our receivers.

Chase is chuckling as he comes up, slapping me on the shoulders and getting into position.

I look at Alister, who nods, his chest rising with a deep breath as he gets into position.

The ball is hiked and I do my part, closing the gap, staying low and fucking strong.

Alister hesitates, and a motherfucker comes around his backside, forcing him to throw the ball away.

I growl, shoving my guy away, and storm up to him as I yank my mouthpiece out. "What the fuck was that?!"

"Harper was in double coverage and Hector was short. I—"

"You could have made the pass," I say, cutting off his excuses.

"I just told you, he was in double coverage!"

I get in his face, knocking my helmet into his. "And I just fucking told you, you could have made that pass!" He starts to shake his head, so I hit his helmet with mine again. "I went back and watched your high school game film. I know all your moves. Fire the fucking ball right where it needs to be."

He glares. "You're asking me to risk an interception on my already minimal stats."

"No." I grip his face mask, my eyes hard on his. "I'm telling you to do what I know you fucking can, so quit with the self-doubt. Make the pass, Howl. Watch the way the crowd stands up for you when you do."

His nostrils flare, and he yanks away, both of us getting ready.

It's fourth fucking down. If we don't get in there this drive, our chances are cut in half. We need three touchdowns to win. We get into the end zone here, and we've got all of the fourth quarter to turn things around.

"You sure about this?" Chase mumbles, arms hanging loose at his sides.

"He can do it. Show him you can too."

Chase gives a hard nod and, when Alister calls the first hut, shifts.

The ball is snapped, I do my job, and not long after, the ball is sailing over my head.

I jerk free, watching as it soars toward the left corner of the end zone.

Chase, once again, is being double-teamed, a guy on each side of him.

The ball starts to drop, Chase's cleats digging into the turf as he runs, arms swinging, the defenders right on him.

He jumps, reaches, and does his fucking job, the ball yanked into his chest, shoulder down as he barrels his way across the one-yard line.

Touchdown.

The crowd flips out, the band plays, and I turn to Alister, grinning like a fool.

He throws his fist in the air, but he doesn't stop to seek the praise like he has done in the past. No, he gives that single show of celebration, but he's already running toward the end zone.

Fuck kicking for that extra point, we're staying on the field and going for two.

And we get it, leaving us just shy of two touchdowns.

We run to the sidelines, and the team is on their feet, giving Alister the credit he deserves while the kickoff team takes the field.

I smile to myself, meeting Mason's eye when he claps my shoulder as I walk toward the water table.

I tear my helmet off, wiping my head, and take a long drink, my eyes scanning the crowd until they land on my favorite girl.

Only this time when I find her, she's not looking at me.

She's smiling at him.

───────────

We won.

The team is still celebrating, running around and saying hi to their families, and I do the same, searching for the others where the girls were sitting.

Sure enough, Mason and Chase are already over there, hugging Mason's parents and laughing with the girls.

Mason takes Deaton from his mama's arms and turns, setting him down on the field. The two jog out to the end zone, and my chest warms as I watch little D run his fastest, his little legs pumping as he tries to catch up to his dad.

"That was him not all that long ago." Mason's dad, Evan, claps me on the shoulder. "Of course, I was playing some adult rec league trying to relive my college days at that point, so it wasn't as cool as this, but man, that kid thought I was the coolest thing in the world."

"Little D sees him the same." I smile, turning to give his wife, Mason's mom, Vivian, a sweaty hug.

She kisses my temple. "That's from your mama, and this"— she kisses my hair with a wink—"is from me. Good job out there."

"Thank you. Thank you, you guys, for coming to watch even though Mase couldn't play."

"Pssh." She waves. "We have three sons on this team, not just one. Chase, honey, come give me a hug."

"Yes, ma'am." He squeezes around me, his shoulder pads still on.

Vivian wraps her arms around him, whispering in his ear something I can't hear, and my brows pull when I notice her eyes are growing misty.

Wonder what that's about.

Chase simply nods and turns around, ignoring everyone as he hops back over the railing, heading for the tunnel.

That's when I spot them, and my ears grow warm.

Cameron is leaning over the guard, and Alister is smiling up at her like she's an angel that just popped out of the damn sky. He's talking animatedly, laughing and nodding, and then her hands are moving, explaining the play the way she saw it, if I had my guess.

They both laugh now, and I watch as they forget to speak, simply staring at each other a moment.

There's a little kick behind my ribs that draws a frown to my face, so I start to turn around, but then an older couple climbs down the stairs, and Alister looks up. His grin is broad, clearly happily surprised at the sight of them. He jumps onto the wide cement guard, offering the younger boy with them a hug before leaning into the adults' embrace as well.

Looks like his family came out to see him after all.

A small smile tugs at my lips, but there's this strain in my chest that tightens when I look back to the blond girl standing all sweet and shyly at his side.

"What am I missing, son?" Evan mutters, and I can feel his gaze when it lands on my face.

Don't ask me why, but I'm pretty sure a flush is threatening to crawl up my chest—no, a blush. I don't blush, so I clear my throat and put on my best grin, turning away so I don't have to watch her get introduced to the dude's family.

"Come on now, Evan. I thought you were as good a mind reader as I am," I tease. "Or maybe that's just your wife."

The moment the words leave me, though, I regret them because now his gaze is gauging, roaming across my features to try and figure out what he, in fact, is missing.

We didn't exactly tell our family we were fake dating and I'm 90 percent positive Alister's name has never been purposefully mentioned to any of our parents. If I say something now, I'll have to admit that there's a word in that little equation that no longer fits, and I'm not sure I'm ready to say that out loud.

It doesn't matter, though, because he's already nodding, his dad senses kicking in, I'm sure. Somehow parents just...know.

When he returns his attention to where I know Cameron to be standing, he frowns. "Why does she look like she's about to cry?"

My entire body yanks around, eyes narrowing.

What the hell?

Cameron is walking back this way, her lips pressed tight, eyes immediately seeking mine.

"Interesting," he muses, but I don't wait to hear what comes next.

I'm already moving, squeezing between people, and offering friendly but quick hellos to the AU crowd, but my focus is on one thing and that's getting to her.

It takes a minute, but then I'm hopping over a row of seats and standing before her, tugging her into me for a hug I somehow know she needs. She doesn't care that my undershirt is covered in sweat. Her arms come around me, and she presses her face into my chest with a sigh, like maybe this was all she needed to settle—me.

My gaze snaps to where Alister is still standing, his ex-girlfriend, Allana, now right beside him, but his eyes? They're on the girl in my arms and then they move to me.

He wants to come over here. He doesn't want her to assume something is going on that isn't. It's all right there in his eyes.

A plea from him to me.

Don't let her think this is more than it is. That's what he's asking me.

My muscles coil, my teeth clamping tight, but I'm not sure why. Who the hell is he to ask me this? As far as he knows, she's mine.

Is he not threatened by that?

212

Does he not believe she could ever be with a man like me?

Why do I agree?

What is happening in my head right now?

Shaking the thoughts as she pulls back, I glance down at her, her chin now resting between my pecs.

She and I seem to look at each other at the same time, and she hits me with the softest of smiles. It does a little something to me, so as much as I want to be selfish, I just can't be. Not when all she ever looks at me with is complete and total confidence.

So I shift us slightly. That way, if she looks to her right, she'll see them again, and like I knew she would, she can't help but take a peek.

She's drawn to him the way I wish someone were drawn to me.

No, not someone...

I clear my throat, and I hold her tighter, running my fingers through the length of her hair.

"They're just talking, Cammie Baby," I reassure her, the words like acid on my tongue.

She nods but doesn't say anything. She just...keeps staring. Finally, her tired blue eyes meet mine. "Come on, Big Guy. Let's go. We've got a party to get ready for."

"Wanna tell me what you're gonna dress up as?"

"Not a chance."

I chuckle, and finally, her smile reaches her eyes. I kiss her forehead, then lead her toward the others.

We say our goodbyes, and I hop back onto the field just as Mason passes Deaton over to his dad.

Us guys move back to the tunnel to get changed and deal with after-game interviews, Alister jogging and falling in place beside us.

I don't look his way, even though he's waiting for me to.

I did what he wanted.

I did what was right for her, tried to ease her spinning mind and remind her it's her he wants.

I told her I'd help her, give her the time and distraction she needed to work through her own thoughts. Maybe she has.

Maybe she's finally realized what I've known for a while now.

She doesn't need a fake boyfriend anymore—not when she's ready for a real one.

CHAPTER 27
BRADY

The team is hyped. Drinks are already flowing, and it's easy to see it's going to be a long, loud night here at the football house. Nearly everyone is home, showered, and changed into their costumes, the sorority across the street having taken on the task of setting up for the Halloween party tonight while we were at the game.

There's not too much to the decorations, just some black lights and neon-green spiderwebs tacked along the walls, a few streamers and things hanging, and one of those foil fridge curtain things you have to push aside to slip in the door.

Someone vetoed the "Monster Mash" shit they had playing, so it's back to the repeated party playlist.

Chase steps through the patio door, spotting me across the bonfire, and we both start laughing.

"Bro, did I step back in time?" He grins, slapping my shoulder and taking a cup from the table, filling it to the brim with foamy beer.

"I look good, yeah?" I smirk, holding my arms out, the cheap faux-fur robe-like thing clipped around my neck nearly sliding off my shoulders.

"You look like you're in your element." He chuckles and I join in.

"Right? Can't wait for Cameron to see."

Chase is dressed as Maverick from *Top Gun*, the aviators a

damn good look on him, and he's got the perfect hair for it. He raises a brow at my comment, and I shrug.

"Inside joke."

"Oh, you've got those now, huh?" His green eyes are teasing as he meets mine over the rim of his cup.

I flip him off, bending slightly to look in the kitchen when it gets a little louder, and spot the source of the commotion. Alister has made his way down, grinning and dapping people up—full acceptance in the house for what might be the first time. Someone hands him a beer, another stops him for a shot, and I can't help but watch.

"What's he supposed to be, Hugh Hefner?" Chase wonders.

My eyes fall to the velvety robe he's got on, and I throw my head back and laugh.

Oh, Cammie Girl. Fucking hilarious. At least I know they won't match. Ain't no way is she showing up with bunny ears on.

"Let me guess." Chase studies me. "Another inside joke?"

"You heard from the girls yet?" I ignore his question, looking around to avoid his grin.

"Nah, I talked to Mason though, and he said he's walking them over, but they had to wait for his parents to get back with food first. Guess they didn't feel like eating at the game."

I nod, settling into one of the chairs.

I'm on my second beer when Mason walks out and everyone around laughs.

He grins good-naturedly, sticking his hand out and shooting silly string all over with a laugh.

"Fucking Spidey!"

He gives a full spin, wearing a tight-as-shit onesie.

"Holy shit, bro, you actually wore it!"

"Dude, Deaton picked it out. What was I supposed to do, tell him no?"

I chuckle. Poor guy's got no chance when it comes to that little man. "Hope you're wearing a cup, my boy, or else everyone

216

here is gonna know what you're packing in there. What's your woman gonna say about that?"

He frowns. "Don't remind me about people seeing too much," he mumbles. "Just...wait for it."

Before I can question him, whistles and catcalls sound, and he huffs, but there's a small smile on his lips.

Then the girls are sauntering through the door—first Payton, then Paige, and lastly mine.

I mean Cameron.

My brows jump, my jaw might drop, and what is this fire in my stomach?

Chase glares, suddenly really thirsty as he gulps down his drink, and I can't even stalk forward like I planned, give her a little show of my own.

No, my eyes have locked on to the perfect pigtails Cameron's sporting. They're pinned up high, one solid, smooth curl spun in each, thin baby blue ribbons tied in bows holding them in place.

Her outfit is best described as shrink-wrap, a tiny strip of the same shade of blue bound around her chest. It's only high enough to cover the swell of her breast, no longer than where the edge of a swimsuit would reach at the bottom, pressed tight against her ribs. Her toned stomach is glimmering, her sun-kissed skin having been rubbed in some sort of sparkly shit, the little flecks blinding as she moves and the fire bounces off her.

Her belly ring is a little ghost dangling, the tip of it teasing along her bottoms—and what the actual fuck, man?

I glare at her lower half. How is she even walking in that?

At first, I think she got the parts mixed up and the thin little strip covering her is meant to be the top...but the top is even smaller.

That little thing is not a skirt.

She does a cute little spin, and... *Nope. Uh-uh.*

I dart forward, my arm snaking around her waist from behind, and haul her to me.

She squeals, a giggly, girlie sound I'm not sure I've heard from her before but already want more of, and grips my arm, tipping her head a bit as I bury my face in her neck.

"What in the heaven's little devil are you doing to me?" I ask.

"It's the pigtails, isn't it?"

"You mean these perfect handlebars on your head? No…"

She hits me with a grin over her shoulder, none of her earlier sadness to be found. "You wanna grab on, Boyfriend?"

"I want to cover you in my fur so no one can look at you." No one but me.

"Call me Bubbles."

"Bubbles?"

"Yeah, you know the Powerpuff Girls?" When I say nothing, she laughs, spinning around and freeing herself. "Did you not notice Payton's red wig and Paige's cute little black one?"

I look up, scanning the other girls' outfits, that no, I did not notice when they came in. Looks like my eyes went straight to Cameron.

"Okay." I nod. "But Payton's actually covers some of her skin, and Paige…" I pause. All right, so she's about as covered as Cameron is, but a frowning Chase is hovering awfully, *obviously*, close to her, even if he is pretending she doesn't exist at the same time, so there's that.

"Wait." Cameron pushes off my chest, moving farther away, finally getting a good look at my outfit.

Her mouth drops open, her hand lifting to cover it as she laughs. Blue eyes wide and pleased, she stomps her boots in excitement—leather boots that go up past her knee, I might fucking add.

Her smile is infectious, intoxicating, and now it's my turn to pose.

I make a fist, showing off the leather cuff things tight across my forearms, the fake metal clicking around my waist where my fake sword and knife hang. I've even got a temporary tattoo covering

218

my entire shoulder on the side where the feldr, as the dude who sold it to me called it, lies. I call it a fucking furry shawl for men.

I spin then, and she starts laughing loudly, in that way where I know, if I were looking at her, her eyes would be glossy, her head tipped back, exposing that silky, slender neck of hers.

"Shut up!" She reaches up, her dainty fingers running along the miniature clipped-in braid I somehow got to stick to my short hair. It's light enough, only hangs to my neck, and feels annoying as hell, but her reaction makes it worth it.

She shakes her head, shoving the shawl thing back a little to run her eyes over the tattoo stamped there.

"I fucking knew you were born in the wrong time," she teases, beaming up at me. "You are giving Ragnar Lothbrok some *serious* competition." Her eyes trail over me slowly, from head to fucking toe, and a light buzz slithers along my spine.

Mason steps forward, holding out his phone. "Look at these two," he says to no one in particular, and we all shuffle in.

It's a picture of Ari and Noah in their costumes, angel wings on the back of Ari's white dress, metal cuffs covering Noah's shoulders. They're posed so he's facing her, lips pressed to her hand as she smiles at him, so I can't see much of what he's wearing, but there's something about the pose and clothing that's familiar. As I'm staring, a second picture comes through, and I throw my head back with a laugh.

"Wait, are they...?" Chase scowls, not sure he's got it right.

"Romeo and Juliet?" Cameron smiles. "Yes, yes, they are."

"The Leo DiCaprio version."

"Classic." Mason grins, shoving his phone...I don't even know where in that Spidey costume. "All right. We've got a sitter for the night. Let's not waste it."

He pulls Payton close, kissing her temple, and shuffles toward the house.

The rest of us follow behind, the girls already dancing around as we enter and the music gets louder.

We make drinks and head over to the room with the dartboards, playing a few rounds. We chat and laugh, and about an hour in, the girls are already two drinks ahead of us, our little group leading them to the kegs for their fourth round of flat beer.

"So we gonna just watch and see how all this plays out?" I tease.

"Not sure I've ever seen Paige drink more than a half a beer before." Chase looks our way, frowning at whatever he sees. "Not that I pay attention or anything, I just—What?" he finally snaps.

Me and Mason laugh, bumping each other as the girls start belting out the lyrics to the Spice Girls "Wannabe" using their cups as pretend mics, and all I can think is yeah …

I wanna be.

"Pretty sure Cameron had a shot or two before I picked them up, but she seems to be handling herself just fine." Mason meets my gaze a moment before looking back to the girls. "Payton, on the other hand, never drinks, so I might have to steal her away after this one." Mason's eyes trail his woman's every move.

"And would you be taking her back to her studio, where your mama and daddy are waiting for you, along with baby boy?"

Mason smirks, shaking his head nice and slow. "Nope." He claps his hand on my shoulder. "Stay outta my room tonight, boys."

"You mean no sleepover?"

"There will be zero sleeping for us tonight, my man." He waggles his brows. "How about you?"

I don't realize he's talking to me until I look over and find Chase is staring at me expectantly too.

Now it's my turn to snap. "Wait, what?"

"How far do these boyfriend duties of yours go?"

"You left out a word," I deadpan.

"Yeah." Chase's grin widens. "But so did she."

I frown, not sure what he's talking about when her little tease from earlier comes back to mind, and he's right. She did call me

220

"boyfriend," leaving off the *fake*. My hand tightens on my cup, and I force a shoulder to shrug. "People are around, that's all. It's not like that."

"And if you guys get a little needy and decide you want it to be like that?" Mason teases.

I swing my eyes to his and hold them, his losing some of the amusement the longer he stares.

"You still haven't told the girls?"

"Wait, really?" Chase's head whips back this way.

He's not talking about the shit going on in my head lately— that has now started to take a little trip south, if you know what I mean. No, he's talking about something else entirely.

I grumble. "It's not exactly a conversation you have at the dinner table."

Mason nods slowly, gaze assessing. "But you don't want her to know. Do you?"

"What would be the point of telling her?"

"What's the point of keeping it a secret?"

"I'm not embarrassed if that's what you're getting at."

Mason frowns. "It's not and you know it. Chase." He looks Chase's way. "Help me out here?"

I meet Chase's eyes, and he lifts a shoulder.

"Look, man, shit happens. Most of the time when you least expect it, so maybe just think about it. That way, if you find yourself diving a little deeper, it's not a whole-ass thing."

I stare at my half-empty cup of warm beer I'm not even drinking.

I have thought about it. A lot, but if I'm honest, it only started to cross my mind over the last few weeks.

And what does that tell you, dumb-ass?

"All right, I think it's time," Mason says, splitting through the mess in my mind, and I look over just as Payton tips her cup all the way back, trying to get something to magically come out when it's clearly empty. "I might ask her to leave the wig on. At least for round one." He smirks and walks away, lifting his woman off her feet, her laughter all that's left as they disappear around the corner as we approach the last two standing.

Paige looks at her watch once they're out of eyesight. "I should probably go too."

"Already?" Cameron whines.

Paige gives her an apologetic expression. "If I don't go now, I'll have to wait another hour for the campus safety shuttle, and I'm not sure I want to be on it when it's people who are going to be carried on and given puke bags."

"You can come home with me and Brady. Take Ari's bed or the couch?" Cameron suggests, hiccupping slightly. "Or you can take Brady's bed. He has a lock on the door, so you'll be safe."

Chase chokes on his drink, looking from Cameron to Paige.

I fight a grin. "Yeah, Paige. Take my bed. I'm room four, second floor."

Chase swings his eyes my way, narrowing them on me.

I wink at him and his frown deepens. Has he not figured out he likes her yet?

Man. My friends are slow to the ball when it comes to women.

So glad I'm not like them.

"Okay, yeah." Paige nods. "One or the other will work. Thanks."

I nod, meeting Cameron's mischievous gaze when she looks back at me, happy her little scheme is working out.

She presses into my chest, and I bend to whisper in her ear.

"I take it she's unaware I have a roommate named Chase Harper?"

"Shh," she laughs, spotting someone to the side and calling out to them with a smile.

She slips away, drunkenly tugging Paige along as she moves over to hug a girl with pink hair dressed in a catsuit.

A few of our teammates join us, and we bullshit for a while. At one point, Chase disappears and then the others walk off too. Unfortunately for me, a gang of girls appear in front of me next.

"Hey, Brady," they singsong, swinging props around and sliding in as close as possible.

"Ladies." I look over their costumes of choice. We've got a nurse, policeman, firefighter, convict, and every other outfit along that line, each one the "sexy," near-naked version. "I've been a good boy. No need for the cuffs," I tease when the cop girl swings her fluffy cuffs around her finger.

"Saw your girlfriend with the new quarterback earlier. Did you guys break up?" one asks.

I open my mouth, but then her words register, and my eyes snap to where I last saw Cameron. I spot Paige and the girl they went over to say hello to, but she's nowhere to be seen.

My pulse jumps for some reason, and I slip through the group, for once not bothering with an excuse about why I'm leaving them standing there.

I circle the main room, the kitchen, and the game room but don't spot her anywhere. Tension tugs at my muscles with each passing minute. I pause at the stairs, wondering if I want to go up to his room and see if she's there. I shouldn't.

I should just...leave them alone.

I take the stairs two at a time, round the corner, and just as I lift my fist to knock, I spin on my fucking heels and hurry back down with a groan.

Unease wraps around my shoulders and I shake my head.

What are you doing, bro?

Quit with the bullshit already. You did your job.

You gave her time.

It's like you fucking knew.

Time is up.

Instead of moving toward the keg, I hit the kitchen, letting one of the freshmen pour me a double of something dark.

I throw it back, snag a bottled water, and push through the back patio door.

It's louder than normal back here, barrels lit up with bonfires, but I tear past them both, moving for a quieter spot in the dark across the yard.

My feet jerk to a stop when a pair of perfect pigtails come into view.

My heart hammers behind my ribs as I watch her.

She's sitting alone, staring across the fire.

Slowly, I make my way over, nerves I don't quite understand twisting in my gut, but there's another feeling in there too. Relief.

My eyes lift, seeking out the sight that has her looking so sad, and I spot him almost instantly. The knot in my stomach seems to tighten, but I'm not sure I understand why. This is good, right?

Was my first thought bad?

I swallow, shaking my head to try and make some sense of what's running through it, but my thoughts are too all over the damn place for me to figure it out. I drop to my knee behind her chair, my hand coming up to squeeze her arm.

"Hey," she whispers, her attention going right back to the guy across the fire.

He's laughing with a few guys from the team, completely ignoring the girls that are clearly trying to get his attention.

Cameron sighs, slowly slumping back in her chair, and my arms push through the loops of the plastic seat and wrap around her.

"You okay?" I whisper into her hair.

Cameron nods. "I'm happy for him. As much as he pissed me off last year, he had an even rougher time—second-string, a cheating girlfriend, a house full of guys who only knew him to be the asshole he was acting like. I hope he can make new friends and find a place on the team he can be proud of."

"I'm sure he will." I pause, then add in a whisper, "Having you around could help."

Why did I say that?

"I thought those were his parents at the game today," she says softly, ignoring my comment. "He had told Ari his family wouldn't be there, and then he saw that couple and young boy, and he was…so happy. I thought it was his parents, maybe a brother. Turned out they were her parents and that was her little brother."

I wince, remembering how excited he seemed to see them.

"Did you know he was with her since they were young? Like thirteen or some shit." She sighs again. "That's a lot of history, lots of shared family holidays."

"Yeah," I agree, swallowing hard, and force myself to be the support she needs. "But we have a lot of room in our extended family. You could always add someone new to it, you know? No one would judge you, Cammie Girl."

Cameron leans to the side a bit so she can see me, her gaze roaming my face before settling on my eyes. "You're kind of perfect, you know that?"

"I try."

She smiles and slowly moves to stand, tugging me up with her.

She slips her arm around my middle, inside my furry shawl thing, her slender, freezing fingers resting along my ribs, or as much of them as she can reach.

I jolt at the chill of her touch, and she chuckles, a low, raspy sound. She folds herself around my naked torso, burrowing deeper into the warm part of my costume.

I bend and sweep her up, bridal style, spinning the fur thing around so it's lying across her like a blanket, and start walking toward the sliding door.

She huddles into my body, and I can't help but haul her higher, her face now in my neck.

She peeks up at me again, those big blue eyes glossy and holding mine hostage. There's glitter swept across them, thick black lines curving up and making the blue seem even brighter. Her lashes are long and full, lips painted a pretty pink tonight.

She's beautiful, my Cameron.

I lean down with the intent to kiss her cheek, but she turns at the last second, pressing her lips to mine.

My feet stop moving, muscles locking in surprise.

Her mouth presses against mine more firmly, more certainly, and an instant heat crawls up my groin, fanning across my stomach. My fingers dig into her thighs a little, and she opens up for me, her exhale filling my starved lungs, our tongues meeting for a soft, silky sweep.

Maybe the boys are right. Maybe I should tell her I'm not the wanton man she thinks I am but a waiting one.

She smiles against my mouth, and I nip at her lips in response, wanting more. *Needing more.*

Maybe I've just been waiting for this. For…her.

Cameron chuckles, eyes still closed as she pushes her face back into my neck, her hand pressed to my chest.

A smirk tugs at my lips, and I stand a little taller, my head a little higher, as I walk toward the door, but before my left foot lifts to follow my right, my eyes do. And the rest of me freezes.

Alister Howl is standing there, staring right at us.

Or more, *at her.*

Suddenly it all makes sense.

She had been watching him before, but he didn't know it.

She must have realized she had his attention now.

She knew he was looking and that's why she kissed me.

She kissed me so he would see, but that's okay. That's good. Perfect.

That's what I'm here for.

It's what I agreed to.

My team won our game tonight.

So why does it feel like I lost?

CHAPTER 28
CAMERON

I hit Submit on the last slide for phase four of the Instructional Design project, hoping our most recent idea is as strong as the others have been.

With a sigh, I lean back against the couch, closing my eyes a moment.

I'm not feeling the best today. I thought it was but a massive hangover from one too many beers mixed with Jell-O shots on Saturday night, but it's Wednesday and I'm still feeling like shit.

I finish off my water bottle and open the syllabus, scanning over this week's lecture points one more time just in case.

"Are we going to talk about Saturday?" Alister asks suddenly.

My fingers freeze over the track pad, eyes darting to meet his.

"What do you mean?" *Okay, that was not the smartest question to lead with.*

He gives me a knowing look, and I put my hands under the table, running my suddenly sweaty palms over my leggings.

"You kind of freaked out when Allana came over to say hi." He shifts on the carpet, facing me a little more.

"I hope the words 'understandably so' are about to leave your mouth next?"

He nods and remains quiet for a few seconds too long. "I wanted to introduce you."

The scoff that leaves me can't be stopped, and I shake my

head. "You wanted to introduce me to your ex-girlfriend and her family?"

"Not necessarily her, but her parents, yes."

I gape at him. "Do you not see how fucking odd that statement alone is, not to mention the actual act of doing so?"

Alister nods again, his gaze falling to his lap briefly. "I do, but…they're important to me."

My eyes slide his way, and I want to ask him what that has to do with me, but that's just me being pissy.

"Her parents were there for me when I didn't have anyone," he shares. "You know they didn't even know she was pregnant until I flipped out and accused them of tricking me into coming here."

I'm not sure I want to talk about this, but the topic isn't as uncomfortable as it used to be.

Is that progress or something else entirely?

I swallow. "Did they trick you?"

He shakes his head. "No. They were just excited that I loved her so much I was willing to risk my football career to be with her. Once they found out she'd been lying to all of us, they offered to take out a second mortgage to cover my tuition if I wanted to try to transfer somewhere else."

"That was nice of them."

He smiles slightly, propping his chin on his palm. "Can I ask you something?"

Unease washes over me, and I fold my arms over my knees, shrugging a shoulder.

"Do you think you would be with Brady now if I didn't screw things up?"

I tense, gaze narrowing. "What…what kind of question is that? I mean, how would I even answer? You and I would either still be together, or we wouldn't, and who is to say what would have happened after? I'm not a cheater, if that's what you mean."

"It's not." He watches me closely.

228

Too closely.

I shoot to my feet, taking quick steps into the kitchen, and I hear him move to join me.

"I guess I'm just wondering if there has always been something between you two." He comes around the little bar top, leaning back against the counter as I take a soda from the fridge and pop it open.

Turning away from him, I take a few small drinks.

I guess that's a fair question when you think about it. He knows I've known Brady for forever. Just like him and Allana.

Of course, he has no idea what Brady and I have isn't real.

I mean, what we are to each other is real, but *we're* not.

That makes sense, right?

Suddenly, there's a hard chest at my back and I tense.

Alister is my height, so when I look over my shoulder, I don't have to tilt my head up to meet his eyes like I do with Brady.

"What are you doing?" I rasp.

His hands finds my hips, and I drop my gaze to my sock-covered feet. "Cameron," he whispers, his forehead falling to the back of my head. "Am I too late?"

For what? I want to ask. Isn't it obvious he's too late? He thinks I'm dating Brady. Should that not answer his question?

He doesn't know we're fake. That all the times Brady and I have kissed, Brady felt nothing.

I mean, *we* felt nothing.

Fuck, I can't think with him so close.

I spin, pressing my arms to his chest.

The door swings open and my head snaps left, eyes locking on a pair of brown ones.

Brady freezes there, an *oomph* sounding behind him, followed by laughter.

"Brady, what the heck," Ari chuckles. "Move."

He doesn't move. His eyes move from mine to my hands. I look down too, realizing they are still plastered to Alister's chest.

He's still holding on to my waist.

I tear away and fly backward so fast I nearly slip, catching myself on the counter behind me.

Ari snakes around Brady then, smiling until she looks this way. Her face falls.

"Oops," she mutters, but then her keen eyes take in the scene, narrowing as she looks between us all.

I don't know what the fuck she sees because I can't even figure out what I see.

"Hi," I say lamely. "We were working on our class project."

Brady nods, his expression smoothing out to one of impassiveness, and I decide I hate that look on him. He looks away, not acknowledging Alister at all, and walks into the space. He sets a few bags down on the counter and turns back for the door.

"I was just carrying these up," he says, his hand on the doorknob. He takes a step, and panic flares in my gut, my stomach sucking in, but then he stops.

I let out the breath I didn't know I was holding when he looks over.

His grin is instant. "Call me when you're ready for our date."

My brows snap together, and he yanks his head forward, breaking eye contact as he walks out, closing the door softly behind him.

Date?

We don't have any plans tonight...

It hits me then: He only stopped to say something to keep up the façade, because it would be weird if a boyfriend saw another man—an ex at that—in his girl's dorm room and just left without a word.

He had to say something, or the ruse would be over.

He didn't care that Alister was in here alone with me or that he saw me with my hands on the man's chest.

I mean, why would he?

Better question...

Why do I feel like he should?

Ari walks into the kitchen, smiling tightly as she squeezes past Alister, who moves back to where his bag is. He starts to put his computer away, and Ari's eyes snap my way, eyebrows lifting in question.

"Want me to go?" she whispers.

"No. We just finished," I whisper back, my attention moving to Alister just as he steps this way.

"I'll see you tomorrow?" he asks with an unmistakable hopefulness that makes my stomach clench with unease. "I could get you coffee, and we could walk over together?"

"No, I'll be out already. I'll see you in class."

With a final nod, he slips out the door, and I groan loudly, dropping my head onto the counter.

"I can feel you staring at me," I mumble into my arms.

"Do you have anything you want to share with me?" she says slowly. "Maybe something you need a little help working out?"

Do I?

I shake my head no.

"Are you sure, Cameron?" There's worry in her tone, and something tells me it's not all for me.

I stand, nodding again, and avoid her gaze as I move into my room.

I crawl into bed, hitting my pillows and flipping them over several times to try to find a comfortable position, but apparently there isn't one.

Maybe I need a heated blanket.

Maybe you need a warm chest to sleep on.

The thought stops me cold, and I moan, throwing all the pillows onto the floor.

I tug the blanket over my head and sigh.

Yeah, okay.

Sleeping alone suddenly sucks.

And the next few days don't get any fucking better.

231

I'm sicker than a fucking dog.

I frown at my word choice.

I know it's something I've heard my family say a thousand times over, but what does it mean?

"Jesus, Cameron," I groan. "You're clearly bored to shit."

I sigh, kicking my covers off and flipping onto my back.

I hate feeling like shit.

To make matters worse, Ari and the others followed the team bus out of town yesterday; they're playing a team that's only a six-hour drive up north. It was a morning game today, but Ari, Paige, and Payton decided to stay one more night so they could take Deaton to the zoo tomorrow. The boys should get back in later tonight sometime, though.

Picking up my phone, my finger hovers over Brady's name, but I'm not sure why.

We haven't talked much since Wednesday, what with me being home sick and him hitting the road Friday afternoon. When we did, his responses were pretty basic. I haven't bothered him today because I didn't wake up until a few minutes after the game started and after another few hours of in-and-out, shitty sleep, I figured he was knocked out on the bus. On the chance that he was, I didn't want to wake him. It's hard enough to sleep on that thing from what the boys have said.

I text Ari back, letting her know I'm fine and not to have too much fun without me. Just as I let it fall on my chest, it starts to ring, the dorm RA's picture flashing on the screen.

"Hey, Cameron," she chirps the second I answer, and I cringe at her chipper sound. Love her, but my head feels like it's made friends with the concrete.

"Hey, Frankie. What's up?"

"Mrs. Garrett is here to see you again. You in?"

I smile, slowly peeling myself from the bed. "Yeah, send her up, please."

She hangs up and I quickly go pee, pulling a robe on over my Hello Kitty sleep shirt. I lost the shorts at some point, and she doesn't want to see that.

There's a soft knock on my door just as I shiver my way into the living room.

I pull the door open and Granny Grace smiles at me, thrusting a bag into my hands. The contents are warm, and I sigh. "More soup?" I ask hopefully.

"Chicken noodle. The noodles are in a little baggie. Take what you think you'll eat, put it in a smaller bowl, and add what you want to that. If you put all the noodles in now and don't eat it, you'll be left without a drop of broth."

I smile at the woman. "Thank you, Granny Grace, but you didn't have to do this. Yesterday was already a surprise and too much."

"You think I'm too old to ride an elevator and pass a piece of Tupperware?" She raises a white brow.

I chuckle and she winks.

"Enjoy, honey. Hope to see you back this week. The kids miss you." She turns around, and I smile after her, softly closing the door when she leaves.

I grab a spoon and head to my room, too lazy to do what she suggested. I only get a fraction of the way through it before my stomach starts to turn and I'm rushing to the bathroom and getting sick.

I drop my head back against the wall with a sigh. "This blows."

I close my eyes, and I must fall asleep like that because the next thing I know, warm hands are pressing against my forehead.

My eyes peel open, and I blink tiredly into a pair of worried brown eyes.

"Hey, Cammie Baby," he whispers, stretching past me and turning on the shower.

"Hey, Big Guy." I smile weakly, reaching up to touch him but then recoiling when I remember my hand was all over the toilet bowl.

He chuckles lightly and wedges himself beside me on the floor, pulling off my socks.

It feels heavenly, and I sigh, closing my eyes again.

"How long you been sitting here?" he murmurs, pushing my hair from my forehead.

I shrug against the wall.

"You take anything yet?"

"Tylenol last night."

There's another shuffle, and when I open my eyes, he's walking out.

A few minutes later, he's back with a water bottle and a little plastic cup with something purple in it.

"No…"

"Yes," he says sternly. "It'll help."

"But, Daddy, no." I whine some more.

Brady chuckles again, and a small smile pulls at my lips. "Keep it up, Hellcat. I'm not above a good ass-smacking."

"I bet you're not," I tease. "I bet it's one of your favorite things in bed."

"Wouldn't know," he mumbles under his breath, but then he looks up with a grin, and it makes mine grow, my head hanging to the side a bit. "This is how I thought Sunday morning last week would go, but you haven't even been drinking and you're puking."

"I didn't get sick that night."

"I know. I was there," he replies. "Thought for sure you'd be praying to the porcelain god by dawn."

"Meh." I shrug, and my eyes drink in the sight of him as he bends again, holding the nasty-ass liquid in front of my face. "I wasn't even that drunk."

His eyes snap up to mine, narrowing, searching. "No?"

What is it you're looking for?

I shake my head, and he holds my stare a moment.

I pull in a lungful of air and cringe, looking at the offending liquid.

"All right." He pushes closer. "Come on, girl. I've got water right here, but you need to take this, and you need to hold it down."

I groan, about to push him away when his eyes harden.

Why is it hot?

That's weird, right?

My mouth opens, ready for him to pour what he wishes inside.

OMG. Okay.

Do not picture his pierced dick while he's about to slide something warm into your mouth.

Thank fuck for my fever, as I'm pretty sure my cheeks are on literal fire.

"You good?" he asks worriedly.

I nod, and he tips the cup into my mouth.

I choke down the liquid, accepting the water he offers quickly. With a groan, I swipe my mouth with the back of my hand. "Why is that shit so nasty?"

He doesn't respond, just nods, staring at my mouth, a small, almost prideful smile tugging at his lips as he processes that I did as he asked. "Okay, next is a shower. Can you stand up?"

I nod, holding my hand out, and he tows me up gently, his arm going around my back to steal a quick hug.

I close my eyes, breathing him in, but he pulls away too quickly, and my lungs feel a little shorted.

"Climb in, but don't turn the water any hotter. You need to cool down a little."

I don't argue, aware I likely smell like a frat house the morning after initiation, and shrug out of my robe as the door closes behind him. My shirt is next, and since I didn't have any panties on to begin with, I step inside.

My muscles clench, back aching at the first spray of the water against my skin, but after a moment, it feels nothing short of amazing.

The sheer amount of sweat covering my body is disgusting, and I pull on all my strength to wash effectively, working on my hair last. I let the conditioner sit for a minute, then just lean my head back and let the pressure of the spray do all the work getting it out.

I climb from the shower, too weak to do much but pat at my hair and quickly dry what I can. I slip back into my robe and shuffle out.

The moment the door opens, Brady calls from my room, "In here!"

I move in, expecting to find him lying down, but when I enter, he's fluffing the last of all eight of my pillows. My eyes fall to the pile of blankets on the floor and move back to the bed.

The plum-colored sheets have been stripped, replaced with my white-and-lavender set.

Brady pulls the blankets down to the foot of the bed, revealing the matching lavender sheets. Looks like he even changed the mattress pad out for the brand-new one I had at the top of my closet. I haven't changed that since I moved in.

Finally, he looks back, doing a double take when he realizes I'm just standing here staring.

"You gonna come sit down or what?" he teases, patting the puffiest pillow settled against the headboard.

I want to run and jump into the pile. There is nothing better than fresh bedding, except maybe fresh bedding *and* freshly shaved legs. But we won't talk about that right now and if I try to run—even two steps—I'm afraid I'll get sick.

I walk over, climbing into the pile of pillows, and my eyes close on a heavy exhale, but then Brady is hauling me up.

"Don't be mean. Let me sleep," I whine, and he chuckles, settling in behind me.

"Almost. Just gotta brush your hair."

236

"Fine." I pout.

He gathers my hair, making sure it's all hanging down my back, and I wait for him to hand me the brush, but he doesn't do that.

Starting at the tips like some kind of professional, Brady begins combing through the tangles in my hair. Little by little, he moves higher in the length, until he makes his way to the scalp.

He's gentle around my face, brushing it back in a slicking motion and working through the length. He does this over and over, the bristles of the brush a massage against my scalp.

"God, that feels so good," I moan.

His hand slips slightly, scraping the edge of my ear, and I yelp, making a throaty chuckle leave him. "I think the tangles are out now. Ready to get some sleep?"

I nod, though I'm not sure I'm all that tired. I feel exhausted, but I've done nothing but sleep all weekend. Terrible, tossy-turny sleep, but sleep nonetheless.

Brady kisses my head and stands, jerking his chin for me to move up to the pillows.

"Wait." I reach out, gripping his fingers in case he tries to go. "You're leaving?"

He raises a brow, his hand turning in mine until our fingers are laced together. "You think I put clean, germless sheets on for your sake?"

I press my tongue behind my teeth to fight a smile, scowling playfully.

"All right, fine, that was all for you, but no, I'm not leaving. I do need to shower, though, and I can sleep on the couch if you want your bed to yourself. I just need to be here to make sure you're good." He reaches out, running his knuckles along my forehead before putting one under my chin, tipping my head up so he can look at me better. "Too many days alone. You're dehydrated."

"I don't want to sleep alone, but I don't want you to get sick," I admit.

"Let me worry about me, all right?" His voice is almost a whisper.

His fingers squeeze mine, and then he turns and walks out of the room, the door to the bathroom closing a moment later.

I drop back onto the pillows with a sigh, stretching my hands until I can reach the remote on the bedside table. I flip through some movie options, but nothing catches my attention, and I decide Brady can pick.

My eyes move to the wall on the left. He's on the other side, clearly having come here straight off the team bus. I'm sure he showered after the game, but there's something about a long car ride that demands another rinse.

It was sweet of him to come by but not surprising. He's always looking out for us girls. Well, I guess we all look out for each other, but Brady's just…different. Better.

Speak of the devil, Brady walks in, black boxer briefs and a white tank top stretched tight against his skin.

"Okay." He sets his dirty clothes in a pile and plops down, eyes closing and a long sigh leaving him the second he does. When his eyes open, they rise to meet mine, a smile on his face. "Hi."

"Hi," I laugh lightly, looking at his wet hair. I want to smooth it from his forehead, run my hands along his fade, and see how it feels when it flits across my palm. So I do exactly that, smiling at how soft it is against my fingers. "Good game today. Still leading in stats, my badass baller."

He rolls onto his stomach, propping himself up on his elbows. "You watched?"

"Of course I watched. You know we always watch."

"Yeah, but no one was here with you, and you're sick and… yeah."

I narrow my eyes teasingly. "And yeah, what?"

Brady shrugs his massive shoulders, the depths of his muscles somehow looking even more defined, but there's a hint of tension tugging at his brows that gives him away.

"Brady?" I push.

"Nothing, it's just Mason was back in the game tonight and whatnot, so…" Another shrug.

"Whatnot so…what?" *What's he getting at?*

He nods, slowing bringing his eyes back to mine, and when they lock together, his gaze pins me there. "And Alister was sidelined the entire game."

I push up on my hand, tugging his hair a little harder than necessary. "Are you for real right now?"

He holds my gaze, a steady blankness to his own, but he can only manage it a solid three seconds and then he's laughing, his head dropping to the blankets before looking back up with a grin. "Sorry, couldn't help it."

"You're an ass." I shove him but he doesn't budge, flipping over and laying his head on my lap as he snags the remote.

"Movie to watch or movie to fall asleep to?"

"Aren't you exhausted?" I ask.

"I slept on the bus but can pass out if you just want to turn it off?" He looks up at me from his place in my lap.

I never noticed how long his eyelashes are. And dark compared to his dirty-blond hair color. "Nah, let's watch something. I've basically slept for two days."

A small crease forms between his brows. "The medicine help at all yet?"

"I think so. The shower definitely did."

"Good." He nods, looking over my face.

"Did you bring the medicine with you?"

He nods. "Grabbed it at the gas station on the bus's last stop."

Warmth flows through me at his thoughtfulness, and I settle back onto the pile of pillows. Brady turns to the TV and hits Play on a movie.

"Should I order something to eat?" he asks, getting comfortable.

"I don't think I can eat much right now, but I did have something earlier." When he looks up at me, I tell him, "I had to call in at the day care, and Granny Grace made me some soup. Twice actually."

"That was nice of her."

"Yeah, I'm her favorite so…"

Brady scoffs playfully. "Course you are. You are a notorious teacher's pet."

"Hey, all you gotta do is smile a little, give a compliment here and there, and bam."

"Pretty sure if I did that here, they'd think I was hitting on them."

I chuckle, taking a small drink of water when he passes me a bottle with the lid off. The coolness feels so good along my heated throat. "Yeah, it's a little trickier when you're an adult being taught by hot adults."

His eyes snap my way, narrowing. "Whoa, what? Who?"

"Professor Falcon. He was my English professor first semester. The man is *fine*."

Brady glares.

"What?" I grin. "I didn't say we hooked up but…I'm not saying I would have regretted it if we had."

"Cameron Cox."

A loud laugh leaves me. "Wait, have you ever slept with an older woman before?"

Brady instantly looks away, and I gape at him, wiggling until I can slide free, and his head hits the pillow. I'm on my knees, shoving at his shoulder in seconds.

"You filthy boy, you have, haven't you? Was she good? Like better than girls our age? Did she want to go all night like they make cougars seem in the movies?"

"Oh my god," he chuckles, shifting and looking over at me without turning his head my way. Only his eyes. "Quit it. No, I haven't slept with an older woman."

"Okay, fine. You haven't fucked one, but have you hooked up with one?"

240

"No."

My shoulders fall. But I nod. Makes sense. His mom isn't exactly old, so that might be weird for him. I gasp, waggling my brows. "Okay, so how old was the oldest person you slept with?"

"We are not doing this."

"Oh, come on! It's fun."

"No," he scoffs a stiff laugh. "Not fun. Keep it up and I'm sleeping in Ari's room."

"Her bed sucks. You'll be back in mine in minutes."

He shakes his head. "You're annoying."

"And yet you missed me."

He looks over, now sitting up beside me. "Yeah," he says quietly. "I did."

A sudden shyness washes over me, and I look away, fighting a grin as I focus on the TV, pretending I don't hear his throaty chuckle that follows.

Brady grabs some snacks from his bag and sets them between us. I pick at the crackers a bit, leaving the Skittles to him.

After a while, he moves them aside, his arm coming to settle on the pile of pillows at our backs, and I lean into his side, curling my legs up.

He's got the blankets tugged up to his hips, so I grab a handful of the down comforter and tuck it under my chin to get even more comfortable.

His hand comes up, and he touches the back of it to my forehead, checking to see if I'm warm. He doesn't say anything, but his lips slide across the same spot a moment later, and I smile to myself.

Guess the fever has finally broken.

My neck starts to hurt after a while and I stretch, turning onto my back, noticing his feet are hanging off the bed with all the pillows we've got stacked.

I sit up, and he pushes onto his elbow, looking at me in concern.

"Come on, let's scoot up so you don't feel like the big bad wolf lying in Grandma's bed."

He smiles, sitting up, and we toss several pillows to the floor.

He scoots back first, his eyes closing with a sigh as soon as he's settled.

I knew he was getting tired. I dig around in the blankets, searching for the remote.

"Woman. Get up here."

"I can't find the remote." I flip the edge of the blanket up, looking around near his feet.

"Leave it. The next movie will play automatically."

"I was going to turn it down so you can sleep—ah!" I cut off with a squeal when he flies up, his arm coming around me and hauling me into his chest.

He shifts slightly so he can tuck me beside him. The movement has his hand slipping along my fluffy robe. It slides through the fold where it's tied closed, and we both freeze when a gasp leaves me.

His hand is massive, fingers reaching my ribs, the edge of his thumb frozen in the place it landed—*right beneath* my nipple.

"Cameron," he rasps, and my toes seem to curl.

"Y—" I swallow and try again. "Yeah?"

"Are you naked under this?"

"Yeah…"

Neither of us moves, and we sure as hell don't speak.

But then Brady's forehead falls to the side of my head, his lips right above my ear. His breath is so warm as it fans over my neck that goose bumps erupt, tickling along my flesh as they spread all over.

"Can—" he begins but says nothing else.

I can't find any words, unsure of what's happening here but too curious to move.

Slowly, his thumb skates higher, the textured pad a featherlike touch against the bottom curve of my nipple.

242

My cheeks flame when it starts to pebble from the tiny bit of attention.

His swallow echoes in my ears, and my pulse thumps in response. His thumb stretches a little higher, and he finds what he was looking for.

His muscles clench under me, fingers along my ribs twitching.

"Barbell," he murmurs, more to himself than me. He explores the jewelry further, his thumb no longer on my breast, but I feel the slight movement of the piercing. "And...spikes?"

I chew on my inner lip, nodding.

A throaty sound leaves him, and this time, his touch is more sure, more deliberate as he presses at the little spike, his thumb dragging across my hardened nipple to the other side.

A low, pulsing need flares in my core, and my heart beats a little faster.

It's confusing. It's invigorating.

"Are they... Do they stay this way?" He glides his finger along the underside of my nipple.

Hard. Do they stay hard, that's what he's asking. My neck burns in embarrassment, because no, no, they do not.

He made them hard.

But I mean, so does the cold, so it's not that big of a deal. Right?

He nods against my head, a soft hum in his throat that tells me I'm wrong.

He likes that he's made them stand to attention.

He lifts his head then, and I can feel his eyes burning into my cheek, but I don't look away from the TV. No idea what's on it, but that's where my eyes remain glued.

His hand leaves my skin, and my chest hollows, willing it back.

And then he flicks my nipple ring.

My entire body spasms, my gasp mixed with a strangled moan loud in the room.

Brady stays perfectly still for a moment before slowly pulling his hand out of my robe.

He grips my hips and shifts me until I'm facing the wall away from him and lies down, pressing at my upper arm for me to do the same.

I do.

Closing my eyes, I try to hide the way I'm breathing, but it's hard when it's stuttering and fast.

It takes an embarrassingly long time, but I manage to calm my heart rate back to a reasonable level, and I no longer feel his harsh exhales in my hair either.

Natural reactions, that's all.

I'm lying so stiffly, so I try to stretch a little, shimmying back, but Brady's hold on my hip turns to steel, pinning me in place.

"Don't," he rasps. "Stay right there."

My pulse thumps, so easy to read between the lines—I can't scoot back because if I do, I'll feel him.

I'll feel him because he's *hard*.

I swallow, shifting, but this time so I'm lying on my belly, and slowly, he lets me go, his arm sliding beneath my pillow.

We lie there for several long minutes, and finally, sleep starts to set in again.

"Thank you for coming over, Brady."

"Don't thank me for taking care of you."

I smile to myself, finding his hand under the pillow and pressing mine against it. "You're really good at it."

"Good. Then you know what you should expect from a man," he says quietly. "If he's anything less than that, he doesn't deserve you. He's not worth calling yours."

Something stirs in my chest, and I welcome the warmth it brings. Eyes closing as I burrow deeper into the pillow. "Good thing I already have a boyfriend, then, huh?"

"Fake boyfriend, Cammie Baby," he murmurs. "Make sure you demand the same from the real one."

I try to turn over to face him, something inside me driven with the need to see the expression on his face in this moment, but his arm comes around me again, holding me still.

"Sleep," he whispers.

I try. I really, really do, but it's not working.

I have no idea how long it takes, but his breathing grows deeper, and a wave of gratitude hits me.

This man had to be exhausted from two days of travel and a hard-played game, yet he still came here to make sure I was okay.

He's always there. So attentive.

So responsive.

Cameron. Stop. Jesus.

Brady is asleep, but sleep is the furthest thing from my mind.

I'm overheating and losing the battle with my willpower—or lack thereof.

My eyes stay shut, but my mind is in marathon mode and shows no sign of slowing down. It's full force ahead with no finish line in sight.

I have no idea how much time passes, but his every exhale rolls over my skin. It's warm and enticing, a tingling sensation that starts at the nape of my neck and prickles its way down.

Suddenly, I'm not just warm and cozy.

I'm hot all over, and this time, it has nothing to do with a fucking fever.

My body, it's aching, my pussy begging to be put out of her misery, the need his mouth created doubling down with the feel of his bare legs tangled with mine.

God, what would he say if he knew? What the hell is wrong with me?

This is Brady!

My Brady.

Maybe it's not about him exactly but more my body's natural reaction to being touched. To be fair, it has been a while.

My eyes flick open at the thought.

Oh my god. It's been a hot minute for me, yeah, but I've gone months without sex, and it was no big thing, but Brady?

This must feel like a lifetime to him. It has to be some sort of record for my insatiable friend.

I wonder if he fucks his hand often.

Aaand now I'm thinking about him stroking himself, taking his thick dick in his massive hand and tugging the way he likes. I bet he's a firm-grip kind of guy. The kind who likes you to take him by the balls and squeeze while you bite at the tip—when giving head, I mean. I've got a long neck, so my head game is strong.

I wonder if I could take all of him.

OMG, off track. Stop thinking about deep throating the man who knows you used to piss your pants as a little girl.

I close my eyes again, letting out a long, controlled sigh in an attempt to send a wave through my brain that will wash the images flashing around away.

It doesn't help, and I drift back to thoughts of him pleasuring himself.

I guarantee he takes himself hard and fast but probably stops right before he's about to come, waiting for the burning to ease before starting all over again. Yeah, he's definitely that sweet, sweet torture type. The kill-me-softly sort of man.

I wonder if he's a cucumber or an eggplant. Straight and solid or curved and firm.

I bet he sounds like a wild animal when he comes, all throaty and chest deep and… *God, my god, Cameron, what the hell!*

Stop it.

Except I can't.

I can fucking see it, and when I close my eyes this time, the images only become more vivid. Brady with his head thrown back, that plump, plush lip—the color you get when you've been eating pomegranate seeds—between his teeth. Eyes screwed shut tightly and muscles clamping, every inch of his body primed and prepped for release. And right before he comes, his long-lashed eyes flick open, buttery-brown gaze locking on mine.

My core pulses, and before I know what I'm doing, my hand is between my legs.

I toy with myself first, the pads of my fingers brushing teasingly over my clit and making my toes curl. I ease a little lower, sliding one finger through my slit, and I bite into my cheek at the wanton feeling that blooms inside me.

Eyes still closed, I get lost in my imagination, my fingers swirling slightly, playing the torturous role tonight to match my fantasy of the man behind me.

My orgasm builds and builds, my arm starting to shake lightly as I seek out the release, ass cheeks clenching.

I imagine his lips dragging along my neck. They're heavy and warm. Perfectly puffy and a teeny bit chapped, creating a provocative, velvety bite. And he does bite. It's light, more of a graze of teeth as he tugs the skin of my neck into his mouth before sucking it raw.

A small sound escapes my throat and his hold on me tightens.

And I fucking freeze, ice shooting down my veins as my eyes fly open wide.

He's… Oh god, he's…

"Don't stop," he murmurs, biting again. Because it wasn't my imagination at all.

"Brady…" I start to shake my head.

His hand moves under the covers, gripping my hip, and my stomach hollows out.

"Shhh," he whispers, nose gliding along my neck until it's tracing the shell of my ear. I shiver at the feeling, fucking starved for this.

For him?

"It's all right. We're playing pretend, remember?"

"Pretend?"

"Mm-hmm." He pushes my hair from my face, and my eyes flutter closed again. "But this time, I'm not your fake boyfriend. I'm just a guy you met at the bar."

A croaky chuckle leaves me, my clit crying for attention. "The Brady I know would never allow me to leave with a guy from the bar."

"He doesn't know you're here, Hellcat. This is our little secret." He squeezes my hip, pressing himself closer. "He'll never ask you about this because he doesn't know…"

In other words, *we won't have to talk about this tomorrow.*

I should stop. I should laugh and own it and put a fucking pillow between us.

I don't do that.

I tip my head back, giving this stranger from the bar more access to my neck, and in turn, he takes my wrist and pushes it back between my legs.

Why is that so hot?

I wait for him to release me, but he doesn't. His fingers stay wrapped around my wrist, pushing so my touch can't possibly be featherlight but rather rough.

Closing my eyes, I give in to the need inside me. My fingers dance against my clit, swirling and pressing, and he licks along my collarbone, making me moan.

"Yes," he mumbles, biting and kissing and squeezing until I'm a shaking mess in his arms.

He takes my ear between his teeth, his free hand sliding under my pillow, palm swallowing mine and folding our fingers together.

A moan comes from deep within my chest and then he's gripping my chin. He turns my head, his warm mouth coming down on mine with a ferocity, his groans thick and heady.

I feel him harden against me, and I gasp into his mouth, choking on his tongue as he plunges deep inside. I press back into him and he allows it.

248

Heat licks across my spine, down my every limb, and they lock up, preparing for the big finale.

"Come, Cammie Baby. Come for me," he begs.

I come on command, body shaking and breath ragged as I tear free of his mouth, panting into the dark room as wave after wave crashes over me.

My eyelids grow heavy, exhaustion suddenly hitting me so hard that there is no time for embarrassment or afterthoughts about what I just did.

What *we* just did.

My eyelids flutter closed, the man behind me snuggles even closer, and in what feels like seconds, sleep wins out.

CHAPTER 29
CAMERON

"How, exactly did we get roped into this again?" Ari sighs, falling onto her back on the grass.

I laugh, pushing off the paper and sitting on my heels, paintbrush in my hand. "It's extra credit, and with the way my professor grades my written responses, I'm as good as fucked on my research paper. I need all the extra credit I can get."

"Okay, correction. How did *I* get roped into this?"

I stick my fingers in the clean bowl of water and flick it at her.

She squeals, rolling over and looking down at her top.

"You're lucky I just changed out the water!" I tease, dipping my paintbrush in it and shaking it around until it's a thick, cloudy blue.

I stare at the poster. Okay, so the words are a little crooked, but at least its drying fast. "Come on, let's finish the rest of the table and then fingers crossed this can be hung up."

"I'm ready for a burger."

"The burgers are for the high school kids."

"We didn't get burgers when we visited the school."

I pause, thinking back to our senior-year campus tour trip. "Oh yeah. But we got to eat in the cafeteria. That's way better."

"Yeah, but we were starved by then. Bet they get a burger *and* cafeteria trip at the end."

"You've got a real fascination with food lately, my dear. Don't skip your cardio."

"Fuck off," she laughs, tossing a crumpled receipt at me. "Okay, so candy in the bowls, flyers on the little stands, and what about the raffle basket?"

"If you can just go see if the boys have some tape we can use for the poster. That way, we know if we have to run somewhere else really fast or not. I'll get the rest going."

"Got it."

I dig into the wagon, pulling out the basket for the raffle, and add the final touches. Unfortunately, all Granny Grace and Junie had to offer for the campus visits starting today were diapers and other baby-related items. But we don't want to look like we're encouraging the youth to go out and have unprotected sex while they're here, so I vetoed that.

I may not have showed them the basket I did make though, that may or may not have a box of condoms in it.

I think it's hilarious, seeing as the brochures I'll be passing out today are for careers in child development. To be fair, Mason gave me a few swag pieces out of his prize box for the football team's toss-game giveaway, so there are some AU-related items. I kept the beanie for myself, but no one needs to know that.

I set the basket on the left corner of the table, the ticket box beside it, and grab the bowls for the candy. I tear one bag open, pouring it into the dish, then bite the other, trying to use my teeth to get the damn thing to open. I tug and tug, and the damn plastic finally gives. But it splits down the center, and the contents pour out before I can stop it, half of it rolling off into the grass.

I groan, dropping to pick them up one by one so no loose grass gets into the bowl.

Ari comes back, laughing at the sight, and drops down by me. "I'm gone for five minutes and bam, disaster."

"See? Proof I'm a mess without you. Don't leave me again."

"Cam..."

The soft tone of her voice has my head snapping up, and I laugh. "Oh my god, I'm kidding. I'm so happy for you and Noah.

Promise. I love that he's this mega rich boy now who can fly you out on the weekends to whatever bougie stadium he's at next. Goals, girl. Goals."

She smirks, narrowing her eyes playfully. "Liar. You hate traveling."

"But I love going on vacation."

"True, but you want a house with a big yard, and chickens with a dog best friend, and hot apple pie in the oven."

I glare at her. "I don't even like apple pie." I pause, adding, "But the dog-and-chicken-best-friend thing sounds legit."

Ari laughs loudly, and we drop onto our butts, picking up my mess.

But why did I have to pick single-wrapped Starburst?

We get everything settled, the horrible poster taped to the end of the table, and then take our seats behind it, just as a few waves of what look to be high school students walk down the path.

Ari starts playing on her phone, and I look around at some of the other booths, but it's the one a good hundred yards over that catches my attention.

The library booth, sitting right across from the football team's.

Brady's little library girl stands there, a big wicker basket in her hands. She's talking to another girl, and that one keeps looking across the way. Finally, she stands and gives the redhead a little push. She stumbles on her feet a bit, tucking her hair behind an ear as she crosses the walking path.

My eyes lock on to her as she moves, and I can't tell from here, but I bet her cheeks are blazing as she approaches her target.

Brady spots her rather quickly, and when he does, his smile is so wide, I couldn't possibly miss it.

He has a football in his hands, and he tucks it under his arm, stepping closer to her.

She's mini. A teeny, tiny thing. Pretty in every sense of the word. Her red hair is in a sweet, loose braid over her shoulder, and her dress, while formfitting, is long, the sleeves wrapping around her hands.

She lifts the basket a little, and his attention falls to what's inside.

He smiles again, reaching in and pulling out some sort of treat. He stares at her, saying something as he opens and makes a show of eating it.

Her gaze falls to her feet, so I can only assume he's being his usual flirty self. I wonder if he likes shy girls. This one is really shy.

"Do you think she's his type?"

Ari looks at me, confused, then follows my gaze. She watches the pair.

"You know, if Brady has a type, like if he met someone that made him want to date someone for real, do you think it would be someone like her?"

When she doesn't say anything, I look her way, finding her watching me closely.

I frown. "What?"

She opens her mouth but closes it, offering a small shrug instead. "Okay, so what do you mean 'someone like her'?"

"You know, shy. Sweet and…innocent." I swallow on the last word.

All things that I am not.

There was nothing innocent about what I did the other night.

"What makes you think she's any of those things?" Ari says, a sort of softness in her voice that has me looking her way, but strangely, she's staring at me, not the hot librarian girl…who is still standing there talking to Brady, by the way. "She could be a raging bitch."

An unexpected laugh leaves me, and I glance up, my eyes locking with Brady's down the path.

He lifts the hand still holding on to the other half of the treat—probably one she made with her great-grandma's secret family recipe—giving me a little wave.

We haven't seen each other much this week, and we've texted even less. He's been a busy bee this week, locked down with school and football.

He's told me so twice since he left my dorm the morning after I came to the sound of his voice, the feel of his touch. His teeth.

Do not blush, Cameron. He might be avoiding you a little.

Swallowing, I wave back, focusing once again on my friend.

"Anything you want to talk about?" she asks for the second time in the last couple weeks, but this time, there's a spark in her eye.

"No. Why?"

Ari nods, looks toward the guys again, and then stands. "All right, I have to go. Paige should be here to pick me up in a little bit."

"Have fun. Don't wear protection." I hug her and Ari laughs into my ear.

"Don't worry. I won't." She winks, waving as she walks toward her twin and the others to say goodbye.

It's technically a joke, but at the same time it's sort of not. After the loss she and Noah unexpectedly faced our freshman year, I can't think of a better way to close that part of their lives than by bringing in a new one.

A pang of sadness hits me, but I force it away, stand up, and start going through the wagon one more time, making sure I didn't leave anything in the bags that should be on the table.

Hands come around my waist a minute later, and I fight the smile threatening to take over because I know who it is without looking. His touch is that familiar.

"Try this." He thrusts a half-eaten cookie toward my mouth, and the smile that wanted to appear is long gone.

I don't want to try library girl's cookie. I can't bake. I don't care that she can and he likes it so much he wanted to show it off.

Jesus fucking Christ girl, what?!

Shut up.

254

I bite the damn cookie.

And then I gag, spitting it into my palm as Brady's shoulders shake in silent laughter.

"So bad, right?" He presses his cheek to mine before pulling away, and I turn to face him. "Anywhere I can throw this out without her seeing?"

"What makes you think she's watching you?" I raise a brow.

"Pshh." He smirks. "Don't you know what you've got here, Cammie Baby?" he teases, sneakily dropping the remainder of the cookie in the bag of plastic wrap in the wagon.

When I glance past him, sure enough, she is looking, but her head whips the other way the moment she sees that I am.

Does she not know he has a girlfriend?

Fake. Fake girlfriend.

I think I'm still sick. Or something.

Brady drops into the chair Ari vacated, and slowly, I lower into mine.

I feel a sort of tension, a small sense of unease that has been there a few days now, but I think I'm the only one.

Brady seems as cool as a cucumber sitting there in yet another AU football hoodie.

The morning classes start to let out, and soon the pathways are filled with students, both from AU and the high school visitors. An hour in, and we're nearly out of candy *and* flyers, *and* we have over a hundred entries for the raffle.

Yet another group of girls comes up, all smiles and giggles as they ask my table partner about careers in the child development areas.

Same as he's done the entire day, he gives me his full attention, his dimple gleaming back at me as he smirks. "Girlfriend, tell them all about it."

I fight a laugh, looking to the girls and the tight smiles that have now taken over their flirty ones. I simply lift up the candy bowl. "Have a piece. We're out of brochures."

We're not—they are sitting right in the center of the table, but they don't notice. They take their candy and gladly giggle their way away.

Brady chuckles once they're out of earshot, and I sit back with a sigh. "Holy shit. If you're bringing all this attention, I would hate to be the guys at the football table."

Brady frowns instantly. "Are you saying there's someone better-looking than me over there, 'cause I was voted fan favorite last year and I intend to win it this year too."

I smile, shaking my head. "You're insufferable."

"Yeah." He wraps his arm around me, kissing my temple. "But you like that about me."

I do.

"You know"—I look up at him—"having a 'girlfriend' might hurt your chances of that one."

His eyes move between mine, and then he says, "Worth it."

A comforting, pleasant feeling stirs within me at his words. His mossy-brown eyes hold mine a moment longer, and he opens his mouth to speak, but then his name is called.

He jolts, and we both look down the path.

His coach is standing there, his arms in the air in a gesture that can only mean *what the hell do you think you're doing?*

Brady chuckles and pushes to his feet. "Gotta go, but you're coming to the ice cream thing later, right?"

I nod and the smile he gives me…

Jesus, I'm fucked up today.

I think I need a side of vodka with my ice cream.

Little did I know, I was about to need *a lot more* than that.

CHAPTER 30
CAMERON

"Is it just me, or do the girls seem a little more feral than normal tonight?"

Payton and Paige look in the direction I'm staring, low laughs leaving them both.

"They are definitely hovering around the athletics station." Paige nods, taking a bite of her matcha ice cream. "But they do have the most topping options."

I scoff, leaning back on my hands and watching the women laugh and giggle with the guys. "You are so cute, sweet, and innocent, Paigey. They are not there for the toppings. They're there to see who they want to *be* topping."

Paige turns ten shades of red, and Payton chokes on her boring vanilla cone.

She wipes her mouth, smiling from us to the athletics table. "I say it's all about the hot dad. I don't know what it is, but guys with babies seem to draw the hottest of women."

"Mm." I nod. "Yup. It's catnip for our pussycats."

"Oh my god," Payton chuckles, and Paige is now the color of a tomato.

We look over again, laughing as Mason lifts Deaton up onto the chair and does his best to scoop a pile of sprinkles, half of them missing the girl's ice cream bowl and landing all over the table when he serves it to her.

She and all her friends giggle and make the universal *he's so cute* sounds.

Mason grins at his son, kissing his cheek before his eyes move this way. He winks at Payton, then goes back to serving ice cream.

"Are they working the table all night?" Paige asks.

"Nah." I look across the room. "Xavier and the other baseball players are already here. They should be taking over soon."

"Why did they decide on ice cream again?" Paige asks, digging into her jacket pocket when her phone dings. "Why not hot chocolate or something?"

"It's from the local creamery downtown. They donate pretty much everything. We got a few big tubs for the day care this morning too, and Junie was telling me about it."

Paige sighs, and I look over to see her frowning at her screen, chewing on her fingernail nervously.

"Hey," Payton says. "Everything okay?"

Paige looks at the two of us, her shoulders falling. "So I finally got the estimate on how much it's going to cost to fix the damages at my studio, and it's…insane. I was only able to buy it because it was in foreclosure, and with what I had left of my dad's life insurance after school expenses, I knew I could only afford to keep the lights on and pay property taxes until I graduate next year, but I was okay with that. Something like this didn't even cross my mind."

"You couldn't afford the insurance," I realize, and her eyes cloud with tears as she shakes her head. "Shit, Paige. I'm so sorry." I reach out, squeezing her shoulder.

"So does that mean you're going to have to let it go?" Payton asks softly.

Paige blows out a long breath. "You know how my long-lost grandfather just popped up out of nowhere?" We nod, and she lets out a sad, humorless laugh. "He says I have an inheritance waiting for me."

I turn toward her. "That's awesome." Payton gives me a quick look, and I rethink my answer. "I mean…that will help, right?"

Paige nods. "Yeah, it would."

"There's a but, isn't there?"

"A huge, massive *but*." She shakes her head again, stuffing her phone back in her pocket. "It's complicated, and I'm still trying to process what he's offering."

"I'm sure it will work out."

Paige nods, climbing to her feet. "I have to go. I have an early lesson tomorrow."

We nod, waving as she walks off, her head ducking as she passes the guys, who are all on their way over here.

"What was that about?" Chase looks in her direction, Deaton hanging half over his shoulder.

"Parental drama."

He only nods, passing the little man over to Brady, who passes him down the line until Little D is smiling and sitting beside his mama, a small bowl of sherbert in his hands.

Mason helps Payton pack up her things, buckles Deaton into his stroller, and they head off. Chase hangs around a little while but then makes his way over to the other side of the cafeteria, where the other football players who came out tonight are lounging.

Brady drops down beside me on top of the picnic-style table, leaning back on his palms to mimic my position. "Kind of crazy we've only got a year and a half left, right? Only one more of these things." He looks around. "Everything we do this year will be the second-to-last."

I bump him with my shoulder. "Getting all sentimental, are we?"

He gives a half smile. "I just want to enjoy it, you know? Before real life comes in and changes things."

Real life.

I swallow, the words twisting in my gut for some reason.

My gaze travels the room, and I smirk, shaking my head at all the team tables. Be it basketball, baseball, football, they all have a buffet of beasts hanging around——male and female. Hell, even the track team seems to have their own groupies.

I watch, chuckling when a girl slides her ice cream cone across one of the football player's lips, leaning in with a smirk to lick it off.

Behind her, I spot Alister. He's smiling and chatting with his teammates, his own bowl in his hands. Someone says something, and he throws his head back, laughing, the others around joining in. He glances this way then, doing a double take and catching my eye.

He smiles and I give him one in return.

From the corner of my eye, I spot Brady watching me, so I turn toward him.

"Want to get out of here?" I ask him.

He stares a moment, then nods, hopping off the table and tugging me to my feet.

We're headed for the exit when a few squeals catch our attention, and we look over to see a different guy dragging an ice-cream-covered finger down another girl's neck.

"Don't you miss that?" I tease.

"Nah." Brady shakes his head.

"Not even a little?"

He glances my way, his eyes on mine. "Not even a little."

"You sure? We can go somewhere off campus where no one knows about us, take home a couple strangers from a bar?" I tease, but the moment it leaves my mouth, images of the other night flash, Brady's words rolling through my mind with a heavy dose of desire.

His eyes flare as if he knows exactly what I'm thinking about, and he sinks his teeth into that bottom lip of his.

Fucking hot.

"I have been cockblocking you for nearly the entire season so far," I say suddenly. "Do you want a hall pass?"

His brows snap together. "I should whoop your ass for suggesting that." He lunges for me, drawing a scream from my lips as his arms circle my thighs and he throws me over his shoulder.

"Now shut it." He smacks my booty nice and hard. "'Cause what I want is all of them to watch me carry *my woman* out of here like a caveman."

I laugh, sliding my hands in his jean pockets, and let him carry my ass out while pretending I'm not enjoying the firmness of his own against my palms.

Shoes come into view as we pass the threshold of the building, and I look up, eyes locking onto a familiar pair for a split second before the door slams closed behind us.

Alister standing on the other side.

ALISTER

I crack my neck, then crack it again, shaking my limbs out as I pace back and forth in front of the training center doors.

With each passing minute, the sun gets higher in the sky, and every part of me grows even antsier. I couldn't sleep last night, and I knew this was where I would end up in the morning.

I've been out here, freezing my ass off since six a.m.

I look to my phone, my back muscles clenching—six thirty on the dot.

I blow out a long breath, rolling my shoulders. I've been patient, sat back and let her have even more space than I'd already given her, figuring that was all she needed—distance from the jerk who treated her like anything less than the prize she is.

Being it was me who screwed up, I knew I had to play by her rules. I was the one in the doghouse and she held the key to the collar that would set me free.

To be honest, after I sat back and forced myself to truly hear what she was saying when she told me she wasn't ready to talk, I understood. I was thankful she wasn't pushing me away completely. Staying away wasn't so bad; doing so didn't change much.

She and I had conflicting schedules from the day we started hooking up as it was—early mornings, late nights, and an occasional Sunday.

Of course, I did weasel my way into her class this semester so I could be close to her. That was sort of a dick move, but I just wanted to spend time with her like a normal guy instead of as someone she wished she never met.

Guess you didn't really give her much of that space after all, did you?

Shaking my head, I look to my watch and start pacing some more.

When she first put on her little show at that party, kissing Brady like that, I was pissed off—until I thought about it. Shockingly, I found myself relieved. Happy even.

She was "dating" one of the guys she had introduced to me in conversation as one of her "*band of overprotective brothers*"?

Perfect.

Great.

It was proof she still had feelings for me, and she was afraid of that fact—self-preservation at its finest.

So the girl whose forgiveness I was seeking had a guy who was overly protective of her pretending to be her boyfriend, in turn keeping the rest of the males of the species away from her while she learned how to forgive me? Couldn't have planned it more perfectly myself.

Only now, he's not just keeping her away from the other guys here who would love a chance with her.

He's keeping her from me.

Every time I want to go to her, he's there. Every time I'm with her, he shows up, and I don't necessarily think he's doing it on purpose. I think he just…wants to be near her.

He even calls when we're studying sometimes, and every now and again, I peek at her phone when she's texting in the middle of class. Often, it's his name I see at the top of the screen.

She smiles when she does this, but what kills me is the guilty look in her eye when she remembers I'm sitting beside her.

She has no reason to feel that, especially not where I'm concerned. We're not together. She has made me no promises—quite the opposite in fact.

So then, why does she? Where did this go wrong? What did I miss?

When did this thing between them go from fake to real because that's what's happened, isn't it?

The crazy part is I like the guy. He's been a huge help the last few weeks. He doesn't hold what I did to his friend over my head like he could, which says a lot about his character. It's kind of annoying, actually, how he seems to be a good guy under the wild-and-reckless-playboy persona he initially gives off. Unfortunately, I'm convinced that was what it was: a persona and one that does not fit the guy I see now that he's with her.

Maybe I'm overthinking everything. They've known each other most of their lives, so maybe all the calls and texts and routine hangouts are normal for their friendship and I just never realized because she and I didn't really get off the ground on the relationship side of things?

Yeah, that could be it.

I think of Allana and the years of friendship we had. We were together all the time; even on holidays, I would walk over to her house and spend the day there. We were best friends for years before love took its place. Is that what's happening?

Is he falling in love with her?

My muscles lock up.

He's falling in love with her.

A humorless laugh leaves me, my hands sliding into my hair and pulling. "Of course he is," I mumble. How could he not?

The doors are thrown open and I jerk away to not get nailed by them.

Mason, Chase, and Brady halt when they first spot me, then start walking again.

"What's up, Howl?" Mason says.

His animosity toward me—all warranted—is as good as gone. He's nothing but a good teammate toward me now, and that makes the shame about how I treated him when I first got here eat at me even more.

I really fucked things up for myself here at Avix U.

I offer Mason a tight smile, but my eyes slide to the largest of the three.

"Can I talk to you for a minute?"

Brady's eye twitches, but he cools his expression quickly. He passes his bag to Chase and nods for them to go ahead of him.

We watch them as they walk over to Mason's Tahoe, tossing the bags inside.

When I face him again, he's looking at me. He says nothing, likely aware of why I'm standing here and not about to make it easy on me.

"I'm going to go for her, Brady."

His face remains completely blank. The man doesn't even blink, and I force myself to keep talking.

"I'm going to talk to her and tell her that I love her. I'm going to beg her to give me another chance and I'm going to swear on my life that I will never do anything to hurt her ever again." I pull in a long breath, waiting for him to speak.

To tell me to fuck off and get lost. To tell me that she's his girlfriend and how dare I, keeping up the ruse—or allowing his panic at losing her to take over.

I'm even braced for a punch to the face.

I get none of that.

The man stares at me, hard, his eyes drilling into mine, the rest of him remaining expressionless. "Do you think she loves you?" he asks in an even tone.

"I know she could."

That gets a slight narrowing of the eyes, but he does blink then, and it's wiped away. Brady looks toward his friends, then back at me. "Trust your instincts, Alister." He heads toward the Tahoe.

"I know you're falling for her!" I blurt out.

Brady stops walking.

I wait for him to turn around, to tell me I'm out of line, out of my mind, or reading things wrong.

I *hope* he'll tell me those things.

He doesn't.

He starts moving again, this time in the opposite direction, ignoring his friends when they call his name.

CHAPTER 31
CAMERON

"Bye, Junie! See you Monday."

"Thanks for coming in for a few hours today, Cam. I know it costs a lot to get you out of bed before ten," she teases, waving as she pushes through the door leading her back to the toddler zone.

Smiling, I close the door behind me, happy the sleeves of this hoodie hang past my hands.

When Junie called me last night to tell me that not one but both of the new girls called out for this morning, I knew I couldn't leave her hanging. Unfortunately for me, I hit snooze several times, and when I finally dragged my ass out of bed, the only thing I had time to do was pull on a pair of leggings, some thick, scrunchy socks, and a hoodie.

My hair is on the top of my head in something that resembles a bird's nest, I've got bits of last night's mascara flaking along my lashes, and there was no time for coffee. I had to force myself to drink the nasty stuff Junie makes, and the only option I could scrounge up for creamer was some ancient powdery stuff that was so clumped together, it took several minutes in the cup to break apart.

Honestly, I'm not even sure the regular stuff works for me. I'm too used to a solid three shots of espresso in my drinks and a good half pound of sugar.

I glance at my watch; it isn't even eight thirty in the morning yet, and instead of heading home and crawling back under the covers like I had planned, I make my way to the café.

My shoulders fall when it finally comes into view and I see the line is out the door. "Why didn't I mobile order?" I pout to myself.

With a sigh, I fall in place behind the last person and pull out my phone to help pass the time. I text Ari.

Me: Hi best friend.

Her response only takes a couple minutes.

Bestie: Who died?

I scoff, snapping a quick photo of my ratchet-looking self, duck lips in full effect, and send it through.

Me: No one, asshole, but tell me what a good girl I am for waking up at five a.m.

Bestie: haha. I figured you would be tagging along.

She sends a wink face emoji.
Tagging along?

Bestie: Are you guys already on the road? If not, you should wash your face. And maybe brush your hair.

I can't even laugh and enjoy her teasing; I'm too confused. I hit the FaceTime button, officially prepared to be one of those people who walk around talking like it's not super fucking annoying.

She declines at first, and I start to type out my threat, but before I can pull the trigger on the Send button, her video call comes through.

She's sitting up in bed, a gray T-shirt—that is not hers—pulled over her. My eyes instantly go to the collar, where her hair is still tucked inside it.

"You ho-bag, you were naked, weren't you?" The guy in front of me looks over his shoulder, but I ignore him, staring at my best friend. "Where's Noah?"

Ari smiles tiredly, still tucked in what looks to be quite the lavish bed. She turns the phone his way, and sure enough, the man is shirtless, covers pulled up to his waist.

"Good morning, Cameron." He smiles, tugging so she's tucked half against his chest.

"You're naked under that blanket, aren't you?"

"Really?" someone sasses behind me, but I ignore them too, aware it likely sounds like a throuple thing going on here.

Ari puts a hand over her face, but Noah only chuckles, kissing her hair in that cute little way. It's such a lovers' thing to do.

"Wait, you're not in the truck. Is he on his way?" She yawns.

"Right. Back on track." I scoot a few spaces forward, finally inside the building now. "Who is going where and when, and why did you think I would be tagging along?"

A small frown builds on Ari's brow. "Mase said Brady was headed home for the weekend since it's their first bye week."

My head yanks back. "Home? Like to the beach house in Oceanside home, or home home, like to his parents'?"

"Parents'."

My mouth drops open. "What the hell? He didn't even tell me. I was just with him last night at the ice cream thing. He walked me back to my dorm and didn't say a word."

She glances at Noah before turning back to me. "I'm not sure, Cam. I called Mase to ask him something about Thanksgiving, and he mentioned it."

"When?"

"About an hour ago maybe?"

I lift my head. There are only two people in front of me now. I can practically taste the Caramel Cookie Crumble latte.

I groan, stepping out of line. "Love you, bye." I hang up, pulling up Brady's number.

It goes straight to his voicemail, so I hang up and try texting him instead.

Me: Where are you?

I start walking toward the gym, aware that it would have been his first stop this morning. I halt, looking in that direction.

But if he was going out of town, maybe he wouldn't make time for the gym. Knowing him, he got up super early and hit the road so there was "no wasted time."

OMG, he hasn't answered my text. Is he already on the road?

I call Mason, but it's Payton who answers.

"Hi. Love you, but where's your man?"

"In the shower. Everything okay?"

"Brady isn't there too, is he?"

"No, it's just Mason. Want me to ask him something?"

"No, it's all good. Thanks." I hang up and try the other.

Chase answers on the first ring. "Who died?"

"Why does everyone keep asking me that? I have woken up early before, you know!"

Chase laughs in my ear, and I glare at the wet grass as I take a shortcut around the English Lit building. "What's up?" he asks.

"Are you home?"

"I am, but I'm about to head out for a meeting in the business office."

I stop, brows drawing in. "For what?"

"Just some...you know, I don't really know. What's up, though? I'm walking out the door right now, but I can call you when I'm done if you need something."

"No, no." I shake my head. "But is Brady home?"

Chase is quiet for a few moments, and I have to look to the

screen to see if he hung up in his rush to leave, but we're still connected.

"Chaser."

"Uh…" There's some mumbling in the background, and then he says, "Nah, he's not here."

My eyes narrow, and I pick up the pace. "Who was that?"

"No one, just a teammate. I should be done in about an hour or so. I'll call you then, okay?"

I nod even though he can't see me and hang up the phone. I hold it in my hand in case it rings and make my way toward the football house because something tells me Brady is, in fact, there.

I'm just passing my dorm when a familiar voice calls out.

I look over to see Alister sitting on the benches not thirty yards from the entrance.

My stomach muscles clench with unease, and I'm tempted to tell him I can't talk right now, but he's already jogging this way. I don't want to be an ass, so I quickly text Brady one more time, telling him to call me, and look up just as Alister comes to stop in front of me.

"Hey."

"Hey," he whispers, glancing from my phone to me. "I, uh… You're up early."

A light laugh leaves me, and I nod. "Yeah. Junie needed someone there with her for the early morning drop-offs. The other girls bailed on her."

He nods, sliding his hands into his pockets. "Did you have coffee yet? We could go get one?"

"No, I—" I cut myself off, not wanting to mention the last twenty minutes to him. "Were you waiting out here for me or…?"

He nods, looking anywhere but at me. "Yeah, I, uh…" He meets my gaze. "I didn't expect you to be out this early."

"So were you just going to wait until I popped out?" I tease.

"Yes."

His instant response has my arms lowering to my sides, and

I clutch my phone tighter. "But I don't have classes on Friday," I point out. He knows this, since he memorized my schedule at the start of the year.

"I know."

"Some Fridays I don't even leave my dorm room."

He nods, not taking his gaze off me. "I know that too."

The air seems to thicken around us, and my toes curl in my socks. Unease slides down my spine, and I nibble at my lip, taking a subconscious, backward step.

"Cameron," he whispers, reaching out for me, and I freeze, watching his fingertips as they wrap around the sleeves of the hoodie I'm wearing.

He gives a little tug, and I stumble toward him, my free, hoodie-covered hand planting on his chest.

He pushes the sleeves up and presses our palms together, and I stare at where we're connected, noting I don't have to spread my fingers too wide to make room for his. His skin is soft, comforting, if a little cold.

His other hand comes up, sliding along my cheek, and a small frown builds over my brow.

"Alister." I meet his gaze, my lungs compressing in my chest. "What are you doing?"

"I have been trying to figure out what I wanted to say to you all night, and I thought maybe once I got here, it would finally come to me. Then I saw you walking by, and now that I'm standing here, I can't remember any of it."

"Alister…" I shake my head, shrugging from his hold.

He steps closer, but I shuffle again, putting the distance between us once more.

"We're friends," I breathe, my heart beating a little harder in my chest.

"No, we're not, Cameron," he murmurs, longing clear in his gaze.

"I have a boyfriend." It comes out a little weak, and he's shaking his head.

"No, you don't."

"I do." I clear my throat, and this time it comes out a little stronger. "I do."

"Then why didn't Brady say those same words to me when I talked to him this morning?"

My head yanks back, my frown instant. "What?"

Alister's shoulders fall, and he offers a meek smile. "I talked to Brady today."

My chest caves, and I press the hand holding my phone against it. I feel like I'm in the middle of a maze, hoping the next turn doesn't lead to the end.

The end of what, though, Cameron?

I swallow. "*What* did he say?"

"I told him how I felt."

"And what did he say?"

Creases form between Alister's eyebrows at my question, and his gaze searches mine for a moment. "He didn't punch me when I said I was going to come to you."

A broken laugh leaves me, though there's no joy in it. I feel...I don't even know.

Panicked? Confused?

My mind is muddled, and I can't make sense of any of this.

Alister reaches out again, cupping my cheek, but I don't lean into his touch this time.

My eyes begin to water, but I'm not sure why.

"Cameron," he whispers, leaning closer.

He's going to kiss me. I can see it in his eyes. He's going to kiss me, and I don't know if I'm going to stop him.

My eyes close, a tear warming my skin before the cool air hits it and makes me shiver.

"Cameron," he whispers again, his breath fanning across my lips.

My phone rings, and I jolt, looking down to find Mason's picture flashing across the screen.

"Hey." I answer immediately, turning to the side a little.

"He's turning onto Avix Street, about a mile from the green strip. He's gotta drive right past your dorm to hit the highway."

I nod. "Thanks. I owe you one."

"We'll cash in on that in the form of a toddler."

A choked laugh leaves me, and I sniffle. "Make it easy on me, why don't you?"

Mason chuckles, and I hang up, my gaze snapping to Alister's.

My smile is faint as I whisper, "I'm sorry but I have to go."

I spin on my heels.

"I love you, Cameron."

His words slam into me, and my feet freeze, eyes slamming closed. "No, you don't."

"But I do." The shuffle in the grass tells me he's coming closer. "And if you would just give us a chance, I know you could love me too."

My lip starts to wobble. "I have been honest and up front with you this entire time."

"I know." He nods. "I know but just think about it. Please."

Everything he's saying is the right thing to say. The problem is, it's not a chance he's asking for.

It's a second one.

His hands fold around my forearms, and he shifts us slightly. "Say something."

"I…" I stare into his eyes. It would be easy to give him one.

He says he's sorry. I know he is. I not only see it, but I can feel it.

He was hurting, and that hurt led him to make a poor decision. No one is perfect, especially not brand-new adults in a new place with new people and a broken heart.

He moves in again, and the look in his eyes is too much. They're the wrong color.

The wrong shape.

The wrong man?

273

My gaze moves over his shoulder, and instantly, a familiar truck a few blocks down catches my eye.

I shake my head, pulling away, and give his hand a little squeeze. "I have to go, Alister. I'm sorry but…" I don't say anything else.

I start jogging straight ahead, past the grass and through the parking lot that leads to the main road. Once on the sidewalk, I pause, trying to decide if I should cross or not.

He might not see me if I stay on this side.

I wait for the road to clear and dart to the other side.

He's at the last red light, but he's not looking this way. He's staring in the opposite direction. He's staring at my dorm building.

Thankfully, this light isn't a through street for other cars to cross but a walking path for students, so I run out into the middle of the road and wait.

BRADY

The hundredth fucking sigh leaves me, and I drop my head against the headrest, trying to clear my mind, but it's like a track is skipping, the same damn verse playing on repeat.

I'm going to talk to her and tell her I love her.

Fuck me.

Alister is in love with Cameron. Or at least he thinks he is.

I don't want him to be. I want him to say he's putting the ball down and walking away, waving his white flag of defeat. I want him to go away.

Jesus, Brady, what the hell have you gotten yourself into, man?

It's not like she and I could ever be *real*. Not when I've played into this fake persona the rest of the world has painted me as, and for what? To make things easier on myself? To not be the talk of the team? I'm far from ashamed, the polar fucking opposite in fact, but for it to come out now will make things worse.

How will she look at me when she finds out I'm so far from what she thinks I am?

When she finds out that the infamous playboy she's known all her life is pretty much a preacher's son?

A virgin at twenty years old. By choice, obviously, but what does that matter?

I'm a liar who hates lies.

I clench my eyes tighter and sigh. Not that she'd want to be with me anyway. I'm her friend.

We're *friends*.

Okay, but even if we did have feelings for each other, it wouldn't last. The fun and newness of having something real would wear off, and we'd fall back into the friend routine because it's what we know.

But then again, what do we do now that we didn't do before?

We laugh and have a good-ass time together, but that's nothing new.

I fall asleep holding her in her bed sometimes, but I've done that a hundred times in the past—probably literally a hundred with all the years we've been friends.

She's always had the most comfortable blankets, so no shit I picked her to bunk with when she and Ari weren't sharing a bed. It's not like it was some subconscious part of myself trying to show me what I couldn't see.

And yeah, we've kissed a few times, but not because we just had to fucking go for it. It was just…necessary—to prove a point to the guy she does have feelings for.

The guy who is probably with her right now, pouring his fucking heart out to my girlfriend.

Fake girlfriend.

I groan.

Fuck, man.

But we have kissed because we just had to, haven't we?

That night in her dorm, the way her body shook and the sounds she was making—there was no way I could pretend to stay asleep. I had to see her, touch her, fucking taste her.

"Shit," I hiss, scrubbing my hands down my face.

A horn blares behind me, and I jerk, my eyes flying open, my foot instinctively easing off the pedal. I start to roll, maybe a single inch, and then reality catches up to me, and I slam back on the brakes, eyes crashing into my favorite blue pair.

I throw my truck into park, tracking her movements, glued to her as she jogs over and yanks on the passenger door. Her eyes snap up to mine, blond brows raising.

"Fuck." I lean over, flicking the lock, and she tugs the handle at the same time as I pull it, helping her shove it open.

She climbs in, shivering slightly, and closes it behind her. She puts her seat belt on and blasts the heater, holding her fingers to the vent.

And I just...stare at her, mouth agape.

The horn honks again, and I jolt, quickly putting the car in drive, and start rolling right as the light turns yellow, trapping all the cars behind me at the light yet again.

"What..." is all I can get out, my head yanking from her to the road several times before I finally give up and jerk the truck to the side, parking in a red zone for just a minute.

We look at each other at the same time.

"What the ever-loving hell were you doing standing in the middle of the road?"

"Catching a taxi." She cocks her head. "If you were paying attention, you'd have seen my hand raised and everything."

She's teasing, the little brat, but for real, what the hell?

She should be with Alister right now, not sitting in the passenger seat of my truck.

"You should really get on the road if we want to beat the evening traffic later," she suggests.

I just blink at her, and she flicks off her little fur-lined boots, folding her legs beneath her. "Hold on." I raise my hand, taking a deep breath. "Who told you I was going home?"

"Ari."

I frown. "And how did Ari know?"

"She talked to Mason."

"And how exactly did *Mason* know?"

She shrugs. "Beats me."

"All right, and how did you know where to find me?"

"Mason has your location."

"Goddamn, we have some nosy-ass fucking friends, don't we?"

She laughs at that, and I just…watch her. The way it lights up her eyes, the curve of her lips, the way she nibbles at them as her laughter tapers off. "That we do, Lancaster. Now, are we going to get on the road or what? Because as you can see, I am the hottest of messes."

Damn straight you are. A beautiful mess.

I clear my throat, looking toward her dorm a moment before facing her again. "I'm staying the whole weekend."

"Cool."

"Not coming home till late Sunday night."

She grabs the blanket I keep in here for her and lays it over her legs. "Perfect, but can we stop for coffee first?"

A laugh leaves me, and I shake my head and lick my lips. "You sure you want to come?"

"Dead-ass."

"Did you… Have you…"

"Did I, have I…what?" Her eyes narrow slightly.

Talked to Alister?

Obviously, she hasn't. She definitely wouldn't be here with me if she had.

Would she?

I bite my damn tongue and decide not to tell her. She'll find out soon enough anyway. "You don't even have a bag."

"Please." She smirks, this time kicking her feet up on the dash. "I don't need a bag to go home. I got my phone, which has Apple Pay, and if by some strange coincidence my parents are gone the one weekend I come home, then I'll just borrow something of yours. Wouldn't be the first time I wore one of your shirts as a dress."

"No, it wouldn't."

See? Just doing things we've been doing for years. All's good.

She lifts her chin in triumph, tugging on the string of her hoodie.

My eyes fall to her chest. Correction, *my hoodie.* You know, the one that's resting against spiky-tipped barbells pierced through her perfectly plump nipples and that has my name and number all over it.

All over her.

She's officially allowed to keep it. In fact, I insist.

Oh no.

I shift in my seat.

Thank God I'm wearing fucking jeans.

I hold her gaze. "You really want to go home with me?"

"Sure, Lancaster, I guess I'll go with you. You don't have to beg."

My grin grows, and she gives me a playful little glare.

"But only if you get me coffee first."

A laugh leaves me, and I pull away from the curb.

"One Caramel Cookie Crumble with extra cookie and extra crumble coming right up."

She smiles and faces forward.

Ten minutes later, when we get into the drive-through line at the coffee shop, she scoots into the middle, and that's where she stays for the entire drive home.

My heart gives a little thump, like a fist bump from it to me, as a sense of rightness falls over me. I wouldn't want it any other way.

CHAPTER 32
CAMERON

"What the hell do you mean, you're going to the Bahamas?"

My mom laughs in my ear, and my jaw drops.

"Oh my god, it's starting, isn't it? I'm an adult child now? Just abandoned. Thrown to the wolves."

Both Ben and Tisha laugh, and I can tell Brady is dying for me to look at his shit-eating grin.

"Oh, honey, no, don't be ridiculous." Mom pauses. "Once you give us a grandbaby, then you can come on vacations with us again."

"Mom!" Now I'm laughing. "Well, I'll let you tell my dad that he'll have to wait a good ten years, *if ever*, to have his favorite ski partner on the slopes with him again, then."

"Oh, you're playing dirty, huh? Bringing out the big guns."

I smile. "Is Zeus at least in the backyard? He didn't bark when I knocked."

"No, he's been boarded."

"Boo." I pout. "Well, I guess I should tell you to have the best time, but next time you're hopping on a freaking plane, maybe let your daughter know?"

"Like you let us know you'd be driving down a highway all day today?" she teases. "No, honestly, we just got through security and we're waiting for a spot at the bar. We were going to call you once we got settled, but Ben and Tisha will take care of you."

"Yes, we will!" Tisha answers back.

"Fine. You're off the hook, but I fully expect to be in the car with you in December when it's time to head up the mountain!"

"Wouldn't have it any other way. Love you."

"Love you, bye." I hang up, finally looking to Brady to find his lips pinched to the side. "Go ahead, Big Guy, let it all out."

He does laugh then, putting his arm around my shoulders and hooking my neck in the crook of his arm. "Looks like it's a T-shirt dress in November for you. You're going to freeze your nipples off, summer queen."

"Brady!" his mom chastises. "You leave the poor girl's nipples alone. Last thing a girl wants is to have her headlights on during the daytime."

My cheeks are flaming, and Brady gives me a little shake.

"Hey, Mama, you got the ornaments dangling from your headlights yet?"

My eyes snap toward him, narrowing on the side of his face.

"Don't be silly." She waves him off. "It's not even December, but I'll get them on."

"You could put them on now."

I elbow him in the ribs in warning.

He ignores me, his tone silk fucking smooth as he says, "Cammie Baby, don't you like it when ornaments stay on headlights all year long?"

His mom looks over curiously, and my mouth opens and closes as Brady tries to hide his laughter in my hair.

Tisha tips her head in thought. "You know what? You're right. Maybe I'll get me some of those little eyelashes to keep on year-round. Thanks for the idea!" She walks away, none the wiser that her son's coarse hands have warmed my nipples.

Brady's shoulders shake with silent laughter, and I pull from his hold.

"I hate you," I hiss.

He slips up behind me, those big, strong arms coming around my waist, and he tucks his hands into the front pocket of his hoodie I'm wearing. His palms press into my lower stomach, and his shoulders are so wide compared to my own that he engulfs me completely, drowning me in his rich and spicy scent.

His lips find my ear. "No, you don't," he whispers, and I bite at the inside of my cheek to keep from smiling.

No, I really, really don't...

It seems being home has brought back the more playful Brady, the one that's been a little MIA as of late. I almost forgot the powers of his charm.

Or maybe it's just never hit the same as it does now...

I toss and turn for the millionth time, yanking the covers up over my head with a low groan just as there's a quick knock on the door, but he doesn't wait for me to respond before he's throwing it open.

"Oh, Cammie Baby," he singsongs, and I groan again.

Brady laughs and then the entirety of his weight settles over me.

"Go away, you big brute. You're gonna suffocate me," I whine, holding the blankets tight over my head because I know what comes next.

Sure enough, his fingers fold over the edge, and he tugs it down, forcing me to squint at the bright-ass room around me.

I pout and he smiles, all big and bright and Brady-like.

"Morning."

"What time is it?"

"Little after nine."

I'm already whining, pulling the blankets back up, but he doesn't let me, his grip tightening as he shifts his weight and swings his feet over the edge of the bed.

I look over, seeing he's already dressed and freshly showered like a psycho. "Who is dressed and ready this early on a Saturday?"

As if on cue, Tisha pokes her head in, smiling brightly. "Oh good, he listened." She beams, her little Suzy Homemaker self already as perfect as ever, hair blown out, makeup in place, and a cute little sweater dress on, with an apron wrapped around her waist. "Breakfast will be ready in twenty. Just waiting for my hash-brown pie to brown so I can start the eggs."

She disappears, and I sulk some more.

Brady chuckles, smacking my blankets as he climbs to his feet. "I'm going with my dad to pick up some firewood down the street, but we'll be right back. Raid my drawers for something to wear and don't judge if you find some dirty magazines hidden in any."

"Oh, please. Me and Ari found you guys' stash under Chase's deck storage when we were, like, fifteen."

"What?!" He gapes. "I gotta tell the boys. We always thought his mom found 'em and never said a word!" He's already moving into the hall as he says it, his phone in his hand.

My lips curve, but then I remember it's early and I'm tired, so I let out one last internal cry for my sleepless night, and I climb from the bed to hit the shower.

With a time limit on my head and the real Donna Reed downstairs, I make quick work of getting ready. Not like it's hard with limited options and zero makeup or skin care products.

There's no time to snoop around in Brady's childhood room, so I just scan for something that can work in the closet, knowing his sweats are an immediate no-go since they're far too big. I find an old hoodie with our high school logo on it and pull it on—why didn't I take the time to put a bra on before heading out to help Junie yesterday morning?

It's a charcoal gray and has been washed so many times, the inside isn't as soft as it used to be, but it's still comfortable, and when I push onto my tiptoes to look in the mirror over his dresser, I see the lip of the back doesn't cover my ass.

I sigh and try again, this time picking up one with some

camp logo on it, likely from some football training program they always seemed to join when it was offseason. I repeat the process, smiling when this one manages to hang low enough to not appear scandalous. The hoodie is a forest green, with a white-and-yellow logo, so I grab a pair of long white socks and tug them up, smiling when the tops reach mid-knee.

"This is actually kind of cute." I pinch my lips to the side in thought. "Now what the hell am I supposed to do about underwear?"

Finishing up, I hurry into the bathroom to use the toothbrush sitting on the counter, figuring it's for me, and brush my wet hair out, parting it down the middle. I search the drawers, finding some hair products, and smooth it through the crown of my hair, flattening the part to my head and sweeping it back in a perfect bun. It's the easiest hairstyle a girl can wear and still look like she tried.

I nod at my reflection and make my way down the stairs, the front door opening as I reach the last step.

Ben comes in, smiling my way. "She's alive."

"Yeah, yeah," I chuckle. "Need some help?"

"With the heavy lifting, when I've got a perfectly healthy six-foot-four and 259-pound son to do it?" He raises a dark brow. "Get your butt out of here."

"I'll have you know, I'm strong as shit, Mr. Lancaster."

"Sweetheart, don't *mister* me. It makes me feel old." He continues into the living room, and I smile as I head into the kitchen to see if Tisha needs any help.

She's dancing around to soft classical music, pulling a glass dish from the oven the second I walk in. She looks up and her lips stretch into a smile. "Perfect! And did I hear the boys get back just now too?"

"You did." I nod, looking around the table as she sets the glass down. "Is anyone else coming for breakfast?"

She waves me off with a laugh. "I know it's a lot, but it's

been a few months since I've gotten to make my baby breakfast. Besides, you guys can always take the leftovers back with you tomorrow. Have you heard from your parents? Did they make it okay?"

I sigh, taking a seat when she points at the chairs. "Yes, they sent me a picture of them drinking mimosas out of coconuts this morning."

Tisha smiles, taking a few coffee cups down, and starts filling them.

"Only two, Mama." Brady's voice reaches me, and just as his mom turns around, a frown on her face, a paper cup is set down in front of me.

I tip my head back, looking upside down at Brady behind me.

"It's not Caramel Cookie Crumble with extra cookie and extra crumble," he says. "But it is a Cookie Butter latte with extra caramel."

I blink up at him. "You know my drink from Bebe's Brews?"

"You thought not?"

"I haven't ordered one of these with you around since, what, the day we left for summer after senior year?"

He holds my gaze and I squash my lips to one side to hide a smile, but he sees it. Slowly, a grin makes its way across his handsome face. He winks and moves around the table, and call me Michael Myers because I stalk him all the way. I just can't look away.

He steps up to his mom, kissing her on the cheek as he steals a piece of bacon and makes a dash for it. As he clearly suspected she'd try, her arm darts out to smack him, but she misses...because her eyes are on me, a gentle heat stirring within me at the tenderness there.

"Well, okay then," she says quietly, her smile soft as she passes the other coffee mug to her husband, the two sharing a look before she turns to the fridge.

Brady drops beside me, looking down at my outfit. "That's the hoodie I got at camp the summer before we left for Avix."

"Mine now." I lift a shoulder, and he rolls his eyes playfully.

"Course it is. You're becoming a regular thief over there."

"Get used to it."

"Oh, I'm happy to."

I grin and he grins back. And then I remember there are others in the room and do my damnedest not to blush, but I really feel like I might. It's ridiculous but it's true.

I clear my throat. "You know, you guys were gone at camps way too much. You missed weeks of summer every year."

"Had the boys not gone to that particular camp, you girls never could have gotten away with sneaking off to Tampa that summer without them finding out." Tisha laughs. "They would have had a massive fit if they knew you girls were out there without them to watch over you."

"Oh yeah." Ben looks over. "Didn't your dad tell me something about a guy you met out there ending up being on the team with Brady?"

A stiffness curls along my shoulders, and for some reason, I peek at Brady. "Yeah, Trey Donovan." I nod, unease settling over me, though I'm not sure I understand why. I've never minded talking about him before, so why does it feel sort of wrong to do so right now? "He's...gone now, though. Drafted last year, like Noah."

"Impressive." Ben nods, taking the seat across from me, his wife settling beside him.

Brady clears his throat, reaching out to take a drink of water, and I wait to catch his eye.

"Thanks for this. You didn't have to make a stop just for me."

He shrugs, looking away as quick as possible. "We passed it on the way home. No big deal."

His dad laughs loudly, and Brady shoots him a small glare that has both my and his mom's attention, though neither of us says a word. I certainly don't point out that Bebe's Brews is not, in fact, on the way home from where I know they buy their firewood.

"Let's eat." Tisha claps.

And so we do.

We pile our plates high, and everyone laughs when I skip over all the protein options and go straight for the giant waffles in the middle.

They ask us about school, and Brady talks about the team's strategy for next week's game.

"What a lucky straw you boys drew getting your second bye week Thanksgiving weekend!" Tisha says. "And the fact that Noah's got a Sunday home game that weekend is like icing on the cake."

"I know, I can't wait." Brady leans back, holding his belly. "I'm beating Noah's ass at the turkey competition this year," he says.

His dad laughs. "It's crazy you guys are already taking over the traditions we had while you were all growing up. Makes me feel a bit sentimental to think about. I missed more than I'd have liked over the years."

"Good thing you retired this summer, then. There are still so many memories to be made." Tisha reaches out, squeezing his hand, and he leans her way, kissing her cheek.

"We never felt like you weren't around, Dad. We were proud of you, and you were always home for the important things." Brady's words leave me feeling soft.

I watch the exchange with a smile, catching Brady staring at me from the corner of my eye.

"You know you guys can still change your minds and come out to the beach house." I say this knowing it's already a done deal. All the parentals booked a weeklong cruise for the holiday.

"And be the only people there over thirty?" Ben smirks. "I think not."

"I mean, you really should have said over fifty, but I get it."

Brady and Tisha laugh, but Ben puts his hand over his chest, feigning hurt. It's such a Brady response, I can't help but break the

286

serious façade I was shooting for, my amusement joining in as I look from the man beside me to his dad.

"Man, Brady might not share your features, Ben, but you're basically twins with all your mannerisms. I swear he's one hundred percent you while looking nothing like you." I grin.

Ben nods, a tender smile on his lips as he glances across the table at his son. "He is, isn't he?" The pride in his voice is evident, and a warmth washes over me.

I turn to Brady. "I wonder if the cycle will repeat itself, and it will be the same way if you have a boy."

"It will," Brady says, a sureness in his tone. "He will be exactly the same."

The expression on Brady's face is one of pure gratitude, a deep-seated love only the luckiest are blessed with between father and son.

Ben's smile says the same as he holds his only son's gaze, his arm now wrapped around Tisha's shoulders, but there's a tension around his eyes as they move from Brady to me and back to his son. There's a question within them that, at first, I don't think he'll ask just as his mouth begins to open. "Brady...have you never told her?"

Brady tenses, and so do I.

"Uh, I mean...no?" His son clears his throat.

His dad's brow furrows, and Brady pushes on.

"Just another thing that's never come up," he mutters, and my head yanks his way.

Another thing?

"But the others know." His mom joins the conversation, and now my stomach twists with a sudden anxiousness.

"The boys, yeah." Brady stares at his dad a moment before looking to me. "There's no reason," he starts to tell me, a nervousness to him I'm not used to. "There's just never been a reason to mention it. The guys really only know because we went through a box of shit in the garage when Dad paid us to clean it out one summer. Chase found one of Mom's memory books and it had a picture of her and dad on their first date."

Reluctantly, I sneak a peek at his parents, not really following as I settle my gaze back on Brady. He looks to his dad for help.

But I can't stand the sight of that helpless expression on his face, not when he's the surest, most confident man I know. So I take us back to where we're most comfortable.

"Did Brady tell you he wants to be a Viking when he grows up?"

All eyes snap to me, and while it takes a second, everyone laughs, so I go into a whole explanation that is pretty much nonsense, but it gets the conversation flowing, smoothly shifting things until we're all laughing.

"Oh, honey, did the flowers arrive okay? You never said anything after you asked me to help you find a place."

Brady clears his throat and nods, shoving more food in his mouth.

He sent someone flowers?

There's a little kick in my stomach, but I ignore it.

The doorbell rings, capturing all our attention, and Tisha jumps up. "That's the contractor coming to take a look at the fence."

"I thought me and you were taking care of that winter break?" Brady says to his dad.

Ben shrugs, standing and collecting our plates in a pile. "Yeah, well, your mama thinks I'm too old."

"That is not what I said!" she reprimands. "I said our warranty would cover it and for you not to feel like your man card was pulled when a crew of twenty-five-year-olds show up to do the job." She smirks, spinning in her flats and heading for the door. "Leave the mess, you two. Get out of here and enjoy being in your old stomping grounds!"

I stand and start to pick up the dishes, but Ben takes them from my hands, brow raised.

"You heard the woman. Get out of here. Keys to my truck are hanging up but be careful. It's supposed to rain tonight."

"You're letting us take the hot rod?" A giddiness settles over me. "You never let us take the hot rod."

"Well, you're not high school kids anymore, and it's not five of you trying to squeeze into a three-seater cab." He chuckles.

I actually squeal, and I look to Brady, waggling my brows.

He smirks, pushing to his feet. "Well, come on then, Cammie Baby. Seems we've got some havoc to cause." He bends, motioning for me to jump on his back, my preferred method of transportation, but I skip around him, putting my lips to his ear.

"Sorry. But if I jump up, your dad is going to get a bigger show than he bargained for." Brady tenses, and I slide on by, heading for the door. "I'm driving!"

"Oh hell," both Brady and his dad say at the same time, and I smirk to myself.

See? Same person.

At first, we just cruise around the town, rolling through the high school parking lot, reminiscing. We get some hot chocolate and walk the town's main strip, full of small businesses.

It's a little after two when we hop back into the truck. This time, I don't tell Brady where we're going, but it doesn't take too long for it to become obvious, and an hour later, we're pulling into a familiar gravel driveway.

Brady looks over at me, but I keep my eyes on the road and soon we're weaving around to the back of the house, parking in the space between the detached garage and the barn.

Unbuckling my seat belt, I climb out and Brady follows, catching the keys when I toss them his way.

"Are the renters not home?" he wonders, glancing toward the back deck of the house.

I sigh, shaking my head as I start down the stone path toward the barn, pushing the long, sliding door open and looking inside.

Right now, it's just a bunch of haystacks lining the walls, waiting to be sold off with the rest of this year's harvest.

I take a deep breath, a small smile pulling at my lips.

Brady steps up beside me and I look his way, leading us over to the ladder at the far right. He grabs on to stabilize it and swooshes a hand out. "After you, my lady."

"Uh…no. Get your butt up there unless you want a show."

His smirk is slow, and a low laugh leaves me.

I roll my eyes at myself. "Okay, I walked right into that one."

Brady chuckles but doesn't move. "I need to hold this rickety-ass thing for you if we're going up there. Promise I won't look."

"What if I said I had more body jewelry you haven't seen yet?"

Rich amber eyes snap to mine, and when he speaks, it's with a low tone I've never heard from him before. "Then I'd remind you that I haven't seen *any* of them, so what's one more?"

My mouth is suddenly watering, my hands shaking slightly as I grip the rungs. I climb up one step, then another, and pause, my face just above his with his feet planted firmly on the floor.

Man, his lashes are really long.

"I was kidding by the way," I rush out.

"Now that's a shame," he rasps, holding my gaze. But then he blinks, and his playful self appears as if summoned. "Now get your ass up there." He smacks my butt.

I laugh and hurry up.

Brady joins me only seconds later, and together we slip through the little door my dad built into the roof of the barn, climbing out onto the small platform he put out here for me and Ari when we were kids.

The boys have been up here dozens of times too, this property being the one we would use for big events and things like my parents twentieth anniversary party. We'll likely have a graduation party here next year, and this time, we'll get to hang around inside the house too, since my parents will be back living in it by then.

I sigh, pulling the hoodie under my ass and lowering to the platform, letting my legs hang over the edge. Brady does the same, and for several minutes, we just sit there in comfortable silence, enjoying the view and the noises coming from the creek that we have the most perfect view of.

It runs about thirty feet wide and a good twenty miles long, stretching across several property lines, but as far as I know, we're the only ones with a little bridge that allows you to cross it without getting wet. It's only accessible for the next couple months though, until the snow comes and goes and the creek overflows for a while.

"I forgot how peaceful it is out here."

"I didn't," I say quietly, not wanting to disrupt the birds overhead. They should be migrating soon. "My parents are moving back in after some renovations. They're going to sell the other."

His brows jump. "They've already decided?"

I nod. "Yeah. They told me in September when they came for the family barbecue."

"You sad about that?"

"Not really." I rethink my answer. "I mean I was, but then I stopped and thought about it, and it makes sense. That place was so special because of all of *us*, you know?" I tip my head, looking his way. "But we're not kids anymore. We're grown now and, in a few years, probably sooner for some of us"—I give him a pointed look and ignore his blank blink—"we'll be starting our own adventures, and for the first time, we won't be two houses down or a couple dorms over. We could be in different states. Hell, countries even."

"That sounds terrible," he mumbles, making me laugh suddenly.

"Hey, we'll still have the beach house, though, right?" I say, thinking of the insane gift our blue-collar parents gave us all for high school graduation. "That's why our parents put it in all our names, so we'd all have a place to go to be with each other if life leads us different places like it's bound to do."

"Stop saying that."

I laugh again and Brady gives a half smile.

I pull in a long breath. "So yeah, I think it makes sense for my parents to sell. I mean why would they want to wake up to a view of Chase's house across the street when they can wake up to this every day."

Brady sits back on his hands, bumping his shoulder into mine. "Why do I sense a *but* in there?"

My lips turn up. "Maybe because you know me too well."

"No such thing, Cammie Baby."

I smile to myself and look out over the creek. "I guess I'm a little bummed because I kind of thought *I'd* be the one who ended up here one day, not them."

"Really?" The surprise in his voice has me meeting his gaze. "Have you told them that?"

My eyes move between his, and something soft swims through me. "I haven't told anyone that."

Brady studies me a long moment, then wraps his arms around my middle and tugs me closer. "Can I ask you something?"

"Duh."

He chuckles, then goes quiet for a couple minutes, making me wonder if he's changed his mind. Just when I'm about to fill the silence with some nonsense, he speaks.

"On the phone to your mom yesterday, you said *ten years, if ever* when she teased you about kids. Do you not want to be a mom?"

His question seems so random that I have to pull back a little so I can see him.

"I don't mean to pry," he rushes, a very un-Brady-like thing to say. "I know a lot of people choose not to have kids, and that's perfectly fine. Best to know what you want than have a child and not want or be able to care for it. Not that you would do that either, but I'm just saying."

"I know, relax," I say, enjoying this little frazzled side of him a bit more than I should, considering the conversation. "It's fine, really."

"So…" He waits.

"First, surprised you caught that. I was only teasing because she was teasing, and I know that's a fear of hers seeing as I'm the only child, not that she would ever pressure me for real either way."

He nods. "And with you wanting to be a teacher or have a day care or whatever, I'd understand how those students would all be yours in a way, and one of your own might be hard."

A strong sense of admiration settles over me at his words, bringing with it a hint of vulnerability, but not in a negative way. It's just a little strange, if not exciting, that he seems to see a part of myself I've never really shared—at least not in so many words. "I don't not want kids. Maybe just one, but…"

"What?" he pushes, almost an eagerness to his tone that has me gazing at him curiously.

"This is another one of those things I've never said out loud."

"Tell me," he whispers.

"It's just there are so many kids out there who don't have homes, you know?" His eyes snap between mine, hanging on every word. A sudden sense of uncertainty circles around my shoulders and I give a stiff shrug. "And I mean, I don't really know how my body would do with a pregnancy."

He frowns. "Because your mom had a hard time?"

A sad chuckle leaves me. "That's just another potential roadblock." He waits for more, and I decide to just lay it out there because this is Brady. If my worries are safe with anyone, it's with him. "So…TMI maybe, but I've never had a regular cycle, if you know what I mean, and that one little fact, mixed with my mom's troubles and having to work really hard to keep weight on as it is, so I'm sickly and weak…just feels like a lot of stress. And from what I hear, stress is also a factor making getting pregnant even harder, so it's mission impossible as far as I'm convinced, no matter how you look at it.

"And yeah, you're right. I think all that played a part in my going the teacher route of life. You know, the desire to be a second home for hundreds of kids over my lifetime in case I can't have one of my own." I chance a glance his way, and he's still right there, hanging on my every word.

"Senior year I was transferred from my pediatric doctor to an adult endocrinologist, and in that very first visit, he told me, unsolicited I might add, that even if I could get pregnant with a nearly nonexistent ovulation, my body doesn't offer much room to grow a tiny human. He said my hips aren't 'birthing hips.'"

"Fuck him." Brady glares.

I chuckle. "That's exactly what my dad said after the guy dropped me as his patient later that afternoon." I smile wide. "My dad threatened to kick his ass before we walked out so…fair."

I sigh and shrug a shoulder. "Anyway, I hadn't thought about it too much until after everything that happened to Ari. It's not like I'm ready to be a mom anytime soon anyway, but I don't know. I think it might be dangerous for me, and that just reconfirms what I've thought over the years."

"That you would want to adopt a child who doesn't have a mother to love him?"

My lips curve to one side, and I peek over at him. "Or her."

A throaty chuckle escapes him, and he nods, getting lost in his own thoughts for a while.

A bit later, I start to move, but Brady grabs me.

"Wait," he whispers, tugging me back to him.

I'm between his legs, my chest to his, temple resting against his chin. His arms come around me and he rubs his cheek along mine softly, maybe even subconsciously, as his thumb traces along mine over and over.

In front of us, the sun starts to disappear behind the mountain and I get lost in the sight.

I could sit here all day, but the sun is gone now, and our conversation took a heavy turn that, for some reason, seems to have weighed on him more than I'd expect.

We need a distraction, so I push to my feet. "Come on, Big Guy."

"Where we goin'?"

"To pretend we're still in high school and not over here worrying about adult stuff."

He doesn't ask questions; he just follows, and the second our feet hit the floor of the barn, he takes my hand in his.

It's warm and rough against my own, swallowing my fingers until even that small touch feels like a mountain of armor that nothing could break through.

My steps slow as I consider that thought a little deeper, wondering why it arose in the first place, but it's there nonetheless.

Nothing—*or no one?*

CHAPTER 33
BRADY

"You're kidding?"

She shakes her head, throwing her seat belt off.

I frown in horror, looking out at the dozens of teenagers getting drunk around the firepits. It's barely after five, but teens around here have always used the time change to our advantage and it seems that hasn't changed in the few years we've been gone.

My attention snaps back to Cameron. "They're going to think we're old!"

"Nah." She pushes her door open, grinning wildly at me. "They're gonna think you're a king." She jumps out, slamming the door behind her.

She doesn't just take off into the group of people or wait for me by the bumper. No, that's not her style. Too basic. Too boring.

Cameron's arms are already lifting, her body swaying to the beat of the bass as she dances her away around until she's right there, hips moving under the headlights. She spins around in a cute-ass, little hip roll, pointing at me as she belts out the song playing because, of course, she just so happens to know all the words to it.

I drop back in my seat, completely and terrifyingly fucking *stuck*.

Cameron smiles, her chin meeting her shoulder as she teases, her natural flirty state shining through, something I haven't seen too much from her lately.

She's here tonight, though. Wild on life. High on moonlight.

My little Hellcat.

She tips her head from side to side, neck stretching delicately, and my eyes trace the rhythmic roll that moves through her. Even in my hoodie that hides her figure completely, she is a sight. My gaze falls to the bottom hem, skin prickling at the way it rubs against her upper thighs. I wish it were my hand gliding across her there, my fingers bending slightly between her legs the way that thick cotton is.

Fucking shit. Alister was wrong.

I'm not falling for her.

I already fell so hard my ass has hit the floor, and now all I want to do is tug her down on top of me. I want her to straddle my waist, her soft hands sliding along my skin until she's holding on the way I would be—and I fucking would be.

If given the chance, I'd hold on with everything I've got.

That's a dangerous thought, my boy.

Her arms lift, sleeves falling down her wrists, but my attention snaps to her legs as she spins again. With each inch higher her hands go, more flesh is exposed until I can see the point where her thigh becomes her ass.

I jerk, turning the headlights off.

That works like a charm, and she whips around, waiting for her eyes to adjust so she can see me through the windshield.

Behind her, the edge of the party stares this way, whether it was from her solo dance or the flash of the light disappearing, I can't say.

If I were one of the guys standing over there, it sure as shit wouldn't have been the lights.

I climb out, tucking the keys in my pocket, and meet her where she stands. She smiles innocently, and my own tugs at my lips as I throw my arm around her, tugging her close. "Okay, brat. You're doing the talking here."

"My *pleasure*, Big Guy." She stretches up, kissing my cheek before taking my hand that's around her and leading us straight to the pickup with the keg in the back of it, several small tents off to the right.

A brunette girl and two blond dudes are sitting in folding chairs in front of it, and they look at us wearily, wondering if we're about to narc on them. Little do they know, it was our parents who started this tradition when they were back in high school and the owner of this land used to babysit us both.

"Is the buy-in still ten bucks?" Cameron gets right to it.

One of the blonds narrows his eyes, looking from her to me and back. "It's fifteen for outsiders."

An unexpected laugh leaves me, and he glances over again. This time, his eyes widen. "Wait, I know you," he starts.

Before he can say another word, another shouts, "Bro...dude, it's Lancaster!"

I look toward the voice, finding a guy wearing the same letterman's jacket I've got hanging in my closet sliding up, red Solo cup in hand.

"Yo, you played with my brother, Clayton Miller!" The guy grins. "I'm Calvin." He reaches a hand out, and I take it for a shake. He glances back, a couple others walking up to join us, before facing me. "I was on the freshman team your senior year. Didn't play much then, but I'm starting safety now. Varsity."

"Good for you, man." I smile. Looking across at the others, I say, "Running backs?"

The one on the end gives a drunken smile and raises his cup. "Nailed it."

"Coach still playing his running backs both ways?"

"Yup. Running back on offense, outside linebacker on defense."

I nod, looking to the big guy with his chin lifted all cocky-like. He's a good six two with shoulders that about rival my own. "Let me guess, you're the new me?"

"Depends." He lifts a lazy shoulder. "Who were you?"

Cameron chokes on a laugh, pulling my wallet from my back pocket to pay the keg guard.

"Bro, shut up!" The eager friend shoves him. "You know who he is. You've been trying to break his record for two years now."

The guy glares at his friend, and I fight the smirk that wants to appear.

Little fucker.

"I'll run some drills with you tomorrow morning if you're up for it."

The guy narrows his eyes, trying to decide if he wants to keep the toughness about him, but we're all the same here: small-town boys who want to make our families proud—make ourselves proud.

"Yeah, man." He chooses the right route. "I'm free tomorrow."

"At the field, six a.m.?"

He nods, standing a little taller.

Cameron slips in front of me, passing me a cup with a secret smile. "See?" she whispers. *"King."*

She kisses my jaw, a natural gesture she's done a hundred times over, but this time, the soft press of her lips makes my skin feel tight. I want to hold her there, tip my head to the side and see if she'll keep going, trace a path that she can call her own. Feel the heat of her breath and see if it rivals the heat building in other places. My eyes lower to hers, and she winks, slipping away, and I shift my body so I can keep her in my sight but stay to answer questions about college ball with the new West Coldon High varsity players.

Cameron makes friends fast, and it helps that we're only a couple years older than them. She dances around with several girls before hopping over to dominate the reigning duo at beer pong.

She smiles and laughs and drops down by the fire, talking about god knows what but having a good-ass time while she does it.

I note that the dude I offered to train with tomorrow has

swapped his Solo cup out for a can of grape soda and smile to myself. I wonder if he noticed I passed my cup off, not having had a single drink.

I've just finished a conversation with a guy I remember from high school when Cameron wraps her little arms around my stomach, sticking her hands inside the pocket of my hoodie like I did hers.

"Warm me up, big bear man."

Chuckling, I spin in her arms, hauling her up and holding her to me, being sure to keep her "dress" under her ass, and she knows not to wrap her legs around me this time. "Ready to get out of here? I'm starving and you know my mom's got something good waiting."

"Oh! I hope it's her baked mac and cheese!"

This time, it's me who kisses her cheek. "Of course you do."

She wiggles to be let down, but I'm not ready to let go yet, so I carry her, even in the awkward pencil-like position her outfit demands of her, and deposit her in the passenger seat this time. I jog around the truck and hop in, driving us back to my house.

As soon as we pull back onto the main road, the rains starts coming down, just as my dad said it would. Cameron tucks her feet under her, leaning over until her elbow is brushing mine on the console as she searches for something to listen to on the satellite radio. Facing the road, I cut a quick side glance her way, noting the little frown of concentration as she skips station after station, trying to find the perfect one to match her mood. She has no clue she's touching me, but it was the first thing that registered in my mind.

She settles on hip-hop, bouncing all around as she sings along, pointing my way and doing her damnedest to get me to join in.

I'm shit with lyrics, so I help out with the chorus here and there, and just as we're rolling up to the stop sign before our street, the track changes, and Drake's "In My Feelings" comes on, and her head snaps my way, her slow grin only growing wider and wider.

"Brady."

"No."

"Braaaaa-dyyyyyy," she says, dragging my name out.

"No, woman, it's fuckin' raining!" I laugh, but she's already cranked the radio up to deafening decibels and is throwing the door open. She squeals and starts running around the back of the car.

"Damn it," I laugh, throwing my seat belt off and doing the same, dipping my head like it'll help repel the rain. We high five as we pass the back of the truck and then meet in the middle of the front end. The chorus hits and we sing like lunatics, doing the damn dance she and Ari forced us to learn when this went viral and our parents made us promise not to follow how it's supposed to go but to dance around a parked car rather than a moving one.

She throws her head back and laughs, her arms coming around me just as I reach out to grip her by the waist.

We're sopping fucking wet, standing in the middle of the dark street, headlights beaming around us.

Her smile is wide. Addicting. The kind of smile that has the power to make time stop.

And that's exactly what happens.

The world around me slows, the humor slipping off my face as I stare into her big, baby blues. They hold this mischievous glow, flirting with the idea of teasing me, but unintentionally enough for her to make me wonder if I'm only seeing what I want to see.

She's clueless about where my mind is, head tipped back and mouth open, catching raindrops on her tongue as throaty giggles bubble their way out of her.

My fingers tighten against her, my feet shuffling forward, and her chin lowers, the smile on her face sending a literal thump through my chest.

I can't take it anymore.

Don't fucking want to.

"Brady?"

I let out a long breath, my eyes on hers.

I let her go, taking a step back, gaze traveling over her, dripping wet and drowning in my hoodie.

I clench my eyes closed, and I sense her coming closer. A soft hand finds mine, and my eyes snap open, connecting with hers.

"Fuck it."

I take her face in my palms and crush my mouth to hers.

And my fucking god, does she respond.

Her mouth opens for me instantly, and my tongue eagerly accepts the offer, sweeping over her silkiness and demanding more. I force my fingers into her hair, driving her back until I'm crushing her against the truck.

She melts, hiking one leg up, and I grab hold, pressing into her as I take her mouth like I'm fucking starved.

Her kiss is fierce. Messy. Sinfully sweet.

She starts to shake under my touch, and a deep, throaty groan escapes me. I tear free, nibbling at her lips the way I've wanted to do for so fucking long, biting and sucking and licking. She grips my wrists, my palms still holding her head how I want her.

I dip into her neck, and she moans before I ever touch her skin there, sending a bolt of lightning straight to my dick.

A loud honk has her jumping and tugging back.

I tense, dread weighing down my veins.

What will I see when I look into her eyes right now?

Regret might just about kill me.

Jaw clenched, I prepare for the worst, but before my eyes can even meet hers, her forehead falls to my chest and she laughs, quickly shifting and grabbing my hand as she drags us back to the driver's side. "Come on, before they run us over!"

She yanks the door open and climbs in, flashing me a quick shot of creamy ass cheeks as she hops over the center console, and I swear to god, my dick is an iron rod in my jeans.

I climb in, and Cameron's laughter doubles until she's got

302

tears in her eyes, her hand holding her side, and I finally relax, my own humor mirroring hers.

Ten seconds later, we're parked in my driveway. Cameron is out, dashing for the front door in seconds, laughing as she gets pelted with rain all over again.

I pause for a moment, unsure of what to do.

My pulse is jumping wildly, my mind running a million miles a minute, but the thought that's screaming the loudest has my eyes clamping shut.

I am so fucked.

"Brady!" she yells, and my eyes fly open. "The door is locked." She smiles, shivering.

"Oh shit." I jump out, only now noting my mom's car isn't in the driveway.

"Whose bright idea was it to dance in the rain again?" she jokes, bending to pull her shoes off and tossing them to the side.

"Definitely mine," I play along.

She rewards me with a laugh, and my god, I've gone completely soft—I feel it in my chest. Cameron shoves me out of the way as she runs inside and books it up the stairs.

I can't keep the smile off my face as I lock the door, kicking my shoes off. I go into the kitchen, pouring us both a double shot of whiskey and adding some hot water to it from the dispenser. I cut a lemon and squeeze a good amount into our glasses, stirring them with my finger, spotting a note from my mom on top of a few tinfoil-covered dishes.

It's bingo night tonight. Be home around nine.

I look to the clock, noting it's a little after seven, and peek in on what Mom made for dinner. I smirk, shaking my head, and pick up our glasses.

I take the steps two at a time. "I got us something that should warm us up quick!"

"In here!"

Her voice leads me into the bathroom, and I'm stepping in

303

just as the curtain to the shower is closing, nothing but her fingers in sight.

"Uh, this is divine!" Her hair tie is thrown over the top, and I watch as it lands by my feet—right next to the hoodie and socks she was wearing. I note there is no other item of clothing there with them. No panties. No bra.

She was full commando today.

My eyes fall to the bulge in my jeans, and I give him a mental apology as my muscles clench. I try to rid myself of the thoughts running through my mind, but then she pulls the curtain back a little, part of her coming into view, hair soaked and hanging over her naked shoulder.

"Oh, what's that?" She stares at the glasses in my hand.

"Some shit my dad makes me and the guys sometimes. No idea what it's called, but it's damn good."

She tips her head, and my gaze follows the long piece of golden hair that slides against her arm, sticking to her in ways I want to.

I'd like to take her hair and—

"Bring mine to me?" she asks, but it's the crack in her tone that has my eyes snapping to hers, my breathing getting a little harder.

Probably because I'm holding my breath.

I shuffle closer, handing hers over, and she holds her hand over mine a moment before pulling it away.

"Cheers." She holds it up; we clink glasses and, at the same time, tip our glasses back.

I finish mine in one go, and she only takes a second swallow, blowing out a long breath as she chuckles. She passes it back and then the curtain is hiding her from me again. "That is good."

"Guess what my mom made for dinner."

The curtain yanks back again, this time soapy bubbles clinging to her, and I have to swallow my groan.

She's killing me and she has no fucking idea.

"Don't play with me, Lancaster."

I tug my hoodie over my head, my shirt next, and the rest follows, leaving me in my briefs. Her eyes burn a path down my chest, but before they can travel any lower, I spin on my feet. "Wouldn't dream of it, Cox."

Lie.

I would very much like to play with her. Naked.

But that's a whole other issue in itself, isn't it, you big fucking fake?

CAMERON

I call on my best spying skills and focus on the sound of his footsteps. Only when I can't hear the slightest trace of him do I finally feel I can breathe, my shoulders falling against the tile walls.

Holy shit, he kissed me when no one was watching.

When no one was there to see.

When it wasn't for the benefit of someone else.

Does that mean he feels this new pull between us?

I thought I was imagining it, that our versions of Mr. Hyde—the flirty, sexual seeker version—were just becoming better acquainted with each other while the sane, more conscious parts of our selves knew the score.

I'm starting to think my scoreboard is glitching and I've missed a touchdown or two because the numbers aren't matching up.

Does this mean more than I realize or less than I want it to?

What the actual hell do I want it to?

I know what's going on, and it's somehow equally as intriguing as it is terrifying. It's like the musical cue in a major motion picture has started playing, and all you have to do is keep your eyes glued to the screen to see what big moment happens next.

Do we keep driving down the field or spike the ball and end the play?

I don't know the answer, but what I do know is this is Brady we're talking about.

If there's anyone I can trust blindly, it's him.

That thought washes the unease down the drain with what's left of the suds, and I climb out, smiling when I find a fresh T-shirt and pair of fluffy, green Hulk socks. I tug them on and towel-dry my hair as best I can, comb it out, and head down the stairs.

Brady's just getting the fire lit, two plates on the coffee table that he scooted closer to the fireplace.

He looks up, his mouth open as if he was about to say something but he seems to forget what it was, and then the front door is opening.

"Oh, hello, my sweet babies!" Tisha coos, her hands coming together in front of her like a prayer.

Brady chuckles, raising a brow at his dad, who winks in return.

"Cameron, honey, did you see I made your favorite?" She grips her husband, stumbling as she kicks off her flats. "And Brady's too. I made Brady's favorite. Well, his favorite dinner anyway. I love you two so much, and I'm just so happy you're here."

I fight a smile, glancing at Brady, who wipes his mouth to cover his laugh. "I can't wait to dig in. Thank you."

She walks over, soft hands cupping and patting my cheeks as she smiles at me, her eyes growing misty. "Oh, I can't wait to have a daughter," she sighs happily.

I tense, and Ben starts laughing, walking over to collect his wife.

"Okay," Ben chuckles, wrapping his arm around her middle and turning her toward the stairs. "Let's go on up to bed, shall we?"

"We shall, Mr. Lancaster," she all but purrs, and Brady makes a gagging sound.

His dad just smiles. "Good night, you two."

They start up the stairs, but Tisha stops about halfway up.

"Oh, Cameron, honey. Sorry but we had to put some logs on your bed, so you won't be able to sleep in there tonight."

My brows jump. "Logs? On the bed?"

306

"Mom, what the hell?" Brady chuckles.

Tisha grins and keeps going, but Ben pauses, lifting a hand into the air with a shrug. "She figured the only thing Cam wouldn't move would be logs."

A laugh sputters from me. "And why exactly did she not want me to sleep in the bed?"

Rather than answering, Ben lifts a brow and looks toward his son. "Good night, you two."

Oh. Ohhh.

My cheeks grow red, but I pretend they don't and move to sit on one of the pillows Brady set in front of the coffee table.

Melted, gooey goodness stares back at me in the form of a massive serving of baked mac and cheese, a perfect layer of Tapatio having been sprinkled over the top, just the way I like it.

"Wasn't sure if you'd want any fried pork chop or not. We can have seconds if you do." Brady sits beside me, his plate of mashed potatoes, fried pork chops, and white country gravy poured on top.

I lean in to get a better whiff.

He laughs, and my eyes snap up to his. "I'll take that as a yes, you want some."

"Maybe just a couple bites of yours."

"I'll share if you share."

"Bet."

We start eating, the TV on low in the background and fire popping in front of us.

"Did you take a shower?" I wonder.

Brady nods, chewing quickly so he can answer. "Used my parents' right quick. I don't have those goldilocks to get through, so I'm more of a two-minute man."

"Are you now?"

His head snaps my way, and I swear, his neck flushes a little. "That is not what I meant."

"Mm-hmm, sure."

"Cameron."

I laugh, covering my mouth so I don't spit food all over the place. I swallow, taking a quick drink from the glass of soda sitting there. "Trust me, Brady. I don't think there's a woman on campus who would believe that if they heard it."

"Yeah, well, people shouldn't believe all the things they hear," he mumbles, shoveling food into his mouth.

A small scowl forms, and I think about his words for a moment. "Is it hard?"

"What?"

"Getting that much attention? Having people on you all the time and fighting people off?"

Brady takes another bite before answering. "It is." I wonder if he might not say anymore, but then he continues. "I thought I knew how to handle people, since it was sort of the same in high school, you know, but all that leveled up at Avix to an intensity I hadn't prepared myself for. Suddenly it wasn't shy, or not-so-shy, schoolgirls but grown-ass almost-feral women. They know what they want, and they aren't afraid to go out and try to get it. It's kind of surprising how many people prefer the hook up and hustle out."

"Do you... I mean, is that not..." *What are you trying to say, cringey girl?*

Brady smirks my way. "Is that not...?"

I glare and he chuckles. *Fine, I'll say it.* "Is that not what you want?"

Brady's knife slows as he cuts into the half-gone slab of meat. Slowly, his eyes find mine and hold. "No."

No.

Not *no, not anymore* or *no, I never wanted that.* Just a solid and sure no.

"Oh."

Brady watches me closely, something steeling in his gaze.

"What?"

308

"I want to tell you one of my secrets."

My gaze gentles. "Okay. But if you think you have to because of all my word vomit today or the conversation at breakfast, you don't."

"It's not that—well, it is but…" He pauses, taking a deep breath. "Ben isn't my biological dad."

My brows jump, mouth falling open just slightly, but I can't quite get any words out before he continues, more to himself than me.

He huffs, shaking his head. "I don't even like saying that. The words 'isn't' and 'dad' shouldn't be in the same sentence when it comes to us."

My statement from earlier starts to turn me the color of the flames before us. "I didn't mean anything by what I said this morning, just that you guys are so similar. In the best ways, I—" I swallow my tongue.

He smiles but it's a little brittle. "That was a compliment, Cammie Girl. I'm proud to be like him. I want to be like him because I am his son. In every way that matters to me, I am."

"But if I had known, I never would have made such a splash pointing out you're…"

"Physically different?" he offers. "It's okay. It's obvious to everyone, so much so I'm sure people have wondered over the years but didn't ask."

"That never even crossed my mind, Brady, I swear. This is big and I feel like an asshole right now."

"It's okay," he laughs softly. "Like I said, it's not a bad thing. It's just …I don't really like acknowledging it, you know? Feels a little fucked up." There's a strain over his brows and he turns away, messing with his napkin a bit.

It's clear he doesn't want to talk about it, even if he thought maybe he did, so I reach over, taking his hand and weaving our fingers together, waiting for him to look my way to say, "Thank you for telling me." My voice is low, barely a whisper, and the emotion that it draws to his face is too much, so I give him a small smile to try to lighten the mood. "I mean, even if I basically forced it out of you and I'm the last to know. What am I, chopped liver?"

"Nah." His chuckle is low. "You're at least fried calamari."

Laughter spurts from me but it fades, and I reach out, cupping his cheek.

He leans into my touch, reaching up to hold my wrist in place. "You know I didn't intentionally keep that a secret, right?" he says, clearly worried. "He is my dad, and saying differently just..."

"I know," I assure him. "And you know nothing you tell me could ever change things between us, right?"

"What if I want it to?" he asks suddenly, softly. "What if there are things I want to say, things I want to share, that I hope change a few things?"

My heart hammers behind my ribs. "What kind of things?"

He stares for so long that when his mouth finally lifts on one side, I jolt.

Brady shifts so his body faces mine while I still sit forward, the coffee table in front of me. "Let me feed you."

"What?" I chuckle, his sudden change of subject throwing me off a little.

"You heard me." He reaches down, gripping the pillow under my ass and tugging it the few inches left between us. He stretches his legs out around me, his thighs framing me on both sides.

He picks up the fork and stabs a small piece of pork he already cut and drags it through the potatoes, making sure both are drenched in the white gravy. Brady holds it up expectantly, and a surprising heat crawls up my chest.

Even my hands start to shake a little, so I put them under my legs as my lips part. He doesn't move in slow motion, but it feels that way as he inches closer, his attention locked on me as his fork meets my tongue and I seal my lips around the silverware.

Slowly, he withdraws, and I close my eyes. Not in a flash of food euphoria, though the flavors are amazing as always, but at the foreign intimacy this moment brings me.

It's unfamiliar and full of promise, almost as if right here, right now, we're on the edge of something we've yet to figure out.

It's a little scary because what if this is all wrong?

What if familiarity and comfort are being mistaken for more?

Oh my god, I like-like him. That's what this is.

My eyes flutter open, finding tenderness staring back at me. Brady's hand lifts, thumb swiping along the edge of my lower lip, before it disappears between his own.

My chest feels suddenly heavy, achy, and I want to lean into him…but I don't.

Brady smiles softly, his gaze dropping to his lap for a moment. In the next, he's shoving his fork into my mac and cheese and shoveling a massive bite for himself, smiling with his mouth full when I gape at him.

"I was saving that bite!"

"I know," he laughs, rubbing his stomach dramatically. "It was a really good bite."

"Ass." I shove him in the chest, and he catches my hand, linking our fingers and giving them a little squeeze as he flicks his gaze toward the clock.

"I've gotta get to sleep soon."

"That's right. Coach Brady's coming out to play tomorrow."

He smirks, but neither of us move.

Before I can think too hard, before he can, I sit up, sliding my knees over his until I'm straddling him.

There's a slight frown over his brow, but he says nothing, welcoming me onto his lap with eager arms.

I pepper his jaw with light kisses, tipping his neck back to gently suck on his throat, right over his windpipe, wondering if he'd allow me access to the pipe growing beneath me.

311

"Tell me what we're doing," he rasps, an almost desperate plea to his gravelly tone.

I freeze, but then his hands start to roam, and it works like a charm. I ease, kissing a path to his ear, and whisper, "Pretending…"

CHAPTER 34
BRADY

Pretending.

That's what she said.

Too bad nothing about the way her little nails are digging into my pecs or the greedy glide of her lips across my skin is pretend.

Thank fuck for that, but I am a more than willing participant in this little game of ours.

I drive my fingers into her wet hair, giving it a good pull until she's gasping in my mouth, her lips curving against my throat. "And who are we tonight, Hellcat?"

"Not strangers from the bar." She sinks her teeth into my shoulder, her tongue sliding across the spot and sending a spasm down my spine.

I clamp her hip with my free hand, and she moans into my ear.

"Fuck." My eyes clench at the sound, and I use my grip on her hair to take my turn, tugging her head back until it's my mouth on her throat. She swallows beautifully, and I kiss along her collarbone. "Who are we, Cammie Girl?"

"We're real."

Her words hammer at my heart, and my head flies up, our gazes locking, but this isn't a deep moment that defines us. No, her features aren't soft.

She's on fire. Needy.

And it's me she wants something from.

"Real, huh?" I rasp, shifting and crab-walking us a few feet until my back hits the edge of the couch.

Cameron chuckles, falling against my chest even more, her hands gliding lower until she's pushing the hem of my shirt up, her long, silky fingers ghosting along my abs and making me fucking shiver. "I'm just Cameron, your girl. You're just Brady, my man."

"I see." I wrap her hand around my fist and draw her closer, my dick twitching against her when her lips part. "So we're pretending that this isn't pretend at all, hmm?"

"Ding, ding. We have a winner." She teases, tongue coming out and swiping across my lips.

I sit up slightly and haul my shirt over my head, throwing it I don't even care where, and then I'm grabbing her hands, putting them back on my skin.

She inhales deeply, her legs opening a little wider around me, knees pressing into the crook of the carpet and the bottom frame of the couch.

My hands come around her, squeezing her ass, enjoying the feel of it in my palms. "Well, as your man, it's my job to make sure you feel good, isn't it?"

"Damn straight it is." She smirks, tongue coming out, rolling along the tips of her teeth.

With more sex appeal and sass than one woman should possess, she reaches down, tearing the T-shirt she's wearing over her head.

My eyes snap to her chest in a blink, and my dick fucking cries in jealousy.

Perfect, perky tits stare back at me, needy nipples swollen and begging for my touch, but it isn't the way they go from firm to rock solid right before my eyes that has my hips bucking involuntarily but the little dangling loops that hang from the center of them.

She changed the barbells to half-moons, but the spikes...the spikes are still there, and right now, they're shaking because she is shaking.

"My needy little Hellcat," I murmur and take them in my hands.

They don't overflow but allow me to cover her completely, like a shield of right, claiming them as mine, at least for the length of this little game we're playing.

My thumb follows the curve of her nipple, up and around, and she whimpers. A whimper that turns into a low cry of pleasure when I give the little loops a nice, gentle tug.

"Shit." She shivers. "I had no idea it would feel so—"

"Good?"

"Mm," she mews, pushing her chest into my palms, but then her words catch up to me.

"Wait." I pause and her eyes flick open.

She smirks in triumph and then her knees slide even wider, her pussy now lined right over the length of my dick. "Yes, Big Guy. You're the first man to see them."

My chest rumbles, and I tug her to me. "We're pretending, remember? So you don't say just *first*." I bite her lower lip. "You say *first and last*."

She starts to smile and then I'm kissing her.

It's a wicked dance, and when her hips start to shift, I match her movements, muscles clenching.

Her hands weave around my neck and she pulls me up, leaning back so I'm half hovering over her, forcing mine to spread out, and her ass drops lower, lining my dick up with her heat.

She's completely naked aside from the thick socks covering up to her calves, and I've never seen such a pretty sight.

"You are..." My chest rumbles, eyes locked on the pinkness between her legs.

"Waiting," she answers, and my gaze snaps to hers.

She slides her hands up my chest, digging her little nails into my pecs, and grinds down on me. It's the perfect fucking dance. My toes curl in my socks, and her teeth sink into that lower lip of hers.

I pinch her nipple and her head falls back, so I go in for

more, dipping lower until I can take one in my mouth. She gasps, holding on, and I need more. Fuck, I need everything.

My left hand slides along her side, slowly in case she wants to tell me no.

"Can I touch you, baby?"

She doesn't answer with words but pushes me down faster, slipping my hand right between her legs.

My groan is instant.

She's molten gold, hot to the touch, and "So. Fucking. Soft."

I sit back again, and I dip my fingers between her folds first, trying to picture the shape of her, then settle right over her clit.

"Inside me, Brady," she pleads.

"Patience, Hellcat." I pinch her clit instead, and she cries out, her moan deepening as I start rubbing, figuring out what she likes. "You get what I give you."

She hums her approval. "My bossy man."

"Your whatever you want me to be," I promise, taking her nipple between my teeth as I rub circles over her swollen little clit.

Her face is smashed to my cheek, her moans bleeding into my ear and making my pulse jump wildly. My dick too.

She feels it, and then she's pushing into my hand even more. "I want to feel you."

Fuck.

I clench my eyes closed. Move my hand and take her by the hips.

I lean back, holding her up a little, and wiggle my sweats down, but when she reaches for my boxers, I settle her back in my lap, grinding up into her so she forgets what she was after.

"There you go. Ride me like a pro." I take her mouth, kissing her savagely.

She starts to quiver, her hips moving faster, and I know what that means.

"I'm close too, baby. So close," I murmur as I pull at her nipples, letting my head fall back on the couch cushion as she plants her palm on my chest and grinds her pussy into me like I'm inside her.

It's fucking euphoric.

I groan, my muscles tightening, and she whimpers, legs clamping over me.

She's trembling, her wetness soaking through my briefs, and I'm about to add to the mess.

I'm about to come in my damn underwear and I can't find it in me to be embarrassed about that.

Her orgasm hits her hard, and she drops forward, her chest sweaty against mine, and my ass cheeks tighten, my own coming in quick. I jerk once, twice, and just as I'm about to come all over myself, a warm, soft hand wraps around my length.

My eyes fly open, locking with hers, and she stares right at me as she squeezes.

That's all it takes, and cum rockets out of me, filling the space between us, and when I look down, a rope of white rolls across her thumb.

Never in my life have I ever seen such an intoxicating sight.

My gaze snaps up to hers, but she's not looking at me.

No, she's transfixed on the little black bars that stretch across the underside of my dick. She doesn't say anything, just traces over them, a sated smile on her lips.

Eventually she slips her hand out from where she snuck it, and neither of us says a word as she leans forward and rests against my chest.

I hug her to me, holding her there, and I don't let go.

I couldn't possibly.

At least not until she makes me.

CAMERON

Hopping to his feet with far more energy than I can pretend to have, he yanks me up with him. We clean up our mess and he

317

closes the doors of the fireplace, the two of us heading upstairs, his hand in mine.

He tugs me toward his room, but I drag my feet.

"Wait!" I whisper, grinning when he gives me a questioning look. "I wanna see if there're really logs on the bed."

I tiptoe over to the room closest to his parents' and push the door open.

Sure as shit, there is a pile of wood sitting on top of the damn bed.

"Your mom is..."

"Inventive? Prone to get what she wants? A seer?"

I chuckle, looking over my shoulder. "What?"

"I mean, she clearly assumed we needed a room for something."

"Little did she know we didn't need one at all."

His grin is wide and gorgeous, and I can't stop smiling as I follow him to his room.

He sits down on the foot of the bed as I crawl in it, burying myself in the blankets and claiming the left side.

The distinct sound of his briefs coming down fills the room, and I wait, wondering if maybe he'll forgo a new pair, but his dresser opens and closes a moment later.

Man, there was something seriously addicting about the way he came undone to nothing more than some heavy grinding. I mean, I know how to use my hips, but this is Brady.

I give myself a mental pat on the back.

He climbs in beside me, and my pulse pounds wildly, waiting to see what his next move will be.

Will he stay on his side? Put a pillow between us?

My fears are gone when he slides all the way over until my back is flush with his front.

His arm settles over me on top of the blanket, lying against the curve of my leg. "Night, baby."

Baby.

Not *Cammie Baby* or *baby girl*.

No *Hellcat* or *Cammie Girl*.

Just...*baby*.

Something inside me melts a little, and I smile against my pillow.

"Night, Big Guy."

CHAPTER 35
BRADY

Last night was the worst way to end a night.

Not because of what happened but because of the plans I made for this morning. I had to keep giving my dick a stern talking to. On the football field with a guy I only just met was *not* the time to get a hard-on, but all I could think about was the way she felt.

The sounds she made.

Her ass cheeks and the way they promised to swallow my cock between them, those pretty, perfect nipples when she tossed my shirt over her head. At first, I almost pouted—I've become a bit obsessed with seeing her in my clothes to the point where I'm tempted to fill her dorm closet with more when we get back. But then.

She smirked down at me from the spot that is now officially hers—my lap—and turned into a little devil. God, the way I want to learn every part of her. She's fucking exquisite when she comes. I can't even imagine what she'd look like if it were my cock she creamed all over.

I hated leaving her in the bed this morning. I can't fucking wait to look her in the eye, knowing exactly what I'll be thinking the moment are gazes meet.

What would she do if I bent down and kissed her for my mom and dad to see? A silent claim is what I want to make. Like a kid on show-and-tell day, I want to brag and be like *look at what I got, a one-of-a-kind woman to call my own.*

I need to talk to her, tell her where my head is at. It's the right thing to do.

I need to know where the pretending begins and ends before she becomes even more than my first and last thought each day. Because she is.

I don't know when it happened, but it did. In fact, it might have always been there, far back in my mind, waiting for the time to come forward.

Cameron's the snow and I'm the sleigh—I only make sense with her.

I'm the leather, and she's the lace; we fit to form the perfect union.

I'm going to talk to her and tell her I love her.

Alister's words hit me cold in the chest, and my hand freezes on the door handle to my childhood home.

Shit.

Fuck.

He's going to tell her how he feels.

He's going to tell her how he feels, and she's going to listen with rapt attention because, at the end of the day, all she's been searching for in this little lie of ours is a soft landing on a bed of truths.

Trust and tenderness.

She was waiting for her mind to clear so she could come to terms with how she feels under the pain and anger, and it's easy to see there are no longer any clouds hanging over her head. No, the sky is clear and blue now.

She said it herself—she no longer thinks he intended to hurt her.

But he's not ready for a girl like her. She needs a man with confidence and a secure hand to hold.

I want to be that man.

I want to hold her hand in public, and I want to mean it. I want to kiss her when no one is watching and give her more than I've ever given anyone.

I want to take her like I've taken no other, giving her a part of me no one else has ever had.

I want her to be my first.

"Bro, whoa, slow the fuck down," I mumble, letting go of the door handle and running my hand through my hair.

But I can't. Last night changed things. She didn't try to hide her desire—she leaned into it, crawled on my lap like she's done a hundred times, but without an ounce of the innocence the move has held in the past. No, she knew what she wanted, and she wasn't shy about taking it.

And fuck me, I was ready to give.

I've never ever wanted to say fuck it so bad in my life and just roll on top of her.

She was sweet and soft and delicious.

She sounded like sin and she tasted like mine.

Goddamn it.

I sigh, shaking my head.

"What are you hiding from, Son?"

My eyes fly open, and I spin around, spotting my dad coming up the walkway. There must be a question on my face because he hooks his thumb over his shoulder.

"I was having coffee with Bill." He points to where Chase's dad waves from his porch. "Poor guy's got a lot to work out."

I lift a hand and wave back, watching as he disappears inside. "What do you mean?"

My dad presses his lips together. "Let's not get distracted, hmm?" He comes up and grips my shoulder. "You got a lot on your mind," he says, reading me as he's always been able to.

I nod, looking across the yard toward Cameron's childhood bedroom window. "She, uh, snuck up on me."

"The good ones always do."

Tension tugs in my stomach, and my hazel eyes lock on my father's blue ones. "What if she doesn't understand?" I don't have to break it down—my parents know what I want out of life.

"Come on now," he begins, opening the front door and easing me inside. We pause in the entryway, our eyes called to the back sliding door. The curtains are tied back, Cameron and my mama sitting there in the early morning sun, blankets wrapped around them both.

Cameron says something, and I can only imagine what it was as, in the next second, my mom leans forward to smack her on the knee.

Cameron throws her head back and laughs, coffee cup cradled in her hands. They just look so right sitting there together. They fit.

We fit.

My dad's hand comes down on my shoulder, and he gives a little squeeze. "That look like a girl who won't understand?"

There's a little thump in my chest because no, it doesn't.

She looks like an angel of chaos who wants all my secrets.

Could I tell her? Fillet myself open and let her watch me bleed, the confident, easygoing man she knows me to be turning into a poster child for insecurity right before her eyes?

When she shared with me on the rooftop barn, I almost jumped in and told her, and then last night, I felt compelled to give her a little more, but that conversation was quickly glossed over. For my benefit, of course, because the girl knows me better than any other.

She saw me struggling and gave me an out, which I eagerly took. Maybe I shouldn't have. Maybe I should have just broke things down for her, filled in all the blanks and shared that the future she's considering for herself is not that far off from the one I want for myself.

No—not *want* but *refuse to give up*.

There's a make or break for me, but it's that break part that I'm afraid of.

Still, when I look at her, I wonder if it would have to come to that.

Cameron looks up then, sticking her sock-covered foot out to nudge my mom. They both smile this way, and my low chuckle matches my dad's.

"Looks like we're caught." With one last squeeze, my dad nudges his head in their direction. "Come on. Come sit with your mama for a few minutes before you have to go."

Nodding, I follow a step behind him, a strange turning in my stomach I've never felt when it came to Cameron before but recognize as fear.

Will she blush and avoid my eyes, saying without words that something deeper happened between us last night?

Will she excuse herself and go back inside, giving some explanation that says just as much as her blush would?

I don't have time to work through any more theories, my dad already stepping out, so there's nothing for me to do but follow.

He moves over to my mom while I drop beside Cameron, and we look at each other at the same moment.

She smiles brightly, shifting on the cushion to face me better. "How'd it go?"

It's the perfect reaction, not a single sign that she regrets last night, just fully focused on how my training session went this morning.

As irrational as it is, it pisses me off.

How can she smile at me like it's any other day? Like she didn't have my dick in her hands last night? Like I didn't feel the heat between her legs?

Like she didn't come with those big blue eyes locked on mine?

She's acting like nothing happened, like it's all forgotten, so small of an event that she's completely unfazed by the sight of me when I've been burning at the thought of her all morning, waiting for this moment.

Cameron isn't the one who gets up and makes some excuse to get away.

I am.

CAMERON

He's totally freaking out. Like epically.

I'm not sure what I expected, but based on how annoyed I am right now, clearly it wasn't that. I'm not even sad.

I'm just straight-up pissed.

This is *Brady*. Proud playboy with an entire fan base who have named themselves. For years now, I've watched him with other women. He's the approachable one, the funny guy who is always laughing but never at another's expense. He's built like a god without the complex. I mean, he knows he's fine, but he's not a dick about it. There's just an air about him that tells you you're safe with him, and that goes a long way for a single girl looking to get hers. And from what I hear, the man is a giver.

Right now, all he's giving *me* is rage-y thoughts.

The man is king of casual hookups, and while we might not fit into the casual category, what happened last night wasn't even a full-fledged hookup. If I were a baseball fan, I'd say we slid into third base and the coach started raging because all Brady had to do was round that sucker to hit a home run. The ball was already over the fence.

I wanted it, pretty sure he wanted it, but the man didn't take it.

Why?

Because we had no condom?

Because he didn't want to take things between us that far?

Yet?

I don't know, but I'm not about to make his mama worry just before we take off, so I smile and sit back, bringing my mug to my lips. "My guess is he just realized he forgot to bring me a coffee home and now he's in big trouble."

Tisha laughs loudly, smacking her husband's thigh, buying my

325

little white lie. "Oh, man, Ben has done that many times. Usually, it's the one ingredient I sent him for, and he has to go right back." She shakes her head, drinking her latte in oblivious bliss. "Men, I swear."

I peek at Ben, and he winks at me, tipping his chin in a grateful manner. Clearly, Brady talked to his dad about something, but I guarantee he didn't mention our little third-down pass.

"I'm so sad you guys are leaving today, but it was such a nice surprise. If I hadn't had that third glass of wine last night, I was going to ask if you wanted to get up with us today to watch the sunrise from the hill."

"I don't think I will ever in my life get up to watch the sunrise on purpose. I had to wake up at five in the morning on Friday for a school thing, and it about killed me. Zero stars, do not recommend."

Ben chuckles.

"My grandpa used to wake up at five every single day with nothing to do but watch reruns of *Criminal Minds* and eat Cheerios with bananas. I might cry if that happens to me."

He pulls his wife onto his lap and it's the cutest thing ever. "That's what sunsets are for."

Tisha smiles. "Watching the sunset is like nothing else this world can offer you."

"Yeah?" I listen raptly, pulling my legs up a little higher on the seat.

"Oh, yes, honey. It's like a symbol of hope, reminding us that it will rise again the next day, bringing with it new beginnings. Promises of a brighter tomorrow."

She peeks over her shoulder at her husband, every inch of her softening as she adds, "A sunrise with the person you love is one of those moments, you know? It's fleeting but reminds us that love doesn't fade like the day, but it does change, rekindling anew each morning. The need to watch the sunset is your heart telling you to listen, to stop and savor that moment in time."

I don't realize moisture has built in my eyes until she looks back with a smile and I blink them away. "That's... I mean, you should write poems or something," I tease because I don't know what else to say.

Tisha chuckles, leaning back into her husband. "I've been known to write a sonnet or two in my day."

My lips curve up as I stare at the happy couple, and it makes me wish my parents were home this weekend too. I sit back, looking around the yard I've played in hundreds of times at dozens of barbecues and birthdays. My eyes travel over to the back side of my home in the distance, and a surge of grief sweeps through me unexpectedly.

I'm really going to miss this.

My eyes grow cloudy again, and a hand pats at my knee. My lips press together so I don't cry, and I smile at Ben.

The sliding door opens, and we all look up at Brady. He's showered and changed into an AU sweatsuit, my clothes I wore here in a clean and neat pile in his hands. "Mom washed these for you if you want to be a little more comfortable for the ride back to campus."

"Yeah, it will be nice to have some underwear for once."

Brady's lips tip up to one side and his parents chuckle. He moves to the side so I can slip through the door, but he squeezes my fingers as I pass, and the little act of reassurance makes me smile.

Everything is going to be okay.

We're going to be okay.

We watched the sunset together.

I tense, shaking the thought from my mind, and rush to get ready.

I'm changed and coming down the stairs in less than five minutes. Brady and his parents are gathered by the door, saying their goodbyes.

They turn to me and I lean in, giving Ben a hug first and then Tisha.

She squeezes me tight, whispering in my ear, "Trust your instincts, honey."

My brows pull, eyes finding Brady's over her shoulder, but then she pulls back, smiling sweetly. "Brady's got last night's leftovers packed away in a little ice chest in the truck already, and I made some muffins this morning. They're in the bag with some more snacks for the road—candy, cookies, chips."

I squeeze her hand. "Thank you and thank you guys for such an amazing weekend. I didn't realize how much I missed home and home cooking."

"Hey, you know you don't have to go to every football game. You can always come home on the weekends and watch it on TV with the rest of us old people."

"I might take you up on that."

"What? No!" Brady gapes, and I look at him. "You have to come to my games."

"Do I?"

"Yes."

"And why is that?" I tease, tipping my head to the side.

His eyes narrow in challenge, and I can't help but laugh.

"Don't worry, Big Guy." I walk over, patting his chest. "I wouldn't miss watching you play for a lifetime supply of Cookie Crumble coffees, let alone to hang out with old people on game days."

"Hey." Ben feigns offense, and this time, I give him a wink.

With a final wave, I leave Brady to his goodbyes and head out to the truck, but he's right on my tail, our doors closing in unison.

He turns the music on, and I take that as a sign he doesn't feel like talking yet, so I pull my phone out and play around a little.

When I look up again, we're pulling into the drive-through of Bebe's Brews.

Our eyes meet, neither of us saying a word, and finally he sighs, reaching over and unlocking my seat belt. He grips me by my thigh and pulls, my ass sliding across the seat until I'm in the middle. He buckles me in beside him. When it's our turn he orders for us both, and we're back on the road within ten minutes, warm breakfast burritos and coffees in hand.

I peel the wrapper back on his and pass it to him, following suit with my own. Before I take a bite, I look his way, burrito in one hand and salsa cup in the other. "You sure you don't want to feed me mine?"

Brady scoffs, sliding a grin my way. "Eat, brat."

Smiling to myself, I do just that.

The first few hours go by pretty quickly, and then the afternoon seems to drag. We stop twice so baby-bladder Brady can piss and a third time for gas.

It's dark by the time we're pulling into the parking lot of my dorm, a little rainstorm seeming to be rolling in with us. It's kind of ominous considering Brady had gone quiet about a half hour ago.

As he swings around the curved drive, his eyes are darting all around.

"Looking for someone?" I tease.

"Huh?" His head snaps my way. "No."

I feel a frown threatening but I let it go, my mouth stretching into a yawn as I unbuckle and start pulling on my shoes.

"You want to come up?"

He glances out the front window, shaking his head slightly. "No, I don't think I should."

"Afraid I might get a little needy again?"

His eyes snap my way, but I falter when he doesn't smile.

"Look, Brady," I begin. We avoided this topic the whole drive, but I guess it has to be discussed now. "Don't make this weird, all right? It's fine if you regret letting it get that far."

A huffed laugh leaves him, and he shakes his head. "It's not that."

"Well, it's something."

He drops his head sideways against the glass, a long exhale leaving him, but when he looks my way, his expression doesn't match the heaviness in his body language. He's got his megawatt

Brady grin in place, and I kind of want to smack it off him. "I've had a lot of fun, Fake Girlfriend."

A sinking sensation weighs down my stomach at his words because I know there are more coming, and I don't think I want to hear them.

"I think it's time to put you back on the market."

Yeah, he totally freaked out this morning.

It takes me a moment, but I nod. "Okay," I say, agreeing despite the disappointment in my gut. I'm not really sure what to do with it, but this is something only he can work out.

"Okay?"

Why is he fighting a frown when he's the one who suggested it?

"If that's what you want, then yeah. Okay."

"It's just that there's a man out there who wants to be the real deal."

A scowl starts before I realize what he means because at first all I hear is *I don't want to be the real deal*.

That's not it, though. He's talking about Alister.

"Okay." I force the word out again, my smile as real as his is as I quickly slide over and climb out. I snag the bag of goods from the floorboard. "I'm keeping these. You can have the leftover mac."

Brady watches, a small crease between his brows.

I force my lips higher. "See you in class tomorrow."

I turn around and walk away, closing my eyes as the weight in my stomach threatens to knock me over and wondering at what point exactly I stopped seeing Brady as my friend but rather something more.

Way to go, girl. Another guy you can't keep.

First Trey, then Alister, and now Brady.

How does it go in baseball—three strikes and you're out?

My feet stop just inside the entrance, Alister's words from before I took off with Brady for the weekend coming back to me.

He didn't punch me when I said I was going to come to you, he had said.

Alister talked to Brady the same day he told me he loved me. The same day that Brady suddenly needed to escape campus and fully intended on doing so alone until I forced my way into his little trip.

He was running away, not wanting to be here when Alister and I did talk, unaware we already had.

We'd talked before Brady kissed me when no one was watching.

We'd talked before I climbed onto his lap and all but demanded he take what I wanted to give.

Realization hits me and I don't know if I want to laugh or cry.

Brady didn't want to end this thing between us. He thought I would once I heard what his teammate had to say.

He's wrong.

CHAPTER 36
CAMERON

We're all chilling at Payton's studio, having just finished the meal Ari cooked for us while following along to Noah via FaceTime. Noah who, two hours later, is still on the screen on her phone that's propped up on a candle, plugged in to keep charged.

"I already went to the store to get everything but the turkeys," Noah says with a smirk, looking over at Brady.

"Yeah, you stay away from my turkey, my man. I'm beating you this year, watch."

Noah chuckles. "What do you think I'm going to do? Inject it with something before you get there?"

"See how easy he came up with that!" Brady snaps, trying to get us all on his side. "I'm telling you I should have won last year."

Noah fights a grin, disappearing from the screen for a moment.

Deaton runs by with his stuffed elephant, and I reach out, pulling him in for some love.

"Well, with both of you making turkey and Noah's ham, we should have plenty of meat." Chase looks around. "We just need to double up on sides."

"And dessert!" Paige lifts a pencil in the air, taking notes like she'll be tested on this later.

"And dessert." He nods. "Noah, you bake too or what?"

"I can," he says, coming back into view with a glass of water. "Or I can ask Nate if his mom might be willing to make something for us," he says, referring to Ari and Mason's cousin. He plays for

USD, so he and Noah share an apartment since it's close to the NFL team Noah plays for. "Unless someone else wants to volunteer..." When no one says anything, he chuckles. "Paige?"

We look toward the little ballerina, whose cheeks are as pink as her fingernails.

"You bake?" Chase asks.

"A little." She tucks her hair behind her ear. "I'm happy to make a few things if there's room in the kitchen."

"You can always come down to my brother's with us," Payton suggests. "Or even Lolli's place."

Lolli is Nate's future wife, and she and Parker, Payton's brother, own beach houses just down the road from the one our parents gifted us.

"Okay, perfect." Paige smiles, going back to her homework.

"Wait. You're not staying in your room, Mase?" Ari asks her twin.

He shakes his head. "Deaton has a room at Parker's, so we won't have to bring anything from here, and with more people coming than just our crew this time around, it just makes sense. You guys are going to need all the extra space."

"How many people are we talking?" I tickle Deaton, locking him in my arms as he wiggles like crazy, trying to get free but not really wanting to.

"Calmy, no!" He giggles, arching his back when I blow raspberries against his neck.

"No?" I flip him into my arms until I'm cradling him like an infant. "But Calmy wants all the love bugs."

"Wuv bugs?!" he laughs, wiggling until I set him free, and darts across the carpet until he's throwing himself in his mama's arms.

Chase looks to Mason. "Fernando, Jeremy, Cedric, and... um." He clears his throat, his eyes moving to Brady.

Brady's gaze skates past mine and he lifts a shoulder, his attention going back to his phone. "Maybe one or two others, not sure yet."

"Okay, so obviously Noah is with me." Ari smiles, looking over at her man on screen. "And, Paige, you're still using Lolli's spare room when you go back and forth from here to Oceanside, right?"

"I am." She looks up with a smile. "How do we feel about pumpkin cheesecake with candied pecans?"

Several of us chuckle, and she blushes all over again, sliding down in the chair and going back to her notebook.

Chase shakes his head, fighting a grin. "Okay, so Mason's room is free," he reiterates.

"Fernando and Jeremy are already roommates, so we can put them both in there," Mason says.

"So that leaves possibly three people." Noah pulls his hoodie over his head, leaning closer in the camera view.

The room goes quiet, and when I look around, Chase, Mason, Ari, *and* Noah are looking at me. "What?"

"Nothing," Ari says quickly.

Too quickly.

I glare at my best friend.

Noah clears his throat. "Well, I can attest to the couch being pretty comfortable. That covers one more."

"Then we're all good." Brady looks up, shoving his phone in his pocket.

"Are we?" Chase asks.

I make a silly face at Deaton, and he covers his face with his tiny hands, pulling them away a moment later and trying to make the same one back. I laugh and make another.

"Paige at Lolli's, Mason at Payton's, Noah with Ari, and me with Cam."

I freeze, my eyes snapping to Brady. "What?"

He frowns. "What?"

"Okay, then, it's settled." Ari claps her hands and jumps up. "Noah, love you. I'll call you when we get back in our dorm."

She hangs up, takes my hand, and yanks me to my feet, tugging me right out the door.

We get to the sidewalk before I think to pull myself free, spinning to face Ari. "Did he just say we're rooming together this weekend?"

"He did."

"For three days?"

Ari scrunches her nose and nods.

"Jesus fuck." I drop my head back. "He's trying to kill me."

Ari loops her arm in mine and drags me down the path toward our dorm. "Well, let's look at the bright side."

"What bright side would that be?"

And then she blows my damn mind.

BRADY

I blink, then blink again.

"What just happened?"

"Didn't you two 'break up'?" Chase smirks.

"Fuck off, we weren't really together, but yeah, we're not pretending anymore. Why? What's that have to do with anything?"

Mason laughs, and I swing a glare his way.

"Is someone going to talk or not, assholes?"

"Well, Cam didn't seem to think you two would be sharing a room together."

My head tugs back. "Yeah, that's because she doesn't need to think about it. It's just what we do."

"It's what you did."

I lean forward, resting my elbows on my knees. "What am I missing here?"

"Oh, Brady." It's Paige who talks, and I look up to find her packing her things in her book bag before hanging it over her shoulder. She walks over, putting her hand on my arm with a little pat. "You're in for a ride."

I frown, trailing her as she walks over to Payton, kissing Deaton on the head before walking out. "Wait. How did you know we ended our fake-dating shit?"

Chase turns to Mason, who glances at his girl.

Payton opens her mouth, but nothing comes out, a small shrug following. "She may have told Ari, and Ari might have let it slip when I picked up Deaton on Tuesday."

"Why would she tell Ari?" I ask. "You guys knew what we were doing since day one."

"Because, my man." Mason drops down on the couch next to Payton, hauling his son into his lap. "Girls tell their friends when things are sad, bad, and ugly."

"Yeah, well, that doesn't match anything about us."

"Oh, you're an us again?"

I throw a pillow at Chase's head, flipping him off when he laughs.

"Come on, man, just say it." He digs into a bag of chips.

"Say what?"

"That you like her."

"I love her."

Their eyes grow wide.

"No, I mean I love her like I love all the girls," I rush to say. "Like you love her. Stop smiling!"

They're all laughing now, and I sit back in the chair.

"You guys are idiots." I sigh, glancing over at Payton. "Think she told anyone else our little deal was off?"

"I don't know." She offers a small smile. "But I think if you're asking that question, then you're hoping she hasn't."

I face my boys, both of them staring with easy, open expressions. Understanding. Acceptance. Unity.

I push out of the chair and walk out, but I don't go back to the house. I roam around until I find myself walking through the gate of the practice field.

I climb up into the bleachers, choosing the section the girls sit in when they come to study while we practice just because they want to be there for us.

Cameron is always there for me.

Smiling and laughing and playing along in any and all of my nonsense. She'll jump on my back or grab my arm, and just like that, we'll be the life of our little party. She's cheered me on with women, on the field, and off it. Never once has she judged me for what she's seen or heard.

Never would she.

I close my eyes, a frustrated sigh leaving me.

She is gonna be pissed at me when she finds out what I did, even if I did it for her. She'll forgive me, though, after giving me shit of course. It's in her nature.

My sweet and sour Hellcat.

My lips twitch, and I take out my phone, pulling up her name.

I haven't actually talked to her since I opened my big-ass mouth the Sunday before last, outside of the *hey* and *what's up* and *see you later*. We fell right into the school week and practice, had an away game, and this week started the same. Sure, we had Monday classes together, but it's not like her class with Alister where we work as partners. No, we're stuck staring at the overhead, listening to lectures. But it wasn't awkward, was it?

It's Tuesday now, and tomorrow afternoon, we'll load up as a group and make the drive to Oceanside for Thanksgiving weekend.

It'll be the first time we'll be around others together outside our little friend family. If they don't know we're "no longer together" already, they will soon enough.

I dread that moment.

I'm not good at this stuff—vulnerability and the unknown.

I like to know the score before I join the game, and if that's not possible, then I make sure it's one I can win regardless of the facts.

This is different.

The game is complicated—has one too many players and no rule book.

There are no plays to pick from and I've already used my time-outs.

The only thing I can do now is let the clock run out and see who takes it all in the end.

Alister or me.

The visitor…or the home team.

CHAPTER 37
CAMERON

I restack the boxes of diapers in the supply closet and add ointment to the rolling cart before closing the door, making my way to the changing stations. After refilling each of the sizes, I move on to the wipe dispensers, filling them to the brim and snapping the lids closed. Once all that is done, I put the cart back and head over to the laundry room to fold the blankets.

Stacking a massive pile in my hands, I place one on each cot.

"Those new blankets are so much better," I tell Junie, picking up Abby when she gives me grabby hands.

I sway her slightly, and she giggles wildly. "Okay, so I finished the list, but I still have a half hour before I need to head back to my dorm. Is there anything else you need help with before I take off?"

"All good here, but maybe check with Granny Grace?"

"Yep." I set Abby down next to the play kitchen and head toward the front. "See you next week, Junie!" I call before pushing through the swinging door into the check in, check out area.

Granny Grace is filling the cubbies with the little handprint turkeys the toddlers made earlier this week as I walk in. She looks up at me with a smile. "You headed off?"

"Almost. Just checking to see if you want some help first."

"I'm all set in here. If you do anything else, I'll be bored."

I smile, hopping up on the counter behind her desk, noticing a vase full of pretty pink and white flowers. I run my pinky along the edge of one of the silky petals. "What are these, Granny Grace?"

She looks back, her expression soft. "Those are gardenias."

The sentiment in her voice isn't missed. "Are they your favorite?"

She nods. "Same ones my husband used to bring me every other Friday when he'd pick up his check. This is the first bunch I've gotten since Frankie passed. I about broke down when the deliveryman said they were for me."

"They're beautiful."

"As was the gesture." Her eyes gloss over, and she looks to the photo on her desk. "Unnecessary but appreciated more than words can say. I'm surprised with how long they lasted. That little feed packet sure did make a difference."

"When did you buy them?" I wonder, bending slightly to see what they smell like. There's a hint of spiciness I didn't expect but not at all unpleasant.

When she doesn't answer, I look over at her and find her staring at me with her head tipped slightly.

"Huh," she says, then turns back to her task.

I smile as I hop down. Old women are so funny with their secret thoughts. Grabbing my bag from under the counter, I take my jacket off the hook and tug it on.

"Okay, well, I'm out of here. Have a nice Thanksgiving, Granny Grace."

"You too, honey."

I go to walk out, but as I pass her desk, I pause, taking a few backward steps, my eyes going to the photo.

Granny Grace is in her prime, maybe thirty years old with her handsome husband beside her as they lean against his old Chevy pickup, a bouquet of pink and white gardenias in her hands.

My heart does a little jump, and I yank my head around so I can look at the older woman, finding she's watching me.

She smiles but says nothing, whistling as she gets back to work.

With one last wave, I leave the center and make the walk back to my dorm.

As I come up the small hill, I find the guys are already pulled against the curb, my bag hanging from Brady's hands. He steps up to Mason's Tahoe and puts it in the back, taking Ari's from Chase and stacking it on top.

They turn toward each other and start talking. I'm almost to them when another car pulls up behind the two already parked there. Their teammates file out, shoving and laughing, all ready for a little break from campus.

Ari and Paige come out of the dorm doors and spot me, walking over.

"Hey!" Ari beams. "I don't know if you want to run up and make sure you didn't forget anything, but we grabbed both of the bags you put by the door."

I nod, glancing over at the line of vehicles.

"Mase and Payton are on their way here in Payton's car, and Brady's driving the Tahoe with all of us. The others are split between the pickups, because one of the guys works at the pizza place part-time and couldn't get his Saturday shift covered."

"Sounds good."

"Hey."

We turn toward the guys.

"We're ready to pile in when you are," Brady tells us, but he's looking at me. "I gave the others the address, so we don't have to worry about following each other the whole way. They're taking off now to hit the gas station."

"Perfect." Ari nods. "Well, let's get ready so we can just roll out when Mase gets here. I want to be there before Noah."

"Cool." He nods, and Chase elbows him in the ribs, widening his eyes at his friend. Brady looks back to me then, and after a moment, a sigh leaves him.

"What?" I ask.

He sighs again. "We're not the only ones who are going to be at the beach house this weekend."

I chew the inside of my cheek, anxiety rolling off me in waves. On one hand, I don't want him to jump to conclusions; on the other, I kind of want to see how he acts about it. "I know."

His eyes narrow. "You know?"

I nod, trying to get a read on him, and if I'm right, it's irritation and maybe a little disappointment that he's feeling.

"All right." He nods, frown pulling low. "No point in talking about it, then."

Isn't there?

The drive is like any other. We head out, stopping forty-five minutes later for food because boys "aren't hungry" when you ask them but magically become so after ten minutes on the road. Thankfully, we only stop one other time after that for gas, Deaton having passed out for the final stretch and allowing us to continue the rest of the way through.

The excitement cannot be tamed as we pull into the driveway, both Ari and I itching to get out and run inside our home away from home.

Brady has barely gotten the thing in park when we're shoving the doors open and racing up the path to the front door, but while Ari runs to the front, I take off around the corner, running along the wraparound porch to the back and down into the sand. I keep going until the sandy hill levels out and its nothing but ocean for miles.

I kick off my slides and hold up the legs of my sweatpants, not caring that my socks are getting wet, and walk right up to the water's edge, letting myself fall back on my ass.

I drop back into the sand, smiling up at the sky, and pull in a full breath of salty ocean air.

"Cheater!" Ari screams from somewhere behind me and then she's at my side, mimicking my position.

We sit there in silence, just enjoying being home.

"Ari?" I ask her after a moment.

"Yeah?"

"Promise me no matter where life takes us, we'll use this house the way our parents intended."

"You're stuck with me forever, sister." She grabs my hand, folding our fingers together.

We turn to face each other, sand imbedding itself in our hair, water from the wet sand soaking into my pants.

"Do you and Noah watch the sunset together?"

She nods. "We do. He has a spot he likes to go, somewhere his mom used to take him, but we haven't been there since he left. Why?"

My lips curve but I just look up at the sky, a sadness slipping over me.

"Cam." Ari smiles softly. "You ready for this?"

Inhaling until my lungs are stretched to the max, I nod. "As ready as can be."

"Good. Because Noah just turned onto our street."

Well then. Here we go.

We walk back to the house, chucking our socks on the deck and slipping inside with bare feet, sand in our hair, and wet spots on our pants. Ari runs straight through when she could have just gone around, throwing the door open and bursting outside.

I hold back, sliding my fingers through my hair, and tie it up in a quick, high pony, cringing at the wet, sandy strands clustered together. My leg begins to bounce, and I roll my eyes at myself, walking back the way I came and into the kitchen.

Lolli came over yesterday and waited for the grocery delivery to get here. She was nice enough to not only put away the cold foods but the whole-ass load, so I go straight for a chilled Capri-Sun, making a mental note to walk down to the store tomorrow to get another box so an adorable little boy doesn't catch me drinking all of his. I stab the straw in, sucking the thing dry as I take inventory of what we've got in case I want to tiptoe down for something sweet in the middle of the night. It's a momentary break from the bittersweet undercut whirling in my stomach as I wait for our guests to come inside.

There's a hint of excitement streaming through my veins, but right behind is an icy chill of anxiousness—of unease, because I know how this is going to make a certain man feel. In part I want to avoid that all together, but again…that anticipation is still there.

Huffing, I close the fridge, yelping when I find a man standing there. Not just any man but a man with familiar green eyes.

I cough, slapping at my chest. "What—"

"You good?"

I jump out of my skin when a second person makes themselves known, whipping around and narrowing my eyes on a different man.

Brady's brow jumps, and he speaks a slow, slightly fearful—as it should be—"What?"

I open my mouth, knowing what comes out is going to hurt someone's feelings, probably my own, because what the actual fuck?

But before I can say a word, a figure appears over his shoulder, and my eyes slide that way.

They freeze there, and my heart gives a little nostalgic thump. Ever so slowly, I feel my smile stretch.

The third man to step into the room smiles back, arms opening wide in invitation.

"Trey."

BRADY

She did not just say what I think she did.

I want to turn around and see if my subconscious is conjuring some sort of fuckery, but I can't seem to tear my eyes away from the girl in front of me, not when she's smiling like that—with her whole body. Her eyes are the brightest of blues, her cheeks stretched high and tinted a pretty pink. Her shoulders have gone lax.

She's happy to see him.

Her bare feet carry her past me, my pulse pounding harder every step she takes. She moves into his open arms, and the moment his close around her, lifting her off her feet the way I like to, a fire lights in the pit of my stomach.

It burns, a physical heat that scalds all the way up and into my throat, demanding I say something because who the hell does he think he is, holding someone else's girl like that?

She was his first, a voice in my head screams, but I strangle it the way I'm imagining strangling him.

And, man, that's unfortunate, because I really like the guy. I got to know him my first year at AU, back when he was the talk of our defense.

It used to be his name the broadcasters said when they wanted to talk about the magic of the Sharks' defense.

It's mine now.

Just like she is.

Fuck.

My eyes finally leave the back of her head, shifting to look at Trey.

I forgot what a big fucker he is, and he only looks stronger than the last time I saw him.

Finally, he lets her go, and satisfaction serves as a bucket of water for the burning sensation in my gut when she takes a few small steps back.

Distance. Yes. That's good.

He smiles at her, and I'm reminded Alister is here when he appears beside me.

Trey grins at Cameron. "Why do I get the feeling you're not surprised I'm here?"

Yeah, why?

A frown falls over my face.

345

"Ari might have given me a little warning," Cameron admits.

"A warning, huh?" He smirks. "Do you think you needed one, or was she just being her sweet little self."

"Meh, maybe a little bit of both," she says, playing along.

"Should I be hurt you didn't feel the need to get all dolled up for me?" he teases, and they both laugh.

"Nah, I only play that game before they bite. Why waste a good worm when you've already landed the fish, right?"

She's not flirting, she's just being Cameron, and Trey grins.

"The dirty sweats, bare feet, and sandy hair are a hazard of a completely necessary dash down to the water, so I guess I looked a tad better about five minutes before you got here."

"You look perfect."

All heads turn to me, and I realize that wasn't just my internal monologue talking.

The answering smile she gives me makes me wish I said it on purpose.

"What's up, Lancaster?" Trey finally realizes it's not just him and her in here and walks over, dapping me up with a grin. "Been watching your highlights. Moving over to my side of the ball was the move for you, man."

"Thanks, bro." I look to Cameron, subtly giving a nod toward Alister, figuring it's her job to introduce the guy, but she's busy biting her nails, staring between us all.

Two men she's dated and the one she pretended to all standing in the kitchen together, silently sizing each other up, and not necessarily because of the beautiful blond staring at us.

Her brows pull tighter, but then she comes closer, waving a hand between the two. "Trey, this is Alister Howl. Alister, this is Trey Donovan."

"That's it?" Trey goads her, and I find myself hiding a smirk. "No details? You gonna make me guess, 'cause I'll tell you, Butterfly, the fact that you're the one introducing and not the teammate he's standing beside is pretty telling."

Alister stands taller, accepting Trey's handshake when he offers it.

"Nice to meet you, man," Alister says respectfully.

Trey chuckles again, knowing it is not, in fact, nice to meet the guy the girl you're into used to date. "You too. I take it you're on the team?"

"Team, bench, same thing," Alister jokes.

Trey nods his head. "I know how that is. I was a red-card player once upon a time. Had to sit out and watch. That shit's hard."

Noah comes around the corner then, and I grin, meeting him for a bro hug. "Good to fucking see you, my guy." I step back, gripping his shoulder with a serious expression. "Don't get your panties twisted when I whoop your ass tomorrow."

"Deal." Noah grins, striding up to Alister with a hand out. "Noah."

"I know," Alister laughs, shaking his head. "Sorry, but I'm a little starstruck right now."

Noah, ever the humble man, doesn't say anything about that, not wanting to talk about himself or how badass of a ball player he is. "I'm glad you could make it. You're going to like it here."

Alister nods like an eager puppy, and I roll my eyes at him.

"Okay, so, I'm going to steal Brady so we can go put away our things." Cameron grips the sleeve of my hoodie and yanks, dragging me through the space, around the corner, and past the back of the couch. She releases me, only to step behind and nudge me until I start to climb the stairs, my shoulders shaking in silent laughter at her antics.

"Oh, ho, get all the laughs out now, because you are not about to be laughing, Brady freaking Lancaster." We reach her room, and she shoves me inside.

She closes the door, then whirls on me, a sexy little fire in her eyes I don't quite get but like.

347

"What?"

"What?" she deadpans, coming back with sass. "You know what! Why is Alister in the kitchen?"

"I'm sure he's stepped outside by now."

"Brady!" she hisses, coming closer until she's right in front of me. "Why is he here? How is he here, and before you say something like 'he rode with who the hell ever'—smooth by the way—just...don't."

I smile at her, reaching out to push stray strands of hair behind her ear. "I was hoping you'd be happy to see him."

A small frown pulls at her brows, and she leans into my knuckles when they slide along her cheek. "Were you?"

"No," I admit.

A surprised chuckle leaves her, and she sighs, her shoulders falling as she stares at me, the tense tenderness in her gaze almost too much.

"Honestly, I'm just enjoying the fact that you told Trey we were sharing a room too much to pick up what you're putting down right now."

She rolls her eyes, but her lips twitch. "That is not what I said."

Wrapping my arms around her waist, I twist my hips and gently tackle her to the mattress. "In man talk, that is exactly what you said."

She fights a smile, but it tugs at her lips regardless, and I reach out, pressing at the corner and lifting it a little higher. She laughs lightly, opening her mouth and snapping her teeth at me, but I pull back before she can catch me.

Not sure why.

I want her to catch me.

I want to tear up that metaphorical worm she spoke about.

We stare at each other for a few minutes and when the longing in my chest gets to be too much, I drop my head back on the pillow.

"He has no one," I tell her. "We were talking about our plans for the weekend and what we're all up to, and he mentioned he'd be staying back at the school. Chase told him he should go home if he could, rest up for the last stretch of the season and all that, and he said the only people back home were Allana's family." I look down, meeting her gaze. "I got the feeling he didn't want to go there because he figured it could hurt or disappoint you. He doesn't want to do that, Cammie Baby, and I couldn't let him be alone when he didn't have to be."

Her expression softens, then it's her turn to reach out and run her hands through my hair. "You are something else, Big Guy."

I want to be yours.

I watch her closely, but then I remember this morning and sit back with a small frown. "Wait, why are you acting surprised he's here?"

Her brows snap together. "Because I had no idea he would be. I nearly choked on Pacific Cooler when I saw him standing there."

"But you said you already knew." Her confusion prompts me to continue. "This morning. I told you it wasn't just going to be us, and you said you knew."

She goes to open her mouth but then her face softens, and it only grows more and more gentle the longer she stares. "I wasn't referring to Alister…"

"Trey."

She nods, watching me closely—too closely.

So I pull myself off the bed and turn away.

She knew he was coming.

Is that why she acted how she did when I said we'd room together? Did she not want to so he wouldn't get the wrong idea?

"You didn't know he was coming, did you?" she whispers.

A humorless laugh leaves me before I can stop it, and I shake my head. "No. I did not."

"Brady," she begins, but I hold my hand up and slowly slip from the room.

I can't do this right now.

I'm not sure I'll ever be able to.

CHAPTER 38
CAMERON

The night was long and restless, sleeping next to Brady without sleeping next to Brady. He stayed downstairs as long as possible, tiptoeing in well into the night and passing out on top of the covers.

When I woke, he was already out of the room. That was a couple of hours ago now, and the hustle and bustle of Thanksgiving morning, turned afternoon, has slowed some. That means I can no longer hide behind a long list of tasks.

Sucking it up, I step out the back door, walking over to where Alister is leaning against the deck, looking down the beach.

He does a double take, a small smile forming on his lips. "Hey, beautiful."

"Hey." I tip my head. "Take a walk with me?"

He holds my gaze a long moment, his chest rising in a full breath because he knows what this is. "Yeah, I'd like that."

We head the way that leads to Parker's and Lolli's houses, moving closer to the water as we go.

"I hope you're not upset I'm here." He glances over. "I should have asked you first."

"No." I grip his arm, squeezing. "No, I'm glad you came. I would have been upset if I found out you were going to be by yourself and only turned down the invite because of me."

"Me, turn down a chance at being near you?" He smirks my way, but there's no mirth to it.

"Ha-ha." I shove him, and he grins for real this time.

We grow quiet again, and I see Mason up ahead, my favorite curly head of dark hair walking beside him in the sand.

My lips curve and I pause, shifting to face the ocean.

"Cameron, it's okay," Alister says. "You don't have to do all this. I know where things with us are, and I understand."

My eyes grow watery, and I bite at my inner lip. "I know, but I just…be real with me. I was honest with you from the start, right?" I worry. "I don't mean before shit hit the fan but after. I told you I couldn't trust you and trust is…"

"Everything in a relationship?" he offers softly. "If you can trust anything I say, let it be that I do understand that—all too well. I just couldn't let go of that little bit of hope."

Of course. It was a break in trust from the one he loved that led him to me in the first place.

We all do dumb things when we're hurt or scared, don't we?

Brady flashes in my mind, but I force myself to focus. "But you never felt like I was leading you on or anything? I know there were a few times when you came close and I let you, and I can't help but feel like I gave you all the wrong signs."

"You didn't. Like I said, I was holding on to what we had, and I knew reminding you of our chemistry was my only shot. I took it knowing the chance was slim, and you never gave me any indication we could be more than a stolen moment or two."

I nod, a heavy breath leaving me.

"In hindsight, I should have seen this coming. Your dad did try to let me down gently, but I didn't exactly understand it at the time."

That has my head yanking his way again. "My dad? When did you talk to my dad?"

His smile is sheepish. "When I had a shirt full of sprinkled ice cream and even that wasn't enough for me to stop staring at you all afternoon."

The barbecue back in September. "Well...what did he say?"

Alister smiles a bit, looking over at the others. "He said, you know, the heart's a tricky thing. Sometimes the people who stand closest to you are the hardest to see, but my daughter? She's not blind. Stubborn, but not blind. Be careful, young man. I can tell she's the one who's upset right now, but something tells me she won't be the one hurt in the end."

He looks over, a bit of bashfulness in his eyes. "I might have repeated the words to myself several times trying to figure out what he was trying to tell me." He looks to Brady. "Turns out he wasn't really talking about me at all."

Man, I love my dad.

I drop my eyes to my lap.

"I'm sorry if I made things harder for you," he says. "But I had to try. If I didn't, it would have been another regret to add to the first one."

"Thank you for believing I was worth the time."

"You're worth a lot more, Cameron Cox, and if I thought for even a second I had a shot, I would keep trying to take it." He reaches over, squeezing my hand.

I hold on to it for a moment before both our arms fall to our sides, and we start the trek back to the house.

When we get closer, some of the guys are outside, throwing the ball around.

We stand back and watch, and after a few minutes, Alister glances my way.

"So." He raises a brow. "That's *the* Trey Donovan, huh?"

"Yep."

"Man," he says. "I must be *really* good-looking, considering you have impeccable taste in men."

Laughter flies from me, instantly gaining the attention of a certain beastly man, but I don't look Brady's way, even though he continues to stare.

"I pulled up his social media pages last night," Alister admits, and now it's my turn to raise a brow. "Think Lancaster knows what a big night Trey had after his team's win last week?"

I smirk to myself. "Nope."

"You gonna tell him?"

"Nope."

Now it's Alister who laughs, and I can't help the smile that blooms.

I'm happy we can do this, that things didn't get so misconstrued along the way where it ended with him hurt and me an epic, deceiving asshole.

Alister knew the score. He's known since day one that he was fighting a losing battle, but I commend him for trying. Respect it even, and in a way, it's made my feelings for him into something more genuine, just not in the way he hoped for.

"Thank you, Alister," I say softly, turning to wrap him in a hug. "Thank you for hanging around long enough to show me what a good man you really are."

"I'm going to miss you, beautiful," he whispers.

Tears form in my eyes, and I smile, kissing his cheek as I pull away. "I'll be around...but you should probably just call me Cameron now."

He lets out a heavy exhale, but his smile doesn't go away. "Yeah, you're right. Well, I guess I should go show these dudes how a real pass is supposed to be made."

I chuckle, pushing him toward the game.

When I look over, Brady is still standing there watching me.

And he doesn't look away.

BRADY

Most of us are in the kitchen, running around and getting things ready, with several conversations going on at once, but I'm only half tuned in. My eyes are glued to the sand hill just outside the floor-to-ceiling windows. I only came inside to check on my turkey and see if the others needed any help with their dishes, but now it seems I'm glued in place.

Trey and Cameron are standing there, chatting with an older couple walking by with a dog. He's got a football in his hands, and she's got a smile on her face. I bet those strangers think they're two young kids in love.

"Guys," I mumble.

"Let's move that down there," I hear Mason say.

"Can we put on Christmas music?" Paige asks someone.

"Guys." I say it a little louder this time, and I look up, finding they all stopped what they're doing and are now staring at me. "I'm jealous."

A few chuckles and a few girlie awws.

I glare. "Not helpful. How do I stop?"

Mason grins, going back to filling the ice chests so they're ready to be taken down to the bonfire later. "It's too late for that, my man. There's only one answer here."

The others nod, and I look around, waiting. "Well, is anyone gonna tell me what it is? 'Cause I'm all fucking ears, here."

It's Noah who walks over to stand beside me. He looks where I was focused and nods his head as he glances my way. "His team flew into town yesterday, and his family has a big dinner back home, so it's just him and his teammates out here this weekend. It didn't feel right not to extend the invite, but now I'm wishing I hadn't."

"Nah," I sigh, shaking my head. "You did the right thing. Shit, why do you think Howl is here?"

Noah chuckles, gripping my shoulder, and lowers his voice so not everyone can hear. "Sometimes it really sucks to be the good guy. It would be a lot easier to be selfish, but easy doesn't always mean right."

I nod, his words making sense, especially considering the drama he, Ari, and Chase went through not all that long ago.

Sighing, I look his way. "Now I'm just annoyed I didn't realize it was his team you were playing on Sunday, and I'd have to watch her watch *him* play."

"Yeah." Noah nods, a sly grin appearing. "But it's you she'll be sitting next to."

I smirk, chuckling as I cut him a glance. "You've got a little savagery in you, Riley."

He laughs, moving back to the kitchen. "This isn't going to be your excuse when I win the turkey competition, right?"

"Oh, kiss my ass, Prince Charming. I got this in the bag."

Six hours later, the sun is gone, and I'm lifting my third beer to my lips, shoulders slumped in a full-ass pout.

I did not have it in the bag.

My turkey was good, great even, but Chef Noah's was the best shit I ever tasted. Even better than last year, that fucker.

My lips turn up. Love that guy.

Alister sits down on the patio lounger beside me, reaching into the cooler at my feet, and pulls out two beers. He offers me one, but I lift mine to show it's still half-full, and he keeps both for himself.

Yeah, I feel that.

Right here, we have the perfect view of the others, laughing and dancing around the kitchen, tasting all of Paige's desserts.

"You know, I've shared a table with her on Thanksgiving my entire life." No need to state specifically who I'm talking about. We're both watching the same blond. "Every single one, every single year."

"That's a lot of history."

I scowl at the night. "Yeah."

Closing my eyes, I push to my feet, tossing my beer bottle in the plastic recycle bin. "Just...don't hurt her, man."

"Funny." Our eyes meet. "I was going to tell you the same thing."

Unease curls around my ribs, not only from his words or

the heavy tone of them but the look of acceptance on his face. "Alister?"

His lips twitch but not necessarily in a smile, and he stands, his own chest rising. "I'm catching a ride back to campus with Fernando in the morning. I'll be gone before she wakes up."

"If this is because of Trey..." I shake my head, my mouth growing sour at the thought of him. "He'll be gone again soon."

"It's not, man." He shakes his head, taking a deep breath. "She told me a long time ago there was nothing left for us, and I just refused to hear it."

"But why are you walking away now? What's changed?"

"When I told her I was going to fight for her, she was available." His eyes hold mine. "She's not anymore."

My heart starts beating wildly as realization sets in. "You told her already."

"I did."

"And she...?"

"Didn't say it back? No." He lets out a low laugh. "No, she didn't. She said she had to go." He sighs. "And then she ran out into the middle of the road and hopped in the truck with you."

Ran into the middle of the road...

"Wait." I push closer. "When did you tell her?"

"Maybe an hour after I told you."

My muscles lock, eyes frozen on his.

He told her.

She knew he was in love with her before she came home with me that day. Before I kissed her outside my truck and before everything that came after.

A slow thump starts in my chest, and it only grows louder, faster.

Alister smiles and grips my shoulder as he goes to walk by, but I spin.

"Wait." Discomfort draws lines to my forehead. "This isn't why I invited you here, you know, to see if she'd turn you down or whatever. I was raised better than that. It was an honest invitation because I didn't like the thought of you, or anyone for that matter, being alone on a holiday."

"And that says a lot about you, Lancaster. I appreciate it, and I had a great time, but I am going to go. Before I do, though, let me be the one to do something kind for you." He pauses, and my brows dip in the center. "Don't leave yourself open for regrets."

"It's...complicated."

Alister smiles, looking up at the back deck of the house, where my friends, my *family*, are drinking and laughing and enjoying each other's company. "I don't know, man." He brings his attention back to me. "Looks pretty simple to me."

With one last pat on the shoulder, he walks off, and my eyes go back to our crew.

Ari is standing there with a smile, Noah's arms wrapped around her with his lips pressed to her hair. Payton is leaning against the railing with a blanket pulled around her shoulders, watching Mason from across the way, the father and son duo dancing to some country song.

I've never been prouder of a best friend than I was the day he claimed that little boy as his own. He has no idea what that will mean to Deaton one day, and I know Mason will spend his life making sure that kid never feels like anything less than his son.

My chest rises and falls on a long breath, gaze continuing along the others.

Mason's cousin Nate is here with his girl, Payton's brother with his fiancé, who also happens to be Nate's sister.

I look for the rest of our crew, finding Paige is off the deck, sitting on a rock by the firepit, Fernando standing across from her telling a story that has her laughing a bit, but her eyes keep moving across the flames, and what do you know? It's my other best friend she's looking at.

He's glaring right back but not at her—at his teammate who's talking to her.

Huh. Seems that most of us are all coupled up, just a few of us left to figure out where life is going to lead us—to the person we want or some other unknown.

My eyes go to Cameron, standing by the fire too, with Trey at her side.

She's got a pair of baggy sweats on, the bottoms all bunched up and shoved as best as she could manage into a pair or fuzzy boots in an attempt to keep the sand out. It won't work. Her upper body is drowning in a hoodie, and I hate that it's lacking my name or number. Her hair is tied up on her head in a mess of blond, little pieces blowing free around her face.

I want to push them away, tuck them back behind her ear.

How do I tell her I'm gone on her?

That she's all I can fucking think about and how I hate that I no longer get to say she's mine, *show she is*.

I want to make her mine in every way, but this is fucking monumental for me, and I'm downright terrified.

When I give myself to someone, fully and completely, it has to be endgame, like a franchise player who signs on the dotted line and stays there until his very last play.

I'd be asking a lot of her, expecting even more. There are things I need in my future that I can't *not* have, but I need to fucking have her too.

The music is turned up a little louder, and I glance up just as the others file down into the sand. Noah grabs Ari and starts spinning her around, and Mason follows his lead, both his little man and little mama in his arms.

My eyes lift, finding Cameron watching them all with a small smile, and my gaze narrows at the strain between her brows.

What's the matter, baby?

Suddenly, my view of her is blocked by a large frame—large but smaller than mine.

I glare as Trey holds a hand out and gives a little bow that has her lips curving.

She puts her hand in his and he tugs her toward the dance floor that doesn't exist but our friends pretend is there.

Her hand falls on his shoulder, and he gently grips her hip, and no.

Uh-uh. I'm already on my feet, moving across the sand.

Someone claps my back as I walk by, and someone—maybe a few someones—chuckle, but I ignore them all, attention locked in on a certain blond.

I'm about four feet from her when those pretty eyes of hers pop up, colliding with mine. I wait for a gasp, for shock or certainty, but I get none of that.

She simply stares, an almost curious if not impatient expression etched across her perfect face, like she wants to hit fast-forward, but someone else is hogging the remote.

I step up so I'm facing them, and Trey glances over with a grin.

"Hey, man."

"She's not available," I tell him, my eyes moving to hers. She raises a bratty little brow, and I slip into the small space between the two. "You're just not."

Her chin rises, going tough, little Cammie on me, but I see the softness she tries to hide. It bleeds from her every pore...but maybe it's only for me to see.

"Is that right?" she sasses, her voice strong, but there's a thickness to it that isn't usually there.

Hope?

"Yeah, baby," I whisper, everyone else fading into the background as I step up to her, one hand cupping her neck, the other pressing on the small of her back to draw her closer. "That's right."

I don't give her any time to decide, but she doesn't seem to need any.

We meet halfway, mouths colliding with a desperate need to claim.

It's not messy or clumsy. We're in sync, the perfect pairing—the ocean and the sun, me and football.

Me and my girl.

Because that's what she is.

Mine.

And I want to show her what that means.

Bending, I swoop her up, and she giggles, a sweet fucking sound that goes right to my dick. I carry her into the house and up the stairs, kicking the bedroom door closed and trusting that the others will know not to go into Ari's room—the one right next door that's connected by a bathroom.

I toss her on the bed, and she smiles up at me from the pile of purple pillows.

"Took you long enough," she teases.

I nod, the words I want to say not coming but no longer from nerves. I suddenly have no fear here. Cameron will accept me for the things I am and the things I'm not alike—just like she always has.

This will be no different.

She'll still be her, and I'll still be me, but we'll get to do filthy things to each other now. And goddamn, do I want to do so many dirty things to this woman.

"I'm a liar," I tell her.

She fights a grin. "Are you now?"

"Yes. I told you someone else wanted to be the real deal to you, but what I didn't say was I did too."

"I see." She smashes her lips to one side, amusement bright in her baby blues.

"Everyone sees me as a campus playboy." A small frown starts to form across her forehead, but I keep going. "Ask around, and you'll be told I slept my way through the sorority houses my first year here."

That little frown deepens, and she starts to shake her head. "Brady—"

"They're wrong. I did hook up with…enough of them."

"Brady, I know who you are. You don't have to tell me any of this."

"I didn't sleep with any of them," I admit, heart pounding in my chest.

Cameron's brows snap together, and I know that look. "You don't have to say that, Brady. There's nothing about you that I would ever judge you for."

"I know." I nod, trying to pack as much truth into those two words as humanly possible because I do know this. It's why we're in this room together right now in the first place.

"Then why lie?" she whispers.

It's a fair question and there is a lie in there, but it's not the words I spoke. "I have lied, mostly without saying a word. By letting people talk and leading them to believe. But I'm not lying to you now."

"Brady, you've slept with some of them."

"I've slept with none of them."

Her brows snap together, the air in the room shifting. She's getting upset and rightfully so. "You're—"

"A virgin."

If there were a picture of shock, it would be Cameron's face in the frame.

CHAPTER 39
CAMERON

Virgin.

Six letters. Two syllables.

Defined as a person who is innocent, naive, or inexperienced.

Brady is none of those things.

He's filthy mouthed and a relentless flirt. Inexperienced?

Yeah right. The man's tongue fucks like a god. With his hands and that voice.

His body and his handsome fucking face.

He is a walking, talking real-life sex toy. All the fantasies I never knew I had come to life.

Maybe that's why you're obsessed with him?

Being near him—hell, thinking about him—is like being barricaded in a whirlpool of want, forever on the cusp of drowning, but the invisible safety vest his presence emits keeps your head hovering above water. I'm not just talking want that stems from lust—that's just a given at this point—but deeper desires.

Scary ones.

The kind that reset your soul with someone else inside it.

But he's always sort of been there, hasn't he?

That's a special sort of experience, right?

A connection rivaled by nothing else. By no other.

A virgin?

"Can I explain?" he asks softly, finally lowering onto the mattress at the foot of the bed.

I offer him a soft smile, so he knows I'm not discrediting his words.

As much of a shock as they are, as hard as they may seem to believe, all things considered, he would never say them to me if they weren't 100 percent true. I trust him.

"Please." I reach out, and he entwines his fingers with mine across the space.

Brady stares down at our hands a moment, flipping them over so he can watch as he draws a few small, soothing circles along the inside of my palm.

"A fear of mine has always been that I would fall for the wrong girl, and I'd give her more than I meant to give, and she'd take what would only be half hers."

Bronze eyes lift to mine and hold.

It takes a moment, but I make sense of his words. "A baby?" I frown, a little lost but not wanting to appear negative.

"A baby," he confirms, almost a little shy, but in his next breath he's as sure as ever. "Cameron, I told you my father is my father by choice."

"Aren't all parents?"

His nod is a little sad. "Yeah, I guess that's true, but the man who got my mother pregnant with me decided a kid wasn't in his plans."

I offer as much of an encouraging expression as possible. "Thank god for that, right?"

A surprised, low laugh leaves him, almost as if he never really thought of it that way, and he smiles. It's wide and happy, and I climb across the bed, sitting with my legs folded right in front of him. Instantly, his strong arms come around me, loosely holding me close.

"My dad met my mom when she was eight months pregnant. She was working at a bank, and he was getting ready to ship out. He asked if he could write her and she said yes. He showed up at the hospital the day after I was born. Married her a week after that, and even though they put his name on my birth certificate, he wanted it to be official, so he adopted me as soon as the paperwork was ready."

"Brady." My heart clenches but not in sadness.

"Never, not for a single moment in my entire life, have I ever felt like less than Ben Lancaster's son. Never have I lacked a damn thing a father is supposed to offer their son, their children in general. That's why I never outright told anyone. Not from embarrassment or shame but because speaking the words out loud when they aren't true felt wrong, disrespectful to him even. He is my dad, you know?" He lifts his head, his right hand coming up to cup my cheek.

"I have waited to sleep with someone because I need to be able to trust that person with everything I have, Cameron. I refuse to risk the chance that any child of mine could possibly lose a parent from choice. If I were sleeping around, I'd have no way of knowing if someone out there ended up pregnant and either couldn't find me to tell me or simply decided not to. I know that sounds crazy. I'm young as hell and maybe this isn't something that should have even crossed my mind yet. And I just said I lost nothing with Ben as my father. It's true that I have everything I could ever need in my parents, but I also know that not everyone has someone else come along who can give as freely and wholeheartedly as my dad has. But it's not only that, and maybe this is the craziest part."

Brady pauses, his shoulders lowering a little, like he thinks this might be what changes things. "I want to give to another child out there somewhere what my dad gave to me simply by being nothing more than the man he is. I will adopt one day," he says surely. "It's a lot, I know, but it's something I've known about myself for a very long time."

My tears are falling, and when I lean forward, gently pressing my lips to his, he kisses me back the same.

It's tender. It's sweet.

It's loving.

It's my Brady.

"I think I'm in love with you," I whisper.

Brady goes tense, but not a breath later, his entire being seems to settle. He leans forward, pressing the world's most precious kiss to my lips.

"That's good, baby, because I know now I've been in love with you for a lot longer than I even realized."

I run my nose along his, and he nips at my lips.

"It's you, Hellcat. The girl, the woman, I can trust with everything I am today and the man I hope to become."

I run my fingers across his cheeks, gripping his face in my hand and leaning up to press a soft kiss to the corner of his mouth. His eyes close and he leans into my touch.

My big, strong man. My beastly...boyfriend.

He was afraid to tell me this, likely worried I would judge, or worse, walk away.

Deep down though, in that part of him where a part of me lives, he knew. It's why he held on.

It's why we're here right now, because he understood that fear is natural, worry is inevitable, but trust...trust is everything.

"You know all my secrets now," he whispers, turning his head slightly to kiss my wrist, those brilliant eyes meeting mine. "You know what that means?"

"What?"

His forehead meets mine. "I get to keep you."

His words draw more tears to my eyes, and I melt into him, my eyes closing.

I don't have to pretend he didn't quickly become my everything anymore, because I'm his too. I want this. Us.

Him and the life he's planned.

"Brady?"

"Yeah, baby?"

"Can we have sex now?"

Brady goes stiff but only for a millisecond, and then he throws his head back with a laugh, and just like that, our future is settled.

My man tackles me onto the mattress.

If I'm lucky, that's where we'll stay for the rest of the weekend.

CHAPTER 40
CAMERON

Six months later

Brady comes barreling out the front of my dorm building with the final box in his hands. It's move-out day, marking the end of our third year here at Avix University.

"Last one!" I clap, cheering him on from my seat like the proper passenger princess he's forced me to be today. I did at least bring down what I could carry on my way to my spot in the cab of his truck.

He finishes his game of packing *Tetris*, fixing the last box into the back beside his, and lifts his hands into the air in victory.

I give him a celebratory cheer, and he flexes his muscles like he's on a stage at some sort of muscle-man competition.

A few people around honk and whistle, and Brady grins, eating up the attention, but the only one he really cares about watching is me.

And I am glued to the man.

My man.

My man who finished out the season as the number-one defensive end in all of college football. I'm so fucking proud of him.

He closes the tailgate and walks over to the grass pathway before heading back and hopping into the cab of the truck. He tugs me to the middle, into *my* seat, and when he turns to face me, he has two dandelions in his hands, the petals long gone, leaving only the white wisps behind. He holds one out to me as he rolls his window down all the way and smiles. "Make a wish."

I smile at my gentle giant and close my eyes, making a quick wish. Together we blow the little seeds, watching as they float away out the window.

"What did you wish for?" I ask as soon as we're buckled.

He merely smirks and presses a quick kiss to my temple. He prepares to pull away, but before he can, I reach out and set something on his dash.

His hand freezes on the gearstick, eyes glued to the little clay molding. His head snaps from it to me and back again before he reaches out and takes it in his hands.

He inspects it a little closer, and I laugh when his fingers glide over the sharpest point.

"Brady!" I smack him and he grins.

"Did you make me a mold of your body, baby?"

"It's my boobs and pierced nipples, but yes, yes, I did." I smile, proud. "Remember back in, like, I don't even know, October maybe, when I told you I made you something in class?"

Brady's jaw drops. "No."

"Yes."

He sits back so he's half leaning on the door, frowning at me. "You mean to tell me I could have had the mental image of my favorite part of you in my head for all those long showers I had to take after you started torturing me with pretend mouth fucking?"

"That is exactly what I mean. Too bad it got lost in my room at some point and I forgot about it." I grin, taking it back and grimacing at how bad my molding skills were back at the start of the semester. "I literally just found it today under the bed."

Brady swipes it from my hands, pressing a hard peck to my lips. "Mine," he mumbles against them, then sets the little clay boobs on the opposite side where I can't reach.

I sit back with a smile, and we're on the road a minute later, this time without having to stop for coffee before hitting the highway because he already had one in here waiting for me to claim it.

Ari, Mason, and the others left ahead of us, but Brady needed some extra time, so of course I hung around until he was ready. He said he had another stop to make before he could be here, but we aren't all that far behind.

"So Mom said they have all the rooms set up at the house—Ari and me in the master, Chase and Noah are in the spare, and Paige in what was my room before we moved to the city house. Mason, Payton, and the baby aren't staying; they'll come for the party tomorrow but go back to his parents' at the end of the night, and because Vivian and Evan aren't pretending their kids are wearing chastity belts—though I'm starting to wonder if I have on an invisible one and no one's told me"—I give him a pointed look, but he only smirks at the road—"anyway, they get to sleep together in Mason's room, and Vivian has a spot for Deaton all set up in Ari's."

"How do you think Noah's going to do not getting to share a bed with Ari when today marks day twenty since he's seen her and day one of their only two months of uninterrupted time they'll get all year?"

"About as well as you will," I tease.

"Yeah, I notice you didn't mention my name in there anywhere. Where am I supposed to sleep?" He smiles.

I think back on what my mom relayed, not catching she left him out completely. "Huh." I tip my head, staring at his profile. "Maybe my dad made you a pallet next to his side of the bed?"

Brady laughs, his right hand coming down to clench around my thigh. "I wouldn't put it past him, but he didn't sound all that surprised when we told them we're together on Christmas break."

"Pretty sure your mom talked to my mom the second we pulled out of your driveway back in November. She kept giving me those mom eyes, you know?" I think about it. "How they get

370

all dopey and cartoon-like, round and glossy but in a cute way. She definitely saw something we hadn't fully figured out yet."

"Oh, I'd figured it out." Brady smirks. "I basically told my dad I wanted you, and he pretty much told me I already had you."

I gape. "What? How? What did he say?"

He peeks at me a moment. "I might have gotten in my head a little and worried you wouldn't understand some of my choices. He was quick to tell me I was wrong."

"Brady..." I whisper, but he only grins, wrapping his arm around my shoulders this time so he can tug me over and kiss my head without taking his eyes off the highway.

"I love you, baby," he promises.

And he says it at least five more times in the six or so hours it takes us to get home.

"I did not!"

"Oh, sweetie, you did." My mom laughs. "You pissed, and you were wearing a summer dress, so it got all over the bottom of the playpen, and when we picked Brady up so we could get everything cleaned, we realized it had somehow gotten on him too. His little shorts were all wet on the one side."

I glare at my mother as everyone around laughs, and Brady tugs me down onto his lap, not caring that everyone is around not even pausing to think about it. It's just second nature, his need to be close. To have me close.

I do blush a little, though, and my mom doesn't pretend to not notice the way the other moms do.

"Aw, she's blushing."

"I am not blushing," I lie.

"It's just a little piss, Cam. Nothing to be embarrassed about." Ari grins.

"Bitch, I'm not embarrassed about peeing while I was sleeping when I was three." I smirk, settling in Brady's arms more. "Besides, clearly young me was smart, marking her territory and all."

"You mean like I did on Thanksgiving when Trey tried to dance with you…and everyone but me knew he had gotten engaged on live television a week before that?" Brady cocks a brow.

That gets a laugh out of everyone, and then the conversation turns from me to the next person. It's Ari's parents' turn to tell embarrassing stories.

Brady's arms curl around me, his nose running along my cheek and drawing goose bumps to my flesh.

We still haven't had sex, but our foreplay is stuff for the playbooks.

We are on point and in tune with the other person in ways I can't imagine others could be. It's *that good*.

"I, for one, like it when you blush," he whispers, his hands pushing a little firmer against my lower belly. "My favorite is when you blush all over. I had no idea that was possible."

I turn my head, smiling at him over my shoulder. "Anything is possible if you just believe."

"I love it when you quote Gen Z movies to me."

"I'd like to quote some X movies to you, if you know what I mean."

Brady waggles his brows, and I choke back a laugh when his dick twitches against my ass.

Someone slaps my arm, and I look over to find my best friend raising a brow at me.

"Can you not dry hump in front of my mom?" she jokes, her voice for only us.

Brady shakes with silent laughter, and I give a little hip roll just to be a brat, loving the hiss that fills my ear. "Don't be jelly that your man is too much of a gentleman to pull you on his lap in front of your daddy."

Noah leans across her lap, having heard, his own dark brow

raised in challenge. "I can be a gentleman and still do dirty, dirty things in private."

I open my mouth in shocked glee. "Noah Riley, I am *so* proud of you right now."

He chuckles, and it only deepens when Ari's neck flushes red, but she gives me a little side smirk.

Go, bestie.

Over the next few hours, good food and great conversation flow, my dad on the barbecue tonight. The only person we're missing is Chase's mom, but when Mason asked about her, no one said a word, so we haven't mentioned it again.

Night falls and all of our parents, with Mason and his little fam in tow, head back to the city while the rest of us pile into the house, rearranging the room assignments to fit our agendas. After a movie and a couple games of cards, Brady wraps his arms around me, lowering his chin to my shoulder. "Walk with me, baby."

I turn instantly, following him out the back of the house and down the little path that leads to the barn. The doors are already pushed open, the place mostly cleared out while it waits to be filled with this year's harvest anytime now.

Brady heads over to the ladder and motions for me to hop on. I slip between his body and the wood to start to climb, but he halts me when my hands wrap around the old wood.

"Not so fast, baby," he rasps, his voice thick and husky, letting me know playtime is coming.

My baby is needy, and I'm eager to please. "Tell me what you want, man of mine."

His hands come around the front of me, an AU beanie with his number on it in his hands. "Close your eyes."

I do so instantly, and he slips the knit cap over my head, pulling it down over my eyes.

He gives my ass a little smack. "Now, climb."

I start up, the heat of his body enveloping mine as he scales with me, a safety shadow at my back.

"Just feel around and hike on up," he says when I reach the top.

Instantly, I recognize something different. My palms come down not on old wood but thick, plush pillowing. There's a moment's hesitation when I notice this, and Brady laughs lightly.

"Go on, baby. Up." His voice is a velvety command.

My pussy flutters and I bite at the inside of my lip.

Once I'm up, he guides me with a hand on my hip until I'm shuffled a little to the left.

There's movement around me, a soft click, and then his knuckles brush my cheeks as he lifts the makeshift blindfold.

I blink, my eyes adjusting. The first thing I catch sight of is the wall along the back of the loft. A curtain of purple lights is hung from top to bottom in long, twinkling strips. The second are the stars dangling from the roof, a slight glow to each of them. Beneath my palm is a padding not unlike what you'd find in a window seat, but it stretches across the entire area. In the back corner are mismatched pillows in an array of colors and a few stacks of blankets beside them.

The slight creak of wood draws my attention, and I turn as Brady pushes open the little door that leads to the rooftop, the moon bright beyond it.

The creek flows behind outside, the stream a lot calmer than it was in November.

Brady looks back my way, an almost shy smile on his lips. He runs his hand over the back of his hair, looking across the space. "I want to add a little fridge, maybe some speakers, but—"

His words die in his throat when I lean forward and crawl his way.

His pupils blow wide, and he goes from his knees to his ass, waiting with eager hands for me to reach him.

His large palms come around my ass as soon as I do, and I give Ari a silent thank-you for suggesting we wear sweat shorts instead of pajamas.

I'm straddling his lap in seconds, and my mouth comes down on his with a hard, possessive kiss. I lick his lips, biting at his tongue, and he groans, his dick hardening beneath me.

"It's perfect, Brady. Thank you."

"Thank you," he whispers, dipping into my neck and kissing what I think might be his favorite spot. He's basically tattooed his name there with his rough tongue and teeth alone.

"For?"

"Existing."

I melt a little—mostly from my pussy, my panties getting wetter by the second.

I need this man like a flower needs watering.

I want him to water me, to plant me, prune me, and pick me.

I'm a shaking mess already, and he hasn't even gotten started yet.

Just as I think it, I'm flipped onto my back, giggling like a schoolgirl—a sound I'd be embarrassed about if anyone else were here to hear it.

But it's just us.

And there's no time for embarrassment because he's already on me, dipping down and taking the top of my tank with him. His puffy lips close over my nipple ring, and I gasp into the space, his tongue rough like sandpaper.

My core is already clenching, desperate for something to grip on to.

He knows, his massive fingers coming down to play their part.

He slides right past my bottoms with expert skill, slipping inside with precision.

I arch, pushing into him until I feel the bottom of his fingers and there's nowhere else to go.

"Always so wet for me, my dirty girl. Wet and ready." He bites my nipple, teeth scraping along the piercing point and making me quake.

I drop my hands into his sweatpants, and he eagerly lifts his hips, letting me tear every bit of his clothing away. He wastes no time sliding his hard length into my open palm.

The black metal beads of his dick piercing roll against my thumb, and his heated groan washes over my chest.

We've done everything there is to do outside of straight-up penetration. Sex without sex.

He's fucked the slit of my pussy, the cheeks of my ass, my mouth, and the shallow space between my breasts. I've ridden his hands and face, and he's not intimidated by a good toy or two, but I've yet to feel myself stretch around his dick.

Brady pulls back, sliding his dick from my hands, and we're both naked in seconds.

"Baby," he rasps, settling over me and taking my mouth with his.

The kiss he gives me is slow and languid.

It's a love language only we know how to speak.

"Brady..."

"Shh," he whispers. "It's me and you, Hellcat. I feel it right here." He taps his chest, over his heart. "You asked me what I wished for the other night, and the answer is this. For years, every wish I've ever made was that there was someone out there made just for me who understood—who *understands*." He smiles softly. "That's you."

I open my mouth, but I don't know what to say, and he chuckles.

"Don't worry, baby. I know." He kisses me, this time a little longer and a lot dirtier, and when he pulls back, it's with a long lick up my throat. "Now that the sugary stuff is out of the way, let's get filthy."

"Yes, fucking please."

He chuckles, his hips shifting so he can slide over my clit, and I sigh at the feeling of his thickness between my legs.

I tug my hips back, twisting a little so he's lined up right where I want him—no, need him, and his muscles tense the slightest bit.

He lifts his head, and our eyes lock.

"Trust me?" I whisper.

His grin is slow, and then he's sliding inside me. "Always," he promises, pushing the rest of the way in in one long thrust.

I gasp, my back arching off the cushion, eyes shooting wide and watering.

My man, he is thick. Long. And holy sweet heaven. The piercing! It's cold against warm.

It's a fire inside me.

Fucking perfection.

His arms shake a little and his forehead falls to mine, harsh, heavy pants rolling over my lips as he pauses to take in the feeling.

I'm stretched to the max, a slight sting of my pussy walls I can't wait to explore more of. It's that good hurt, a deep pressure that tells me how epic this is about to be.

I can't wait to do it again and we haven't even started yet.

"I should warn you," he groans, flexing inside me. "I might be a minute man after all, but don't worry." He lifts his head with a deadly grin. "I'm a dedicated man when it comes to practice."

"Quiet, Big Guy." I wrap my legs around his back, and his eyes widen with a rumble when the move drives him even deeper. "There is no doubt in my mind that you're a natural." I roll my hips and his breath leaves him in a rush. "Besides, I'm not a virgin. I don't need a break before round two." I grin and he's all over me.

"Remember you said that, baby, because I'm about to fuck you the way I've imagined for months."

I lift up, lick at his lips, and whisper, "Prove it."

He doesn't have to be told twice, and he doesn't start slow.

No, he lifts his hips and slams them into me with the full force of his weight.

My moan is embarrassing, and I'm pretty sure you could hear it for miles. But my god. "Your piercing," I gasp, hooking my hips higher.

My body slides up the cushions and I reach back, pressing my hands against the wood, asking for more.

"You like that, naughty girl?" Brady nips at my throat and does it again. And again. And it can't have been a minute but I'm already about to come.

I dig my nails into his back, holding myself to him, and he shifts a little, dropping back on his knees.

The move drives him impossibly deeper.

We both gasp.

"Fuck." Brady shakes, hips shoving up into me. "It's so fucking deep like this."

I can't even talk. I let my head fall back, my entire body trembling when he runs his callused hand across my chest, pushing me back while holding me up.

He fucks up into me, his movements hard and long but not hurried. I feel him swelling inside me, and I clench him in response.

"Oh, fuck. What was that?" he groans, dropping me back on the cushion and pushing my legs back. He shoves his hips forward, his eyes nearly black as he leans down to kiss me. "Again," he demands.

I do it again, and he groans like a caveman, dipping to my neck and sucking until it stings.

"Mine. All fucking mine." He bucks his hips faster and faster until I'm clenching everywhere. "No," he snaps, tearing out of me and sitting back. "Not yet."

I actually whine, and my pussy quite literally aches at the loss of him.

He covers me again, but he doesn't slide back inside. He pushes my sweaty hair from my face and nips at my lips. "Can I take you how I want you, my gorgeous fucking girl?" He kisses me softly, speaking against my lips. "I promise I'll let you come this time."

I push on his chest, and he moves willingly.

I don't have to ask him how he wants me.

I know what he likes.

I know his favorite way to "fuck" me without having actually been inside, though I know for a fact he's been tempted a time or two.

I flip onto my stomach, leaving my breasts to the mattress as I rise up on my knees, pushing my ass back into his face.

"Fuck, I love you." He's on me in a second, gripping my ass cheeks and pushing them aside. His hands shake as he lines himself up and then I'm full again, nipples dragging along the cushion beneath me making me moan.

He bends over me, folding his upper half across my body, and starts to rock.

Slow and steady.

Torture, torture, torture, but the orgasm that builds... I know before it hits it's going to be fucking life-altering.

Brady's breaths are ragged now and his full, long sweeps inside me grow shorter. He's hip to ass, unable to get closer, but still he bucks.

He shakes.

He grips my chin in the gentlest of fingers and draws my eyes to his.

Sweat drips from his forehead to mine. Our lips touch.

"Come with me, Hellcat."

I do.

My entire body convulses as his seizes up.

His hips buck and my pussy spasms, and it just keeps on coming.

Minutes that feel like hours later, we collapse onto the cushions, truly and completely fucking spent.

"See," I pant, and our heads roll toward each other. I grin, hitting his sweaty chest, and he catches my hand, bringing it to his lips. "Natural."

Brady chuckles and I close my eyes.

Fuck.

My boyfriend is basically a natural-born porn star.

Yay me.

I chuckle and let my eyes close.

We've been lying here in silence, basking in the *literal best sex ever* glow, when my phone pings and pings again.

I groan, and Brady chuckles, reaching over to grab it from wherever the hell it ended up. Worry claws at my throat when I see it's from Granny Grace. Why would she be texting me?

"What's the matter, mama?" he rumbles sleepily, wrapping his arms around me. "I felt you tense."

"Granny Grace," I mumble, quickly unlocking my phone and waiting for the message to load.

I'm greeted with a gorgeous bouquet of light pink and white gardenias, exactly like the last one but this time with a little yellow bow instead of a blue one. A frown forms, but then it all comes back.

Brady and his mom's question about the flowers. Granny Grace and her cryptic wording about where they came from.

Today and the stop he had to make.

This must be what the Grinch felt like when he was overcome with love because I literally feel an overflow of emotions as if my heart is growing two sizes.

I sit up, my hair falling over my shoulder as I look down at the man beside me, a soft smile on his handsome face. "Brady..."

"You been saying my name like that a lot."

"You've been blowing my mind a lot."

"I'm ready to do it again if you are," he teases, pushing my hair from my face so he has an unobstructed view.

"The gardenias."

He nods against the pillow, and I look down to admire my nail marks on his neck for a moment. "She was good to you."

My brows pull, and I roll so I'm half on his chest. "What do you mean?"

"You were sick. I couldn't be there to take care of you, but she took the time to make you soup, not once but twice, and she brought it to you without a soul asking her to. I couldn't not say thank you."

"But you didn't even sign the card."

He shrugs. "It's not about the recognition. She went out of her way, and it was the least I could do."

"You have no idea what those flowers mean to her."

He runs his knuckle across my lower lip, lifting to kiss me. "I think I do."

"I think I want to do nasty, nasty things to you to show you what it means to *me*."

He grips my ass, hauling me up until I'm settling over his hard-on. "Well, go on, real girlfriend. Show me what you've got."

I do.

And then I do it again.

It's crazy how much has happened over the last three years at Avix University.

I, for one, cannot *wait* to see what our last year brings.

READ ABOUT THE OTHER
BOYS OF AVIX AND THEIR
LOVES IN MEAGAN BRANDY'S

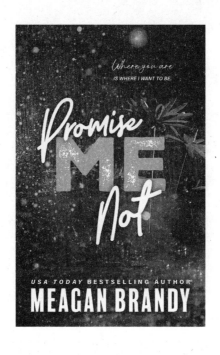

CHAPTER 1
PAYTON

Now, July 2

Deaton cries, arching his back and kicking his feet all around, doing his absolute best to fight against the fresh onesie I'm sliding his arms into, his third outfit change of the day. And mine.

"Okay, okay, little man." I manage to get the two outside buttons done and decide the middle one isn't necessary. Tickling his tiny, sock-covered feet, I grab ahold, wiggling them back and forth with a big smile to pretend we're playing a game. It works like a charm, and he stops flailing for half a second, just long enough for me to quickly slide on his cotton shorts.

He screams then, his arms stretched out, fists opening and closing over and over, making grabby hands to let me know he wants me to pick him back up.

"One second, mister." I turn to my own mess of a wardrobe in search of another clean top, but my drawer is empty aside from the T-shirts I wear to bed, and when I look in my closet, bare hangers stare back. That is, on the side dedicated to the clothes that actually fit. My eyes fall to the clean basket of laundry at the foot of the bed, and I sigh, reaching in and digging around for the least wrinkled one. I still need to shower, so what's the point of worrying about ironing or, hell, matching.

Ironing. I scoff. Yeah right. The most I'll take the time to do is throw the entire load back in the dryer and hope it works out the mess I created by tossing them carelessly into the basket in the first place.

"Well, mister man, looks like we're officially adding laundry back to the never-ending to-do list."

Deaton cries harder, reminding me why it's so important to keep him to his normal routine no matter what's going on outside of it.

"I know, I know. It's my fault you missed your nap, and we're all going to pay for it." I yank the shirt over my head, my lack of finesse causing it to tug the bun I seem to be living in down with it, but I don't bother to pull the now loose strands out from under the thin cotton, let alone fix the damn thing.

I scoop up the little boy who suddenly hates being put down for any and every reason that doesn't include water. Foolishly, I thought he'd grow more independent with age, but it seems the opposite is true. Too bad I can only give him so many baths a day to free up my hands, and even then, it's not to get anything done. It's the ten-ish minutes of sitting on the tile floor with zero responsibilities that make the fight to dry him off and put on his diaper and clothes worth it.

Well, no responsibilities other than the ever-present fear I'll mistakenly look away for the split second it would take for him to twist and slip under the water.

Yeah, baths aren't all that relaxing, but the little smile when he splashes water all over the place is better than any restful moment could be.

I bounce around the room, walking back and forth from one corner to the next, but Deaton continues to fuss, rubbing his face in my chest and playing with the curls of his hair.

"Are you tired, sweet boy?" I kiss his head, cradling him against me, but my little man hates to miss a thing. The moment he recognizes the move for what it is—my attempt to sway him until he's sleeping—he lifts his little head, blowing air between his lips and sending drool sliding down his chin.

"Oh, we're blowing bubbles while we cry, huh?" I swiftly snag a bib and snap it into place, not once pausing the bouncing of my body. My eyes catch the clock and widen. "Shit."

My lips snap closed, and I sigh. I was supposed to be ready an hour ago. Knowing what's coming this evening, I suck it up and take a deep breath.

"It's now or never, mister man." Blanket flung over my shoulder and a toy in my hand, I slide into a pair of flip-flops, doing what I told myself I wouldn't do today.

I head over to Lolli and Nate's house next door.

Inside, I pause to listen, the bickering in the hall cluing me in on where to go, and I throw the door open to Lolli's office.

"Someone, for the love of hot coffee, help. *Please.*" The words leave me before I fully take in the sight, and sadly, I don't even have the energy to gape. Or laugh.

Lolli, the girl terrified of marriage and most anything that has to do with acknowledging feelings, though she is getting better at that, stands on a stool in the center of the room wearing a giant, white wedding gown. Her cousin and new roommate, Mia, kneels beside her with a needle and measuring tape in her hand. Mia is lucky Lolli loves her and wants her new business endeavor as a seamstress to work out, or Lolli would never be caught dead in that gown.

My shoulders fall instantly. So much for sneaking away for five minutes.

"Aw..." Lolli's attention locks on Deaton, and she attempts to step down, but Mia is quick to hold her still.

"Ha! Lolli, get real!" She shakes her head. "Baby puke is another big fat no to be spilled on this dress," she says, as if they've already had this argument.

"Again, Mia, *potentially*. And you're getting on my nerves now." She looks to me, an apology drawing lines to her forehead. "Sorry, she's being full drill sergeant."

"It's fine. I just..." I hesitate, deciding one truth is enough.

"Really wanted to shower before Nate's parents get here. I hate looking like I suck at life when they come." Again.

I look out the large back window, watching as a few people run by on their way to the ocean, and hope she doesn't call me out for any *other* potential reason my stress meter is clearly overflowing today. Thankfully, she doesn't.

"You don't suck at life and know that Sarah and Ian would never judge." Kalani, or Lolli as we call her, reminds me of what I already know.

If she ever decides to give in and let Nate marry her like he wants, she will officially have one of the best sets of in-laws on the planet. Though I have to say, they're tied with another certain set of parents I know. Not mine, of course. *His.*

I swallow, shaking away the thought.

"Bright side is they won't be getting into town until around five," Mia adds with a grin.

"True!" Lolli agrees.

My brows snap together, and I decide they're not joking. Seems I'm not the only one time got away from today. "It's five thirty." I break the bad news.

Lolli swings her glare to Mia, who laughs loudly, and I watch the two as I move Deaton from one arm to the other, swinging slightly as he grows more and more restless.

Fussy baby or not, I can't help but smile as I listen to the two bicker like sisters.

Lolli lets out a little growl. "I gotta get out of this before they get back and—"

"We're back!"

Lolli cuts off at the sudden intruding voice, the shouted words coming from the front of the house, and like being dipped in liquid nitrogen, we freeze instantly.

My stomach drops to my feet, a cool sweat breaking out over my palms.

Oh god. No, no, no...

My eyes snap up, locking with the girls'. The panic whirling its way through me is reflected on both their faces, none of our reactions related to the reasons of the others', but the reason for mine is secret. Not the best kept one, but a secret nonetheless.

A soft thunk snaps us out of our stupor, and at once, we start moving.

Mia hurries to unzip Lolli while Lolli reaches up, yanking clips from her long, dark hair.

I spin on my heels, doing everything I can to escape, my hand wrapping around the handle of the door, fully prepared to race through the back side of the house so no one sees me.

I'm not ready for this. I thought I could put on a brave face, but it turns out I'm not brave. I feel sick at the mere thought, and I just…cannot.

I need a little more—

The door is shoved open from the other side, and I yelp, nearly knocking myself off balance, but then my eyes snap up to the newcomer. I swallow my tongue.

It's as if cement is injected into my veins, every inch of me growing heavy before turning to stone. My pulse pounds, then plummets as my eyes lock on a pair of pensive brown ones so familiar, I could pick them out in a lineup of hundreds.

My fingers curl into Deaton's blanket, and I open my mouth, but nothing comes out.

Those dark eyes narrow, searching, seeing.

Softening.

My stomach flips and twists, and I can't tell if it's unease or elation. Or downright dread.

How can they still turn so tender when trained on me?

"What's wrong?" His words are a low demand, and I want to scream and cry at the same time.

"Nothing." *Everything.* "Everything's fine."

"She needs help with Deaton," Lolli says, calling me out.

"Lolli," I hiss, my head snapping her way briefly. I try to stay focused on her, but it's too obvious, not to mention *hard*, so I slowly move them back to the man before me.

And he is a man. I swear, every time I see him, there's a little something about him that's changed. Sometimes it's subtle, a shorter haircut than the time before or a deeper tan than the one his olive skin keeps all year—a result of the endless hours he puts in on the football field or natural, I couldn't say. Other times it's more than that. His shoulders have grown wider in the year since I met him, his jaw sharper. His hands…

I swallow, unable to break away from the choke hold of his gaze.

If there is one thing that hasn't changed, it's his eyes. The honey-brown irises are as rich as ever, the perfect mix of dark and light, vivid yet grave. A flawless illustration of his character.

Mason Johnson is as fierce as he is tender. He's yin *and* yang.

And after nearly nine weeks of sudden silence, he's standing before me with an expression that threatens to break me down right here, right now.

He doesn't say a word, but he doesn't have to. The slight frown blanketing his features says enough—he's worried, frustrated.

Angry.

It's deeper than that, though. I can see it in his troubled gaze.

Did something happen? Did I do something wrong? Did you change your mind…

Those are just a few of the questions he's asking without opening his mouth, none of which I want to answer right now. To be honest, I'm not so sure I could.

Did something change? I ask myself, swallowing the needles that seem to have appeared in my throat.

Still, angry or not, he's as gentle as ever, shuffling closer, and I know before he so much as lifts his arms, he's going to reach for Deaton.

I hesitate, if only for a split second, but it's long enough for him to notice, and his lips press together more firmly than they already were. I look away as I pass him my little boy and all but run from the room. In the hall, I'm ready to go full sprint, but my feet don't seem to get the message, instead lingering in the hall, out of sight but not earshot.

Mason's voice reaches me instantly, and I know by the lulling in his tone, he's swaying my son just as I was. "What's wrong, little man, hmm?"

A sharp pain stings my chest, and I consider going in and taking him back, but not a second after he speaks, what I couldn't seem to do is done—Deaton stops crying.

I drop my chin to my chest and speedwalk out of there, softly closing the back door behind me so no one in the front of the house is alerted to my escape. It's bad enough I'm clearly going out of my way to avoid everyone who has just arrived, but I can't pause. Pausing will lead to too many thoughts, none of which I'm prepared for right now. At all. In any fashion.

I walk quickly down the deck, across the twenty feet of sand, and back up the deck of the house right next door. Yes, my older brother, Parker, owns the home right next door to his best friend. When Lolli told him she had purchased the home beside this one, it felt like a blessing I didn't deserve. It's how he was able to offer me my own room—and his nephew a nursery once he was born—after I ran away from our mother's place.

It's times like this, though, I wonder if I should have taken my dad's offer to move in with him, as out-of-left-field and awkward as the conversation was, considering we hardly know each other these days. But even as I think it, I know I made the right choice when I gave him the swift and instant answer of a hard no way in hell. My refusal had nothing to do with him on a personal level, though I'm not sure he believed me when I told him so, considering I didn't go into much more details outside of that. If he knew me better, he would have never asked. He would understand living with him would mean going back to Alrick, where my mother lives, where the family that shares my son's last name lives. The last thing I want is my Deaton anywhere near those vile people. They hated their son as much as much as my mother hates me.

Leaving that place was both the best and worst decision I have ever made.

On one hand, my son will never be exposed to the toxicity that is Ava Baylor. On the other, it is the very reason his daddy died.

I am the reason he's dead.

Swallowing, I swiftly lock my bedroom door, dropping my head against it. I no sooner close my eyes than hurried footsteps sound on the hardwood floors in the hall. I hold my breath, the sound of his heavy exhales causing my hand to clench the knob I've yet to let go of.

I know who's on the other side. Of course he followed.

"Where you are is where I want to be..."

I squeeze my lids closed tight.

There's the smallest of raps, as if he lifted his knuckles to knock, to demand an answer or beg for a reason, but changed his mind at the last second. My eyes open, pointed at the floor where the shadow of his shoes sits just inches from my own, watching as it fades into nothing as he walks away a moment later.

I grit my teeth, jump into the shower, and get myself together as quickly as possible, which I've found is a lot faster than I ever would have thought now that every minute is one I can no longer waste.

Smoothing my hair back, I take the front pieces and twist them slightly to allow a small center part before tying it up into a high ponytail. I swiftly braid the thick, wet strands, the long blond length still reaching to midback. Using some wax, I smooth my baby hairs down to my skull, opting for a quick bronzer, blush, mascara, and, at the last minute, a touch of lip gloss.

Nearly nothing I own fits, not that my mother sent all my belongings, but the things she did box up are three sizes too small,

392

even eight months after birth. When I was emancipated last year, I was able to drain my bank account before my mom got ahold of it, but she ignored the court's order to allow me to take my things. In the end, I found material items didn't mean enough anymore if it meant having to look her in the eye and ask for it. She wasn't worth the fight, and that is *all* she was after. A reaction. So I stopped giving her the chance to get one.

The money I had saved from winning pageants she forced me to enter and secret photography contests she knew nothing about was enough to get the things I needed, but only because my brother refuses to accept a penny for rent. Because of that, it should hold me over for another six months or so, longer if Lolli and Parker keep going out of their way to buy things for Deaton and me before I get the chance to do it myself. Not that I want them to, but chances are they won't.

My lack of clothing mixed with the added weight my body seems to want to keep means I've basically been living in stretchy bottoms, loner T-shirts, and lightweight hoodies for the better part of a year. Glancing at myself in the long mirror beside my closet, I sigh at my reflection.

It's a far cry from the girl I was when I first showed up on my brother's doorstep in two-hundred-dollar jeans and a purse that cost more than the down payment on his new truck. I was a certified rich girl, shiny and perfect on the outside, suffocating and starving on the inside—literally, thanks to my mother's need for her version of a trophy daughter. She would let me eat so long as she saw me throw it up after. The only thing I was allowed to keep down was whatever she handed me with the "vitamins" she gave me each morning.

Nothing like an appetite suppressant and a handful of whole natural almonds for breakfast, right, Mom?

About the Author

Meagan Brandy is a *USA Today* and *Wall Street Journal* bestselling author of new adult and sports romance books. Born and raised in California, she is a married mother of three crazy boys who keep her bouncing from one sports field to another, depending on the season, and she wouldn't have it any other way. Coffee is her best friend, and words are her sanity.

Website: meaganbrandy.com
Facebook: meaganbrandyauthor
Facebook group: facebook.com/groups/130865934291300/
Instagram: @meaganbrandyauthor
TikTok: @meaganbrandyauthor
Merch: teepublic.com/user/meaganbrandy